Anywhere But Here

Anywhere But Here

Shawn Marie Graybeal-Sellers

First published 2026
ISBN 979-8-9956354-0-6 (print)
ISBN 978-8-9956354-1-3 (ebook)

Contents

A Note on the Text

This novel is set in Albuquerque, New Mexico, a real city rendered here with as much fidelity as fiction allows. The North Valley, the Rio Grande bosque, the acequia system, and Frontier Restaurant are real places. The characters and events are entirely invented.

Spanish appears throughout the text as it is spoken — naturally, without translation or italics. This is intentional.

This book contains depictions of domestic violence, alcohol addiction, sexual assault, and child abuse. It also addresses human trafficking. While the characters and circumstances are fictional, the experiences they reflect are real and ongoing. Readers who may be affected by these topics are encouraged to approach the material with care.

For Leonard, who walked into my life when it was already full and stayed anyway. For the adventures, the grandchildren, the hard years, and the good ones. Always.

"Now I understood that the same road was to bring us together again. Whatever we had missed, we possessed together the precious, the incommunicable past."
Willa Cather, *My Ántonia* (1918)

Part I: Roots

"When I come back to it, I never have to remind it of anything; I begin just where I left off."
Willa Cather, *O Pioneers!* (1913)

Chapter One
The Note

I sat on the narrow bench in the office, pressed against the wall. My legs were shaking. I pressed my heels into the floor, but they just wouldn't stay still. The clock across the room ticked loudly as I watched the door, waiting for Mom and hoping she would be sober.

Sylvia and I had been passing a note in class. I was telling her about the fight my parents had. Mom had moved too slow with dinner and Dad threw the plate across the room. Both of them were screaming. She started crying, then he threw his beer can at her face. I was sure the neighbors would call the cops again. I thought about climbing out the window and going to her house because the last time the police came, I ended up in foster care for a week with old people who smelled like mothballs and treated me like I was broken.

Then Ms. Reynolds was there. The room went quiet. She took the note from Sylvia's hands and carried it back to her desk. She read it quietly and then she called me out to the hallway. Last period, I was called to the office.

Dad was going to be furious.

The office door opened and Mom walked in, cheeks flushed, eyes too bright. I could smell the alcohol.

"Michelle, get over here. Come on, let's go."

The secretary stepped between us, her smile tight. "I'm sorry, Mrs. Martinez, but the principal needs to speak with you before we can let her leave."

Mom exhaled sharply. "Fine. Let's get this over with. I have things to do."

The secretary knocked once and opened the door. "Mrs. Martinez is here to talk with you about Michelle."

I stood. Mom's hand closed around my upper arm before I could move. Her nails dug into my skin. When I looked at her, she didn't speak. She didn't need to. I knew I needed to keep my mouth shut and let her handle it.

I swallowed, but tears came anyway. I kept my head down.

"Mrs. Martinez, Michelle, have a seat," Mr. Otero said, folding his hands on his desk. His voice was calm, but his eyes moved between us.

He slid the note forward. "Normally note passing is not a concern. Michelle's a good student. I am worried about the content. I wanted to speak with you about it."

Mom laughed lightly, the laugh she used in public. "I'm sorry, Mr. Otero. My husband and I had a disagreement. It's not nearly as serious as this makes it sound. Michelle can be dramatic. I promise there's nothing to worry about."

I stared at the paper. My own handwriting looked strange.

Mom stood before he could answer and held out her hand. Keeping my eyes on the carpet until we reached the door, I followed her past the secretary's desk and out into the parking lot.

The car smelled like cigarettes and coffee with an underlying sweetness from the rum. She started the engine. Gravel snapped under the tires as we pulled away. She didn't turn on the radio and didn't speak or even look at me. The silence worked on my nerves.

I watched the houses go by and wished she would turn left instead of right. Sylvia's house was only a few blocks away. We could sit at the kitchen table and Mama would bring me a warm tortilla. Sylvia and Bobby would be goofing around. I wished we would go there.

We didn't. We turned right and headed to our house. When we pulled into the driveway, Mom sat there, hands on the wheel, staring at the house. Her fingers tapped once, then stopped.

"Get inside," she said.

I stepped out, my backpack hitting my hip, and paused at the door.

Mom came up behind me. "Go."

I opened the door. The living room was dim, lit only by the television's blue light flickering across the walls. Dad was lying back on the couch, a beer bottle resting against his stomach. When the door shut, he opened his eyes.

"What took so long?" he muttered, pushing himself upright.

Mom gave me a look and then smiled at him. "The principal wanted to talk," she said, dropping her keys into the bowl by the door.

Dad's eyes shifted to me. "About what?"

I swallowed.

"Michelle passed a note," Mom said. "Teenage nonsense. They overreacted."

Dad rubbed his face. "Christ, Michelle. You're always causing problems."

I didn't respond, standing still by the door.

Mom moved into the kitchen. Cabinets opened and shut harder than necessary. Dad leaned forward, elbows on his knees.

"Come here."

I crossed the room.

"What'd you write?"

"Nothing. Just… stuff."

"Stuff about us?"

I looked at the carpet.

Mom stood in the doorway with a mug in her hand. "Answer him."

"I was just passing a note to Sylvia," I said. "The teacher took it from her."

"That girl's trouble, her whole family is." Dad said. "And you don't go telling people our business."

"I won't do it again."

Mom cleared her throat softly.

Dad stood. He swayed once, then steadied. "Did you tell them we fight?"

My pulse thudded in my ears. "I was just talking," I mumbled.

He stepped closer. I stepped back.

"You scared of me?" he asked.

I didn't answer.

He watched me for a moment. He reached out and grabbed my arm and backhanded my face. He shook me once and pushed me toward my room.

"Go. Before I change my mind."

I slipped down the hall and closed my bedroom door as quietly as I could. I got a tissue and dabbed the blood from my lower lip.

I sat on the edge of my bed and listened. His voice rose first. Mom answered. A cabinet door slammed in the kitchen, followed by the sound of breaking glass.

I reached for my phone. Sylvia always answered. Her mom would come get me. Dad never stopped me from leaving. Mom depended on it. When I was gone, they could make-up, or at least pretend to.

I opened our messages and stared at Sylvia's name. My thumb hovered over the screen. As I heard another crash from the kitchen I hit call.

Chapter Two
Sanctuary

The phone rang once, twice, then Sylvia answered on the third.

"Hey," she said quietly. "You home?"

"Yeah," I said, my voice barely above a whisper.

"Can you talk?"

A chair scraped hard across the tile. Dad's voice rose, thick and uneven, a cabinet slammed and I startled.

"Okay," she said. "Hang on. Mom's warming up the car."

"I didn't mean to…"

"I know you didn't," she said. "She's already grabbing her purse."

In the background, I heard Mama's voice, calm and already moving. "Tell her I'm leaving now. Five minutes."

Five minutes. Soon enough that they wouldn't notice I was gone.

"Are you sure?" I asked automatically.

Sylvia exhaled. "Michelle, my mom would adopt you if she could. You're not extra. You're ours."

Glass shattered in the kitchen, and I pressed back against the wall.

"She's almost there," Sylvia said. "If you can, wait outside."

"I'll try."

"M&M?"

"Yeah?"

"You're coming home."

I ended the call and moved quickly but quietly, because loud always made things worse. I pulled a hoodie, jeans, and socks from the dresser. The navy sweatshirt lay folded beneath the others, Bobby's, the one he'd handed me outside the movie theater when I said I was cold. "Looks better on you anyway," he had said without looking at me. I packed it without thinking.

Dad's voice rose again, something heavy hit the wall. I crossed to the window, lifted it slowly, and slid out into the flowerbed. Dry stems snapped under my shoes. The air outside was cold. I didn't look back.

A few minutes later, headlights turned onto my street. The silver Honda slowed to the curb, and the passenger door swung open before the engine fully stopped.

"Hop in, sweetheart," Mama called.

She didn't ask what happened or look toward the house. I climbed in and shut the door carefully. The car was warm, the air carrying the aroma of green chile and laundry soap. She reached across the console and squeezed my hand once, her palm steady and warm against mine.

"There you are, mija. Seatbelt."

I clicked it in, and she eased back into the street without hurry. My house receded in the side mirror and slipped out of view. We drove past the corner store, the cracked sidewalk near the old church and then the streets widened as we turned north, cottonwoods closing over the road, the lots growing quieter and further apart. By the second stoplight, my jaw was no longer clenched.

Mama pulled into the driveway. The headlights swept across the front of the house before she turned them off, adobe walls, a portal running along the front, and at the far edge of the property where the corral fence caught the light, the dark shape of a horse standing still, watching. Then the front door opened.

Sylvia ran down the walkway in pajama pants and an oversized hoodie, her hair twisted up, mismatched socks sliding against the concrete. Bobby followed a few steps behind, slower, his arms folded against his chest, his jaw set. Rowdy, their red and white Australian Shepherd, ran out behind him with his stumpy little tail wagging.

"M&M," Sylvia breathed, reaching me before I was fully out of the car. She wrapped both arms around me and held on.

"I'm fine," I said into her shoulder.

"You don't look fine," Bobby said. His hand brushed my shoulder before he pulled back and shoved his hands into his pockets.

Inside, the stove light cast a low yellow glow across the kitchen tile, and green chile stew simmered in a wide pot. The radio played quietly, an old Spanish guitar song, the kind Pops liked. Along the hallway, framed photos held the light: Bobby mid-ride at a rodeo, one arm raised and the other gripping the rope as the bull kicked beneath him, his body forward over the shoulders; Sylvia missing her front teeth in a school picture, grinning wide; Pops in a pressed white shirt at someone's graduation, standing straight and unsmiling. And further down, slightly apart from the others, Grandma Calderon at a long table set for Sunday dinner, her hands folded in front of her, looking directly at the camera.

Bobby eased the door shut behind us, careful not to make a sound.

Mama stepped forward, cupped the back of my head in her hand, and kissed my hair. "¿Tienes hambre?"

I nodded, even though I wasn't sure. She guided me to the table with her hand at my back.

The smell hit me before I sat down. Green chile and warm corn, thick and particular, the kind that existed nowhere else.

I was seven the first time I smelled it. The Calderons had taken me camping somewhere dark enough that the sky was a different sky than the one above our apartment. I remembered sitting close to the fire because the night was cold and asking why the stars were so much brighter out here than at home.

Bobby had looked up from the marshmallow he was trying to fit into his already full mouth. He and his friends were trying to see who could fit the most, which was disgusting and completely serious. He said something about light pollution, perfectly clearly despite the marshmallows. How the city's lights drowned out the starlight. How out here there was nothing between you and them.

Josh said something that was probably a challenge. Bobby's response was incomprehensible.

Sylvia had leaned over and whispered that she was pretty sure Bobby had just swallowed four marshmallows whole and that we should probably be concerned.

I had looked back up at the stars and thought: I didn't know the sky could look like that.

"Sit, mija," Mama said, her hand warm at my back.

I sat.

A bowl of green chile stew, thick with potato and pork, waited for me, along with a tortilla wrapped in a dish towel and a glass of water set near my right hand. I ate slowly, carefully working around the split lip.

Sylvia filled the space with noise like she always did when things felt unsettled, moving through gossip about school, exaggerated impressions of teachers, a dramatic retelling of someone spilling an entire soda in the hallway that somehow lasted ten minutes and involved four witnesses and a custodian named Gerald. Midway through, a car passed outside with bass loud enough to rattle the windows. I stiffened. Sylvia raised her voice by exactly one register and kept going without pausing, as if the sound had been part of her story all along. Every few minutes her knee knocked against mine under the table.

Bobby didn't talk much. He watched. At the table, he had a way of going still, hands wrapped around his glass, eyes moving slowly across the room. When Mama asked if I wanted more, he answered before I could. "She's good," he said quietly.

The front door opened around nine, and cold air came in with Pops, carrying the faint smell of piñon smoke. He shut the door with a firm, controlled click and hung his jacket on the hook without breaking stride. Broad-shouldered and deliberate, he moved through rooms without raising his voice. The house seemed to adjust when he entered.

His eyes moved once across the living room: me on the couch with Rowdy near my feet, Sylvia angled toward me, Bobby standing too still near the doorway. His gaze lingered on my bruised face and swollen lip.

"¿Qué pasó?" he said quietly, his voice low.

"She's staying," Mama said from the kitchen before I could answer.

Pops nodded once. He crossed the room and stopped in front of me, then bent slightly so we were level, his forearms resting loosely on his thighs.

"You're safe here," he said. "If he shows up, you call me first."

I nodded.

Joe and Hector stood in the hallway doorway. Joe was broad through the shoulders, older than Pops by a few years, with the stillness of a man who learned early that the room told you everything if you waited long enough. He and Pops had grown up together on these same streets. Whatever that history held, it had made them the kind of men who showed up without being asked.

Hector leaned against the wall behind him, arms folded, boots still carrying dust, one heel braced against the baseboard. His eyes moved over me, not a long look, just enough, and then away. His expression didn't change as he watched Bobby lean toward me and Sylvia press her shoulder into mine. He had been six years old when he came to Joe, and Joe had given him a roof and work and not much else. Warmth was something he had learned to read in other people's houses.

When Pops said I was safe, Hector's jaw tightened and his eyes moved to Bobby. Bobby met it without speaking. It lasted only a second.

Later, when Sylvia had fallen asleep half across my legs, her breathing slow and steady, Bobby leaned forward from the recliner.

"Want some air?" he asked quietly.

I nodded.

We stepped outside without turning on the porch light. The night air was cold and still. Beyond the porch, the yard stretched dark, the corral fence a low line against the sky. The horse had moved closer to the gate and stood there quietly, breath visible in the cold.

Bobby stood beside me with his hands in his pockets. He didn't look at me right away.

"You don't have to talk," he said. "Just breathe."

I tried.

"I feel like I wrecked it," I said. "The night. All of it."

He turned toward me. "No. That's not on you. What happens in your house, that's their mess. It was already there."

"I don't want to be a problem," I said.

"You're not," he said. Then, after a moment, quieter: "You never have been."

I looked away. The horse shifted at the fence, its hooves soft against the dirt. After a moment Bobby's hand came up slowly, and when I didn't move, his thumb brushed the tear from my cheek.

"You deserve better than being scared all the time," he said.

We stood there until the cold settled in, and then he nudged the door open with his shoulder.

"You're going to freeze," he said.

I followed him back inside.

The heater ran steadily. Sylvia had sunk deeper into the couch, one arm thrown across the blankets. Down the hall, Pops' voice moved in low, measured Spanish.

Hector was in the kitchen, standing with his arms folded, watching Bobby pour two glasses of water. Bobby handed one across without asking.

"You hear from him?" Hector asked.

"Not yet," Bobby said. "Pops already made a call."

Hector took the glass. "Good. If he shows up anyway, I'll deal with it."

"I know," Bobby said.

I stood a few feet from the counter with my arms folded.

Hector looked at me directly. "You gonna be okay?"

"I'm fine."

He held my gaze. "I didn't ask if you were fine."

"Same thing."

"It isn't," he said. "You look like you're about to fall apart."

Bobby set his glass down. "Knock it off. She's been through enough."

"I'm not doing anything," Hector said.

"Good," Bobby said.

The room settled but didn't clear. Hector said he'd crash in Bobby's room just in case, and Bobby nodded. Hector turned toward the hall, then stopped.

"You know you can't keep doing this," he said, looking at me. "Coming here every time it gets bad over there."

I didn't answer.

"Enough," Bobby said.

Hector looked at him, then back at me. "Figure it out," he said, and walked down the hall.

The bedroom door closed.

Bobby looked at me. I looked at the floor.

"He's wrong," Bobby said.

I nodded.

I wrapped myself in the borrowed blanket and stared at the ceiling. Down the hall the heater hummed. Outside, the wind moved through the chimes. Somewhere past the yard, one of the horses shifted in the dark.

That night, I fell asleep without listening for the next sound.

Chapter Three
Lines in the Sand

The smell of breakfast burritos and coffee drifted through the house: warm green chile, eggs hitting a hot pan, and the dark bitter roast Mama bought from the little shop off Central where the barista greeted her by name. The heater hummed quietly through the floor vent. Sunlight came through the blinds in long slanted bars that settled across the blankets around me.

For one second, I forgot where I was.

There was no shouting, no cabinet slamming hard enough to rattle the frames, no crash yanking my body upright before my thoughts caught up, no silence loaded with threat. Just the steady rhythm of a house waking up: dishes clinking, the scrape of a chair, the murmur of morning conversation. The kind of quiet that didn't feel like something waiting to turn.

Then Sylvia rolled over beside me, her curls flattened on one side and wild on the other. She squinted toward the coffee table and groaned, dragging the blanket higher around her shoulders.

"M&M," she muttered, voice thick with sleep. "Your phone is blowing up."

My body tightened before my mind understood why. The vibration came again, sharp and insistent against the wood. I reached for it slowly, already bracing. The screen lit up and the breath left my lungs in a thin, controlled rush.

Fourteen missed calls. Most from Mom, several from Dad, and three from numbers I didn't recognize: blocked, private, disposable. My father went through phones the way most people went through cheap lighters. When he was angry, he called until someone answered. And if they didn't answer, he borrowed someone else's phone so you wouldn't know which voice you were about to hear.

A new message slid across the top of the screen.
YOU COME HOME NOW.

I held the phone tighter than I meant to and shut the screen off. I set it down carefully.

Sylvia was upright now, completely awake, already defensive. The blanket hung off one shoulder. She took one look at my face and didn't ask a single question.

"Nope," she said immediately. "Absolutely not. You're not going anywhere. I will physically tackle you."

The certainty in her voice found something to grip in my chest, though it wasn't enough to stop the slow cold turning in my stomach. If I didn't answer, he would escalate. If I did answer, I would fold. Either way, something would give.

Before I could say anything, Mama appeared in the hallway doorway, already dressed in her sunflower apron, her hair pulled back into a loose bun. Her eyes moved once from my face to the phone on the coffee table and back again.

"Michelle, cariño," she said gently, "come to the kitchen. Eat something warm. It will help."

I stood and followed her down the hallway, my legs feeling slightly out of sync with the rest of me. The house was fully awake. The small television above the refrigerator murmured a Spanish morning show, the hosts laughing about something ordinary. Tortillas warmed on the griddle. Eggs hissed in the pan. A pot lid rattled faintly as steam pushed against metal. The ordinariness of it pressed against my chest in a way that hurt.

I slid into one of the wooden chairs at the kitchen table and folded my hands in my lap. Mama moved with quiet efficiency, spooning eggs into a tortilla, folding it neatly. A mug of coffee sat near her elbow, steam rising. Behind me, Sylvia hovered in the doorway, arms crossed, jaw set, completely alert.

My phone buzzed again. The vibration cut through the kitchen's warmth, abrupt and out of place. I flinched.

Pops stood at the counter pouring coffee into a chipped UNM Lobos mug, unhurried. He was already dressed for the day: dark jeans, heavy boots, a worn henley under a flannel that carried the faint scent of sawdust and cold air. He looked like someone awake for hours, who had already moved through the early morning quietly and returned to this spot without needing to announce it. When he saw the phone vibrating against the table, his jaw tightened. His eyes moved from the screen to my face and held there a second too long.

Mama slid a warm burrito onto a ceramic plate and set it in front of me. She had folded it tight in the pan, the tortilla lightly blistered, edges sealed with melted cheese. Steam lifted from the seam where it split, carrying green chile and eggs and potatoes into the air.

The phone buzzed again. Dad's name flashed across the screen.

Pops held out his hand. "Give it here, mija."

I hesitated, fingers tightening around the phone. "It's okay," I said quietly. "I can just ignore…"

"Michelle."

He didn't raise his voice, but the firmness in it left no space for debate. "Hand it over."

My pulse thudded in my ears. I placed the phone in his palm. It disappeared there, reduced to something smaller than the fear it carried.

He answered without glancing at the screen. He watched me instead.

"Sí," he said calmly. "She's here."

My lungs stalled.

"No," he continued, slower now. "She's not coming back right now."

Pops switched between English and Spanish with quiet precision, his tone even but edged just enough to signal that the conversation had crossed into territory he controlled. He wasn't arguing or reacting so much as directing. Whatever my father was saying, it didn't rattle him.

"No," Pops said again. "You listen to me." His voice dropped lower, not louder. "You put your hands on her again, you deal with me."

Silence followed, thick and deliberate. Pops didn't blink. He didn't look away. He waited.

"I said," he repeated, each word measured, "you deal with me."

Another pause. Longer. Behind him, Mama stilled at the stove. She didn't turn around, but her shoulders squared slightly. Sylvia stood rigid in the doorway. Bobby hadn't moved at all.

"Good," Pops said finally. "Don't call this number again."

He ended the call and slid the phone back in front of me, like the conversation hadn't been anything unusual, then picked up his mug and took a sip of coffee.

"Pops, he's going to…"

"No." He cut in, calm and immediate. "He won't. He won't try anything he can't finish."

Mama let out a slow breath beside the stove. Pops took another measured sip of coffee, as if he had just confirmed a delivery time instead of drawing a line with my father.

After breakfast, he tipped his chin toward the front door. "Come on, mija. Walk with me for a second."

The air outside was sharp and clean, cold enough to bite at my cheeks. The porch boards creaked under our weight, worn smooth by years of kids running in and out without knocking. A stack of firewood leaned neatly against the wall. The street ahead was wide and quiet, cottonwoods lining both sides, their bare branches laced against the pale morning sky. Down the block, piñon smoke threaded through the air. Somewhere along the back of the property, one of the horses moved in the corral, hooves soft and deliberate against the frozen ground. Pops rested his elbows on the railing and studied the street without speaking. In a few hours, kids would ride bikes here. Neighbors would step out with coffee. Dogs would bark behind fences.

"Michelle," he said finally, low enough that only I could hear, "you're family here. You hear me?"

I nodded because I didn't trust my voice.

"You're safe as long as you're under this roof," he continued. "No one touches you."

And if he comes here?" I asked.

Pops kept his eyes on the street. The cottonwoods stood still in the cold air; their branches bare and patient. When he spoke again, his voice was steady, almost casual, the voice of a man who had never needed volume to be heard. "He won't. Because he knows who I am."

He straightened and turned toward me, placing his hand on my shoulder. The weight of it was warm and steady. It didn't claim anything. It just grounded me.

"You are a good girl," he said, softer now. "None of this is your fault."

The words landed harder than anything else that morning. No one at home had ever said that to me. Not once. My vision blurred. I looked down at the porch boards so he wouldn't see. He squeezed my shoulder anyway, pretending not to notice.

"Go on now," he said, practical again. "You all will be late."

Inside, the house felt bright and busy. Cabinets opened and closed. Shoes moved down the hallway. Sylvia stood there already dressed, backpack over one shoulder, finishing the last bite of her burrito. She looked at me carefully, taking in more than I wanted her to.

"You okay?" she asked.

Before I could answer, she grabbed my backpack off the couch and shoved it into my hands. "I put snacks in there. Cafeteria's trash today and you're not eating mystery meat on top of everything else."

I managed a small smile. "Thanks."

She shrugged. "That's what best friends are for." She zipped her jacket and nodded toward the door. "Come on. Bobby's probably outside revving the engine like an idiot."

The cold hit as soon as we stepped outside. The sky over the Sandias was pale, the mountains still dark. Leaves scraped across the driveway as we walked. Bobby's baby-blue Ford idled at the curb, engine rattling the way it always did in cold weather. The passenger door carried its familiar dent. The back panel showed the uneven paint from a repair he'd done himself. He leaned across the bench seat and pushed the passenger door open. His hair was still damp from a shower. He wore the gray Calderon Construction hoodie loose over his shoulders, and in the back seat, half-buried under a jacket, a coiled rope and a pair of worn riding gloves sat where they'd been tossed after the last time he'd used them. Behind the seat, a printout of the upcoming district rodeo schedule was folded and tucked against the window, one corner curling loose.

"Morning, Shell," he said.

My chest tightened at the sound of my name. I had known him most of my life: backyards and camping trips, years of him being just Bobby, easy and familiar, safe in the way older brothers are safe without ever having to try. Somewhere along the way that had shifted, quietly enough that I couldn't point to when it happened. I noticed things now: the way his voice dropped when he was serious, like he was giving the words more room; the way he read a room before committing to it, taking stock of exits and moods and where everyone was standing; the way he said my name, with a small pause before it, like he was making sure he had my attention. I didn't know if any of it meant anything or if I was still just part of the furniture of his life. That uncertainty sat low and constant in my chest, the kind you learn to carry without letting it show.

I slid into the middle of the bench seat, the way I always did because Sylvia didn't want to sit next to her brother. My knee shifted automatically away from the gearshift. The heater blew hot air against my legs. The cab smelled like oil, horses, and cold morning air, familiar in a way that made my throat ache.

Bobby shifted into drive. The truck jerked forward, then steadied as we rolled down the street. Sylvia started talking immediately: Spirit Week, a quiz she was sure was coming, a complaint about Bobby drifting toward the center line. Her voice filled the cab, fast and steady. She was trying to keep things normal. I could hear it in the pace of her words, the way she didn't pause long enough to leave room for anything else. Bobby didn't interrupt her, but he wasn't relaxed either. His left hand rested easy on the wheel while his right tapped once against his knee and stopped, the small contained motion of someone working something out internally that he wasn't going to say out loud. Every few seconds he glanced at me and then back at the road.

At the red light near the school, he lowered his voice. "You doing alright, Shell?"

I kept my eyes on the crosswalk signal as it counted down. "I'm fine," I said. The word sounded thin and rehearsed. He didn't challenge it, but his hand tightened briefly on the steering wheel before he forced his fingers to loosen. I saw it. I didn't know what to do with the way that made me feel.

The truck sputtered into the student parking lot and backfired once, loud enough to turn a few heads. Bobby pulled into an open space beneath a crooked light pole and parked slightly off-center, the way he always did. When he shut off the engine, the sudden quiet pressed in. The heater clicked off. The smell of oil and rope hung in the cab. For a moment, none of us moved. The school building sat ahead: brick and glass and fluorescent light behind double doors. Students crossed the lot in clusters, laughing, adjusting backpacks. My phone sat heavy in my pocket. I kept expecting it to vibrate again.

Bobby shifted in his seat, just enough that his shoulder brushed mine. "If anything feels off," he said quietly, eyes fixed on the windshield, "you tell me. Even if it's stupid. Even if it's nothing."

Part of me wanted to let someone else carry the weight this time. Another part didn't want to need him like that. I wasn't sure which part would win.

Sylvia flung her door open before I could answer. "Strength in numbers," she announced, already halfway out.

I stepped out into the cold. Gravel crunched under my shoes. Bobby reached behind the seat and grabbed his backpack, slinging it over one shoulder. He checked the time on his phone once and then dropped it into his pocket without comment. "Let's go," he said. His tone was casual, but his eyes were not.

The three of us crossed the parking lot in a loose line, breath rising in quick white bursts. Car doors slammed. A group of juniors leaned against a Silverado, loud and half-awake. Bobby reached the front doors first and held one open. Sylvia pulled me ahead of him. The moment we stepped inside, the heat and noise closed in. The hallway smelled like dust and old textbooks. Lockers clanged. Voices overlapped. On any other day, it would have blended into the background. Today, every sound hit harder than it should have. My shoulders tightened. My breathing stayed shallow.

Sylvia didn't let go of my arm. Bobby moved half a step ahead, not blocking anyone, just creating space. When someone brushed past, he shifted without looking like he had.

We turned into the main hallway and something changed. No one stopped, no one pointed. It was quieter than that: glances that lasted a second too long, conversations that dipped when I walked by and picked up again in lower tones. A few kids looked up from their phones, took me in, then dropped their eyes. Two freshmen lingered near the drinking fountain, pretending to scroll while watching over their screens. A cluster of girls from biology leaned close beside a locker covered in stickers. One nudged the other when she saw me. I caught pieces of it as we passed.

"…the note…" "…her mom came drunk…" "…CYFD…" "…probably been like that her whole life…"

My mouth went dry. The last one landed differently from the others. Not about what happened. About me. About who I was before anyone in this hallway had decided to look. Sylvia went stiff beside me, her grip tightening on my arm, her whole body angling toward them before I even had time to react.

"Oh, hell no."

"Sylvia…" I started, already tired, already wishing I could disappear.

"No." She turned fully now, stepping toward them, her voice sharper. "Wanna say it again?"

The girls broke apart quickly, slipping into separate classrooms like they had somewhere else to be. I caught Sylvia's sleeve and pulled her back before she could take another step.

"Please," I said. "Not today."

She let out a hard breath but didn't argue, her shoulders still tight, her eyes tracking them as they disappeared, holding onto it longer than I wanted her to.

Then my phone buzzed in my pocket, long and insistent against my hip.

Mom.

I pulled it out and stared at the screen while it rang, my thumb hovering over it without moving. Around us, the hallway kept going. Lockers slammed. Someone laughed too loudly. Shoes scraped against the tile. None of it slowed.

I let it ring.

The screen went dark.

A message appeared almost immediately.

Michelle, please answer. He's mad. I need you.

Then another.

I can't do this alone. Come home.

Home.

The word didn't feel safe. It felt like something pulling at me, low and familiar, something I knew how to respond to even when I didn't want to. I could see her in the kitchen:

hands twisting together, pacing between the sink and the table, eyes too bright. I could hear him in the background, louder now, the edge already there. Mad meant something specific in our house. It meant doors slammed hard enough to rattle frames, glass breaking, his voice rising until it swallowed the room whole.

I wasn't there.

Someone slammed into my shoulder from behind, knocking my backpack half off and forcing me forward a step. I turned and found myself facing a girl I recognized from the hallway, a junior with a high tight ponytail and glitter eyeliner, who hovered a second too long after apologizing, her gaze moving from my face to the phone in my hand and back again.

"Sorry," she said quickly. "I didn't see you." But she didn't move away. "I heard about your mom," she added, lowering her voice. "I hope you're okay."

It sounded kind. It didn't feel kind. Heat climbed up my neck. I could feel eyes around us, not everyone, but enough.

Before I could find words, Sylvia stepped forward, her body shifting in front of mine. "What did you hear?" she demanded, her voice controlled but sharp. "Go on. Say it again. Out loud."

The girl blinked. "I… I didn't mean…"

"Move," Sylvia said.

The girl stepped back fast enough that her sneaker squeaked against the wet tile. She slipped into the nearest classroom without looking back.

My phone buzzed again in my hand. The messages would keep coming. The calls would keep coming. My cheeks burned, my hands trembled. I wasn't just the girl who passed a note anymore. I was the girl whose mother came drunk to school, the girl whose house the cops might visit, the girl walking around with a swollen mouth, the girl people lowered their voices about when she walked by. And underneath all of it, quieter and more shameful than the rest, was the part of me that still wanted to push back through those double doors and go home to the chaos, because at least there I understood the rules. At least there the danger was predictable. Here it was diffuse and public and sharp in a different way, and I didn't know how to stand in the middle of it without coming apart.

"Shell?"

I turned at the sound of my name and saw Bobby cutting toward us through the shifting bodies and fluorescent glare, moving with deliberate purpose, backpack off one shoulder, sleeves pushed to his elbows, jaw already tight. One look at my face and something in him changed. He stopped close, close enough that his presence pushed back some of what had settled under my skin. "What happened?" he asked, voice low but urgent.

I tried to answer, but my lungs wouldn't cooperate. Instead, I held up my phone. He leaned in, close enough that I could smell laundry soap and the faint trace of rope dust that never quite left him. His eyes scanned the screen quickly. I watched the muscle in his cheek twitch, the thing he did when he was furious and working not to show it. His mouth tightened as he read. When he lifted his gaze back to mine, it was steady.

"Shell," he said quietly, "You're not answering that."

There was no argument in his tone, no lecture. Behind him, at the edge of the hallway, Hector leaned against a bank of lockers with his arms folded. He hadn't wandered there. He was positioned there, his back to the wall, angles open, the particular stance of someone who had chosen his spot before the situation required it. His gaze moved from my face to the phone to the cluster of girls who had scattered, then back. He gave Bobby a look that carried a full conversation in it, and Bobby answered it with the smallest nod.

My phone buzzed again. I flinched. Bobby reached for it.

"Turn it off," he said softly.

The hallway kept moving. Lockers slammed. Someone laughed too loudly over something I didn't hear. Bobby looked back at me.

"No more," he said. "Not today."

He pressed the side button and powered it down. The screen went black. The vibration stopped. Without ceremony, he slid the phone into the front pocket of his hoodie. Hector's eyes tracked the movement. Sylvia let out a slow breath.

I leaned back against the lockers and let them hold the line.

Chapter Four
Impact

For the rest of the day, I moved through school like my body was running a few seconds too slow. The fluorescent lights blazed too bright, flattening every surface until the rooms looked harsh and unreal. The scrape of chairs across the tile made my shoulders jump. Every slammed locker hit too hard.

Bobby walked me to first period and lingered in the doorway longer than he needed to, one hand hooked through the strap of his backpack. He didn't hover or make it obvious. He just stood there, scanning the room with that quiet assessment I had started to recognize in him. He mapped exits, faces, angles. When the bell rang, he met my eyes once like he was marking my location before stepping back into the hall.

Sylvia slid into the desk beside mine even though it wasn't technically her seat. She dropped her bag with deliberate noise and angled her chair so our shoulders touched. She didn't make a speech. She just stayed. When a girl two rows up twisted around to look at me, Sylvia held her gaze without blinking until she turned back around.

Teachers lectured. Projectors hummed. Pencils scratched. I wrote my name at the top of a worksheet and stared at it longer than necessary. The letters looked strange, disconnected from me. Michelle. It felt like the name of someone who hadn't stood in a hallway an hour earlier fighting the urge to run.

Between classes, Hector appeared and disappeared at the edges of my vision. At one point I caught him near my chemistry class, leaning against the lockers with his arms folded, Bobby beside him, the two of them talking in the low focused way they talked when something mattered. The word qualifiers reached me as I passed. Bobby said something back without looking up, his jaw working slightly, and Hector nodded once like that settled it. Neither of them looked my way. They were just two juniors talking about rodeo in a hallway, and the ordinary fact of it, their lives continuing on their own track, separate from whatever was happening in mine, steadied something in me I hadn't known needed steadying.

When a couple of varsity baseball players laughed too loudly in my direction a few minutes later, Hector didn't say anything. He just looked at them. The laughter shifted, softened, redirected.

By lunchtime, exhaustion had settled into my bones. We took our usual table in the far corner of the cafeteria; backs angled toward the wall without ever discussing it. The room buzzed with trays clattering and the high, careless laughter of people who believed their biggest problem was algebra. Sylvia launched into a loud critique of the cafeteria pizza, holding up a limp slice like it was evidence. Bobby reached across my tray and stole half my fries, claiming I owed him gas money in potato form.

I picked at my food, chewing without tasting. Every time the double doors at the far end of the cafeteria swung open, my pulse spiked hard enough to make my vision blur. I imagined my mom standing there, hair unbrushed, eyes frantic. I imagined my dad behind her, scanning the room until he found me.

"Just so you know," Sylvia said suddenly, pointing a fry at me, "if your mom shows up here, I'm tackling her at the door."

"Please don't tackle my mom," I muttered automatically. Saying it made something twist in my chest anyway.

Bobby leaned back in his chair. "I mean. I'm not saying I'd stop her."

The corner of his mouth lifted, teasing, but his eyes were serious. A small laugh slipped out before I could stop it. It felt wrong and right at the same time.

By the last bell, my shoulders were locked in place. When I spotted Bobby's truck where he'd left it that morning, something in my chest loosened all at once.

"Home or home?" Bobby asked.

"Yours," I said.

"Good choice."

The drive back felt shorter than it should have. Sylvia filled the cab with a dramatic breakdown of her math quiz. Bobby let her talk. I leaned my head back and let the motion of the truck carry me. The cab still smelled like rope and cold morning air, the same as it had at dawn, and Rowdy's red and white fur clung to the back of the bench seat where he'd ridden out earlier. Small things. Ordinary things. The kind that didn't require anything from me.

When we turned north and the cottonwoods closed over the road, I felt my breathing slow for the first time all day.

Mama had pulled into the driveway ahead of us. Rowdy met the truck at the gate, circling once with his nose up before settling into his characteristic trot alongside the driver's side as Bobby eased forward. The corral fence ran the length of the property's far edge, and both horses stood at the near rail in the late afternoon light. The property looked exactly as it had that morning and the morning before, unhurried and solid, the kind of place that didn't reorganize itself around whatever had happened elsewhere.

Inside, the house felt warmer than it needed to be. Mama had laid out clean towels. An extra toothbrush sat by the sink. Borrowed pajamas were draped over the couch. No one asked how long I was staying.

We spread our homework across the kitchen table. Textbooks open. Calculators nudged back and forth. The overhead light cast a warm circle over us. Sylvia complained about her essay. Bobby worked through a construction drafting assignment, a floor plan spread flat beside his textbook, a pencil moving in careful measured lines. He smelled faintly of horses and laundry soap, the particular combination that meant he'd been out to the corral before school and hadn't quite scrubbed it all the way off. I underlined sentences without really seeing them.

My phone was on the table beside my notebook.

It buzzed.

You made me look bad. Why would you tell them? You're my daughter. You're supposed to be on my side.

Then:

I'm sorry. I didn't mean it. Come home. We can start over.

Each message pulled differently. Bobby's foot nudged mine under the table.

"You know you don't have to read those."

"I know."

I left the phone where it was.

After dinner, Sylvia put on a dumb comedy. She stretched across the couch with her head in my lap, reading memes aloud. Bobby sat in the recliner, pretending to be annoyed while still laughing. I let my fingers move through Sylvia's hair, giving my hands something to do. Rowdy had settled on the floor near the couch, his chin resting on his front paws, his eyes moving between the television and the room, his tail sweeping the floor occasionally.

Hector came in around nine. He moved through the room, poured water, and stayed leaning against the counter, watching. His eyes moved from Sylvia to Bobby to me.

"You should figure out something more permanent," he said quietly.

I looked at him. "I'm fine."

"That's not what I said."

Sylvia pushed up. "Hector—"

"Living out of other people's houses isn't a plan."

Bobby set his glass down. "Nobody asked."

"I'm not talking to you."

His eyes stayed on me.

"I said I'm fine." I repeated.

"You keep saying that." He paused. "Doesn't make it true."

Bobby stood, just enough to step between us. "We're done."

Hector looked at him, then back at me.

"Must be nice," he said. "Just walk in and everybody rearranges."

Sylvia sat up. "That's not what this is."

"You sure about that?"

Then to me: "You think this is permanent?"

I didn't answer.

He nodded once.

He walked down the hall to Bobby's room and shut the door.

Bobby stood where he was. He didn't move toward me right away. His eyes stayed on the closed door for a long moment, jaw working once, before he turned back. Something had shifted in his expression, not quite agreement, not quite dismissal. Something in between that he wasn't going to say out loud.

Hector's words stayed, settling in beside my mother's texts and the borrowed pajamas and the toothbrush that hadn't been there yesterday. All the evidence of a life that kept landing in other people's spaces.

Around ten, Mama came in, steady as always. She kissed Sylvia's forehead. She squeezed Bobby's shoulder. She pressed her lips to the top of my head like there was no difference between us.

"You wake me if Michelle needs anything."

Then to me:

"Or if you just want to talk, mija. Any hour."

I nodded.

The house settled into its late-night sounds. The heater clicked on and ran its steady hum through the vents. Outside, the cottonwoods moved in the wind. One of the horses shifted in the corral, hooves soft against the frozen ground.

Rowdy padded across the room and lowered himself beside the couch where I lay. I reached down and curled my fingers into his fur, as I lay there in the dark, Hector's words and my mother's texts sitting side by side in my chest.

Chapter Five
Weather

Over the next few weeks, I didn't go home.

There was no announcement, no meeting around the kitchen table, no sentence that officially marked the shift. It happened quietly. My shoes joined the uneven line by the front door. My hoodie ended up tossed over the back of the couch more often than folded in my backpack. Every afternoon, my backpack landed on their couch with the soft, familiar thud of routine. No one asked where I was sleeping.

If the school or CYFD were involved behind the scenes, they kept it quiet. I heard the word placement once in the hallway when a counselor murmured it to Mr. Alvarez. That word caught in my chest. When they noticed me looking, the language shifted immediately: support, stability, resources. Words meant to smooth sharp edges into something less frightening.

Sometimes Mom called. Sometimes she texted. Sometimes she disappeared for days and then returned in a rush of messages that felt like they'd been building pressure behind a wall.

Your father says this is your fault. He's saying things about me. You know they aren't true, right? We're supposed to be a team.

Other nights the tone shifted entirely.

I miss you. I'm trying, Michelle. I swear I'm trying. I'll quit. I'll pour it all out. You'll see. Just come home.

Home. The word felt unstable if I held it too long. It used to mean endurance. Then it meant fear. Now it was a choice I didn't know how to make without breaking something. If I went back, I would betray the way it felt here. If I stayed, I would betray the woman who had raised me.

I couldn't take the whiplash: the swing from accusation to apology, from *you ruined everything* to *baby, I need you.*

Each shift hit me before my brain could catch up. My stomach turned slow and sick. My pulse spiked every time my screen lit up, even when it wasn't her. At night, lying on Sylvia's floor or half-curled on the couch, I replayed the messages in both voices, the angry one and the soft one. I knew they came from the same place. That was the part that hurt. She could love me and still pull me under.

So, I stayed where the ground felt steady. I learned to let the phone buzz without reaching for it every time. I learned that guilt didn't automatically require action. And slowly, without anyone announcing it, the Calderon house became home. There was homework at the table, Sylvia's commentary running in the background, Bobby's boots by the door still carrying the pale dust of the corral, Pops' low voice on the phone in the evenings. At night when the house went quiet you could hear the acequia running somewhere beyond the yard, steady and indifferent, the sound of water that had been moving through this valley longer than any of us had been here to listen to it. Laughter mixed in with vigilance. Teasing layered over watchfulness.

One night, when my phone buzzed for the fourth time in ten minutes, Bobby leaned forward from the recliner without a word. He picked it up from the coffee table, glanced once at the name flashing across the screen, and walked it into the kitchen. I heard the drawer slide open. Then the soft, contained sound of it landing inside. The drawer shut.

"If it's important," he said, leaning against the doorway on his way back in, "they'll call Pops."

I stared at the closed drawer. "She's still my mom."

"I know," he said. No impatience. No dismissal. "That doesn't mean she's safe."

There was weight in what he said. I hated it instantly because it was true. And because some part of me still wanted it not to be.

A few days later, Sylvia and I were stretched out across her bedroom floor with our geometry books open and completely ignored between us. Her door was closed. Music drifted low from her speakers, soft enough that Mama wouldn't call down the hall about homework. Late afternoon light filtered through the blinds in narrow gold stripes, catching dust in the air. Rowdy was asleep against the foot of Sylvia's bed, chin on his paws, his breathing slow and even. My history composition book lay open beside my elbow, the same black-and-white marbled notebook everyone had bought in August. The corners were bent. The cover was soft from use. The front half was filled with careful notes. The back half used to be mine.

Sylvia noticed before I said anything. "You haven't written back here in a while," she said, nudging the book with her socked foot.

"I've been busy."

"Liar."

I looked up. She wasn't accusing. She was observing. "You're writing safe now," she said. "And it's boring."

"I am not writing safe."

She flipped to the last page I'd filled. The sentences were flat. Measured. Nothing emotional enough to be misunderstood. Nothing that could be lifted out of context by adults with concerned faces. Sylvia closed the notebook slowly and rested her palm on top of it.

"Okay," she said.

"Okay what?"

"We're not writing normal anymore."

I laughed. "That's not a thing."

"It is now." She sat up cross-legged and pulled the notebook between us. There was a spark in her eyes. "If people are going to decide what we mean," she said thoughtfully, "then we stop writing what we mean."

"That makes zero sense."

"It makes perfect sense. We invent it."

"Invent what?"

"A code."

I stared at her. "You've been watching too many spy movies."

She ignored me and flipped to a blank page near the back. "No real names," she declared immediately.

"Why?"

She gave me a look. "Because I do not need Bobby reading something over my shoulder and thinking he knows what it's about."

"You write about Bobby?"

She clutched the notebook to her chest dramatically. "Just an example, Silly."

I laughed despite myself. The sound felt easier than it had in days. She uncapped my pen and leaned over the page.

"Okay," she murmured. "We start with categories."

"Categories?"

"Yes. Themes."

"This feels like homework."

"It's art," she corrected. She wrote one word.

Weather.

I burst out laughing. "Weather?"

"Listen," she said, already delighted with herself. "Weather is neutral. It can mean anything."

"That's not how weather usually works."

"It is in our world." She began writing beneath it, speaking as she went. "If something feels dramatic, Storm. If someone's being weird, Fog. If there's tension, Static."

"That's electricity, not weather."

She flicked the pen at me. "Details."

I leaned closer, drawn in despite myself. "What's good then?"

She paused, thinking harder. "Library," she said finally.

"That's not weather."

"No," she admitted, softer. "But it's safe. Quiet. No one interrupts you."

I didn't argue. She wrote it down carefully.

Library.

The page already looked like coded nonsense. "Okay," I said, warming to it. "If someone makes your stomach flip?"

She didn't hesitate. "Fireflies."

"That's dramatic."

"Exactly."

"And if you're nervous but pretending you're not?"

She thought for a second, then wrote: *thin ice.*

We both leaned back and read it.

Storm in second period. Static near the lockers. Fireflies at lunch. Library after school.

It looked like the emotional forecast of someone unwell. It was perfect.

"And dates are always wrong," Sylvia added.

"Why?"

"So, if anyone tries to line things up, they can't."

I raised an eyebrow. "Who is investigating us?"

"You never know," she said lightly, but I caught something deliberate underneath it.

We didn't write down what any of it meant. No key. No translation. The meanings lived between us, in shared glances, in the way she'd say "Fog?" and I'd nod without explanation. We slipped it into hallway conversations. Sometimes we wrote entire paragraphs in code, laughing at how dramatic it sounded. The notebook still looked like school. Still looked harmless. But tucked into the back pages was something no one else could read. It felt like building a small, private room inside something ordinary.

By the time the light faded from the blinds, geometry was forgotten and the page was full. We closed the notebook and slid it back into my backpack. Rowdy lifted his head at the movement, looked around, and put it back down. Outside, one of the horses shifted in the corral, and the acequia ran on in the dark beyond the yard, steady as it had always been.

"From now on," Sylvia said, satisfied.

"From now on," I agreed.

Chapter Six
Eight Seconds

The rodeo grounds smelled like dust and diesel. The bleachers were still warm when we sat down, heat pressing through the denim of my jeans. Country music crackled through worn speakers. Vendors called out near the concession stand. Behind the chutes, a bull hit the gate hard enough to make the steel rattle.

Sylvia dropped beside me with a lemonade sweating through the paper cup, her braid tight down her back. I wore the black T-shirt Bobby had once told me he liked best. It was soft and thin from too many washes. I told myself I wore it because it was comfortable.

Down near the chutes, Bobby rolled his shoulders beneath his vest, loosening up the way he always did before a ride. Hector stood a few feet away with one boot hooked over the bottom rail, his hand resting on the metal. Bobby glanced toward the stands once, aware of the crowd. Hector didn't look up at all. Pops and Joe stood together, as they had for years, further along the fence, arms crossed, hats low. Rowdy sat between them, with his eyes moving across the arena the way they moved across every space he entered.

"You nervous?" Sylvia asked.

"For who?"

She laughed, raising her eyebrows. "Please."

A rider went before Bobby and got thrown flat on his back. The impact rolled all the way up the bleachers. The bull's hooves came down close enough to make the first row recoil before the bullfighters stepped in. The rider stayed down a few seconds longer than anyone liked.

"Bobby Calderon!" the announcer called.

Pops didn't clap. He didn't move. Rowdy's ears went forward.

Bobby climbed into the chute and settled onto the bull, adjusting his rope with small, precise movements. He nodded.

The gate opened.

The bull came out hard and fast, twisting left and snapping right. Bobby's body followed the motion, his free arm up and steady. The bull kicked high and dropped its front legs hard. Dirt flew.

Two seconds.

Four.

The bull changed direction sharply. Bobby corrected, boots tight against the animal's sides. My hand jerked; lemonade sloshed over the rim, sticky across my fingers. I didn't wipe it off.

Six seconds.

The bull drove forward and twisted again, head down, shoulders rolling. Bobby stayed centered.

Eight.

The buzzer sounded.

Bobby released and hit the ground running. The bull turned toward him before the bullfighters cut in and redirected it. For a moment the space between them was too small. Then Bobby reached the fence and swung himself up.

The crowd stood.

Sylvia hit the railing with her palm. "See? Fine."

Bobby jogged toward the stands a few minutes later, helmet off, sweat dark at his collar. He dropped onto the bench beside us, his thigh brushing mine as he sat. He smelled like dust and sweat and the faint trace of horses that never quite left him. He looked up at the scoreboard, then back at Sylvia with the subtlety of someone who already knows his score and wants her to acknowledge it.

"Eighty-three," he said, as if stating a neutral fact.

"Congratulations," Sylvia said flatly. "You're insufferable."

He didn't disagree. The corner of his mouth lifted. My stomach tightened.

Hector's name came next.

He mounted without flourish, settling into position quickly. The bull beneath him shifted and slammed the gate once. Sylvia sat up straighter beside me. She didn't say anything. She set her lemonade down on the bleacher plank and watched the chute intently, not moving a muscle.

The gate opened.

The bull came out low and driving, no spin at first, just force. It bucked straight up and then cut hard toward the fence. Hector's shoulders snapped sideways before he corrected. His free arm stayed closer to his body than Bobby's had.

Five seconds.

The bull lunged forward, then twisted sharply. Dirt sprayed into the first row.

Six.

Seven.

At eight, the buzzer sounded, but the bull lunged again. Hector came down slightly off balance. He hit the ground on his shoulder and rolled. The bull's hind leg struck dirt close enough to send dirt across his back. For a second he was on the ground with the bull still turning.

He got up fast and moved low and away as the bullfighters stepped in. The bull tossed its head and kicked once more before being pulled off line.

The crowd reacted all at once.

Bobby leaned forward, elbows on his knees, jaw tight, watching until Hector reached the fence. The scoreboard flashed seventy-nine. Bobby let out a slow breath, not disappointment, not satisfaction. Something more complicated than either.

Hector reached the fence and leaned against it, breathing hard, dust streaked across his face. He reached up and pulled off his helmet, running a hand through his hair once, a quick, private motion, before looking up at the stands. His gaze moved across the rows in a way that looked general until it stopped. It stopped on Sylvia.

It lasted less than two seconds. His expression didn't change. He looked away and spat dust onto the dirt and turned back toward the chute area like the moment hadn't happened.

Beside me, Sylvia picked up her lemonade and took a long, slow drink. Her eyes stayed on the arena. Her jaw was set. After a moment she tucked a loose strand of hair behind her ear with the same careful attention she gave to things she was pretending not to think about.

She didn't wave. She didn't look back.

The drive home took twenty minutes on roads that ran north and east, the Sandias catching the last of the sun on their western face, going amber and then dark as we turned. Dust clung to Bobby's jeans and the hem of my shirt, gritty and dry. Sylvia sat between me and the window, her braid coming loose, one knee angled toward the door and the other toward me. The truck smelled like arena dirt and sweat and green chile chips Sylvia had already finished. Bobby kept the radio low. The cottonwoods thickened as we turned north, the lots widening and quieting, the streetlights further apart. By the time the porch light came into view the sky had gone fully dark.

Rowdy met the truck at the gate, circling once before falling into his trot alongside Bobby's door, tail working, nose up, reading the night air.

Hector pulled in behind us a few minutes later, boots still dusty when he came through the door, and went straight to the kitchen without saying much.

The house smelled like chicken and red chile, the heat of it thick in the air, settling into the curtains and the couch cushions. Sylvia and I sat cross-legged on the living room rug with index cards scattered between us, the edges bent and soft from being handled too much. We quizzed each other for history, turning every date into something ridiculous just to make it bearable.

"Treaty of Versailles," Sylvia announced in a deep, dramatic voice, like she was introducing a heavyweight bout.

"Bad decisions in fancy handwriting," I shot back.

She grinned and scribbled something onto the card. "Accurate. Painfully accurate."

From the recliner, Bobby looked up whenever we butchered something beyond redemption. If it was especially bad, he reached for whatever was within reach — a throw pillow, a rolled-up napkin — and lobbed it in our direction with lazy aim. "If you fail this test," he said, leaning his head back against the chair, "don't drag my last name down with you. I've got a reputation to maintain."

"Your C in algebra says otherwise," Sylvia fired back.

He snorted. "Alleged C."

Rowdy had stretched out across the rug between us and the recliner, chin on his paws, eyes tracking every card that hit the floor with the focused attention of a dog who had decided retrieving is beneath him but monitoring wasn't.

Pops sat at the kitchen table beneath the hanging light, sorting receipts into careful stacks. He worked with the same steady rhythm he used for everything, paper squared, numbers checked twice, pen tapping once before each note. Mama moved between the stove and the sink, tasting the sauce, adding a pinch of salt, wiping down the counter with the edge of the dish towel tucked into her apron. She hummed under her breath, something soft and unhurried. Hector had showered and changed. He sat at the far end of the kitchen table with his back to the living room, a glass of water at his elbow, working through something on his phone. Once, Sylvia glanced toward the kitchen when Pops' pen paused and the room went briefly quiet. Hector didn't look up. Pops did, once, in the direction of the living room, before returning to his receipts.

The room was full of small, dependable sounds. Silverware settling into a drawer. The low murmur of Spanish news drifting from the kitchen radio. The scratch of Sylvia's pencil. The quiet creak of Bobby's chair when he shifted his weight.

My phone buzzed once on the coffee table.

The sound cut through the room. I kept my eyes on the card in Sylvia's hand.

It buzzed again. Then again. The glass beside it trembled. Pops' pen paused. The heater clicked off.

I didn't look.

The phone buzzed a fourth time and slid across the wood. The screen lit. I caught the first few letters of her name. My throat tightened.

Sylvia's voice slowed. She lowered the flashcard, tracking my line of sight without turning.

The phone buzzed again.

My pulse answered it. I pressed my hands flat against my knees. Bobby leaned forward, watching the phone.

Rowdy lifted his head from his paws. His ears moved forward, angling toward the front of the house, not the phone. Something outside. Something not here yet.

Pops stopped writing. Mama turned the burner down. The room shifted.

The screen lit again.

Michelle please.

I swallowed. "She'll just keep calling."

The phone vibrated again, sharp and constant.

This time, everyone in the room felt it.

A new message slid onto the screen.

I'm outside. Come out. We're going home.

The warmth drained out of me so fast it left my hands cold and unsteady. "She's here," I said, the words barely holding themselves together. "She's outside."

The shift in the room was immediate and complete. Sylvia sat up so fast the index cards scattered across the rug, sliding under the coffee table and toward the couch. Bobby was on his feet in one motion, all trace of teasing gone from his face. Mama turned off the stove without looking back, the burner clicking sharply as the flame died. Pops pushed away from the table, his chair scraping once across the tile. "Don't open the door," he said to Sylvia and me, already moving down the hallway. "You hear me?"

We nodded. It didn't feel like obedience. It felt like understanding the risk.

Rowdy was already at the door, standing low and quiet, his body angled toward the sound outside. Pops' hand dropped briefly to the dog's head as he passed, and Rowdy fell into step beside him without being told.

Sylvia grabbed my wrist and pulled me toward the side window where the blinds never quite closed. We crouched low, shifting just enough to see a narrow slice of porch and sidewalk. Bobby stood just behind us, close enough that I could feel the heat from him through my shirt, not touching, but ready. Behind him, Hector had come to the hallway doorway. He stood with his shoulder against the frame, arms folded, watching Pops move toward the front door with the particular stillness of someone who has run this kind of calculation before and already knows how it ends.

The front door opened and cold air rushed in, carrying my mother's voice ahead of her.

"Where is she?" she shouted. "Michelle! Get out here right now!"

The words were loud but uneven, blurred at the edges. She stood just beyond the porch light, keys clenched in her fist. Mascara had smeared beneath her eyes. Her hair had slipped halfway out of its clip. One heel caught on the concrete as she shifted her weight. Her car sat crooked at the curb, angled too far in, two tires riding halfway up onto the sidewalk.

"You need to lower your voice, señora," Pops said evenly, Rowdy still at his side. "Kids are sleeping."

"She's my kid!" Mom shot back. "You can't just keep her from me like some thief."

"I'm not keeping anyone," Pops replied. "Michelle doesn't want to go with you tonight. That's all."

"She's my daughter!" Her voice cracked upward. "You people think you're better than us, huh? With your nice little house, your perfect little…"

Her keys slipped from her hand and clattered against the sidewalk, sharp in the cold air. She stared at them for a long second before bending too quickly to pick them up, nearly pitching forward as she grabbed the porch railing for balance.

Inside, guilt came first, heavy and immediate, followed by fear that settled lower and stayed. Sylvia's fingers laced through mine and squeezed hard enough to ground me. "M&M," she whispered, close to my ear, "don't move."

Outside, Pops drew a slow breath, controlled and deliberate. "I'm gonna call you a ride," he said. "You shouldn't drive."

"I'm fine," Mom snapped, straightening herself unevenly. "Don't tell me what I can do."

"Patricia," Pops said quietly, his voice lowering rather than rising, Rowdy steady beside him, "you're drunk. Go home. Sleep."

"I am home!" she shouted back. Then her tone shifted, thinner now, threaded with hurt. "Or I was before you people decided you knew what was best for my kid."

Mama stepped beside Pops, her sweater pulled tight around her shoulders, keeping her distance but holding her ground. "We're just trying to keep her safe," Mama said softly.

"That's my job!" Mom yelled. "Mine. Not yours. Not his." She jabbed a finger toward Pops. "You think you scare me? Everybody's so scared of you. Not me."

Pops didn't react. "I'm not trying to scare you," he said. "I'm trying to keep you from getting arrested. Or hurt. Or worse."

Mom let out a short, broken laugh. "Too late for that."

She stumbled backward toward the car, heel slipping again as she reached for the handle. "Call it in," Mama murmured. Pops didn't argue. He stepped further down the walkway, already dialing, his voice low and even as he gave the dispatcher the street name, the direction of the car, the make and color. He didn't raise his voice. He didn't hurry. He spoke like he was reporting a fallen branch in the road.

Mom yanked open the driver's door and dropped into the seat. The engine coughed once, then turned over rough and loud. Headlights flared across the house, washing the porch and windows in harsh white light. For a second the living room lit up from the outside, our silhouettes thrown against the wall.

"She's going to crash," I said. My voice sounded thin and distant.

Bobby's hand settled on my shoulder, firm and steady. "Pops called it in," he said quietly. "They'll intercept her."

"But what if they don't?" The words tore out before I could shape them. "What if…"

"Michelle." His voice shifted, softer but solid. "Look at me."

I turned because I had to.

"She's making choices you can't stop," he said. "That's not on you. Do you understand?"

I didn't, not in the place where love and fear had lived together so long, they were hard to tell apart. Part of me wanted him to ask rather than tell, wanted the question instead of the answer, but his steadiness was enough for now. I nodded because he was close and because the alternative was coming apart entirely.

Outside, the engine revved too high. The car jerked away from the curb, tires scraping as they dropped off the edge of the sidewalk. The taillights burned red at the end of the street and then vanished around the corner.

Pops came back inside a minute later, phone still in his hand. His face had gone still in that way it did when he was holding something in place. "Units are close," he said. "They'll stop her." No one moved. The heater kicked on again. The pot simmered quietly on the stove. The index cards lay scattered across the rug where they'd fallen.

I stood there counting seconds without meaning to. Ten. Twenty. Thirty. My mind kept running the corner of our street forward: another car, a pedestrian, a tree.

Rowdy pressed against my leg and stayed there.

Ten minutes later, red and blue lights flickered faintly through the front window, washing over the living room wall and then disappearing, then returning again. My stomach dropped.

Pops' phone rang. He answered immediately, stepping a few feet away but not far enough that we couldn't hear the shape of the conversation. "Yes." A pause. "Anyone else involved?" Another pause. "Okay." He ended the call and looked at us. "She hit a parked car," he said. "No one was inside. No one's hurt."

"And her?" I asked. The word caught halfway out. "Is she…?"

"She's alive," Pops said. "They're taking her to the hospital. Then to the station."

The heater ran. The pot simmered. Somewhere outside the acequia moved through the dark.

DWI.

Chapter Seven
Steady Ground

Nothing in my life shifted cleanly. It moved in stages and required paperwork. There were hearings in low-ceilinged rooms where the fluorescent lights hummed too loudly and the air smelled faintly of burnt coffee and carpet cleaner. Long tables. Name placards. Thick binders opened and closed while adults flipped pages as if my life were something to be audited. Every time someone said *this is the last form*, another appeared, clipped neatly to the top of the stack like a stubborn shadow. I learned to sign my name in steady strokes, to keep my voice level when I answered questions about where I felt most stable, as if stability were a preference.

Mom went into rehab, she actually went, and for once it wasn't a sunrise promise that dissolved by dinner. When she called, her voice sounded different. Not cheerful. Not fixed. Just clearer, like something blurred for a long time had sharpened. She talked about group sessions and accountability and doing the work, repeating the phrase as if repetition could build something solid. She described the schedule there, the early mornings, the rules. Sometimes she cried mid-sentence and apologized. Sometimes she asked about school in a careful, measured way, like she was trying to relearn how to be my mother without leaning on guilt or urgency. I listened. I answered. I told her about tests, homework and the weather. After I hung up, I pressed my face into the couch cushions so no one would hear me cry in a way that had nothing to do with sadness alone. Loyalty and anger lived in me at the same time, pressing against each other without canceling out.

All that time, I stayed where I had landed.

My toothbrush took permanent residence in the bathroom, wedged between Sylvia's floral one and Bobby's plain blue. My socks disappeared into Sylvia's laundry basket and returned folded tight, still warm from the dryer. My backpack found its place at the end of the couch every afternoon. Mama called out *"Mija, dinner"* without hesitation. The chair next to Pops at the dinner table became mine, as if it had been waiting. Sunday dinners at Grandma's, I sat in the same chair at the long table.

Sanctuary stopped feeling temporary. It stopped feeling like a favor. It became routine: homework at the table, dishes in the sink, the heater kicking on at night, Sylvia's music down the hall. Routine made it possible to breathe without checking the door. It also made the idea of leaving feel like something that would tear instead of simply change.

One hot, wind-cut afternoon in August, the caseworker pointed up at a beige apartment complex three blocks from school. The paint had faded unevenly in the sun. The metal railings were chipped and warm when I brushed my fingers against them. The building wasn't unsafe, just tired. Laundry hung from a second-floor balcony. A tricycle lay on its side near the curb.

"Unit 2B," she said. "If your mom completes treatment, this is where you'll go."

The brass numbers above the door had dulled with weather. 2B. Plain. The kind of door you could walk past every day and never register.

I stood at the base of the stairwell and tried to build the inside in my head. A narrow living room with secondhand furniture that didn't match. A kitchen where the cabinet doors closed fully and the sink didn't drip. A bedroom with intact drywall. I tried to picture Mom there sober, coffee mug in hand, hair pulled back, no hidden bottles in the trash, no listening for the shift in her voice that meant the night was about to turn. Every version of it felt provisional, like it depended on something outside the frame staying in place.

Hector's voice came back to me the way inconvenient things do, uninvited and precisely timed. *At some point you have to deal with your own situation. You can't just relocate it here.* He had said it weeks ago in the living room, quiet and matter-of-fact, like he was pointing out something obvious. Bobby had shut it down immediately. I had told myself it didn't land.

But standing at the base of the stairwell, staring at the dulled brass numbers above the door, I understood what he had meant and hated that I did. He wasn't wrong. He just said it without any softness, like it was simple. Like fourteen-year-olds with nowhere safe to go get to make clean decisions. Like the place he thought I was running to wasn't the only thing keeping me from disappearing entirely.

But 2B was the answer to his argument, whether he knew it or not. My own door. My own lock. A space that didn't belong to someone else's family. The question was whether I trusted what was supposed to hold it together.

Bobby stood with his hands in his pockets, taking in the parking lot, the neighboring balconies, the street at the end of the block. His gaze moved the way it always did when he was assessing entries, exits, blind spots. Then he looked at me.

"You okay?" he asked.

"I don't know," I said, and it was the most honest answer I had.

"Sylvia said, hands planted on her hips as she looked up at the building. "Three blocks from school. You could walk. That's basically prime real estate."

The wind pushed hard down the walkway, catching loose gravel and sending it skittering against the curb. A section of railing rattled. Somewhere nearby, a screen door slammed and then bounced back against its frame. This wasn't the house with the steady porch light and the sound of Mama in the kitchen. This quiet felt exposed. Shared. Dependent on neighbors and locks and hope.

"Nothing's decided yet," the caseworker added, checking something on her clipboard. "It's just an option."

An option. The word sat strangely in my chest, as if my life had shrunk to a form: stay, return, placement pending.

On the walk back, the Sandias rose sharp and blue against the sky. Dry leaves chased us along the sidewalk. I kept thinking about the space between rescue and independence, about how you could be grateful to be held and still know that eventually you were expected to stand.

Sunday dinner at Grandma's was a regular thing, as if the universe had long ago decided that Sunday afternoon belonged to that house and everyone in it simply showed up because that was what Sundays were for.

The property sat back from the road behind a stand of old cottonwoods, their trunks thick and pale against the afternoon light. A low adobe wall ran along the front, the gate worn smooth at the latch from decades of hands pushing through it. The portal stretched the full length of the house, deep enough to hold chairs and a bench and the particular quality of shade that only comes from walls two feet thick. Hollyhocks grew tall and stubborn along the south side, their colors faded now in the August heat but still present, still reaching. Behind the house, past the kitchen garden Grandma tended with the same focused efficiency she brought to everything, a small pasture held two older horses that belonged to the property the way the cottonwoods belonged to it — as if they had always been there and simply continued to be.

I had been coming here since I was five, trailing behind Sylvia the way I had trailed behind her everywhere, and the house had absorbed me the way it absorbed everything, gradually, completely, without making anything of it. I knew which step on the portal creaked. I knew that the santo in the hallway had a small chip at the base that Grandma had never repaired because her husband had put it there and she saw no reason to erase him. I knew that the kitchen radio stayed on all afternoon and that Grandma's opinion of whatever the hosts were saying came in short, decisive bursts that required no response. I knew my chair at the long table, third from the end on the left side, between Sylvia and the window that looked out toward the pasture. What was different now was that I arrived with the family instead of being collected along the way. The distinction was small and enormous at the same time.

Grandma was already in the kitchen when we came through the door, moving between the stove and the counter with the efficient unhurried motion of someone who had been feeding people in this room for forty years and saw no reason to change her method now. She was small and round and completely in command of every surface she occupied. Her hair was pinned up the way it always was, dark streaked with gray, a few strands loose at the back of her neck from the heat of cooking. She wore a housedress and an apron that had been washed so many times the pattern had faded to something approximate.

The kitchen smelled of red chile and garlic and the warm, quiet darkness of beans simmering since morning. It smelled of candle wax and old wood and the lavender lotion that sat by the bathroom sink and that I associated so completely with this house that sometimes I caught a trace of it somewhere else and felt briefly, inexplicably, safe.

Hector's cat was asleep on the chair in the corner near the stove, a gray tabby of indeterminate age that had arrived at the property some years ago and never left. Nobody explained why it was called Hector's cat. It simply was.

Grandma looked up when we came in, assessed the group in one sweep, and pointed at me.

"You. Wash your hands and come chop these onions."

Not a welcome. An assignment. I was already at the sink before I registered that I'd moved.

Sylvia dropped into a chair at the kitchen table with the ease of someone who had been sitting in that chair her whole life. Bobby went through the back door to check on the horses, screen door banging behind him the way it always did. Pops came into the kitchen and stood near the counter, and something shifted in him that I had never seen shift before. He waited. He stood in his own mother's kitchen and he waited to be told where to go, his hands loose at his sides, the quiet authority that filled every other room he entered held in reserve here, returned to her without argument.

"Sit down," Grandma said, without looking up from the stove. "You're making me nervous standing there."

"Mamá," he said, with a patience that suggested this was an old conversation.

"Sit."

He sat. Mama, who had brought a dish from home wrapped in a towel, set it carefully on the counter and asked where Grandma wanted it, and the two of them moved through the kitchen in the particular calibration of women who respect each other's domain and have worked out over years exactly how much space each requires.

I chopped onions and watched all of it.

Hector came in from outside and nodded once at the room in general, poured himself a glass of water, and sat at the far end of the table with his back to most of it. The cat opened one eye at his arrival, assessed him, and went back to sleep. Sylvia watched him sit down with the careful inattention she had been practicing lately, the kind that required more effort than actual looking.

Bobby came back smelling of horses and summer dust, went to the sink to wash his hands, and told Grandma that the gray mare was favoring her left foreleg slightly. Grandma nodded and told him to tell Pops after dinner. Bobby told Pops right away. Grandma did not comment on this.

The meal arrived in stages, the way meals at that table always did, too much food, never enough room, everything passed across too many hands. Red chile and posole and the beans that had been going since morning, rice Grandma had learned from her own mother, never written down. Tortillas from the comal, still blistered. Sylvia talked her way through three servings. Pops ate with the focused appreciation of a man who knew that this cooking couldn't be replaced. Bobby ate quickly and then slowed down like the food reminded him there was no reason to hurry. Hector ate without a word and accepted a second portion from Grandma before she offered it. I ate everything placed in front of me and felt, as I always did in this kitchen, that the food was doing something beyond feeding me, telling me this is what care looks like when it has been practiced long enough to become instinct.

Afterward, the plates were being cleared. Pops and Bobby talking about the mare. Sylvia telling Mama something about school. Hector reading something on his phone with the cat now relocated to his lap without his apparent permission. Grandma touched my elbow and tilted her head toward the back door.

I followed her out onto the narrow back porch that looked toward the kitchen garden and the pasture beyond. Late afternoon light filtered through the cottonwoods in long, shifting pieces. One horse stood near the fence, head down, unhurried. The air smelled of green chile and dust, and the faint sweetness of whatever Grandma had baked earlier that hadn't made it to the table yet.

She stood beside me, looking out at the pasture for a moment without speaking. Then she said, quietly, not looking at me:

"The ones who find their way here always do."

She went back inside before I could answer.

I stood on the porch for a moment longer, the cottonwood light moving across the ground, the horse still at the fence, the sound of the family drifting through the kitchen window. I wasn't sure if she meant me, or the cat, gray and certain in Hector's lap. Or Hector himself. Maybe she meant all of it. Maybe, in her understanding of the world, those things were the same.

I went back inside.

That night was the back-to-school dance.

I almost didn't go. I sat on Sylvia's bed in a borrowed dress and stared at my reflection in her mirror. My hair was straightened. My makeup was light but deliberate. I looked like any other girl getting ready for a school dance. That felt almost dishonest.

"You're going," Sylvia said, inside the closet, her voice muffled by hanging clothes. She tossed two more shirts onto the bed like she was in the middle of a timed event. "You need loud music and bad lighting. It's medicinal."

"I don't think that's how medicine works," I muttered.

"It is tonight."

Bobby knocked once and leaned into the doorway. He'd traded his usual hoodie for a dark blue button-down, sleeves rolled just below his elbows. His hair was combed back, though it still curled slightly at the ends. He looked older like that. More deliberate.

"You look nice, Shell," he said.

He said it like he meant it, then stopped. The way he looked at me, steady and unhurried, made something in my chest tighten and settle at the same time.

The gym smelled of sweat, fruit punch, and floor polish. Crepe paper drooped from the rafters. The bass from the speakers vibrated through the soles of my shoes. Colored lights moved in slow circles across the floor, shifting everyone from blue to red to white and back again.

I stayed near the wall at first, back pressed to the cool brick, watching the center of the room churn. Girls adjusted dresses. Guys pretended not to care. Teachers hovered near the edges pretending not to supervise.

Bobby stood beside me with his hands in his pockets, watching the floor with the mild competitive attention he brought to most things. "That guy's been doing the same move for twenty minutes," he said, tilting his head toward a junior near the center of the room who was rotating his arms in what appeared to be a personal interpretation of rhythm. "I respect the commitment. I don't respect the execution."

"You could show him how it's done," I said.

"Obviously," he said. "But I'm being generous."

Sylvia appeared from somewhere in the crowd and pointed at him. "Don't you dare. Last time you decided to demonstrate something at a school event, I spent a week explaining it wasn't a seizure."

"One time," Bobby said.

"One memorable time," Sylvia replied, and disappeared back into the crowd.

He watched her go, something between offense and amusement on his face, before turning back to the room. "You gonna hide all night?" he asked.

"Probably."

"Not happening."

He reached for my hand, not grabbing, just closing his fingers around mine, and pulled me gently toward the middle of the floor. The music was loud enough that it blurred everything else. He started moving first, loose and unselfconscious, and after a second, I followed. It wasn't coordinated. It wasn't impressive. It was just movement.

For a few minutes, the only thing that mattered was staying in rhythm. The lights. The sound. The heat of bodies moving around us. The fact that his hand stayed in mine and didn't let go unless I did.

The next song slowed, and the room shifted with it. Laughter dipped. Pairs turned inward. The lights dimmed another notch.

I hesitated.

"You don't have to," he said, leaning close so I could hear him over the music.

"I know."

He lifted his hand again, palm open.

I stepped forward.

His hands settled at my waist, light but certain. Mine rested on his shoulders. We moved in small adjustments, barely noticeable. His shirt was warm beneath my fingers. I kept my eyes down for a moment, watching our feet, until I didn't need to anymore.

"You're not going back there," he said quietly.

"I might have to."

"Then we'll figure it out."

We. He said it as something practical. Like a plan that already existed and just needed to be followed.

I rested my forehead briefly against his collarbone, just enough to feel grounded. The music carried on. Around us, other couples shifted and swayed.

After the dance, long after Sylvia had analyzed every song choice and accused Bobby of having slow-dance posture issues, I found myself sitting on the front steps. It was late. The sky had gone fully dark, the Sandias a flat black line against it. The porch light cast a soft yellow circle over the concrete and the edge of the walkway. I wrapped a blanket around my shoulders and stared at the street. A car rolled past, its headlights briefly painting the street. Somewhere down the block, wind chimes knocked lightly against each other. From the corral, one of the horses shifted in the dark, a soft movement of hooves against the ground. Rowdy lay beside the steps, his chin on his paws, already decided that wherever I was going to be was where he was going to be.

I thought about 2B. About the dulled brass numbers and the chipped railing and the version of my mother I was being asked to believe in. About whether hope was something you could ration carefully enough to survive if it didn't work out. I didn't have an answer; I just sat there with the question.

The door creaked open behind me. Bobby stepped out and sat down beside me without asking. Our shoulders touched. He didn't shift away. He didn't make a show of it.

"So," he said after a minute, his voice low enough not to carry inside, "you thinking about 2B?"

"Yeah."

"You want it?"

I pulled the blanket tighter around myself. "I want her to stay sober," I said. "I want it to work. I don't know if that means I want the apartment. I don't know if I can survive hoping that hard again."

He didn't answer right away. He leaned forward slightly, forearms resting on his knees, looking down the street. I could see him working toward something, the way he worked toward most things — steadily, without rushing, making sure he had it right before he committed.

"You don't have to hope for perfect," he said finally. "Just better. Better's enough to start with."

Start.

The word pressed somewhere tender.

"I'm scared," I said. It felt easier to say it in the dark. "If she falls apart again, I don't know if I can keep choosing her."

"You don't have to choose her over yourself," he said. "Not anymore."

I turned to look at him. The porch light caught in his eyes, making them lighter than they were during the day. He held my gaze for a moment, steady, then looked back down at his hands like he was deciding something. When he looked up again his expression had shifted — less certain than usual, something working its way to the surface that he hadn't quite organized yet.

"I like you," he said. Then stopped. Started again. "I mean, I've always… it's not because things are complicated or because you're here." He exhaled once. "I just always have. That's it. That's the whole thing. I don't want to wait for your life to settle down because it probably won't and I don't care if it doesn't."

A small laugh slipped out before I could stop it. "You're asking me out during rehab limbo."

"Yeah," he said, almost smiling. "Guess I am."

"You idiot."

"Is that a no?"

"It's a yes," I said, softer. "You idiot."

Something in him loosened. It was visible: his shoulders dropping a fraction, the tension easing from his jaw.

He leaned his forehead lightly against mine for a second, not dramatic, not rushed. Just enough to mark it. Then he reached under the blanket, found my hand and held it without saying anything else.

Rowdy's tail swept the step once, slow and satisfied, like he had been waiting for everyone to catch up.

We sat there with the night wide and quiet around us, Pops' voice drifting low from inside and Mama moving through the kitchen and the wind chimes knocking somewhere down the block and the acequia running beyond the yard, steady as it had always been, steady as it would always be.

Chapter Eight
Foundations

We moved into 2B the week before Thanksgiving, when the air had turned sharp and metallic and the wind carried dust and wood smoke through the narrow walkways. The walk from the Calderon house took less than ten minutes: north past the acequia, where the cottonwoods had already dropped most of their leaves and stood pale and bare against the November sky, then east toward the school, then three blocks more to the faded beige building with its mismatched mailboxes and railings that rattled when the gusts came down from the Sandias. The hallway light outside our door flickered, and the stairs creaked every time someone climbed them. The parking lot had potholes deep enough to swallow a tire if you weren't paying attention.

It was perfect.

We didn't have much. A hand-me-down couch with one arm lower than the other. Two mattresses on the floor until Mom could afford bed frames. A wobbly kitchen table someone from church had carried up the stairs. Bare walls. Mismatched dishes. Curtains thin enough that the hallway light leaked through at night. On the kitchen windowsill, Mom had set a small potted rosemary she'd brought from rehab, a cutting someone had let her root in a paper cup. It sat in the thin November light and she watered it every morning before work.

But the first night I lay in my own room, on a mattress pushed against the wall, the window cracked just enough to let in the hum of traffic, I noticed something that made me stop moving. I wasn't listening for his footsteps. I wasn't waiting for the slam of a door. The quiet was just quiet. I stayed awake longer than I needed to, staring at the ceiling and listening to the normal sounds of the building. Someone walking up the stairs. A car starting in the parking lot. A neighbor's television through the wall. Eventually I fell asleep.

Mom moved carefully in that apartment, as if she was still learning how to live inside it. She worked mornings at a bakery and from home for a call center three nights a week. When she came home from the bakery she smelled like sugar and flour. On call center nights she sat at the kitchen table with a headset on, speaking calmly to strangers while the small kitchen light stayed on above her. She went to meetings twice a week and sometimes joined them online from our kitchen table wearing pajama pants and a One Day at a Time T-shirt. The refrigerator slowly filled with magnets and printed slogans from rehab: *Progress Not Perfection, Easy Does It, Keep Coming Back.* At first, I rolled my eyes every time I opened the door. Then I noticed how often she stood there reading them. Not for long. Just a few seconds before work, after a phone call, or on nights when she looked especially tired.

Sometimes she came home exhausted and dropped her bag by the door. "If I ever ask you to pour me a drink again," she'd say, half serious, "slap me." "Which hand?" I'd answer, because joking was easier than trusting. Other nights she sat on the couch with a mug of tea and said quietly, "I'm sorry. I'm so, so sorry." I never knew how to answer that. The apology mattered. I could hear that it was real. But the damage was real too. Years of it had settled into habits I couldn't turn off quickly. Both things were true at the same time.

The bottles never appeared. The recycling stayed empty. Cabinets opened without the sound of glass shifting inside. Weeks passed, then months. The tightening in my chest eased, not gone, just quieter.

Bobby walked me home every afternoon even though it was only three blocks. We fell into the routine without talking about it. When school let out, we met near the parking lot or the front gate and started the short walk back, past the acequia and under the bare cottonwoods, the November cold sharp against our faces. Sometimes Sylvia came with us. Sometimes she had practice or something else and it was just the two of us.

Dating him wasn't dramatic. It was small things repeated until they felt normal. Walking side by side through the hallway at school and letting our hands brush until one of us closed the space. His fingers sliding between mine without either of us making a show of it. His hand resting at the small of my back when we crossed busy streets. It was the kind of relationship that didn't ask for attention from other people.

Thanksgiving that year moved between two places without tension. We ate the main meal at the Calderons' house. Mama filled the table the way she always did, plates appearing faster than anyone could clear them. Pops carved the turkey at the head of the table with calm efficiency while people talked over each other and reached for dishes. Rowdy had stationed himself near the kitchen doorway with the focused, patient optimism of a dog who understood that Thanksgiving rewarded persistence.

Mama made sure my plate never stayed empty for long. "Eat, mija," she said, nudging the serving bowl toward me again. "You're too thin."

"I've had three plates," I said.

"Then you can have four."

Sylvia leaned across the table and pointed her fork at me. "You should listen to her. This is the one day of the year calories don't count."

"That's not scientifically true," Bobby said, reaching over to steal a roll off my plate.

"Give that back," I said.

"You weren't eating it."

"That's because you grabbed it."

Pops glanced up from carving and slid another slice of turkey onto my plate without comment.

Mom sat beside me, quiet at first, her hands wrapped loosely around a glass of iced tea. She watched the room like she was taking it piece by piece: Mama moving between the kitchen and the table, Pops steady at the head, Sylvia talking over everyone, Bobby leaning back in his chair, his hand resting on the back of mine. After a moment she said softly, "This is really nice." Mama set a bowl of green chile stew down and squeezed her shoulder gently. "You're always welcome here," she said. Mom nodded once, blinking quickly before picking up her fork again.

Later that evening, Mom and I went back to 2B with leftovers wrapped in foil. We sat on the floor with paper plates because we still didn't have chairs for both of us at the small table. The apartment was quiet except for the hum of the refrigerator and the occasional car passing outside. We ate pie straight from the container. Mom looked around the room for a moment — the couch, the small table, the bare walls, the rosemary on the windowsill catching the last of the evening light. "I know it's not much yet," she said. "It's enough," I told her. She nodded slowly, like she was letting herself believe that.

Christmas lights went up in both places. At the Calderons' house, the lights were neat and evenly spaced along the roofline because Pops believed in doing things correctly the first time. At our apartment, Sylvia insisted on hanging crooked strands across the window. "It's intentional," she said when Mom raised an eyebrow. "Artistic." Bobby helped Mom carry up a small artificial tree someone from church had donated. The box was heavier than it looked; the branches had to be bent into place one by one. When we plugged the lights in, Mom's eyes filled with tears for a moment before she wiped them quickly. Bobby pretended not to notice. He just adjusted one of the branches and stepped back. For the first time in a long time, the two parts of my life didn't feel like they were competing with each other. It felt like they were both trying to hold space for me.

One afternoon a few days after the tree went up, Mom went to her afternoon meeting. Bobby came over after his last class, still in his jacket, backpack over one shoulder. He'd been doing that more often lately. He dropped his bag by the door and sat on my bedroom floor with his back against the mattress and his legs stretched out in front of him. The lamp by the door was on, throwing a low yellow glow across the walls.

For a few minutes, we didn't say much. I was editing photographs on my laptop, working through a set from the journalism lab. He had his phone but wasn't looking at it, turning it over slowly the way he did when something had been working through him for a while and had finally run out of room.

"You've been somewhere else lately," I said, without looking up from the screen.

He didn't answer right away. The phone turned over once more in his hands. Then he set it face-down on the floor beside him, his hand staying flat against it for a moment like he was making sure it stayed where he put it.

"Pops talked to me," he said. "About rodeo. A few weeks ago."

I looked up from my laptop.

He told me slowly, the way he told stories he was still sorting out. Pops had called him out to the garage on a Sunday afternoon in October, when the season was winding down and the air had started carrying that particular cold that meant the mountains were already thinking about winter. The big door stayed open but their voices stayed low. Pops stood at the workbench with both hands resting on the edge, the way he stood when he was about to explain a set of plans, and he didn't circle the subject. He said Bobby had had his run, that he was good, damn good, but that good didn't build what came next. Bobby said he could do both. Pops said no, he couldn't, and laid it out the way he laid out construction plans: UNM in the fall, business, finance, Calderon Construction expanding, bonding companies, contracts, payroll, equipment. The kind of work that depended on consistency and judgment, not a broken collarbone or a concussion knocking someone out of commission for months. A company like theirs depended on trust, Pops told him. Banks, crews, clients. They were betting on the man in charge.

Bobby had leaned against the opposite side of the workbench with his arms folded, jaw tight. He reminded Pops that he had ridden when he was younger. Pops said he had, and he had stopped when it was time. Bobby said he just didn't like the risk. Pops didn't argue that point. He looked at Bobby for a long moment and then said: *risk is for men who don't have something to lose.*

Bobby stopped talking. His shoulders settled the way they set when he was absorbing something he couldn't argue with.

"So that's it?" I asked. "No more rodeo?"

He exhaled slowly through his nose. "Guess not."

"You're mad."

"Yeah." His hand dragged across the back of his neck, fingers pressing into the tension there. "But he's not wrong."

"Why didn't you tell me?" I asked, quietly. For a few weeks, he'd been carrying this through all of it, the move, the boxes, Thanksgiving, the Christmas lights, and hadn't said a word.

"You had enough happening."

He had waited because he was trying to protect me. It should have felt simple. It didn't.

"You were good," I said instead, keeping my voice low.

Bobby turned his head toward me. The look he gave me held something quieter than frustration, something that looked a little like grief.

"I liked knowing I could get back up," he said.

"You still can."

He reached out without looking away and took my hand, his fingers sliding between mine. His grip tightened slightly. "It's different," he said. Maybe it was. Riding meant stepping into something that could throw you hard and still choosing to climb on anyway. Walking away meant accepting a different kind of risk, one that didn't announce itself with a buzzer or a crowd.

"You're going to UNM," I said. "That's huge."

"Yeah." His eyes stayed on mine. "You'll still be here."

It wasn't phrased like a question, but I could hear the uncertainty inside it.

"I'll still be here," I said.

The apartment felt smaller at that moment. UNM was across the city. That had never seemed like much before. Now it felt like the beginning of something we'd have to choose rather than just fall into.

"You think we'll survive it?" I asked.

"Shell," he said, his voice firm enough to steady something inside me, "I'm not going anywhere."

Later that night, after Mom had gone to bed and the apartment settled into its thin-walled quiet, we moved into the living room. The crooked Christmas lights still hung across the window. They cast a soft gold glow across the ceiling and the far wall. We sat on the floor with our backs against the couch, the room warm from the heater running too often, the air near the window staying cool.

"If I'm not riding anymore," Bobby said after a while, glancing up at the lights, "I guess I need something else to be reckless about."

"That's not reassuring," I murmured.

He shifted closer. His hand came up to my face, his thumb brushing slowly along my jaw, careful and unhurried.

"Maybe this," he said softly.

My stomach tightened in a way that felt half nervous, half something warmer. The kiss wasn't rushed. It started slow, uncertain for a second before settling into something steadier. His hands rested at my waist, warm through the thin fabric of my shirt. My fingers curled into the front of his hoodie, feeling the slight tension in his shoulders ease and then return differently. The heater rattled once in the hallway. A neighbor's television murmured through the wall. Somewhere down the corridor a door closed.

"I'm building something," he said quietly, after. "And I want you in it."

Winter moved into spring. I started working part-time at the main library downtown, and getting more serious about photojournalism. Something about photography grounded me in a way nothing else ever had.

Sylvia started working in the office of Calderon Construction, keeping her earnings in a dented pencil case in her backpack. The case had held markers in seventh grade. Now it held stacks of tens and twenties pressed flat from her counting them over and over. "Evidence," she told me once, catching me watching her. "Evidence of what?" "That I can leave whenever I want."

When she finally had enough, she told me first. Not Mama. Not Bobby. Me. "Come with me," she said one morning, already halfway out the door, her grin bright enough to make it clear something had already been decided.

Joe's garage sat three blocks off Central in a low concrete building that had probably been there since the seventies. The shop smelled like motor oil, hot rubber, and the kind of dust that never really left concrete floors. The big door stood halfway open, sunlight cutting across the shop in a hard white strip. The Tercel sat off to one side near a stack of old tires. The paint had faded unevenly in the sun, one door a slightly darker shade than the others. The back bumper had a shallow dent like someone had tapped it years ago and never bothered fixing it. One hubcap was missing entirely.

Sylvia stopped in front of it and nodded once. "It's perfect."

Joe wiped his hands on a rag and looked at the car. "It runs."

"That's perfection."

She slid into the driver's seat without hesitation and wrapped both hands around the steering wheel like she had already imagined this moment a hundred times. The vinyl seat was warm from the sun and cracked slightly along one edge. The interior smelled faintly like old upholstery and dust. The air conditioner rattled when she turned it on, blowing out air that was only slightly cooler than outside. The radio jumped between stations in bursts of static before settling briefly on a country song. Joe handed her the keys. Sylvia held them up for a second, turning them in the light.

"I am officially unstoppable," she said.

The first drive was uneven and loud and wonderful. She stalled the engine once leaving the lot, burst out laughing, started it again, and nearly clipped the curb in the process. I grabbed the dashboard. "You're going to kill us." "Relax," she said, gripping the wheel tighter. "I'm learning." "You're learning with my life." "Dramatic."

The windows stayed rolled down, the wind feeling better than the struggling AC. Hot air rushed through the car and whipped loose strands of Sylvia's curls from their tie. The engine hummed high and determined as we rattled down the street. From the passenger seat, the city had a different shape. The same streets we had walked for years stretched out farther than they used to. Intersections didn't feel like boundaries anymore. They felt like options. Sylvia kept glancing at the mirrors like she was testing the idea that she was allowed to move.

We drove past the grocery store, past the bus stop where we had waited a hundred times, past the corner where the sidewalks cracked wide enough to trip on if you weren't careful. "Where are we going?" I asked. "Anywhere," she said, her voice steady and full of adventure.

We ended up behind the old elementary school near the cracked basketball court. The chain-link fence leaned in; the hoop sagged from years of kids hanging on it. The asphalt still radiated heat through the soles of my shoes when we stepped out. Cottonwood leaves buzzed overhead in the dry breeze. Sylvia turned off the engine but didn't move right away. Her hands stayed on the steering wheel. The car ticked softly as the engine cooled. "These changes things," she said, quiet but certain.

Within a week, the Tercel became ours in ways no one else would have noticed. We drove places that barely counted as destinations just so we could sit somewhere different. Sometimes it was the gas station lot on Central where the neon lights buzzed after dark and the pavement still held the day's heat. Sometimes it was the empty lot behind the library where the asphalt stayed warm long after sunset and the cottonwoods rattled in the evening wind. We ate fries out of paper bags, windows down, the radio drifting between stations. The heat seeped through the windshield. The car smelled like salt, grease, and warm vinyl. Sylvia always drove with one elbow hooked over the wheel, one hand loose but confident. I stretched my legs across the dashboard and watched the city move past the glass: bus stops, faded storefronts, stoplights blinking red over empty intersections.

And because Sylvia never left anything at simple ownership, she escalated it.

"If something ever goes wrong," she said one evening, the sky turned orange behind the Sandias and cicadas screamed in the trees, "we need a backup."

"For what?" I asked.

"For everything."

She leaned forward, tugging at the back of the driver's seat. The fabric shifted where it met the frame. There was a narrow slit in the seam, barely visible unless you were looking for it. She slipped two fingers into the gap and widened it just enough to create a hidden pocket.

"There," she said. "For notes."

I laughed. "You're unbelievable."

"No," she said calmly. "I'm prepared."

She dug through the glove compartment, found an old receipt, and tore off a corner. She wrote one word.

Library.

She folded it into a tight square and pushed it deep into the seam until it disappeared.

"If we ever can't reach each other," she said, brushing her hands together, "you check here first."

"That's dramatic."

"It's smart."

We built rules the same way we had with the notebook. One note at a time. No full explanations. Dates are always slightly wrong. If it was urgent, Storm. If everything was fine, Library. If it was just the usual chaos, Fireflies.

But Sylvia wasn't finished.

"If someone finds the notebook," she said, tapping the dashboard, "they could still figure it out."

"So?"

"So, we add another layer."

Simple codes. Letter shifts. Number swaps. Enough to turn anything real into something that looked like nothing. We wrote them in the back of the notebook and used them without thinking about it.

"But the key can't stay with the message," Sylvia said.

"Then where?"

She leaned back and smiled. "The library."

The travel section sat in the back where no one our age ever went. Albania. Mongolia. Iceland. Thick guidebooks we opened like we were just curious, slipping folded pages near the spine where no one would look.

"If we ever need it," Sylvia said, sliding one back onto the shelf, "we leave a clue."

Not the answer. Just enough.

By the end of summer, it wasn't a game anymore. Notes in the seat seam. Codes in the notebook. Keys hidden in library stacks.

Late that summer we lay across the hood of the Tercel while the metal still held the warmth of the day. The sky shifted from pink to deep blue, the first stars pushing through.

"If you ever get a car," Sylvia said, "you do the same thing."

"Obviously."

"Same system."
"Same system."

Chapter Nine
Still Brighter Out Here

Fenton Lake in March smelled like pine sap and cold water and the particular sharpness of mountain air that hit different after a winter of breathing valley dust. We had been coming up here since we were small — the same campsite, the same fire ring, the same stretch of bank where the water ran clear over smooth stones. The drive took less than two hours but felt worlds away

Bobby had the fire going by the time Sylvia and I finished setting up the tent. Josh was down at the water's edge throwing rocks. Hector sat on a log at the edge of the firelight, already still, already watching the way he was in every space he occupied.

The mountains held onto cold. We wore jackets to dinner and kept them on after. The fire was the center of everything — the food, the conversation, the shifting light across five faces that had been showing up in each other's lives long enough that the silences between us had stopped requiring explanation.

The conversation moved through all the inconsequential things first, the way it always did. Bobby and Josh argued about something that had happened at a rodeo qualifier two years ago, each version growing further from the other with every retelling. Sylvia provided running commentary on the credibility of both accounts. Hector said nothing but his expression suggested he knew exactly what had happened and had decided the argument was more entertaining than the truth.

I watched all of it through the fire. The light moved across their faces in slow orange shifts. The lake was dark beyond the tree line, the sound of it hiding just beneath the conversation. Above us the sky was filling itself with stars in a way it never managed in the valley, the Milky Way a pale smear from one ridge to the other.

I looked up at it for a long moment.

Bobby caught me looking. He didn't say anything right away. Then, quietly, so only I could hear it: "Still brighter out here."

I nodded. I didn't say anything else and neither did he, because some things had already been said once and didn't need saying again. We were nine and seven and sixteen and fourteen all at once, sitting around different fires in the same mountains, and the stars above us were exactly what they had always been.

The fire dropped lower as the night wore on. That was when Josh told us.

He said it directly, without building toward it. He had enlisted. Marines. He shipped out in June, three weeks after graduation.

The fire popped once. A log shifted and sent a brief column of sparks up into the dark.

Bobby looked at Josh across the coals with the flat assessment of someone taking inventory. The silence lasted exactly long enough to communicate something that neither of them was going to say out loud.

Then he reached across and hit Josh hard once on the shoulder, the kind of hit that carried its own meaning between people who had grown up competing against each other. Not good luck. Something heavier than that, delivered in the only language they had for it. Josh winced. Bobby nodded. That was the whole speech.

Across the fire Hector looked at Josh with a different kind of recognition of someone who understood choosing a road that didn't look like anyone else's road, one that didn't come with a map or a guaranteed return. He didn't say anything. He didn't need to.

Sylvia made Josh promise to call. He said he would. She said she knew the Marines were going to make that complicated and he needed to promise anyway. He promised again, more seriously, which meant she'd gotten what she actually wanted. I watched her face when he said it, how she accepted the promise knowing exactly what it was worth and chose to hold onto it anyway; some things you hold onto even when you know they're fragile.

I reached for my camera where it sat beside me in the dirt.

Josh's face in the firelight, the last time he would look exactly like this in exactly this place. The mountains, cold and dark above us, the lake somewhere beyond the trees, the fire going low the way fires go when the night has gotten serious.

I left the camera where it was.

Some things you don't photograph, because photographing them would mean admitting they're ending. I wanted to keep this one the way memory keeps things, imprecise and permanent, warmer than it probably was.

Later, after the food was gone and the conversation had moved through everything it needed to move through, Josh asked, in the loose way of someone who had already made his own decision and was curious about everyone else's, what Bobby was going to miss most about rodeo.

Bobby looked at the fire. He was quiet long enough that I thought he wasn't going to answer.

Then he said: "Eight seconds. Everything goes quiet. Nothing else does that."

He moved on immediately, reaching for his water bottle, already redirecting. But the sentence stayed in the air above the coals and I turned it over in my mind the way I turned over photographs that were almost right but not quite. I thought I understood something in it that I hadn't had words for before. Why he built things. Why he planned and measured and laid out the future in careful drawings. Building was its own version of those eight seconds. Everything depending on whether you stayed centered, everything quiet when you got it right.

I looked at him across the fire and he was already talking about something else, already forward, already building toward whatever came next. That was who he was. I loved it. I also felt it sometimes like a window I couldn't quite open.

Hector had not spoken in a while.

He sat forward with his elbows on his knees, his eyes on the coals. The quality of his silence had shifted at some point in the last hour, less watchful, more settled, like a decision that had already been made and was waiting for the right moment to be said aloud.

"I'm not walking," he said.

Sylvia's head came up immediately. "What?"

"Graduation." He didn't look at her. "I'm not finishing."

"Hector."

"It's done." Not aggressive. Just final. The way he said everything that was actually final.

The fire crackled. Josh stared at the coals.

Bobby's jaw tightened once before he said: "You talk to Pops?"

"Yeah."

A beat. Something passed between them across the fire, Bobby's expression changing in a way that told me Pops had already known and had said nothing to any of us. Not his news to carry.

"Okay," Bobby said.

Sylvia was not done. "That's it? Okay?" She turned to Hector fully, her body angling toward him. "You have two months. Two months, Hector. You could…"

"Sylvia." His voice was quiet. He looked at her then, directly, the way he rarely looked at anyone directly. "It's done."

She held his gaze for a long moment. I watched the moment she accepted it. She didn't agree with it, didn't like it, but accepted that it was true and that arguing further would cost her something she wasn't willing to spend. She picked up her soda. Took a slow drink. Set it back on her knee. Her hands were still after that, which for Sylvia meant something.

Hector looked back at the fire.

I watched him in the low light, the stillness of him, the way the decision settled on him not like a burden but like something he'd set down in a place where others could finally see it. I understood something about him at that moment that I couldn't have named before. He wasn't choosing against something. He was choosing toward something, even if no one else could see what it was yet.

The fire burned down to coals. The mountains were dark and very close around us. Above the tree line the stars were exactly as bright as they had always been at Fenton, exactly as bright as they had been the first time I looked up at them and didn't know yet that the city had been hiding them from me my whole life.

We didn't stay up much longer after that. The cold had settled in properly and the coals were giving off more warmth in memory than in fact. Bobby banked what was left without being asked, the way he always took care of things that needed taking care of without making anything of it. Josh went to his tent first. Hector followed. Sylvia and I lay in our sleeping bags for a while talking about nothing consequential, our voices low in the dark, the tent walls moving slightly in the mountain wind.

I fell asleep listening to the lake.

Three weeks later Bobby crossed the stage at University Stadium in a cap and gown he wore with the particular discomfort of someone who had dressed up under protest. Mama was crying before his name was called. Pops stood with his chin lifted, hands clasped in front of him, the quiet pride of a man who had planned for this moment and was watching the plan arrive exactly as drawn.

Somewhere during the long reading of names, Sylvia found my hand. Neither of us decided to. It just happened the way things do when you're sitting beside someone you've known your whole life and something is ending and beginning at the same time. She held on and I held back and the names kept coming.

Robert Calderon.

The crowd rose. I watched him cross the stage, his cap slightly crooked, his shoulders loosening out of the formal posture as he shook the principal's hand, already himself again before he'd stepped off the platform. I thought about a photograph I wasn't taking. The light was good. The moment was real. I left the camera in my bag.

Some things you kept differently than that.

Hector was not there. I had known he wouldn't be and had thought I was prepared for it. The empty space where he should have been standing in the line of graduates registered anyway, briefly and precisely, like a note played wrong in a familiar song.

Afterward the families gathered on the grass outside the stadium in the warm May afternoon. Mama held Bobby for a long time before she let him go. Pops gripped his shoulder and said something low that I didn't hear and Bobby nodded once, his jaw working slightly.

Sylvia bought Bobby a cinnamon roll from a vendor near the gate and presented it with the gravity of a significant award. He ate it in three bites. She told him he had no appreciation for ceremony. He said the roll was the ceremony. They argued about this the entire walk back to the cars.

I walked beside them and let the afternoon carry me and tried not to think about June, when Josh would ship out and the group that had gathered at Fenton Lake three weeks ago would never gather in exactly that configuration again.

A week into June Bobby picked me up before seven, which meant he'd already been up for hours. The horses were fed and turned out. He said we were going riding. He didn't ask if I wanted to. He said it like a fact, the way he said things he'd already decided were good ideas and was giving me the courtesy of announcing rather than offering as a choice.

I grabbed my camera and got in the truck.

The property in early morning had a quality the afternoon never managed — the light coming in low and gold across the portal, the corral fence casting long shadows, the horses moving quietly in the near pasture with the unhurried economy of animals that had been living their own lives since before we arrived and would continue after we left. Rowdy met us at the gate and circled Bobby once before falling into step beside him, his nose working the morning air.

Bobby tacked both horses at the corral without hurrying, his hands moving through the familiar sequence of buckles and adjustments with the ease of someone who had been doing this since he was old enough to reach. He checked my stirrups without being asked and adjusted the left one two holes down without comment. He didn't explain why. He'd seen exactly how I'd been sitting before I'd said a word and had simply corrected it.

We rode north along the bosque path with the Rio Grande to our left through the trees. The cottonwoods were fully leafed out, their canopy closing the path into a green corridor that opened occasionally onto stretches of pale morning sky. The horses moved at an easy walk, their hooves soft on the packed dirt. Rowdy ranged ahead of us and doubled back in the perpetual motion of a dog who considered covering the same ground twice to be a reasonable use of energy.

I lifted my camera.

Not at the river. Not at the cottonwoods opening above us. At Bobby, ahead of me on the trail: the set of his shoulders, the easy way he sat the horse. The light was doing something to the moment that I understood I would not see again exactly like this.

The shutter closed.

He glanced back at the sound of it, one eyebrow lifted.

"Evidence," I said.

His mouth curved. He turned back to the path.

We rode farther than I'd expected, past the familiar stretch near the property, past the spot where the river bent and the cottonwoods thinned, out into a longer, quieter section of bosque where the path narrowed and the light changed. Bobby let his horse move into a slow trot and glanced back at me with an expression I recognized as a question that wasn't quite a question.

I nudged the mare forward.

The trot was rougher than I anticipated, the ground uneven, the horse's rhythm demanding my full attention, my hands tightening on the reins before I found the balance point and let my body move with it instead of against it. Bobby slowed when I found it. Not before. The right call, and I noticed it without saying so.

We walked the horses back through the cooling shade of the cottonwoods. The river moved beside us, brown and steady with snowmelt. A hawk circled somewhere above the canopy, its shadow crossing the path twice before it rose out of sight. Rowdy appeared from the undergrowth, tongue out, satisfied with whatever he'd been investigating, and fell into step beside us without breaking stride.

"UNM starts in August," I said.

"Yeah."

"You ready?"

He considered it the way he considered most things — not performing the consideration, just actually thinking. "I know what I'm building," he said. "That helps."

I thought about the Christmas lights. *I'm building something and I want you in it.* The warmth of it and the thing underneath the warmth that I still didn't have words for, the slightly architectural quality of the way he moved toward the future, everything measured and planned and load-bearing. I loved that about him. I also felt it sometimes like a window I couldn't quite open, a question I didn't know how to ask yet.

I looked at the light on the river instead.

"It's a good summer," I said.

"Yeah," he said. "It is."

Chapter Ten
Senior Year

By February of my senior year, the apartment no longer felt like something we were borrowing from the universe. It felt like home.

The beige walls still held faint nail holes from whoever lived there before us, and the hallway light outside 2B still flickered when the wind hit the building. But the space had begun to remember us. My shoes sat beside the door; one pair kicked halfway off the mat. Mom's meeting schedule was taped to the refrigerator in blue ink, the days circled carefully with small notes beside them. A chipped ceramic bowl held our keys on the table by the door, something we'd started doing without ever deciding it out loud.

The place had its own rhythm now.

Her mornings at the bakery began before sunrise. I'd hear the clink of a coffee mug, the hum of the microwave, the quiet shuffle of her shoes while the sky outside was still dark. When she came home in the afternoons the apartment filled with the smell of flour and sugar and warm bread that clung to her apron. Sometimes powdered sugar dusted her sleeve.

For the first time in years, home wasn't something I measured by the absence of shouting. It was something I felt in the small, ordinary things we kept repeating.

That Thursday morning the heater kicked on with its familiar metallic rattle, pushing out dry warmth that carried a faint trace of dust through the vents. I stood at the narrow counter spreading peanut butter onto a tortilla. The counter was barely wide enough for a cutting board and the jar of peanut butter, the knife scraping against the glass as I worked the last bit from the bottom.

The window over the sink held a pale slice of winter light. Outside, the parking lot shimmered with frost, the early sun catching the thin layer of ice on windshields. The rosemary on the windowsill had grown since fall, its stems woody at the base now, filling the narrow sill with its particular sharp green smell. Mom touched it briefly as she reached past it for her travel mug, the way she touched it every morning without thinking about it, the small habitual gesture of someone tending something alive.

Someone's car alarm chirped half-heartedly before going silent again, followed by the muffled slam of a truck door somewhere down the row of apartments.

Mom moved around the kitchen in soft, efficient motions, tying the bakery apron around her waist. She'd let her hair grow longer over the past year, the gray at her temples no longer hidden under dye. There were lines at the corners of her mouth that hadn't been there before rehab, but her eyes were clearer now. Steadier. When she reached for her travel mug, her hand didn't shake.

"You have your ID?" she asked, the question automatic.

"Yes."

"Keys?"

"In my pocket."

"Phone charged?"

I sighed, but the irritation was gone. "Mom. I'm eighteen."

She smiled, tired but genuine, the kind of smile that came easier now than it used to. "Humor me."

Two years ago, that question would have meant something different. Control. Surveillance. Suspicion. Now it meant she was trying to be the kind of parent who remembered the small things that kept a day moving smoothly. The difference still caught me off guard.

She paused before leaving, watching me like she was reading something invisible across my face. "Are you nervous?" she asked.

"About?"

"Everything."

I huffed a quiet laugh and folded the tortilla in half. "Yeah. FAFSA meeting today. And I still haven't finished my journalism portfolio statement."

She leaned one hip against the counter instead of rushing toward the door, giving the conversation the space it deserved. "You've been working on that for weeks," she said.

"I know. I just want it to be right."

"Remind me," she said gently, "which one you're sending."

"The one with the fair photos," I said. "The rodeo shots. And the protest downtown last fall. Mr. Alvarez says the composition's strong."

Her eyebrows lifted slightly. "The bull riding pictures?"

I nodded. "Photojournalism programs like action. They want to see something real happening." I glanced toward the kitchen table where my camera bag sat, the strap draped over the chair. The camera itself had been a birthday gift a few months earlier. Pops handed it to me in a plain box like it was just another practical tool, Mama insisting we take pictures immediately to break it in. Beside it, the documentary photography book the advisor had given me in September, a folded receipt marking the page I kept coming back to.

"I want to tell stories with pictures," I added. "Not just write them. Show them."

Mom watched me for a moment the way she had started watching things lately, carefully, like every piece of who I was becoming mattered. "You've always told stories," she said. "Even when you didn't mean to."

That landed deeper than I expected. I didn't tell her that sometimes telling the truth had nearly wrecked everything. I didn't tell her that sometimes I still woke up convinced that if I looked hard enough, the past would be standing in the doorway again. Instead, I leaned back against the counter.

"I'm proud of you," she said.

I nodded once. "Thanks."

She stepped closer then, hesitating for half a second like she was still learning the boundaries between us. Then she reached up and brushed a loose strand of hair away from my face. It was such a small thing. But two years ago, it would have made every muscle in my body tighten. Now I let myself lean into it, just a little.

She grabbed her bag from the chair by the door and paused again, looking back into the apartment that now held both our lives: coffee mugs in the sink, my camera bag on the table, her meeting notes stuck to the refrigerator with a sunflower magnet, the rosemary on the windowsill catching the morning light. "Don't forget your camera," she said. I glanced at the strap hanging from the chair. "Never." She smiled at that, the kind of smile that held relief in it. Then she stepped out into the cold morning air, the door closing softly behind her, leaving the apartment quiet in a way that now felt normal.

After she left, the apartment settled into its small morning rhythm: pipes clicking behind the walls, a neighbor's television murmuring through thin drywall, traffic humming faintly three blocks over. I wasn't listening for footsteps or measuring silence for danger. The quiet felt like something real, not waiting to change.

My phone buzzed on the counter.

Sylvia: u alive

Sylvia: we're almost there

Sylvia: if you don't come outside, I'm calling the cops

I grabbed my backpack and my camera before heading out. The camera felt natural in my hand now, the weight of it familiar, grounding. The air bit sharp against my face when I stepped outside. February in Albuquerque had that dry, cutting cold that didn't last all day. The sky above the Sandias was pale blue, snow still clinging to the ridges in narrow white streaks. I cut across the gravel behind the church, boots crunching over frozen dirt and bottle caps, when a horn beeped twice.

Bobby's truck rolled along the curb, heater fogging the windshield. The dent on the passenger side was still there. So was the strip of duct tape along the mirror that he insisted was temporary. A UNM parking decal clung to the lower corner of the glass, sun-faded now from a year and a half of Albuquerque winters and summers. I looked at it for a second and thought about what it would feel like to have my own one day. My own reason to be there.

He leaned out of the window and grinned. "Need a ride?" Sylvia hopped out while he was still talking.

"I live three blocks away," I said, crossing to the passenger side and climbing in, Sylvia getting back in behind me.

He shrugged.

The heater pushed warm air at our legs as I shut the door. The cab smelled faintly of motor oil and horses and the pine air freshener Sylvia had hung from the mirror weeks ago. Bobby leaned over and kissed me quick and warm.

Sylvia groaned softly. "Morning," she said. "Glad I could witness that."

Bobby pulled away from the curb, one hand loose on the wheel. His textbooks were stacked on the floorboard near his boots: accounting, business fundamentals, something thick enough to double as a doorstop. He'd thrown himself into his UNM classes, spending long nights reading things with charts and formulas.

"How's college?" I asked.

He tipped his head side to side like he was weighing it. "Busy. But it's good."

I lifted my camera and snapped a picture before he could react.

"Michelle," he said.

"Too late."

He shook his head but didn't push it. After a second, he glanced at me again, more thoughtful. "Still working on your UNM application?"

"Yeah."

"And the journalism program?"

"That's the plan."

He nodded once like that settled something. "You'll get in." The way he said it wasn't encouragement. It sounded like a simple fact, something he had already decided and filed away.

At school, February clung to everything. Posters for FAFSA nights hung crooked on the walls. Someone had written 92 DAYS UNTIL GRADUATION in red marker near the office, updating the number every morning. Seniors talked about prom and apartments and summer jobs like the future was already waiting outside.

I spent lunch in the journalism lab more often than the cafeteria.

The room smelled like printer ink and warm electronics, the particular combination that meant work was happening and had been for a while. The overhead lights buzzed at a frequency you stopped hearing after a few minutes. Computers lined the wall, their screens filled with layout grids and photo files, and the printer in the corner clicked and whirred steadily, spitting out pages that someone would cut and rearrange before the week was out. The advisor's desk sat near the window with its stacks of marked-up drafts and a coffee mug that was never empty, and the walls held framed issues going back decades, photos and headlines from years when the students in them were now older than our parents.

I had a station in the back corner that had become mine without anyone officially assigning it. The monitor there flickered slightly at the lower left edge, a dead pixel cluster nobody had bothered fixing, and the keyboard had a sticky R key from some spill before my time. I didn't mind. I knew exactly how hard to press.

Most days I came in with a memory card full of images from whatever I'd been shooting and worked through them methodically. The process had its own logic I'd had to learn by getting it wrong first: culling what didn't land, keeping the frames where everything came together. Light. Composition. Expression. Timing. You couldn't manufacture any of it. You could only be ready when it happened and make sure the camera was pointed the right direction.

The advisor had given me the documentary photography book in September, a collection from the sixties and seventies, and I'd looked at it so many times the spine had cracked. What I kept coming back to wasn't the famous images. It was the ones that appeared in the back pages, the contact sheets, rows of small identical frames where one shot was circled in grease pencil. All that work, just to find one true moment. All those frames that were almost right but not quite.

What you left out mattered as much as what you chose to keep.

That afternoon I was working through a set from the winter rally downtown, forty or fifty frames from two hours of shooting, most of them wrong in ways I was only starting to understand how to name. Too much sky. Subject caught mid-blink. The moment a half-second gone. I moved through them steadily, marking and discarding, until one made me stop.

A woman near the back of the crowd, older, her sign held low like she'd been carrying it a long time. She wasn't looking at the stage. She was watching the person beside her, a teenager who couldn't have been more than fourteen, and her expression held something I didn't have a clean word for. Not pride exactly, closer to recognition. Like she was watching something she understood.

I sat with it for a while before adjusting anything. Tightened the crop. Brought up the midtones just enough. The image didn't change, exactly. It just became more itself.

The advisor stopped behind me on her way to the printer.

"You've been on that one for a while," she said.

"I'm trying to figure out what it's about," I said.

She leaned in, studying the screen. After a moment she straightened. "It's about her," she said, meaning the woman. "And it's about you a little bit too."

She moved on before I could respond. I looked at the image again. The woman's expression. The thing she was recognizing. I thought about what it meant to watch someone still becoming something and understand exactly what you were seeing.

I saved the file and closed the laptop.

Some afternoons Bobby met me at the apartment so we could study at the kitchen table. Mom would already be in the bedroom with the door pulled mostly closed, her laptop balanced on the dresser for her meeting. Her voice carried through the thin wall clearly enough that we could hear the introductions as people joined. *"Hi, I'm Patricia, and I'm an alcoholic."* The words had stopped feeling shocking months ago. They were part of the routine now, as ordinary as the refrigerator's steady hum or the heater clicking on when the temperature dropped.

Bobby spread his textbooks across the small kitchen table while I worked beside him editing photos. His binders opened into neat columns of numbers and notes in the careful handwriting he'd developed once college started. My laptop screen filled with images from the last few weeks: basketball games, hallway portraits, the rally where the light had hit someone's face just right in the middle of the crowd.

The table was barely big enough for both of us. Our elbows bumped sometimes when one of us reached for a pen or a mouse. Underneath, our knees touched more often than either of us acknowledged. Neither of us moved.

The quiet between us had its own shape. The heater pushed warm air through the vents with a low metallic rattle. The refrigerator ran steadily behind us. From the bedroom, Mom's voice rose and fell as someone else spoke during the meeting, the tone calm and attentive in a way I still noticed every time. Outside, the metal railing along the walkway rattled when the wind came down from the mountains. A car passed slowly through the parking lot, gravel crunching under its tires. Inside, it was warm.

I was adjusting the exposure on a photo when I felt Bobby's attention shift. I looked up. He was watching me. Not in the distracted way people sometimes glance over while thinking about something else. He had stopped writing entirely. His pen rested across the open page of his notebook while his eyes stayed on my face.

"What?" I asked.

He leaned back slightly in his chair, studying me like he was trying to put something into words. "You seem different," he said.

I tilted my head. "Different how?"

He didn't answer right away. His gaze drifted toward the window and then back again. "You seem lighter." The word landed gently, but it stayed there.

"Good lighter?" I asked.

"Yeah." He paused, eyes still on mine. "You don't look like you're waiting for something anymore."

I leaned back slightly in my chair and thought about it. "Maybe I'm not," I said.

He nodded once, slowly. The room settled around us again. Mom's voice drifted through the wall, someone thanking the group for listening. Bobby reached across the table then and rested his hand lightly over my wrist, his thumb brushing once across the inside where my pulse beat. A small touch, steady and familiar now. I turned my hand so my fingers rested loosely against his.

"I like seeing you like this," he said, quietly.

"I like being like this," I admitted.

Something in his shoulders eased when I said it. Not relief exactly. More like confirmation. For a moment neither of us moved.

After a moment Bobby turned back to my laptop screen, the images still open from the afternoon's work. He looked at them the way he looked at most things, without hurry, taking them in one at a time, his eyes moving across each frame with the same steady assessment he brought to a set of construction drawings or a property he was evaluating. Looking for what was load-bearing. Looking for what could be built on. He stopped on the rally photograph, the woman, the teenager, the recognition in the woman's face, and stayed there longer than the others.

I watched him look at it and felt something I didn't quite have words for. He was seeing something real in it, and also what it could become, what it could do, where it could go. That was how he looked at everything he loved, not just as it was but as what it was building toward.

"You're going to do something big with that camera," he said.

I looked at the photograph on the screen. The woman. The girl. The recognition between them had nothing to do with what came next and everything to do with what was happening right now.

"Yeah," I said. "Maybe."

Chapter Eleven
Thin Ice

The night he came back, the apartment looked like something we had earned with blood and exhaustion.

Mom had been cleaning since noon. The counters were scrubbed until the laminate caught the kitchen light in a dull reflection. The thrift-store curtains hung straight. Even the rehab slogans on the refrigerator, edges curling and ink fading, looked deliberate.

One Day at a Time. Progress Not Perfection.

The heater rattled in the hallway, pushing dry warmth through the narrow rooms. Soup simmered in the dented silver pot she'd carried from the old house, steam fogging the window above the sink. Garlic and onion thickened the air over the sharp tang of Pine-Sol still clinging to the floor. The apartment smelled clean and fragile.

I sat at the kitchen table with my laptop open, staring at a blinking cursor at the end of a sentence about resilience I had rewritten three times and still didn't believe. My chest had been tight all evening, a low hum under my skin that refused to settle.

Outside, wind scraped along the siding. A car passed slowly on the street below. Somewhere down the hall a neighbor laughed too loudly and then stopped.

Mom was humming.

She hadn't hummed in years before rehab. Now it came back in soft, tuneless bursts.

The knock hit the door with three sharp raps that pressed against my ribs. Not frantic. Not hesitant. Deliberate.

The reaction was physical before it was conscious. My stomach dropped. My breath caught halfway in. My heart slammed once so hard the edges of the room blurred.

Mom's humming stopped instantly. The spoon in her hand stilled against the pot.

The heater continued its metallic ticking, oblivious to the shift in pressure inside the room.

There was a pause long enough for denial to try to take hold. Wrong apartment. Neighbor's mistake. Someone lost. Then another knock came, softer, almost patient. Nobody knocked on our door at night. The landlord texted. Neighbors called through the stairwell. This knock felt intentional. Controlled. Like someone who knew we were inside and knew we would answer.

"Mom," I said. My voice sounded thin and distant, as if it had traveled across the room without me.

She turned toward the door slowly, confusion moving across her face. She wiped her hands on the dish towel, leaving damp streaks on the fabric, and walked toward it like she expected to find a neighbor or someone from church standing there. I was already on my feet without remembering standing.

The lock turned with a soft metallic click that sounded too loud in the quiet apartment.

The door opened. Cold air rushed in first, sharp and dry, sliding along the floor and up my legs. Then him.

For a moment my brain refused to grasp what I was seeing. He looked thinner. Older. The gray at his temples was more pronounced, his coat hanging loosely from his shoulders. His hands were visible and empty; fingers relaxed at his sides. No bottle. No tremor. But the way he stood, weight balanced evenly, chin slightly lowered, eyes scanning the room once before settling, was exactly the same.

My body recognized him before my mind did. A cold pressure spread through my chest so quickly it felt like the air had been pulled out of the apartment.

"Pat," he said quietly.

The sound of his voice entered the room like something that had waited outside for years.

Mom froze. The dish towel slipped halfway from her fingers as her hand lifted toward her mouth. For a moment she simply stared at him, her expression blank with shock, as if her mind needed time to rearrange the shape of the world.

"Mark?" she whispered.

He nodded once. Then his eyes moved past her. They found me immediately.

"Michelle."

Hearing my name on his lips made my throat close. For years that sound had been followed by anger, or disappointment, or the thick blur of alcohol. My brain searched for the smell automatically, the sour sweetness of whiskey that used to announce him before he even spoke. There was nothing. Just cold air. Just his voice. Just the fact of him standing inside the rectangle of our doorway like the last two years had been a long pause instead of an ending.

"I know this is sudden," he said. His voice was gentle and controlled. The kind of careful that made my stomach twist harder. "I've been sober two months. Meetings every day. I've had time to think about things. About what I did." Each sentence sounded deliberate, like words learned somewhere else and brought here.

Mom's eyes filled with tears so quickly it looked as though they had been waiting for permission. "You look…" Her voice trembled. "You look different."

Mark nodded again. "I'm trying," he said quietly.

My hands had curled into fists without me realizing it. My nails pressed hard into my palms. "You need to leave," I said. The words tore out of me before I could soften them.

Both of them turned toward me.

My heart was beating so hard it hurt. My lungs felt too tight to pull in a full breath. Dad shifted his attention toward me slowly, careful in a way that made something deep in my body recoil. I recognized that carefulness. The way he approached a moment when the room had gone quiet. "I know I hurt you," he said softly. "I know that. I'm trying to fix it."

Mom's shoulders shook once. "He's sober," she said quietly, her voice almost pleading. "Michelle. He's sober."

Before I could say anything else, she stepped backward. Just one step. Small. But it opened the doorway. "Come in," she said.

The words hit me like something physical. I wanted to grab her arm. I wanted to pull her back across the threshold. I wanted to slam the door so hard the frame cracked. Instead, I stood there, frozen, breath shallow, every nerve in my body registering that something irreversible was happening. He stepped forward, not aggressively, not quickly, just enough that the line between outside and inside disappeared. The cold air sealed itself out behind him. The apartment, our apartment, the one we had rebuilt from almost nothing, wrapped around him like it had been waiting.

And that was how he stepped back inside.

The first week felt almost convincing, and that frightened me more than if he had slammed a door or thrown a glass.

Dad moved through the apartment with restraint. He washed dishes after dinner without being asked, sleeves rolled neatly to his forearms. He fixed the flickering hallway bulb that had buzzed for months, standing on a chair while Mom steadied it and looked up at him with quiet relief. One afternoon he knelt beside the bathroom wall, running his thumb along a hairline crack in the drywall like it bothered him personally.

When he spoke to me his voice stayed low. He asked about school, my classes, the college applications spread across the kitchen table. The questions sounded gentle, but something in them felt practiced. Every kindness carried a trace of calculation.

The first few nights he slept on the couch. Mom insisted on extra blankets, fussing over the pillow like hospitality might smooth the past. He stretched out along the cushions with his boots lined neatly beside the coffee table while the television murmured low in the background.

By the second week he was no longer on the couch. One night I woke to the quiet creak of Mom's bedroom door and voices I couldn't make out. The next morning the blankets were folded and gone from the living room. His boots sat outside her door instead.

No one said anything about it.

Mom moved like someone starving for proof that redemption might still be possible. She cooked more, stretching the grocery money farther than it should have gone. Garlic in oil. Onions softening. Chicken simmered until the broth thickened. She wiped the counter between steps, checked the pot too often, straightened things that didn't need straightening.

She laughed more, too. Too bright. Too quick.

At night she sat beside him on the couch, their knees touching, her shoulder angled toward his. She started saying *we* again. *We will figure this out. We just need time. We deserve another chance.*

The word hung in the air like something fragile.

I watched everything.

He never fully settled into a chair. His eyes moved through the apartment in a quiet pattern. Door. Hallway. Window. Kitchen. Not enough for Mom to notice, but enough that I did.

Sometimes he watched me when he thought I wasn't looking. Just a second too long.

My body adjusted before I had made any decisions. I started sleeping in my jeans and a sweatshirt, my phone under my pillow, the way I used to when the house had been unpredictable. Sometimes my shoes stayed beside the bed instead of in the closet. I told myself it was habit. Convenience, nothing more.

But muscle memory does not care about promises.

By the second week Mom skipped a meeting. She said she was tired. She said she did not feel like sitting in a folding chair and rehashing things that were already behind her. She said she was doing well and did not need to prove it every night to a room full of strangers who did not know her life. Dad did not argue. He did not encourage her either. He simply nodded slightly when she mentioned it and the subject drifted away. By the third week she said she did not need meetings at all. She said she was past that phase. She said the program had done what it needed to do. By the fourth week the subject disappeared entirely, like something quietly removed from the apartment without acknowledgment.

The rosemary on the windowsill had not been watered in days. The soil had pulled away from the edges of the pot and the needles had gone slightly dry, still alive but stressed, the way things look when someone has stopped paying attention to them. I noticed it one morning and didn't say anything. There was nothing to say.

The smell returned, gradually. At first it was faint enough that I almost convinced myself I imagined it. A sweetness under the bathroom sink when I reached for the cleaning spray. A sharper note in the trash can. Something thin and sour that clung to the air after she passed me in the hallway. It did not arrive all at once. It seeped. The first bottle I found was tucked behind the cleaning supplies under the bathroom sink. It was half empty and warm from the pipes running through the wall. My hand trembled when I lifted it into the light. Mom did not look shocked when I confronted her. She did not look angry either. She just looked tired. Bone deep tired. "It's just to take the edge off," she said quietly. "You don't know how hard this is."

Dad stood in the doorway while we argued. His arms were folded loosely across his chest and his expression stayed calm and unreadable. He did not raise his voice. He did not tell her to stop. He did not tell me to calm down. He simply watched the exchange unfold like something predictable and inevitable, as if the scene confirmed a theory he had already tested.

The apartment began shrinking in ways that had nothing to do with square footage. The heater's rattle sounded harsher at night. It no longer blended into the background. The walls seemed thinner. I could hear the neighbor's footsteps above us, the television murmuring through the drywall, the pipes knocking softly in the early morning hours.

Dad never yelled. That was the part that unsettled me most. There was no eruption to brace for and no explosion to mark the boundary between safe and unsafe. Instead, he asked small questions at dinner in a tone so casual they almost sounded like concern.

"You still seeing that Calderon boy?" he asked one evening, tearing a piece of bread slowly between his fingers.

I did not answer.

"His family know everything about you?"

The words hung in the air. Quiet. Patient. He did not need to finish the thought.

Mom began turning her frustration toward me instead of him. If I mentioned meetings, she said I was living in the past. If I questioned Dad's sudden sobriety, she said I was sabotaging something good. If I suggested he might not have changed, she said I was refusing to let anyone grow. "Don't start," she said sharply one night, her eyes flashing with something that looked more like fear than anger. "Don't ruin this."

Ruin this.

As though what we had built was fragile glass and I was the one pressing too hard.

The dread did not explode. It accumulated. It gathered slowly in the corners of the apartment and lingered in the quiet after forced laughter. It lived in the space between their voices when they spoke too softly in the bedroom at night. It crept into the hours after midnight when the heater clicked off and the building went quiet. It pressed against my ribs as I lay awake, fully dressed, staring at the dark ceiling and listening. Listening for the shift, in his breathing, in her tone, in the quiet, careful way control returned to the room.

Sylvia noticed before I said anything.

By then, it was early April, the kind of Albuquerque spring that never quite decided what it wanted to be. The mountains still carried streaks of snow near their peaks, thin white lines against darker rock, but down in the valley the wind had turned restless and abrasive. It pushed dust along the sidewalks in uneven gusts and chased loose paper across the parking lot before letting it fall again.

School felt different in April. Seniors moved through the hallways with a strange mix of exhaustion and anticipation, hovering in that uneasy space between obligation and escape. FAFSA deadlines had come and gone. Prom posters hung crookedly on locker doors, the tape curling at the corners. Teachers spoke in countdowns now. Thirty-five days. Twenty-nine. Almost there. Conversations overlapped in waves. Someone laughed too loudly near the science wing. A cart squeaked past the library doors. Everything felt transitional, like the building itself understood that half the people in it were already halfway gone.

By then I carried my camera everywhere. The lens gave me rules. Aperture. Shutter speed. Framing. Through it, the world behaved. I could decide what belonged inside the border and what stayed outside it. If I focused long enough, the noise of everything else went quiet.

That afternoon the camera hung unused against my hip.

I stood near the vending machines staring at a scuffed patch of tile on the floor like it might steady me if I focused hard enough. The hallway noise blurred around the edges. Lockers slammed. Sneakers squeaked against the waxed floor. The fluorescent lights hummed overhead in that constant electrical buzz that only became noticeable when you stopped moving and had nothing else to occupy your attention.

Sylvia stopped in front of me. She didn't speak right away. She just looked at me. Really looked. Her eyes moved slowly across my face, searching with the careful attention she used when she was trying to figure out whether someone was telling the truth. Her gaze lingered on my eyes, then my mouth, then the way my shoulders were set.

"You're not here," she said finally. Her voice wasn't sharp or accusing. It was certain.

I shrugged automatically, a reflex I had perfected over years whenever I needed a conversation to end before it started.

Sylvia's expression tightened immediately. "Don't do that," she said quietly. "Don't give me the shrug."

"What's going on?" she asked. No impatience. Just insistence.

I hesitated. The hesitation was enough. I watched recognition move across her face, not sudden but inevitable, like she had been circling the truth for days and had finally reached the center of it.

"He's back," she said. It wasn't a question.

I swallowed and nodded.

"Since when?"

"Early March," I said quietly. "Almost a month."

Sylvia blinked once. Then again. "A month." She repeated it slowly, like she was trying to understand how something that large could have existed beside her without her seeing it. "You've been walking around like this for a month. And you didn't tell us."

The disappointment in her voice landed harder than anger. I tried to build something that sounded like an explanation. "He said he was sober. At first, he was calm. Mom seemed steady. I thought if I didn't make it bigger, maybe it wouldn't become bigger." Even as the words left my mouth, the logic sounded thin.

Sylvia stared at me; arms folded tightly across her chest. "That's not how this works," she said. "You don't wait for him to do something. And you promised me." Her voice stayed low, but the words carried weight that reached past this hallway, past this moment. "After everything that happened before. After all those nights we sat in the kitchen talking about how you weren't going to disappear into it again. You promised you wouldn't go quiet like that."

She still wasn't yelling. That somehow made it worse.

"And your mom?" she asked after a moment.

"She stopped meetings in week two," I said. "By week three she was drinking again."

Sylvia closed her eyes briefly. When she opened them the concern in her face had hardened into something sharper. "Does Bobby know?"

"No."

She shook her head once. "You're doing it again," she said. "You're deciding for everyone what they're allowed to know."

The truth of it landed hard enough that I couldn't answer.

"I'll tell him tonight," I said finally. "We're going out. I'll tell him everything."

Sylvia studied my face for a long moment. "You swear."

"I swear."

She held my gaze for another second, then nodded once. The anger hadn't disappeared. Neither had the disappointment. But she was still standing there, and the fact that she hadn't walked away told me just how serious she believed this had become.

Bobby didn't take me to the diner that night.

He drove past the turn without slowing down. The neon sign flickered once in the distance and disappeared behind us. Streetlights thinned. The neighborhoods gave way to scrub and dark yards where the wind pushed through dry grass. The city opened beneath us as we climbed, the grid of lights spreading wide.

He didn't say anything.

That alone made my stomach tighten. Bobby was rarely quiet for long. Tonight he just drove, both hands on the wheel, eyes fixed ahead.

By the time we reached the overlook, the wind was strong enough to rock the truck. He parked and killed the engine. The metal ticked as it cooled. The city lights shimmered below us.

My leg was bouncing. I didn't notice until the engine stopped. When I forced it still, the tension shifted into my shoulders, my jaw, the tight space at the base of my throat.

Bobby kept his hands on the wheel, staring out through the windshield. The silence stretched long enough that I almost spoke first.

"Something's wrong at the apartment," he said. Not a question. "I don't know what it is. You haven't told me. But I've been watching you for three weeks. The way you answer your phone. The way you go quiet when someone mentions going home."

He paused.

"And you haven't said a word."

I opened my mouth.

"Don't." He turned then, and the anger in his face was quiet and steady. "Don't tell me everything's fine."

The wind hit the truck again.

"I'm not stupid, Michelle. And I'm not fragile. Whatever's happening, I can handle knowing about it. What I can't handle is you deciding I don't need to."

The words settled between us.

I stared through the windshield.

"My dad's back," I said.

Bobby didn't move. Then his fingers tightened slowly on the steering wheel. "How long."

"Four weeks."

He let out a short breath. "Four weeks." He turned toward me. "We've gone out. Sat across from each other. And you said nothing."

The hurt in his voice landed harder than the anger.

"I thought I could manage it," I said.

"That's not the point." His voice sharpened. "You decided I didn't need to know."

I swallowed.

"I didn't want you showing up there. I didn't want it to get bigger."

"And if something had happened?" he asked quietly.

I didn't answer.

He looked back out at the city. His jaw tightened once.

"You don't get to decide that I only get the easy parts of your life."

I forced the rest out before I lost it. "She's drinking again."

He went still.

"She stopped meetings in week two. By week three there were bottles again. He acts like he doesn't see it," I said. My hands curled into fists. "I sleep in my jeans. My phone's under my pillow. I listen to them at night trying to figure out if something's about to turn."

The wind slammed against the truck.

"I keep thinking if I catch it early enough, I can stop it."

Bobby leaned back slowly. For a long moment he didn't speak.

"You've been living like that for a month," he said finally.

"I didn't want to ruin the time we had."

He let out a breath. "Michelle." His voice had softened, but the hurt was still there. "You didn't ruin anything by telling me the truth."

He looked at me.

"What hurt is realizing you were carrying all of that and decided I didn't need to know."

I reached for his hand. His fingers were cold and tense. After a moment, they loosened.

"I was scared," I said.

He looked down at our hands. "You should have told me the first night," he said quietly. "I would have come."

"I know."

"No," he said. "You didn't."

The wind rocked the truck again.

After a moment, he turned his hand under mine and laced our fingers together.

"I'm not just the guy you go to dinner with," he said. "I'm the guy who stands next to you when things get ugly."

His hand tightened on mine and his eyes moved briefly to the city lights spread below us, the grid of streets and intersections, already calculating something — where she was, what the apartment looked like right now, what needed to happen next. The look lasted only a second. He brought it back to me. But I had seen it, the way his mind had already moved ahead of the moment into what came after, and I held onto his hand and didn't say anything because he was right and he was here and that was enough for now.

When I walked back into the apartment that night, the heater was running, the lamp was on, and everything looked exactly the way it had that morning.

Mom and Dad sat close together on the couch. Her shoulder leaned into him like she needed balance, her body angled toward his. His arm stretched across the back of the couch behind her, loose and casual, the posture of someone comfortable in his own home. But the way his arm curved there took up space. It boxed her in without touching her directly. His hand rested just behind her shoulder, fingers relaxed.

The heater rattled again in the hallway. My shoulders tightened. My ears sharpened. The sound landed like a signal, not just background noise. Every small noise in the apartment suddenly mattered. The hum of the refrigerator. The faint buzz of the television screen. The whisper of wind pushing along the siding outside.

The air smelled faintly sweet. Not food-sweet. Not soap. Something underneath. The thin sour sweetness of alcohol that had been in the room recently enough to leave a trace but not long enough to fully disappear.

I stood in the doorway half a second too long.

Mom looked up first. Her smile appeared instantly, too quick to be genuine, like it had been waiting on her face before she even saw me. Her eyes were shiny. Not falling-down drunk, not sloppy. Just softened around the edges. Slightly unfocused. "Hey, baby," she said lightly. "We saved you some soup." Her voice carried a brightness that felt rehearsed.

Dad's gaze followed a moment later. He lifted his eyes from the television and looked at me slowly, deliberately, like he had all the time in the world. His expression was calm, not angry or surprised. Satisfied.

The look of someone who had already measured the room and knew exactly where everything stood inside it. "Long day?" he asked. His voice was casual. Smooth. The same tone he used with neighbors, waitresses, strangers who would never see the other version of him.

My heartbeat slammed against the back of my throat.

His eyes stayed on me longer than necessary, then shifted, first to my hands, to the strap of my bag and back to my face. The motion was subtle enough that Mom wouldn't catch it. But I recognized the pattern. Assessment. The quiet habit of a man who studies people the way other people study rooms.

Mom shifted slightly beside him, leaning more firmly into the space his arm created behind her. Her smile flickered for a fraction of a second before she rebuilt it. "You must be freezing," she said quickly. "The wind's awful tonight."

Dad didn't look at her. He kept looking at me.

The past month wasn't peace. Each small repair around the apartment, each calm dinner, each gentle question had moved the room one degree at a time until the door closed behind him and nobody noticed it happening. He hadn't forced his way back in. He had waited until the apartment arranged itself around him.

Standing in the doorway with my key still in my hand, I understood what I was looking at.

He hadn't come home. He had reclaimed territory. And he was waiting to see what I would do about it.

Chapter Twelve
The Night Everything Breaks

I stayed late with Mr. Alvarez in the photography room, the blinds tilted so the last of the April light slipped through in narrow gold bands across the tables. Dust drifted above the chemical sink. The room smelled faintly of fixer and old paper.

My portfolio lay spread across the black laminate surface. Stairwells. Empty bleachers. The Sandias in that purple hour before dark. Sylvia laughing mid-sentence, her curls caught in the wind. Bobby's truck against a pale winter sky.

For a little while, we talked about aperture and narrative voice and the journalism program at UNM like August was already set, like survival was already handled.

Mr. Alvarez leaned over one of the prints and tapped the edge with his finger.

"You photograph what people try not to see," he said.

I carried that sentence with me down the hallway when I left the building, holding it carefully in my thoughts like something fragile. For a few minutes, I let myself believe that there might be a future where I framed danger through a lens instead of living inside it. The sky outside the school had shifted toward evening. The parking lot lights flickered on in pale circles.

By the time I reached our building, the light had drained from the sky. What remained was that flat blue color that comes just before full dark settles in. The wind that had been pushing dust through the city all afternoon had died down completely. The stillness felt wrong.

The hallway outside 2B smelled like cigarettes and fried food drifting up from the apartments below. Even before I slid my key into the lock, my chest tightened. It happened automatically now. My body had learned the pattern and did not bother asking my mind for permission. The brass numbers above the door caught the porch light. They looked harmless, but my pulse had already begun to climb.

I opened the door slowly, the way you test something cracked before you trust it to hold your weight.

The apartment was dim. Only the television lit the room. Its blue light flickered against the walls and furniture so that everything seemed to shift slightly as the scene changed. The air felt heavy and stale. The smell of whiskey hung thick in the room, sweet and sour at the same time, soaked into the carpet and the drywall.

For a moment I imagined he might be asleep. If he were asleep, I could cross the room quietly. I could reach my bedroom. I could close the door and keep the fragile illusion that I still controlled where I could exist in this apartment.

"Where the hell have you been?"

The voice came out of the dark with quiet clarity.

My body reacted instantly. My spine locked. My breath stopped halfway in. The muscles in my shoulders tightened so sharply it felt like a wire had been pulled through them. He rose slowly from the couch, unfolding himself with steady control. The whiskey bottle on the coffee table caught the blue television light and flashed as he moved. His eyes were red and heavy at the edges, but the way they landed on me was precise.

"I was just…"

My backpack slid from my shoulder and hit the floor with a dull thud that sounded far too loud in the quiet room.

"I wasn't…"

"Lyin' again," he said. The word came out slow and thick. The alcohol softened the edges of his voice, but something underneath it remained sharp. "Sneakin' around like you're too good for this house." The slur was there, but controlled. He stepped closer. The smell of whiskey reached me before he did. It burned the back of my throat.

"I didn't lie," I said quietly. Even after everything, some part of me still believed correcting him might slow things down.

He tilted his head slightly. "What did you say?"

Before I could answer, movement staggered in from the kitchen doorway. My mother appeared gripping the doorframe. Her fingers were white against the wood. Her balance looked uncertain. Her eyeliner had smeared beneath her eyes and her cheeks were flushed too bright. Her gaze moved from him to me.

"I knew where she was," she said, her voice shaking but loud. "Leave her alone, Mark."

The boldness in her voice sounded thin. Fragile. Like something propped up by alcohol rather than strength. He turned toward her quickly. "You?" he said, laughing harshly. "You're gonna tell me what's enough? You can't even…"

She stepped between us.

Her hands landed against his chest; they trembled but stayed there. For one suspended second the room froze around the image. Her smaller body squared against his. Her shoulders lifted in resistance she had not shown in months.

"That's enough."

The punch came without warning.

His fist cut through the blue television light and struck her with a dull sound that echoed in the room. Her head snapped sideways. Her body slammed against the wall hard enough to shake the picture frame beside her. The frame tore free and shattered across the carpet.

For a moment the world tilted. Then the blood appeared. A thin line at first along her lip. Then more. I moved toward her instinctively but his arm shot out and hit my chest. It stopped me instantly. The movement was quick and efficient, like moving a chair out of the way.

"Stay back," he said.

My mother tried to stand straight but her knees gave slightly. He grabbed her arm and jerked her upright. Before she found her balance his hand struck her again. The sound was sharper this time. Blood burst from her nose and sprayed across his shirt and the beige wall behind him.

Her hand flew to her face. Through tears and blood, she looked directly at me. For the first time in weeks her eyes were clear. Clear of alcohol. Clear of denial.

"Run, Shelly," she said.

The words were quiet.

She wrenched free from him and grabbed her keys from the counter. Her shoulder slammed into the door as she jerked it open and stumbled into the hallway. He lunged after her but caught his leg on the coffee table. The whiskey bottle crashed to the carpet, shattering into shards. The smell of alcohol poured into the room.

She was already halfway down the hallway when he regained his footing. Her footsteps echoed away. He turned back toward me.

Not wild. Focused.

And in the way his eyes narrowed, in the way the apartment seemed to close in around us, I understood something with terrible clarity. This was not another night to survive. Something had broken.

I ran.

I don't remember unlocking the door.

I remember the stairwell.

The door slammed open behind me hard enough to crack against the concrete wall and rattle on its hinges. The fluorescent bulb flickered overhead, casting a sick yellow light over everything. I took the steps two at a time, my hand skidding along the railing. My backpack caught on the chair where it had fallen. Without thinking, my hand grabbed the strap and yanked it free. I couldn't leave my camera behind.

My lungs burned by the second flight. The stairwell smelled like dust and old concrete. Somewhere behind me, his voice carried through the walls. Close enough that my body treated every second like he was right there.

I did not look back. Looking back was how you got caught.

My shoes pounded the steps. The railing rattled under my palm. I hit the final landing and shoved through the front door.

Cold air hit my face hard enough to sting. For a second it forced my lungs open. I dragged in a breath that scraped all the way down my chest.

Then I moved again.

Across the parking lot. Past the fence. Past the parked cars under humming lights. My backpack thudded against my shoulder with every step.

I ran until I reached the corner store.

The neon sign above it flickered red and white against the dark street, buzzing steadily above it. The sound filled the space around me like a machine that never stopped running. I bent forward with my hands braced against my knees, trying to drag air into my lungs. My chest burned. My throat tasted metallic and raw. My hands shook so violently I dropped my phone the first time I tried to unlock it. It hit the pavement and slid before I grabbed it again. When the screen lit up, the brightness of it looked wrong against the darkness of the street, like something from a different world.

I tapped Sylvia's name. She answered on the second ring.

"Sylvia," I said, but the word broke apart halfway through my throat. My voice sounded thin and raw.

She did not ask what happened. "I'm coming," she said immediately. I could hear movement behind her. A chair scraping across the floor. A door opening. Fast footsteps. "Don't move. Bobby's grabbing the truck."

The line went dead.

I stood under the neon sign while the red light pulsed across the pavement and the front of the store in slow flashes. My hands would not stop shaking. Every car that passed at the end of the street made my shoulders jump. Every shadow made my stomach tighten. I kept expecting him to appear at the corner of the block. I kept expecting his voice to tear through the quiet again.

Headlights swung around the corner faster than they should have.

The sound of Bobby's Ford reached me before the truck itself did. The engine rattled loudly as it came down the street and braked hard in front of the store. Gravel spat under the tires as the truck stopped. The passenger door opened before the engine finished idling.

Bobby was already out of the driver's seat.

"Shell," he said.

The word came out low and controlled, but the fear underneath it was unmistakable. His jacket was already in his hands. He stepped close and wrapped it around my shoulders, pulling it tight. His fingers moved quickly across my face, brushing my cheek, my temple, my jaw. "You're safe," he said quietly. His voice was rough. "You're safe. I've got you."

I did not decide to move toward him. My body did it for me.

My hands clenched the front of his hoodie, twisting the fabric like it might vanish if I let go. He pulled me against him immediately, his arms closing around my shoulders with steady pressure. His chest was warm. His heartbeat was solid and slow beneath my cheek. I pressed my face against him and breathed in the familiar smell of laundry soap and cold air and the faint metallic scent that always clung to his truck.

For a few seconds the world narrowed to that contact.

Then Sylvia was there too. Her hand slid into my hair at the back of my head, her fingers tightening slightly. "We're here," she said softly. "We're here."

They guided me toward the truck carefully, moving slowly like I might break if they rushed. Bobby kept one hand on my shoulder while Sylvia opened the passenger door wider. The heater blasted warm air that smelled faintly dusty. Bobby drove with one hand on the wheel and the other resting on my knee. He did not grip. His hand stayed there quietly, steady and solid.

Streetlights slid past the window in long streaks of yellow. Traffic lights cycled through red and green. Houses passed in dark shapes. The city looked perfectly normal. I stared at the passing lights and tried to force my mind to accept what was happening. That the truck was moving. That the distance between me and that apartment was growing. That I was no longer standing in the living room with blue television light and blood on the wall. That I had gotten out.

My body was still running long after the truck turned onto the Calderons' street. Even after the familiar shape of the house appeared at the end of the block, the porch light glowing steady and warm the way it always had. Even as Bobby slowed the truck and pulled into the driveway, even as the engine dropped into a quiet idle and the headlights washed across the adobe wall, something inside me refused to slow down. My heart still hammered as if I were sprinting. My lungs kept pulling air too fast. I did not feel like I had arrived anywhere. I felt suspended, as if the ground beneath me had already given way and my body simply had not caught up yet.

The house looked exactly the way it always did at night. The porch light cast its soft yellow circle across the driveway and the front steps. The wind chimes hanging beside the door moved gently in the cold air, their small metal notes brushing together in a thin rhythm. The sound was painfully ordinary. For years that porch light had meant safety. It meant dinner already on the stove. It meant Mama's voice drifting out from the kitchen and Pops' low voice answering somewhere deeper in the house. Seeing it now felt unreal, like stepping into a photograph from another life.

Rowdy was at the gate before Bobby had the engine fully off. He didn't circle or bark. He came directly to me when I stepped out of the truck and pressed himself against my leg and stayed there, warm and solid and completely still.

Mama was already opening the door before we reached the porch. She must have heard the engine or the tires on the gravel because she appeared in the doorway almost immediately, barefoot in her robe, her hair loose around her shoulders. The porch light caught the worry on her face and deepened every line around her eyes. She did not ask what happened. She did not hesitate. The moment I stepped onto the porch she reached for me.

"Mija," she breathed, pulling me into her arms with sudden force. "Dios santo… ven aquí."

Her embrace came immediately, unyielding and absolute. Both arms wrapped around me, tight and certain, like she had already decided whatever had happened was serious enough that explanations could wait. My body folded into her before my mind had time to decide anything. The contact loosened something that had been clenched tight since the stairwell.

Inside, warmth rushed over me. The house smelled like green chile and toasted corn and the faint sweetness of something that had simmered earlier in the evening. The heat from the kitchen wrapped around my shoulders as we stepped inside. The television murmured softly in the living room, a telenovela paused mid-argument, bright colors flickering across the walls.

Sylvia guided me to the couch before my knees had the chance to give out. She pulled a blanket from the back of a chair and wrapped it around my shoulders, tucking the edges beneath my chin the way someone might wrap a child coming in from the cold. Her hands moved quickly but carefully, practical and controlled. Mama disappeared into the kitchen and returned a moment later with a mug of manzanilla tea, pressing it into my hands. "Despacio," she murmured softly. The ceramic was warm enough to sting my palms slightly. Steam rose in thin white curls that brushed my face. I watched it because it was easier than letting my mind replay the apartment.

Hector was sitting in the armchair near the far wall. I had not noticed him at first. He had been there the whole time, leaning forward slightly with his elbows on his knees, hands loosely clasped together. When we came through the door his eyes lifted and followed the movement quietly. He did not stand. He did not ask questions. He did not speak. When our eyes met for a second, he gave the smallest nod, almost invisible, and then looked away again.

Pops moved through the kitchen with slow, deliberate precision. He did not rush. Cabinets opened and closed softly. A burner clicked and flared to life. Every motion felt intentional, like a man aligning himself before stepping into something that would not be undone. When he came back into the living room he closed the front door firmly behind him. The latch slid into place with a quiet but final sound that seemed to settle the entire house. He stood in front of me for a moment, studying my face with the kind of attention that looked past panic and straight into facts.

"Did he put hands on you?" he asked. His voice was low, steady, a quiet anchor in the room.

I shook my head.

His shoulders eased only slightly. Not relief. Adjustment. "Good," he said quietly. "Sit. Eat a little."

He turned back toward the stove and warmed a tortilla directly over the flame until it blistered and puffed. The smell of corn and char drifted through the room. When it was ready he placed it on a small plate and brought it back to me, setting it carefully in my hands. "Just a bite," he said.

Because he asked like it mattered, because in this house food was both comfort and instruction, I tore off a piece and forced it into my mouth. My jaw moved slowly. My stomach recoiled and then accepted it anyway. The ordinary act felt enormous.

Time thickened. It stopped moving forward and settled into the room, pressing quietly against the walls.

Lamplight rested across the carpet and the low table. The warmth felt contained, like the house was holding something fragile in place. Beyond the windows the yard stretched cold and still. The wind chimes stirred now and then, their metal notes brushing together before fading back into silence.

Bobby paced behind the couch in slow, tight circuits. Each step landed carefully, but the tension in him filled the room. His jaw stayed clenched. His hands opened and closed as he walked. Every few steps his eyes flicked to me. Quick checks. Counting.

Sylvia stayed pressed against my side, her shoulder firm against mine. Her fingers were threaded through my hand, tight enough that neither of us could have pulled away. Every few seconds her thumb moved against my skin, a small, steady signal.

Mama sat on my other side, one arm around my shoulders, her hand moving through my hair in slow, even strokes. The motion was familiar in a way that cut deeper than comfort could reach. It was how my mother used to touch me when I was small enough to curl into her lap without thinking. Before everything fractured.

The mug had gone cold. I didn't remember setting it down.

Then Pops' phone rang.

The sound cut through the room with an unnatural sharpness. For a moment no one moved. The wind chimes outside tapped faintly against one another in the cold air. The television's silent glow flickered across the wall. But the air in the room tightened immediately.

Pops looked down at the phone in his hand. "Ay," he said quietly. "Es Sheryl."

My heart misfired so violently, it felt as though it had left my chest and forgotten how to return. A sudden hollow opening under my ribs. A drop before the fall.

Pops stepped into the kitchen to answer the call. He moved deliberately, not wanting the conversation to fall in the center of the room. His voice carried anyway.

"Yes… sí… I understand."

A pause followed. Then another. The silence between his words was not empty. It held weight. His voice did not rise. It grew heavier instead, slower, each word placed carefully as if he were steadying something fragile with nothing but control. I could not hear the voice on the other end of the line, but I heard enough in the pauses. In the thinning breath between his responses. In the slight shift in his tone that meant something irreversible had already been spoken.

I turned my head toward the kitchen doorway without realizing I had moved. My body felt distant, like it belonged to someone else sitting on the couch wrapped in a blanket.

There was a long stretch where Pops did not speak at all.

Through the doorway I saw him lift one hand slowly to his forehead. He pressed it there, not dramatically, just firmly, as though he were holding something inside his skull that threatened to break loose. His shoulders curved forward slightly. His breath caught once. Small. Tight.

That was when I knew.

Mama's hand froze in my hair.

Sylvia's fingers tightened around mine so suddenly it hurt.

Behind the couch Bobby stopped pacing mid-step. His entire body went still, as if someone had cut the thread that allowed him to move.

When Pops came back into the living room he did not hesitate. He did not pace or search for words. He walked straight to me and lowered himself onto one knee in front of the couch, bringing himself down so I would not have to look up. "Michelle," he said gently. "Mija…"

The word trembled.

I already knew.

My body knew it from the first silence in the kitchen. My pulse had begun racing long before the sentence formed. He took my hands in his. His palms were warm and steady. His thumbs pressed firmly against my knuckles.

"Your aunt called," he said quietly. "There was an accident."

The room tilted slightly. Not visibly. Not dramatically. Just enough that the edges of my vision narrowed.

"Your mother ran a red light," he continued, each word slow and careful. "Another car hit her."

He paused.

Not for effect.

For mercy.

"She didn't make it."

Something tore loose inside my chest. It was not a sob. Not a cry. My body folded forward before I could stop it. The blanket slid from my shoulders. My elbow caught the mug on the coffee table as I went and it shattered against the hardwood floor, tea spreading across the boards unnoticed.

Pops caught me before I could collapse completely. His arms closed firmly around my back, steady and unshaking. Mama wrapped herself around both of us, her robe warm against my cheek. Sylvia pressed into my shoulder and began to cry openly, her breath breaking into uneven gasps. Bobby dropped to his knees beside the couch, his hands at my arms and waist, his eyes bright and wet.

In the armchair across the room, Hector leaned forward and pressed both hands over his face and stayed that way.

Something broke. The room stayed, lamplight, voices, hands, but what felt real was the absence.

Chapter Thirteen
Devastation

The days after Mom died blurred together. Time stopped making sense. Morning arrived without meaning. Night settled without rest.

I slept wherever the house allowed me to. The first night was the couch, wrapped in a quilt that smelled faintly of fabric softener and green chile. The second night Sylvia pulled me into her bed and slept with one arm draped across my waist, like she thought I might disappear if she let go. By the third night Mama had quietly arranged a small corner room for me, clearing space as if she had already decided I belonged there for as long as I needed.

I barely ate. Barely spoke. I moved only when someone guided me from one room to another, something fragile that required steady hands.

Pops made phone calls in the kitchen with the door half closed, his voice low and formal, the kind that meant paperwork was being signed and arrangements confirmed, that official words were already being spoken about my mother in the past tense.

Mama brewed tea I could not swallow, pressing warm mugs into my hands anyway as if heat alone might stitch something back together.

Sylvia stayed close enough that I could hear her breathing even when I wasn't looking, her presence steady and deliberate.

Bobby drove me everywhere without comment. First to the funeral home, where the air smelled faintly of lilies and furniture polish and the quiet felt unnatural, like sound itself had been discouraged. Then to school, where teachers needed signatures and forms and someone from the office spoke to me with careful sympathy that made the whole building feel unfamiliar.

The day after the service he drove me to the river. We sat on a low bank where the water moved past the cottonwoods. I cried until my throat burned and the sound coming out of me stopped resembling language.

Bobby sat beside me the entire time. He did not try to fill the silence. He did not ask questions. He simply stayed.

I did not return to the apartment.

Not the night Mom died. Not the next morning when people spoke in hushed voices about services and liability and what would happen with the lease. Not while adults discussed belongings as if objects could be separated neatly from memory. Each time Pops asked quietly, "Mija, if you want, I'll go with you," I shook my head before the sentence even finished. The thought of stepping back through that door made my stomach twist sharply. My body recoiled before my mind could even form the image. The apartment no longer felt like a place. It felt like a wound that had not finished bleeding.

Grief does not move forward politely. It circles, doubles back, and arrives in quiet moments and insists on being answered.

Four or five days after the funeral I woke with an urgency so sharp it felt like panic. My eyes opened and the thought was already there. I needed my things. The clothes I recognized without thinking. The shoebox under my bed filled with notes Sylvia and I had passed since middle school, folded into careful squares. The Polaroids taped around my mirror. The sweater Mom wore in the mornings before everything unraveled, the one that still held a faint trace of her shampoo if you pressed your face into the sleeve.

The need was irrational and overwhelming at the same time. If I didn't go back and gather those pieces, it felt like they would disappear. Like the last evidence of who we had been before everything fractured would dissolve if I waited too long.

Mama was folding towels in the hallway when she saw me lacing my shoes. The house smelled like coffee and laundry detergent. The radio in the kitchen was playing softly; the same station Pops left on most mornings. Everything inside the house felt steady and ordinary, the quiet routines moving from room to room like nothing had broken the week before.

"Michelle?" she asked gently. "Where are you going, cariño?"

"To the apartment," I said. My voice sounded rough, like it had been scraped raw. "Just for a few minutes."

She stopped folding the towel and looked at me. Not quickly. Carefully. Her eyes moved across my face like she was checking something she could not quite see but already understood. "Do you want someone with you?" she asked.

The question sat between us in the hallway. For a moment I almost said yes. The word was already forming in my throat. Part of me wanted someone beside me. Someone to walk through the door first. Someone to stand between me and whatever waited inside. But the habit was stronger than the fear. I shook my head too quickly. "I'll be fine."

The lie came out easily. I had said it for years without thinking.

Mama knew it was a lie. I could see it in her face. The worry deepened around her eyes, but she did not argue. She held my gaze for another second and then nodded slowly, like she was allowing something she did not believe was safe but could not stop. "Come back soon," she said.

Outside, the air felt dry and restless. Wind moved down the street in uneven bursts, pushing dust across the sidewalk and against my shoes. The sky was bright and empty. The mountains stood sharp in the distance. The light made everything too clear. Nothing softened under it.

The world kept moving.

Mom was gone.

The thought wouldn't settle. It kept striking the same place in my chest, without landing anywhere that made sense. Cars passed. A neighbor watered a small patch of grass two houses down. A screen door slammed somewhere on the block. Each sound hit my body before my mind could catch up.

I told myself Dad wouldn't be there. If he was there, he'd probably be asleep. If he wasn't asleep, he'd ignore me. If he didn't ignore me, I'd leave. I repeated the sequence again and again as I walked, building it into something that felt like a plan.

The building came into view at the end of the block, and my steps slowed. The siding looked dull in the afternoon light. The windows were dark; the curtains were pulled closed tight across the glass. The front door was open. Not wide, just enough that it did not sit against the frame.

I stopped on the sidewalk, staring at it.

The wind pushed against it and it shifted slightly, the hinge making a tired creaking sound that carried across the empty walkway. No voices came from inside. No music. No movement anywhere in the building. The whole place felt quiet in the wrong way.

For a second, I thought about turning around and walking back to Mama's house. I imagined the smell of coffee again. The warmth of the kitchen. Sylvia sitting at the table with her homework spread out. Bobby leaning against the counter. The normal rhythm of their house. But my things were still inside. The pieces of my life that had existed before everything broke open. If I did not go in, they would disappear too.

I walked up the path slowly. Each step made the tight feeling in my chest grow heavier. By the time I reached the door, my hands had started to shake. I pushed it open and stepped inside.

The change in my body was immediate. Every muscle tightened at once, the way it used to when I was a kid trying to listen through walls for the sound of his footsteps. My breathing slowed. The air inside the apartment felt stale and heavy. It smelled like beer, sweat, and something sour that had soaked into the carpet and furniture. The curtains were pulled completely shut across the windows, blocking out the afternoon sun, so the room was dim except for the television. Its blue light flickered across the walls and ceiling, turning everything the same cold shade.

Dad sat at the kitchen table.

Three men sat with him.

Empty cans and half-finished bottles crowded the table. Wet rings of condensation spread across the wood where the cans had been sitting. One of the men leaned back in his chair with his boots hooked on the rung, rocking slightly like he had settled in for the afternoon. Another turned his head immediately when the door opened, his eyes locking onto me with a sharp attention that made my stomach drop. The third watched more slowly, his gaze moving over me with open curiosity before his mouth pulled into a small smile.

Dad looked thinner than the last time I had seen him. Not weak. Just carved down. The skin around his jaw hung looser, the lines beside his mouth deeper, but his eyes were steady. When he saw me, his face hardened for a moment. Then the corner of his mouth lifted into a slow, familiar sneer.

"Well," he said thickly, pushing his chair back. "Look who crawled out of the Calderons' place."

He stood up, steadying himself briefly on the chair before straightening. "Come to grab your stuff and leave me too?"

"I just need my things," I said. My voice slid automatically into the careful tone I had learned to use around him years ago. Quiet. Neutral. The tone meant to keep things from turning.

"You think you're better than me?" he asked, stepping closer. The smell of alcohol reached me, sharp enough to sting my eyes. "Your mom thought she was too." His mouth twisted. "Look how that turned out."

The words hit me so hard the air left my chest; for a moment I could not breathe at all.

"I'm not here to fight," I said.

Even as I said it, I knew the sentence meant nothing.

Dad gave a short laugh without humor. He did not stop looking at me when he lifted his hand and gestured loosely toward the men at the table. "Teach her not to run her mouth."

For a second the sentence made no sense. Then the meaning settled in all at once.

"No," I said quickly. The word sounded small and thin. "Dad—"

But he had already turned away. He walked to the refrigerator like the conversation was finished. He opened it, pulled out a beer, and cracked the tab with a soft metallic snap that sounded too loud in the quiet room. Then he leaned back against the counter and folded his arms across his chest.

Watching.

Behind me chairs scraped across the floor. One of the men laughed quietly. Another muttered something I could not hear. Their movements filled the room slowly, deliberately, like they had all the time in the world.

My body locked first. My shoulders stiffened, my hands went cold. My heart began pounding so hard in my ears that the rest of the room sounded distant. I looked toward the kitchen. Toward Dad. He stood there with the beer in his hand, leaning back against the counter, his eyes fixed on the room in front of him. He did not move. He did not speak. He did not look away.

That was when the fear settled fully into my chest. Not the sharp panic that makes you run. Something heavier than that. The kind that comes when you understand the person who should stop something has already decided not to.

After that the room broke apart into fragments that I still cannot line up cleanly. The scrape of a chair. Someone's hand on my arm. The television light flashing across the ceiling in uneven pulses. My breath came too fast. My body pulled away from itself just enough to keep going.

Survival reduced itself to one instruction: endure it.

When it was finally quiet again the apartment felt unnaturally still. The television continued flickering in the corner. The wind outside pushed dust against the siding. My whole body shook so badly I could barely move. When I tried to push myself upright my arms slipped against the floor. My mouth tasted like metal.

I found my shirt on the floor near the hallway. I pulled it on without looking at it, fingers shaking so badly it took three tries to get my arms through. The fabric hung wrong where it had torn at the shoulder seam. I didn't try to fix it. I just pulled it as straight as I could manage and held it closed with my hand.

Dad did not look up.

That was the last thing I saw when I turned toward the door. Him, still leaning against the counter, staring past me at something that didn't exist. That was deliberate too.

I moved toward the door because movement was the only option left. My legs carried me forward before my mind had caught up. I don't remember leaving the apartment. I don't remember going down the stairs or pushing through the building door. The first clear thing I remember is the corner store's neon sign buzzing above me and the brick wall against my back as I slid down it and landed on the pavement.

The April wind moved through the street in dry bursts, pushing grit across the sidewalk and against my shoes. Cars passed without slowing. A man walked out of the store with a soda and stepped around me without looking twice. Somewhere across the street someone laughed. The world continued in bright afternoon daylight while I sat there, trying to breathe inside a body that no longer felt fully attached to me. My hands shook violently. My knuckles were scraped and smeared with drying blood. The shirt hung loose where it had torn at the shoulder, the seam stretched open. Dirt streaked across my jeans and darker stains had already begun to stiffen the denim. My cheek throbbed where the swelling had begun to spread and every breath pulled tight against my ribs like something inside them had been bruised or cracked.

I pulled my phone out with fingers that barely obeyed me and dialed Sylvia. The screen blurred and sharpened in uneven waves. I blinked hard until I could see her name clearly enough to press call. She answered before the second ring finished.

"M&M? Michelle? What's wrong?"

I tried to answer her. My mouth opened but nothing came out except air that caught halfway in my throat. For a second there was only my breathing on the line. Then the sound tore loose from somewhere deep in my chest. A broken sob that I could not swallow back once it started.

"Oh God," Sylvia said.

I heard the moment she understood. The moment her voice changed from confusion to certainty. A door slammed somewhere behind her. "I'm calling Bobby," she said. "Don't move. Please don't move."

The line went dead.

I curled tighter against the brick wall beneath the neon sign, pulling my knees toward my chest and pressing my forehead into the rough mortar. The buzzing light above me vibrated through the wall and into my skull. Dust scraped along the curb and lifted against my bare ankles. My hands would not stop shaking. Every passing car made my body tense automatically. The daylight felt harsh and exposed, like the whole street could see me sitting there and simply chose not to.

The truck came fast.

I heard the engine before I saw it. Bobby's Ford roared around the corner too quickly, tires spitting gravel as it braked hard in front of the store. Bobby was already out of the driver's seat before the engine settled. Sylvia came around from the passenger side.

He ran toward me.

The urgency in his movement slowed the moment he got close enough to see me clearly. He stopped a few feet away like he had run into something invisible. For a second, he just stared. The color drained from his face so quickly it left him pale and tight around the mouth. Then the blood rushed back just as fast, spreading across his cheeks and neck. His eyes moved over me once, quickly. The torn shirt. The blood on my hands. The bruising already darkened along my cheek. His jaw tightened so hard the muscle jumped beneath the skin.

"Jesus," he whispered.

He took one careful step closer. "Shell," he said. "Hey. Look at me."

I tried to lift my head. The movement made my ribs burn and I sucked in a breath that came out sharp. His eyes changed immediately when he heard it. He reached toward me without thinking and his fingers brushed my arm.

I flinched violently. My whole body jerked sideways and I nearly lost my balance.

He pulled his hand back instantly. "Okay." he said quickly. "Okay. I'm sorry." He lifted both hands where I could see them. "I won't touch you. I won't. I'm right here."

His voice shook despite the effort he was making to control it. His eyes kept moving over me in quick, panicked checks, trying to understand what had been done without forcing me to say it.

Sylvia dropped beside me. She pulled me against her immediately, one arm around my shoulders and the other bracing my back. My body went rigid at first but she held on anyway. "We've got you," she whispered into my hair. "You're safe. You're safe."

Bobby crouched in front of us. The anger in his face was unmistakable now, but it was buried under something heavier. Fear. Control. The effort of holding himself together. "I'm going to lift you," he said. "Okay?" He waited. When I didn't pull away, he moved slowly, sliding one arm beneath my knees and the other behind my back. When he lifted me, he did it carefully, like he was afraid of hurting me more. My head dropped against his chest and stayed there.

He carried me to the truck and got in on the passenger side, pulling me in with him so I was in his lap against the door. Sylvia came around and climbed behind the wheel. "Hospital?" she asked. "Yes," Bobby said. She pulled the truck into the street and accelerated hard.

Bobby settled back against the seat with me in his lap, one arm wrapped around my shoulders and the other braced across my back. His jacket came off his shoulders and wrapped around mine, covering the torn fabric without a word about it. "I've got you," he said. The words were steady but the tension in his body was not. His chest rose and fell too quickly beneath my cheek. One hand stayed against the back of my head the entire drive, holding me there gently but firmly.

Sylvia drove fast, weaving through traffic without hesitation. The city blurred past the windows in bright streaks of afternoon light. By the time the hospital came into view, Bobby had not loosened his hold on me once. When the truck stopped under the emergency entrance, he opened the door and carried me inside.

I remember fluorescent lights. I remember forms being placed in front of me and a pen pushed gently into my hand. My fingers would not close around it properly.

Sylvia answered most of the questions before the nurse finished asking them, her steady voice making the room feel slightly less chaotic. When someone asked me something directly, I tried to answer, but the words moved slowly through my mouth, as if they belonged to someone else.

Nurses moved in and out with quiet efficiency. One cleaned my hands, wiping dried blood from my knuckles with slow, deliberate movements. Another swabbed my cheek and asked questions in a calm, repeating tone. What happened? Where did it happen? Did I know the people involved? Did I want to speak to someone from the police department?

Sometimes I answered. Sometimes my mouth would not cooperate and the silence stretched until Sylvia stepped in and filled it.

Bobby stood beside the bed the entire time. He did not sit. He did not pace. He stood there with his hands clenched so tightly his knuckles had gone white.

At first, he tried to look at me. I saw him try. His eyes moved over the bruises on my face, the torn fabric of my shirt, the places where dried blood had stiffened against my skin. Then his jaw tightened, and his gaze shifted away. After that he stared at the wall beside the bed like it required his full attention.

Looking at me hurt him too much. Not looking hurt him, too. But it was the only way he could keep himself still.

Pops arrived before dawn, Hector a step behind him.

Outside the hospital windows, the sky had just begun to pale when they walked through the doors together. Hector took up a position near the wall and stayed there, saying nothing. Pops spoke with the nurse at the desk and then with someone from hospital administration, his voice low and controlled, each word deliberate. When a police officer arrived, he stepped into the hallway with him and spoke in that same steady tone. There was no raised voice, no visible anger, yet the tension in his shoulders was unmistakable.

Bobby stood nearby while they spoke. At one point he said, "It was him." Pops did not look at him. He only nodded once, small and controlled, as if placing something carefully onto a shelf where it would stay until he decided what to do with it.

Dad was gone by the time Bobby and Hector went to the apartment. I did not learn the details until later. Only that Pops insisted they not go alone. Hector's face had been unreadable when he left the house. Bobby's hands were shaking when he grabbed his keys and walked out the door.

When they reached the apartment, the place was empty, but still thick with the aftermath of the night. Beer cans were scattered across the floor and the kitchen table. The curtains were still drawn tight across the windows. The television still plugged in and humming in the corner. Dad was gone. The men who had been with him were gone too. But the room held what had happened anyway. My jacket lay on the floor near the hallway, exactly where it had fallen when I came in. One of the men had left a belt on the counter. Neither Bobby nor Hector touched either of them.

Bobby stood in the middle of the room for a long moment without moving. Hector crossed to the window and stood with his back to the room. Neither of them spoke.

They did not search for anyone. They did not go looking for a fight. They moved straight to my room and packed everything in silence. Clothes from the closet went into garbage bags first. The shoebox beneath the bed with every folded note Sylvia and I had passed since middle school went carefully into a cardboard box. The Polaroids taped around my mirror were peeled away one by one. The sweater, still carrying the faint smell of my mother, was folded carefully and placed on top of the pile.

In the kitchen, Bobby stopped at the windowsill. The rosemary sat there in its pot, the soil pulled away from the edges, the needles still faintly alive despite the weeks of neglect. He stood there for a moment. Then he picked it up and carried it out with the rest.

Bobby told me later it felt like collecting bones from a wreck.

They didn't linger. They didn't speak to anyone in the building. They carried everything out in garbage bags and cardboard boxes, loaded it into the truck, and drove away. When they brought my things back to the house, they carried them upstairs and set them at the foot of Sylvia's bed. They didn't open the bags. They didn't ask where anything should go. They simply placed the pieces of my life there.

By the time I was discharged from the hospital, the sky was turning gray with early morning light. Sylvia drove us home.

When the truck pulled into the driveway, Pops opened the door before the engine had shut off. He stepped onto the porch and looked straight at me as Bobby helped me down. Something inside him went utterly still. His jaw tightened. His shoulders squared slightly. The air around him hardened with a quiet rage that did not need to be spoken.

Rowdy was at the base of the porch steps, still and close, his eyes on me. He didn't circle or demand anything. He simply stood there the way he always stood when the household had taken damage — present, steady, already decided.

Mama crossed the porch in two quick steps and folded me into her arms the second my feet touched the ground. Her embrace was warm and steady. Sylvia stayed pressed against my side, one hand gripping my arm. Bobby hovered just behind me, close enough that I could feel the heat of him at my back.

No one asked for details or pushed for explanations.
They simply made space.

Sylvia cleared half her dresser without ceremony. One
afternoon I came back from a follow-up appointment and
found drawers emptied, my clothes folded neatly inside as if
they had always belonged there. She didn't make a speech
about it. She just shrugged and said it made more sense this
way.

Mama made food I couldn't eat and left it on the table
anyway. Some nights I managed a few bites because she was
watching too closely to refuse. Most nights the plate sat
untouched until someone carried it away.

Pops handled everything that required adult language:
paperwork, calls, conversations with people whose titles
sounded official and distant. I heard fragments of those words
drifting through the kitchen at night: statements, charges,
reports, words I could not carry without feeling like my ribs
would crack open.

Bobby did not leave unless I forced him to. He drove
me to follow-up appointments and waited in the parking lot
with the engine off until I came back out. When nightmares
woke me up shaking and sick, he sat on the floor outside the
bathroom door while I leaned against the tile and tried to
breathe through the nausea.

He washed my clothes without asking which ones I
wanted saved and which ones I wanted erased. Sometimes I
caught him standing in the laundry room doorway, holding one
of my shirts for a long time before dropping it into the
machine. He watched me constantly, the way someone watches
a thing they are afraid of losing.

College stopped existing in my mind almost overnight.
The brochures stacked on Sylvia's desk went untouched. My

camera sat on the dresser where Bobby had placed it when they brought my things back from the apartment, the strap curled loosely beside it, the memory card still inside from the last morning everything had been ordinary. Mr. Alvarez emailed once asking if I was okay and whether I still planned to submit my portfolio to UNM. I read the message three times and then closed the laptop without answering. Photography had once felt like oxygen, something that kept the world sharp and visible. Now the idea of pointing a lens at anything felt unbearable. I could not imagine documenting anything ever again.

The Calderons held me together piece by piece. They were safe, love, and home.

But Albuquerque wasn't.

Every siren jolted through me. Every street corner felt wrong. Even the wind dragging dust across the pavement made my shoulders tighten. The city no longer felt like a place. It felt like something I had survived.

If I stayed, the ghosts would not fade. They would settle in.

Chapter Fourteen
The Plan

Quietly, without telling anyone, I made a decision.

It did not feel brave. It did not feel dramatic. It felt like instinct, like something inside me had finally stopped arguing and started listening. The feeling stayed. It settled under my ribs and refused to move.

Healing was uneven. Some mornings I woke up and the world did not hurt immediately. Those mornings felt like small miracles. I could sit between Sylvia and Bobby in the courtyard at lunch and let their voices blur together until it almost sounded like normal life again. I could ride in the middle seat of Bobby's truck and pretend, for a few minutes at a time, that nothing had been broken beyond repair. At night Mama braided my hair before bed, her fingers moving slowly, separating the strands and tugging only when necessary.

In those moments my body almost felt like it belonged to me again.

And then it would collapse.

A siren would cut through the air, and my heart slammed so hard that I tasted metal. A locker would crash shut and my shoulders would jerk upward before my brain caught up. The sharp smell of whiskey would pass and the room would tilt just enough to feel unsafe again. My body reacted before thought had time to follow.

The Calderons noticed everything without saying they did. Sylvia shifted closer to doors. Mama lowered her voice when I went quiet and pretended not to see when I pushed food around my plate. Pops watched every room like he was already calculating how it could change. Bobby stayed near in a way that was careful and almost reverent, like attention alone might keep the world from touching me again.

They gave me something real. Something I could lean on. But they also anchored me to a city that no longer felt safe to stay in. The more they gathered around me, the harder it became to ignore the thought that kept returning: if I stayed, I might break again, and this time I would not be the only one who felt it.

My father was still somewhere in Albuquerque.

Somewhere inside the same grid of streets. Somewhere moving through the same gas stations and liquor stores and side roads the rest of us moved through every day. The city was not large enough to disappear inside. Every slow car near the house made my pulse spike. Every unfamiliar shape at the end of the street forced my body to brace before my mind could catch up.

And if he came back, he would not only reach for me. He would reach into their lives too.

Once that settled into place, it stopped feeling like a possibility and became something closer to fact.

The decision settled and hardened about three weeks before graduation, though it never felt like a choice so much as an understanding that had finally stopped pretending to be anything else. I had already been saving money long before everything collapsed. My part-time job shelving books at the library had turned into a quiet envelope of folded bills tucked into the bottom of my backpack behind worksheets and an old spiral notebook. One night I sat on Sylvia's bedroom floor and counted it. The room was dark, lit only by the small lamp on her desk. She had fallen asleep hours earlier, one arm thrown across her pillow. Bobby had gone home for the night after insisting twice that I wake him if anything felt wrong. The house was quiet in the way only very late hours allowed. I counted the money slowly. When I finished, the realization sat in my hands heavier than the envelope itself. This was not college money. This was an escape.

That same week I noticed the rosemary on the kitchen windowsill. It was alive. Someone had watered it, set it in the light, done what needed doing without making anything of it. I didn't ask how it had gotten there. I already knew. I stood there for a moment with my coffee going cold in my hand and looked at it and felt the decision in my chest harden and ache at the same time.

Two weeks before graduation, I walked to Joe's garage.

The building smelled like oil and hot metal and sun-warmed rubber. A fan rattled in the corner and a radio hummed low near the tool bench. Joe was halfway under the hood of a pickup when I stepped inside. He slid out, wiped his hands on a rag, and looked at me.

He studied my face long enough that my throat tightened. When I told him I needed a car, he didn't laugh. He asked one question.

"You tell Pops?"

"No."

The word felt heavy coming out of my mouth.

Joe exhaled through his nose, then jerked his chin toward the back lot.

The car he showed me wasn't impressive. An older four-door sedan with faded dark blue paint dulled by the sun. The driver's door was a slightly different shade where it had been replaced. The rear quarter panel carried a long crease, and one of the wheel covers was missing. The seats were worn but not torn, the fabric flattened from use. The interior smelled faintly of dust, old upholstery, and stale cigarette smoke.

It wasn't much, but when Joe turned the key, the engine started immediately and settled into an even idle.

He named a price. I had it saved.

When I handed him the envelope, he didn't open it. He looked at me instead. Something shifted behind his eyes, less judgment than recognition. Finally, he nodded once.

"I'll make sure it's roadworthy," he said. "Tires. Brakes. Fluids. You won't leave in something that won't carry you."

I thanked him. He waved it off like it didn't matter. Then he leaned against the fender and studied me again, slower this time, like he was deciding whether the next words were worth saying.

"You're leaving clean?" he said. "Not running."

For a second, I almost told him the truth. That leaving the Calderons felt like tearing something out of my chest. That Bobby would wake up and realize I was gone. That Sylvia would be furious and hurt and still understand. That Mama would worry, and Pops would know exactly why I had done it even if I never explained.

But if I said any of it out loud, I might not be able to follow through.

So, I stood there in the heat and the smell of oil and rubber and said nothing. I let him believe what he wanted.

After that, everything became deliberate.

I packed light. Jeans. A hoodie. Socks. Toiletries. My ID. My Social Security card, sealed in plastic. The shoebox of notes Sylvia and I had passed since middle school, folded and refolded until the creases had become permanent. Leaving those behind felt like erasing proof that I had once been loved without complication. My camera went into the bag next. I hesitated over it for a moment before zipping the pocket closed. A single photo of the three of us, me, Sylvia, Bobby, slipped into the side pocket, and I didn't let myself look at it long enough to reconsider.

I hid the duffel in the shed behind the house. The shed was cool and dim, smelling of old wood and pine smoke from camping gear that hadn't been moved in years. A sleeping bag folded at the bottom still carried that smell, the particular mixture of campfire and mountain cold. I pushed the duffel underneath it and pulled the sleeping bag back into place. The zipper sounded too loud in the quiet afternoon air. My hands shook the entire time even though no one was watching. The shaking wasn't about getting caught; it was something deeper than that. My body understood what my mind refused to say out loud. Every step I took toward leaving tightened something in my chest. Every step loosened something too.

The hardest part was pretending nothing had changed.

Life in the house continued with the steady rhythm the Calderons had built around me. Pops made coffee early in the morning and read the paper at the kitchen table. Mama moved through the house cooking and folding laundry and touching my shoulder whenever she passed, the gesture small and steady. Sylvia talked about graduation decorations, senior pranks, and who was secretly hooking up with who, her voice filling the spaces where silence might otherwise settle. I sat there with them and laughed when the conversation required it, nodding at the right moments, letting the warmth of the room wrap around me while the decision sat in the back of my mind like something already finished.

Bobby stayed close.

Sometimes he drove me nowhere in particular, just slow loops through neighborhoods with the radio low and the windows cracked open. Other times we ended up near the river where the cottonwoods leaned toward the water and the dirt paths twisted through tall grass. It was the one place in the city that still felt almost neutral. The sound of the river moving over stones softened everything else.

One evening we parked near the trail and walked down to the bank without saying much. Rowdy ranged ahead of us on the path, nose down, following whatever the afternoon had left in the dirt, doubling back when the distance got too large and then ranging out again. The sky was beginning to dim and the air smelled faintly of damp earth and leaves. Bobby skipped a small rock across the water and watched it sink.

"You've been somewhere else lately," he said.

I kept my eyes on the river. "I'm right here."

"You are," he said. "But not all the way."

The words settled between us. I felt his eyes on me. Careful. Patient. The way he had looked at me since the hospital, like he was always checking that I hadn't drifted somewhere he couldn't reach.

"You don't have to pretend with me," he added.

"I'm not pretending."

He let out a slow breath and rubbed the back of his neck. "Shell, I know you. You go quiet when something's eating at you."

The river moved steadily in front of us, brown water sliding around rocks and fallen branches. Rowdy came back and sat beside Bobby without being asked, his shoulder against Bobby's leg.

"I just don't know what the future looks like right now," I said.

That part at least was true.

He nodded, accepting the answer even though it clearly wasn't the whole one. "You don't have to figure it out all at once," he said. "You've got time." Then, quieter: "We'll figure it out."

We. The word pressed against my ribs. He had already moved forward into planning, into the shape of what came next, and I understood that this was how he loved, by building toward something, by making room in the future for both of us. It was generous and true and it was also not quite what I needed right now. I needed him to stay here on this bank for one more minute without solving anything. I didn't say so. I just let the moment be what it was.

I swallowed and nodded because anything else might have broken something open that I couldn't repair. Bobby squeezed my hand once and let the silence return, both of us watching the river move past like it had nowhere urgent to be. Rowdy put his chin on his paws in the dirt beside us and closed his eyes.

Graduation was two weeks away.

I would walk across that stage. I would smile for photographs. I would stand beside Sylvia while the family clapped.

And then I would leave. Before the city closed in again. Before my father reappeared somewhere inside it. Before they made it impossible to go.

Chapter Fifteen
Joe's Promise

I went back to Joe's garage after school on a Wednesday in May, taking the long way through side streets so no one would notice where I was headed.

Spring in Albuquerque never arrived gently; it came with wind that carried dust and impatience. The air pushed at my hoodie and dragged grit across my lips, leaving that dry taste that made everything feel brittle, like the whole city had been sitting in the sun too long.

My backpack was heavy, though it held nothing unusual: papers, notebooks, and my camera. The weight was in the decision I was carrying. Each step toward the garage felt like walking deeper into something that would not reverse itself.

I kept telling myself I could still stop. Turn around. Go back to the Calderons' house. Sit at the kitchen table while Mama asked how school went and Bobby leaned against the counter pretending he wasn't watching me too closely. I could stay. I could let the future arrive the way everyone expected it to.

But my feet kept moving.

Joe's place sat where it always had, wedged between a sagging chain-link fence and a row of tired storefronts that never quite lost the smell of grease. The bay door was half open, the interior dim against the bright afternoon.

Joe had known me since I was small enough to wander into his shop just to delay going back home. He'd hand me a rag and let me pretend I was helping while he worked and never asked why I lingered. But he knew.

I remembered being seven or eight, slipping through that same bay door on afternoons when going home felt like a bad idea. Joe would be under a hood or flat on his back beneath something rusted and enormous, and he'd slide out just enough to look at me. He never asked, just handed me a clean rag and pointed me toward a hubcap that didn't need wiping and let me work beside him in silence until the light changed. Sometimes he'd explain what he was doing, not to teach me, just to fill the quiet with something useful. Hector was usually there too, already knowing which tool was which, handing things over before Joe finished asking. He never paid much attention to me. I used to think if I stayed long enough, the afternoon would run out and I'd never have to go home. Joe never rushed me. He just worked, and I stayed beside him, and neither of us said anything about why.

When I stepped inside, the temperature shifted immediately. The air was thicker, warm with oil and coolant baked into the concrete. A country station crackled from an old radio perched on a shelf. Somewhere deeper in the shop, a wrench tapped against steel. Joe rolled out from under the hood of a Chevy when he heard my footsteps. He pushed himself up, wiped his hands on a rag that had long ago surrendered to grease, and looked at me without speaking.

"You okay, kid?"

"Yeah," I said too quickly.

He didn't challenge it. Joe never wasted time pretending he didn't understand things, but he also never forced people to say them out loud. He just waited, eyes steady, giving silence room to settle.

"I came about the car," I said.

He nodded once. "She's ready. New plugs. Fixed the hose. Window won't drop on you halfway up I-25." He jerked his chin toward the back lot. "Engine's clean. She'll run."

Relief moved through my chest.

"You sure about this?" he asked.

"I can't stay."

"That ain't what I asked."

The wind rattled the sheet metal along the storage wall. Dust curled through the doorway before settling again. Joe stood there waiting, patient in a way that meant he would accept whatever answer came next, but he wasn't going to help me avoid it.

"I'm sure," I said.

He studied my face for a long moment, then nodded once.

"When?"

"After graduation."

"Day after?"

"Yes."

He nodded again, slow and deliberate, like he was tightening something invisible.

"I'm not waitin' for you to show up here," he said. "Too many eyes. Too many mouths. Too many folks still talk to your old man's crowd."

The words settled in my stomach.

"I'll park it for you."

"Where?"

"You remember the old basketball court behind the elementary school? Fence half down. Rim hangin' crooked."

I nodded. We used to ride our bikes there in the summer when the playground was empty and the asphalt still held the day's heat. Sylvia had parked the Tercel there the first time she drove it anywhere, and we had sat on the hood while the engine cooled and she said *this changes things* like she already knew something I was still figuring out.

"Graduation night," he said. "After dark. I'll leave it by the big cottonwood on the east side. Keys under the driver's mat. Title in the glove box. You walk over. You get in. You go."

He said it like he was describing a routine errand. Simple. Direct.

My throat burned. "Joe—"

"It's safer," he cut in. "You don't come back here the next morning lookin' like you're boltin'. You disappear when everybody's busy celebratin'."

There was no drama in his voice. No sympathy either. Just practicality. That made it heavier somehow.

"They'll know by morning," I said.

"Yeah." He didn't soften it. "But if you leave when you're supposed to, you'll be past Santa Fe before anybody finishes their coffee."

The radio hissed as it slipped between stations. For a moment the shop filled with static.

Joe lowered his voice. "Bring what you can carry easy. Don't weigh it down with things that'll make you hesitate." He paused. "You can miss stuff later. Missin' ain't the same as goin' back."

Silence stretched between us. Not uncomfortable. Just real.

"You break down, you call me," he said. "I don't care where you are."

"Why are you helping me?"

Joe looked at me for a long time. Something sharp flickered behind his eyes.

"Because we didn't step in soon enough," he said. "And because you're not the kind of kid who asks."

He turned back to the Chevy and picked up his wrench, giving me space.

"Walk like you've got somewhere to be," he said over his shoulder. "Don't rush. Don't look scared. You go to that ceremony, you smile for the people who matter, and when it gets loud you slip out."

He glanced at me once more, quick and certain.

"Don't make it memorable."

The wind pushed through the garage again, warm and gritty, rattling loose metal near the door.

"You get one clean start," Joe said. "This is yours."

That was all.

I stood in the doorway for a moment before stepping back out into the May afternoon. The brightness hit me immediately after the dim interior. The wind was still going.

Dust moved across the street in low patterns. Somewhere down the block a car door slammed and a dog barked twice and went quiet. The city continued exactly as it always had, indifferent to the fact that I had just arranged my own disappearance from it.

I pulled my hoodie tighter and walked back the long way, the same side streets, the same unhurried pace.

Walk like you've got somewhere to be.

Chapter Sixteen
Leaving

Graduation night was supposed to feel like freedom. That was what everyone kept saying. Teachers smiled too widely beneath stiff gowns. Parents fanned themselves with folded programs in the warm May air. Classmates shouted about dorms and summer jobs as if the future were already waiting just beyond the stadium gates.

The words floated everywhere, light and celebratory.

Sylvia stood beside me in line, her cap tilted crooked, her tassel tangled in her curls the way it always caught on everything. She bumped her shoulder into mine and whispered that if she tripped in her heels, she was taking at least five people down with her.

I laughed. The sound felt real enough, but something heavier sat low in my chest.

We had started kindergarten holding hands because the world felt too large. Now we crossed the stage the same way, close enough that our gowns brushed, our steps unconsciously matched. Our names were called seconds apart. Applause rose and blurred into one warm roar.

I found the Calderons in the crowd. Mama was already crying. Pops clapped with his chin lifted in quiet pride. Bobby whistled so loudly someone turned around.

When Sylvia and I threw our caps into the violet Albuquerque sky, they spun above the stadium lights against the fading line of the Sandias. Everyone cheered.

I felt something closer to gravity than freedom.

Afterward the hugs came in waves. Mama kissed both my cheeks and called me her girl. Pops rested his hand at the back of my neck and told me he was proud of me.

Bobby pulled me into him last. He smelled like laundry soap and motor oil and summer heat. I held on a second longer than I meant to, long enough to memorize the shape of his shoulders beneath my hands. Long enough that he shifted slightly, like he felt something different in my grip but couldn't name it.

Sylvia caught my wrist before I drifted too far inward.

"We did it," she said.

We.

The word followed me through the rest of the night.

Dinner was loud and bright and full of celebration. Plates clattered. Glasses sweated on the table. Bobby kept raising his soda in mock toasts. Sylvia narrated every bite like it was part of a competition.

Mama kept reaching across the table just to squeeze my fingers.

Pops leaned back once and said, "You'll always have a home here."

He didn't say it for effect. He said it like everything that mattered.

Calm. Certain.

It nearly broke something in me.

I excused myself and locked the bathroom door, pressing my forehead against the cool metal divider until my breathing steadied. Staying meant building a life in soil that remembered too much. Leaving meant tearing myself away from the only place I had ever felt chosen.

Both hurt.

Only one felt survivable.

Back at the house, Sylvia insisted on a movie marathon because she refused to let graduation end in tears. Bobby burned the first batch of popcorn on purpose just to make her complain. Mama made hot chocolate anyway, humming softly as she moved around the kitchen. Pops kissed our foreheads one by one and headed down the hallway, his heavy steps grounding the house.

The night turned into something dangerously normal.

Sylvia stretched across the couch, half asleep but still talking. Bobby sat close enough that his knee rested lightly against mine. The television flickered blue across the walls.

I watched all of them carefully.

When Sylvia finally drifted off and Mama's breathing deepened in her chair, Bobby and I were the only ones still awake.

He leaned forward, elbows on his knees, studying me.

"You feel it too," he said.

"Feel what?"

"That things are about to change." He paused. "You've been looking at everything like you're memorizing it."

Silence stretched.

"You planning something?"

The truth rose fast. I forced it down.

"I don't know what's next," I said.

He watched me for a long moment.

"If you go somewhere," he said, "I won't stop you." After a short hesitation, he said, "I just need to know if I'm part of it. Or if I'm the part you leave behind."

I looked down at his hands instead of his face.

"I don't know yet."

He nodded slowly, like he was accepting something he already understood.

Then he leaned in and kissed me.

Slow. Certain. Like he was committing it to memory.

His hand rested warm at the back of my neck. I kissed him back with something softer. Something that felt too much like goodbye.

When we pulled apart, his forehead rested lightly against mine.

"I love you," he said softly.

My throat tightened.

"I know," I whispered.

It wasn't the answer he deserved. It was the only one I could give.

By two in the morning, the house had sunk into quiet. Sylvia slept with one arm thrown across my leg. Bobby had fallen asleep in the recliner, one hand hanging loosely toward the couch, palm open.

I stood beside him for a long time.

In sleep, he looked younger.

I reached down slowly and brushed my fingers against his hand. His skin was warm. My thumb moved lightly across the center of his palm. For a moment his fingers shifted, curling faintly.

I froze.

If he woke up, if he said my name, I wouldn't be able to leave.

I eased my hand away.

In the kitchen, I wrote the note and slid it beneath Pops' coffee mug. I didn't reread it. If I had, I might not have left.

Outside, the night was warm and still. The cottonwoods whispered above the broken basketball court. Joe had parked the car exactly where he said he would.

I slid into the driver's seat and closed the door carefully. The engine turned on the second try and held.

I looked once toward the Calderon house. The porch light glowed through the trees.

"I'm sorry," I whispered.

At the stop sign, I hesitated. I could turn around. I could go back inside. I could stay.

My hands tightened on the wheel until my knuckles hurt.

If I went back now, I would never leave.

I pressed the gas.

The house shrank in the rearview mirror until it was just another porch light.

I drove past dark storefronts and intersections that held too many memories. Past the hospital. Past the apartment I refused to look at.

The city thinned behind me. The mountains faded. The sky began to pale.
I didn't look back again.

Part II: Distance

"But whenever my consciousness was quickened, all those early friends were quickened within it, and in some strange way they accompanied me through all my new experiences. They were so much alive in me that I scarcely stopped to wonder whether they were alive anywhere else."
Willa Cather, *My Ántonia* (1918)

Chapter One
The Return

As I drove north on Rio Grande Boulevard toward the North Valley, the cottonwoods closed over the road the way they always had in early fall, their leaves gone yellow at the edges, catching the afternoon light in small restless pieces. Early fall in New Mexico came in warm afternoons and cool evenings, roasting chile in the air, light on adobe walls that existed nowhere else in the world quite like this. For a moment it felt less like a memory and more like something still alive.

I hadn't planned my return around the season. My schedule had been built around rodeo stops for the last six months. Cheyenne, Pendleton, Amarillo. Each town blurred into arenas of grit, leather, and eight-second rides. My life ran on entry lists and press passes, on hauling my gear from one county fairground to another, on sleeping in the narrow bed of my RV with my cameras lined neatly along the shelf above my head. I lived by the rhythm of livestock trailers and floodlights and men who bet their bones against bulls.

I didn't stay long enough anywhere for the air to settle.

But New Mexico had a way of getting under your skin whether you invited it or not.

The road narrowed as I moved north, the lots widening on either side, the houses set further back behind adobe walls and old fencing. Irrigation ditches ran alongside the road, the acequia system that had been moving water through this valley since before anyone now living could remember. The surface was smoother than the highway I had just left, the kind of road that didn't need to rush. My RV hummed steadily beneath me. The vibration in the steering wheel grounded me, something solid beneath the layers of dust and distance I had wrapped around myself over the years.

A mile past the church I reached the turn.

The property sat back from the road behind a stand of old cottonwoods, their trunks pale and thick in the afternoon light. A low adobe wall ran along the front, the gate latch worn smooth from decades of hands. I pulled into the gravel drive and shut off the engine.

The world went quiet.

I sat for a moment before getting out. Through the windshield the property revealed itself in pieces. The portal running the full length of the house, its shade deep and deliberate. The kitchen garden along the south wall, still producing something in the fall heat. A large clay planter on the portal, overflowing with rosemary that had gone woody at the base and spread wide over the years, its silver-green sprawl catching the light. The pasture fence running along the property's far edge, two horses visible near the rail in the late afternoon.

My eyes moved to the gate before I opened the door. Instinct, looking for a red and white dog who had been gone for years.

What I found instead was a blue merle Australian shepherd sitting alertly watching me. His pale eyes tracked me through the windshield without blinking.

I climbed down from the RV. My boots hit the gravel and the dog stood immediately, his whole back end moving with the tail. Not barking. Assessing.

"Hey," I said.

He pushed his nose through the gate and then pulled it back, dancing. Still deciding.

This had been Grandma Calderon's place. Back when the screen door slammed all day and the air smelled like tortillas and incense. Back when lavender lotion sat by the bathroom sink and Sylvia and I sprawled across the living room floor with notebooks and cheap nail polish, the two of us invented entire languages out of ordinary words while Bobby pretended we were annoying and kept walking through the room to check. Back when Bobby pretended not to notice how

I watched him. I hadn't been here in more than a decade, back before leaving had meant something permanent.

The porch boards creaked before I saw him. Bobby stepped out into the fading light, one hand resting on the doorframe. He wore jeans and a gray T-shirt dusted faintly at the shoulders, like he had come in from work not long ago. His boots were gone, his bare feet against the worn boards. Life had reshaped him. His shoulders were broader, his arms heavier with muscle earned from work instead of high school lifting sessions. A clean black line of ink ran from beneath his sleeve down his forearm. His face wore harder lines now. Sun at the corners of his eyes. Responsibility in the set of his jaw. But his eyes were the same.

Dark. Steady. Unflinching.

He said something to the dog in a low voice. The dog stepped back from the gate and sat, his eyes still on me but his body language shifted. Permission granted.

I pushed open the gate. The metal latch scraped softly against the post, the sound too familiar.

"Hey, Bobby."

"Hey."

He stepped off the porch and crossed the yard. Up close he smelled faintly of sawdust and sun, the kind of clean dust that comes from long hours outside. For a moment he just looked at me, like he was confirming I was actually there. Then he pulled me into a hug. I felt the rough cotton of his shirt against my cheek and the warmth of his skin beneath it. One of his hands rested briefly between my shoulders before dropping again. I let myself stay against him for one second longer than I meant to before stepping back.

The dog circled us once and then sat again, satisfied.

"Rowdy?" I asked.

Something moved across Bobby's face. Small and contained, the way he contained things. "Three years ago," he said. "Good long life."

I nodded. There wasn't anything else to say about it. Some losses you just place somewhere and leave them.

"This is Cisco," Bobby said. The dog's ears lifted at his name. "He's still deciding if he likes most people."

"But he's decided about me?"

"Jury's out," Bobby said. "He let you through the gate. That's more than he gives most."

Cisco looked between us with the alert intelligence of a dog eavesdropping on a conversation he had strong opinions about. I held my hand out and he came forward and pressed his nose against my palm once, deliberate and assessing, then stepped back.

"He'll come around," Bobby said, quietly.

"You said you weren't coming back," he said then, the shift in subject smooth and immediate, like the dog had served as a soft landing.

"I wasn't."

He nodded once, accepting that without argument. "Sylvia called," I said. "About a month ago. She sounded scared. Said she needed my help. I was in the middle of something but got here as soon as I could. But she isn't answering my calls."

I watched his face go dark. He looked past me toward the RV sitting in the gravel drive, like he was measuring the distance I had traveled and the reason for it. Then his gaze came back to mine. He stepped back and turned toward the door.

"C'mon in."

I followed him up the steps and across the portal. The rosemary brushed my arm as I passed the planter, releasing its sharp, particular scent. I slowed, without quite stopping. The plant was large and established, woody at the base the way rosemary grows after years in good soil, its branches spread wide. I had last seen it in a paper cup on a windowsill. Bobby didn't look back. He had already opened the screen door.

Inside, the force of memories nearly pushed me back outside. The screen door creaked the way it always had, softer now but unmistakable. The adobe had changed. The dark paneling was gone, replaced with white walls that caught the evening light. The old carpet had been ripped out and replaced with wood flooring. The space felt more open than it used to.

But the past lingered in the corners. The ceramic rooster still perched above the stove. A cracked gold-framed mirror hung near the hallway. A rosary draped over a lamp. On the side table sat a faded photo of Mama and Pops at Elephant Butte, their arms around each other, sunlight flashing off the lake behind them. Beside it, in a smaller frame I hadn't seen before, was a photo of the three of us. Sylvia in the middle with both arms thrown wide, pulling Bobby and me toward her the way she always did when she sensed distance growing, grinning like she had just won something.

And on the kitchen windowsill, in a small clay pot that looked like it had been there a long time, sat a gray tabby cat of indeterminate age, watching me with the particular self-possession of an animal that had been here longer than most things and saw no reason to move. Hector's cat. Still here. Of course.

The house had learned to live with its ghosts.

"You redid it," I said.

"Bit by bit," he replied. "After Grandma passed. Most of the family came by and took her things. I kept a couple of pieces but you can walk around in here now."

He leaned against the kitchen counter, folding his arms across his chest. The distance between us felt deliberate.

"You didn't call," he said.

"I didn't know how," I answered.

"That makes sense." He shifted his weight slightly against the counter. His eyes stayed on me, steady and unreadable. He didn't say he'd tried. He didn't say he'd waited. He didn't say he hadn't.

"Sylvia and I talked," I offered. "Sometimes."

"Yes."

"She didn't say much about you."

"I didn't ask her to."

"I didn't ask her to give me updates either."

For a moment neither of us moved. The kitchen light hummed above us. Outside, Cisco had taken up a position near the gate, monitoring the RV with professional suspicion. The silence didn't feel hostile. Just unfamiliar. Like standing in a room you once knew by heart and realizing the shape of it had changed.

"I didn't leave because of you," I said.

"I know," he said. "And I wasn't going to chase you."

He turned toward the counter, poured two glasses of iced tea, and slid one across to me. Condensation gathered along the sides of the glass.

"You still take it unsweet?"

"Yes."

He nodded once, like that detail mattered.

"You still shooting?" he asked after a moment.

"Rodeo circuit mostly. Bull riding. Barrel racing. I sell to a few western magazines and a couple wire services." I shrugged. "It pays. And it moves."

"You move a lot."

"Every few months."

"Why?"

I met his eyes across the kitchen table. The late light coming through the window caught the edge of his forearm, the dark line of ink there sharper against his skin. "Because staying starts to feel like roots and roots feel like traps."

He leaned back slightly, considering that. Not arguing. Not trying to soften the words. "I stayed," he said. "I didn't feel like leaving." His voice carried the same quiet certainty it always had. Not defensive. Just true. He glanced around the room for a moment, the new flooring, the white walls, the small pieces of the past that had survived the changes. The difference between us settled plainly between the glasses of tea on the table.

Outside the kitchen window, the sky deepened toward amber. Cottonwood leaves stirred in the evening air. Cisco had abandoned the gate and was now moving along the pasture fence in quick purposeful sweeps, running the horses the way young Aussies run everything because they can and because stillness is a form of failure.

Bobby reached for the pitcher and refilled my glass without asking.

"You weren't surprised," I said. "When I pulled in."

He considered that for a moment, his hand still on the pitcher. "Sylvia called me too," he said. "Told me what she'd found. Said she'd reached out to you." He set the pitcher down. "After she went quiet, I figured it was only a matter of time. You were always going to come when she needed you."

"You could have called me yourself."

"Yes," he said. Just that. No apology. No explanation. The word carrying the full weight of ten years of choosing not to.

I looked at my glass.

"Josh still in?" I asked after a moment.

Bobby nodded. "Okinawa. Career. Makes sergeant next year if everything goes the way Hector says it will."

"Hector keeps up with him?"

"More than I do." Something shifted in his expression, not quite a smile. "You know how Hector is. He doesn't announce things. He just knows them."

He pushed off the counter and opened the cabinet above the stove. Peanut butter. Honey. He pulled two plates from the shelf without asking, the motion easy and automatic, like this was something his hands knew how to do when conversation got to a certain weight.

"You remember Fenton?" he said, not looking at me as he unscrewed the peanut butter lid.

"Which part?"

"The hill."

I laughed then. Genuinely, the sound arriving before I decided to let it. "Josh pushed me down a hill."

"Josh pushed you down a hill," Bobby confirmed, "and you came up ready to fight a boy who had six inches and forty pounds on you." He spread peanut butter across a slice of bread with the focused attention of someone who took sandwiches seriously. "Nine years old. Fists up. Absolutely certain you were going to win."

"I might have won."

"You weren't going to win." He drizzled honey over the peanut butter and pressed the second slice down. "Hector just looked at him. That was it. Josh apologized so fast he tripped over his own feet."

"I didn't need Hector to fight my battles."

"No," Bobby said. He set the plate in front of me and leaned against the counter with his own sandwich, looking at me with something that had been sitting behind his eyes since I walked through the gate. "But you were nine and you came up off that hill like nothing in the world was going to stop you." He paused. "Crazy lil spitfire."

The words landed like old things do, carried a long time. Not surprising. Just present. Like something that had been waiting in a drawer for ten years and was exactly where it had been left.

I looked down at the sandwich.

"I forgot you called me that," I said.

"I didn't," he said simply.

The kitchen was quiet for a moment. Hector's cat dropped from the windowsill with the dignified thud of an animal deciding the conversation was interesting enough to relocate for. It wound once around the leg of my chair and then settled under the table with the air of someone who had always planned to be exactly there.

I picked up the sandwich. The honey was local, the kind that tasted distinctly of New Mexico high desert, dark and faintly sharp. I hadn't had it in ten years. My throat tightened in a way I wasn't prepared for.

Bobby watched me for a second and then looked away, giving me the moment without making anything of it.

"Hector," I said, when I trusted my voice again. "What's he doing these days?"

"Works for Pops some. Works for Joe some. Builds custom Harleys out of a shop on 4th. Runs with that crowd." He paused.

"What happened to Sylvia?" I asked.

His jaw tightened slightly. "I don't know. She disappeared. I don't think she ran. She would have called one of us if she had." He set the pitcher down. "We need to figure this out. I have a few leads and I suspect she gave you something to work with too."

I took a long drink of the tea. "Do you know what she found? All she told me was that it was something strange and that she needed help figuring out what to do. She said there weren't many people she could trust."

"Inventory that didn't match shipments. Trucks coming in after hours. People watching her too closely." He took a slow drink before setting the glass back on the counter. "She thought it was drug smuggling. She called me. She called you."

"She said she didn't trust anyone local. Are the police looking?"

"They looked at first. After a few days they concluded she probably took off. Couldn't find signs of a struggle or anything odd at work. Her boss said she was on vacation." He shook his head once. "She left her cats. Didn't feed them before she went. Her suitcase was in the closet. Her purse on the counter. Sylvia doesn't go anywhere without that purse. It's the one with the broken clasp she kept meaning to fix." Something moved across his face when he said it, a small involuntary thing, like the detail had arrived before he could decide whether to say it. "I pointed all that out to the police but they had nothing to work with. I doubt they've closed the case but they aren't looking hard."

"You know your dad died?" he said after a moment.

"I don't really care. That bastard died the night he decided to let his friends have me."

"They're all dead."

"Sylvia told me." I looked at him for a moment. It had been a long time since anyone had spoken about me like that, like I was someone worth protecting after the fact.

"Get some sleep tonight," he said. "Tomorrow, we go to Frontier, then we need to go by and see my folks. Then I'll take you by her place and see if you notice anything that makes sense."

"That sounds good. I'm pretty tired." I started to move toward the door but Bobby stood and stopped me. "Shell, you can stay in the house. I have a spare room."

"I'm not ready for this, Bobby. And I don't sleep well. It'll be better if I'm in my own space."

"Okay." He nodded once. "Door's unlocked if you need anything."

He walked me back outside as the evening cooled. Gravel shifted beneath our feet and the smell of dust and cottonwood hung in the air. The rosemary on the portal caught the last light, its silver-green color gone gray in the dusk. The horses had moved away from the fence. Cisco materialized from somewhere near the shed and fell into step beside Bobby without being asked.

"You don't have to be alone," he said.

"I'm not alone," I said. "I just need control over my own space."

His eyes softened slightly. "I get that." He stepped closer, not touching me, just close enough that I could feel the warmth of him in the cooling air. The porch light behind him threw a soft edge of gold across his shoulders. "Frontier in the morning," he said. "Burritos and cinnamon rolls."

"Obviously."

He reached up and touched my cheek once, then turned and walked back into his house. Cisco followed him to the porch and then sat, watching me cross the yard to the RV with those pale eyes that had apparently decided that I was acceptable.

Before I went inside, I stopped briefly to turn on the propane tank. I opened the door and lit the candles. The narrow space wrapped around me, deliberate and contained. I had rebuilt this interior over several years, replaced the thin cushions with a pillow-top mattress, splurged on good linens, draped fabric across the ceiling in a way that made the low space feel intentional rather than cramped. Thick blankets lay folded across the foot of the bed, soft from years of washing in laundromats across half the country. My cameras rested in their padded cases on the shelf above the bed. My boots sat neatly beneath the small bench. A stack of rodeo programs lay beside my laptop; their corners bent from travel.

The candles flickered and I turned on the small stove to heat water for tea. On the shelf above the stove, tucked between a road atlas and a spare battery pack, was a folded piece of paper I had carried since the morning I left. Sylvia's handwriting. A note she had pressed into my jacket pocket at some point during graduation, which I had not found until I was already past Santa Fe. It said only: Library. Iceland. Page 47. I had not needed to look it up. I already knew what it meant.

I was here. She had called. That was enough.

I knew I was never going to sleep tonight.

Chapter Two
The Night That Wouldn't Let Me Sleep

I didn't sleep.

I tried in all the quiet, deliberate ways I've taught myself over the years. I stretched out on the narrow mattress I rebuilt piece by piece until it felt like something I could trust. I pulled the heavy quilt to my chin, the one I stitched during a Wyoming winter when snow pinned the RV outside a rodeo ground and I needed something steady for my hands. I lit the small candles I carry everywhere. I brewed chamomile and held the mug beneath my nose until the steam faded. I slowed my breathing and closed my eyes.

None of it worked.

The RV is usually my sanctuary: locks I control, doors that close when I decide, a life small enough to carry.

Tonight, it felt different.

Seeing Bobby had loosened something. Saying Sylvia's name out loud, admitting she wasn't just busy or distracted but missing, had loosened something else. The silence inside the RV no longer felt protective.

It felt like it was waiting.

Every time I closed my eyes the past came back. Quiet at first. Then closer. Like it had been standing outside the door for years.

Bobby at fifteen on that Calderon trip to San Diego. The ocean was colder than we expected. Sylvia complained about sand in her shoes like it was a personal attack. Bobby walked up to me on the boardwalk holding a shell necklace, pretending it didn't matter. His ears red when he shrugged and said it was stupid. He called me Seashell for a long time after that trip. I wore it until the string broke.

Seventeen. A hallway at school. Someone said something about my family just loud enough. Bobby stepped between us. Not loud. Not violent. Just present long enough that the boy backed down.

By the time he started college, he was still living at home, driving back from UNM every afternoon with dust on his boots and textbooks in the back seat. He would lean in the doorway of whatever room I was in and talk about professors, assignments, bad coffee. He never acted like he was doing me a favor. He was just always there.

I stared at the curved ceiling of the RV. The gold stitching caught the candlelight in small patterns.

Nostalgia can weigh more than grief. Grief cuts clean. Nostalgia lingers.

The apartment. The hallway smelled of cigarettes and fried food. The television's blue light cut across the room, the kind I still associate with danger. My father's voice came out of the dark, already coiled. My mother stepped between us with shaking hands and more bravery than sense. She had been drinking, but her voice was clear.

The sound of his fist.

Her head snapping sideways.

"Run, Shelly."

The cold air when I hit the street. The neon hum of the corner store. My phone, slick in my hands. Sylvia answered before the first ring finished. *I'm coming.* And Bobby. Because he had been there then too. His truck pulled up before the engine settled. His jacket around my shoulders before he asked a question. His voice was low when he said I was safe.

The Calderon house glowing like something sacred.

Mama's arms. Pops pacing. The smell of green chile still lingering from dinner.

And then the phone call. The way Pops' shoulders curved before he spoke. Your mother ran a red light. Drunk. Dead. That never comes straight. It comes in fragments.

I turned onto my side, willing my body to settle. It didn't.

Then the memory I don't revisit. The apartment days later. Door open. Curtains drawn. Men at the table. My father watching. Something in me breaking in a way that never set right. I don't need the details. They never left.

What I do remember clearly is Bobby's truck arriving too fast after I called. The way he froze when he saw me, the way he stopped himself when I flinched and knelt instead, the way he carried me without asking for something I couldn't give.

Outside, the cottonwoods shifted in the wind. Across the yard, a light flicked on in the house and then off again. In the moonlight below the porch, Cisco turned his head toward it, ears forward, watching until the window went dark again. Then he lowered his head back onto his paws.

Bobby didn't sleep well when something was wrong.

He never had.

Another memory surfaced. Fenton Lake at night, years before everything broke. The fire gone low. The sky was so full of stars it looked crowded, the Milky Way a pale wash from ridge to ridge. The same stars I had first asked about at seven years old over a campfire, not understanding yet why they disappeared when we went home. Still brighter out here. Some things stayed true no matter how much else changed.

Another memory after that, closer and warmer. A field behind his parents' house. Tall grass brushing our legs. His hands warm at my waist. My back against his chest. The world was wide and manageable. He kissed me like there was time.

That memory didn't hurt.

It unsettled me because it still felt possible.

I sat up and crossed the narrow space to crack the door open. Moonlight washed across the yard. The smell of alfalfa drifted in. Cisco lay near the base of the porch steps, his eyes catching the light for a moment before he looked awayt. For a moment I thought about crossing the gravel. Knocking. Stepping back into something familiar.

Instead, I closed the door.

I reached for my phone. Sylvia's last message sat near the top of the thread. Three weeks ago.

Three words.

Remember the code.

I stared at it.

I spent ten years building a life that moves. Rodeo arenas under open sky. Dust rising beneath hooves. The thunder of bulls and the quiet afterward when I crouch in the dirt to photograph a rider catching his breath. I tell other people's stories and leave before anyone asks for mine. It is a good life that belongs to me.

But Sylvia reached across ten years because something frightened her enough to break her silence. Not because Bobby wasn't there. He was. He had always been there.

Because I wasn't.

And whatever she found, she trusted the code to reach me. Which means she had been preparing for this longer than I understood.

Distance is not the same as healing.

"Come on, Sylvia," I whispered into the dark. "Where are you?"

Chapter Three
Morning Coffee and Old Ghosts

I woke to the sound of someone knocking on the RV door.

For a few seconds, I didn't know where I was. The night had been long and restless, my mind circling old memories that refused to settle. Sunlight sliced through the narrow blinds in bright bands, striping the walls and catching dust in the air. The RV felt smaller in the morning, less like a sanctuary and more like a box holding everything I hadn't decided how to face.

The knock came again, steady and familiar.

I pushed myself upright, head thick from too little sleep, and padded barefoot across the cool floor. Candle wax still lingered from the night before, mixing with coffee grounds and propane.

I peered through the small window.

Bobby stood outside, one hand raised mid-knock, the other in his jacket pocket. Cisco sat at his heel, ears forward, watching the RV door. The early light softened the harder lines time had carved into Bobby's face. For a moment he looked almost like he had at nineteen.

I opened the door.

He ducked instinctively as he stepped inside, careful of the low ceiling. His eyes moved slowly around the space. The bed built into the wall. The narrow shelves lined with worn paperbacks and camera lenses. The candles burned nearly to their base. The folded quilt at the foot of the mattress.

"This is nice," he said after a moment. "You've put a lot of work into it."

"It's where I live," I said, turning toward the kitchenette. "Might as well make it feel like mine."

I filled the percolator and set it on the burner, twisting the knob until the propane caught with a soft click and hiss.

The small rituals steadied me. The measured scoop of grounds. The lid snapping into place. The quiet gurgle as the water began to heat.

He lowered himself onto the narrow bench at the table, one knee bouncing once before he caught it and stilled it.

"So, this thing's mostly off-grid?" he asked.

"Mostly. I plug in when I need to. Laundry. Laptop backups. A microwave if I'm feeling indulgent. The fridge, stove, water heater all run on propane." I shrugged. "As long as the tank's full, I'm fine. Candles do the rest."

The coffee finished with a soft burble. I poured two mugs without thinking, adding cream and sugar before I even realized what I was doing.

He noticed.

"I can't believe you still remember how I take it," he said, a small smile at the corner of his mouth.

"It's the same way I take mine," I said. "That's your fault. You made mine like yours for years. I guess it stuck."

The memory slipped between us quietly. Late nights at the Calderon kitchen table after Sylvia had gone to bed. Coffee warming our hands while we talked about everything and nothing.

He took a sip and nodded once. "Still perfect."

The silence that followed wasn't uncomfortable, but it wasn't easy either. Ten years had weight. It sat between us like another presence at the table.

"You hungry?" he asked eventually, setting his mug down. "Frontier's open."

I didn't hesitate. "When am I not? If there are cinnamon rolls involved, I'll follow you anywhere."

"And green chile," he added.

"I almost came back a dozen times just for the chile," I admitted before I could stop myself.

Something warm flickered in his eyes. "Come on, then."

He stepped out first. As he passed, his hand brushed lightly across my shoulders. Casual. Easy. But the contact lingered.

I dressed quickly: jeans, tennis shoes, hair pulled back into something manageable. I turned off the propane tank, checked the cabinet latches, and locked the door behind me. Small motions that reminded me I controlled my exits.

Bobby was waiting on the porch, leaning against the railing. Cisco had relocated to the top porch step and was watching the horses at the far fence with professional interest, his back to us, already on to the next thing.

He still drove the old Ford.

The sight of it loosened something in my chest. I remembered the day he bought it, driving all the way to Durango to meet a man selling a spray-painted light-blue 4x4 that sounded like it might come apart at the seams. Bobby had stood there grinning like he'd just adopted a stray dog.

"I can't believe you're still driving this thing," I said as I climbed into the passenger seat.

"Why not?" he said, sliding in behind the wheel. "She runs great. Ain't a hill she won't climb." He patted the dash once. "I've got a car at Mom's if I need something civilized."

I buckled in. For years, I had always sat in the middle. Sylvia refused to sit next to him, so I ended up squeezed between them while they argued about music or directions. Now I took the passenger seat without thinking, and the space between us felt careful. Intentional.

He turned the key. The engine rumbled awake, shuddered once, then settled into its familiar growl. The stereo crackled before catching a Chris Stapleton song, and Bobby sang along under his breath, tapping the steering wheel in time. Every few minutes he glanced at me like he was confirming I was still there.

We drove mostly in silence.

The North Valley opened around us as we headed south, the cottonwoods thinning as we left the river corridor, the bosque giving way to older neighborhoods and then the familiar density of the city. The Rio Grande caught the morning light through a gap in the trees for one brief moment before the road curved away from it. Ahead the city thickened, low adobe neighborhoods giving way to older commercial strips and then the bustle of Central.

"The city's grown," I said, watching new developments slide past the window.

"You really haven't been back?" he asked.

"I said I wouldn't." Then, softer, "And if I had, I would've called you."

"Would you?" he asked. "I know you talked to Sylvia sometimes. Why didn't you ever call me?"

I looked out the window. Traffic moved past in steady lines, morning sun flashing off windshields.

"I didn't call her that often either."

"That's not what I asked."

He didn't push after that, reaching forward to turn the radio up a notch. The music filled the cab, loud enough to make conversation optional. I was grateful for it.

The truth sat heavy in my chest anyway. I hadn't called him because he was threaded through too many of the worst nights of my life. Because loving him had once felt like safety, and I had never figured out how to separate that safety from everything that came after. Leaving had been the only thing I knew how to do.

We turned east onto Central, the familiar strip of neon and old storefronts sliding past the windshield, then onto Cornell and into the Frontier parking lot. Bobby eased the truck into a narrow space and shut off the engine. Sudden quiet filled the cab.

For a second neither of us moved. Then we got out.

He came around the front of the truck as I stepped down, and when I fell into step beside him he reached over and took my hand without comment, his fingers closing around mine the way they used to. I didn't pull away. We walked toward the entrance that way, neither of us saying anything about it.

Inside, the Frontier hummed with its usual morning chaos. Students clustered around tables with paper cups of coffee. Families steered children through the narrow aisles. The smell of green chile and sugar hung thick in the air. Noise wrapped around me instantly, a rush of sound and scent like stepping into an old photograph.

Bobby ordered without hesitation, two breakfast burritos, two cinnamon rolls, two fresh-squeezed orange juices. We carried the juice to a small table near the wall. The number board flickered overhead while people drifted in and out of line. I felt his eyes on me and looked up to find him already watching.

When our number was called, he stood. "Stay," he said. "I've got it."

He came back balancing the trays with practiced ease. The food hit the table in a cloud of heat and scent. I took a bite of the burrito and closed my eyes. The chile was sharp and bright, potatoes soft, melted cheese pulling everything together. It tasted exactly the same.

For a moment the years collapsed.

We didn't talk while we ate. There was something almost ceremonial about it, like acknowledging that some things didn't need words.

When I moved on to the cinnamon roll, I slowed down, peeling it apart layer by layer. Butter soaked into the dough. Sugar clung to my fingers. I scraped the icing with my fork until there was almost nothing left.

"Are you going to lick the plate too?" Bobby asked, watching me with open amusement.

"I might," I said seriously.

I dragged the fork through the last streak of frosting and licked it clean. "There is nothing in the world like this."

He laughed then, fully and without restraint. The sound filled our corner of the Frontier the way it always had, like it belonged there.

I watched him for a moment before looking back down at my plate.

Bobby was still smiling when I looked up. Something in his expression shifted when he saw mine. No questions, just present, the way he had always known how to be.

"We should get moving," he said.

"Yeah," I agreed.

But neither of us stood up right away.

Chapter Four
Where the Valley Still Remembers

"Man," I said softly as we drove past our high school, its low buildings and chain-link fences stubborn and unchanged, "that place hasn't moved at all."

The words carried more weight than I expected. The building looked smaller now, sun-bleached and practical, but the angles were the same. The courtyard. The buses lining up in the same loop. Even the cracked stretch of sidewalk near the entrance was still there.

Bobby gave a quiet laugh. "Some things around here don't," he said. "They just wait."

The North Valley unfolded around us in slow layers. Cottonwoods leaned across the road, their leaves flashing silver-green in the morning light. Irrigation ditches ran beside narrow streets, water sliding over stone. Older houses sat back behind tall fences and sagging gates. The air smelled like damp earth and fresh-cut grass, and somewhere faintly, green chile roasting.

This part of Albuquerque never rushed. It endured.

Farther along, though, the land began to shift. Where the bosque corridor had once been open — scrub and cottonwood and the kind of space that existed because nobody had gotten around to filling it yet — neat stucco homes now sat on carefully raked gravel lots. The acequia still ran along the east side of the road but the land beside it had been parceled and sold and built over, the old field where we'd spent entire summers pretending we were invincible reduced to somebody's backyard.

"Wow," I murmured, leaning forward slightly. "They really built over everything."

Bobby's mouth tilted. "Guess we weren't subtle."

I let out a quiet breath of laughter. "You remember that night the cops showed up?"

He barked a laugh. "How could I forget?"

The memory came back so clearly that I could almost taste the cheap beer and dust.

We had built a small fire in the middle of the field, just bright enough to see each other's faces. Music played low from someone's truck speakers. We were seventeen and certain the world didn't apply to us. Sylvia paced the edge of the firelight complaining about mosquitoes while Bobby and I sat in the tall grass, his arm warm and heavy across my lap.

We'd kissed under that enormous sky like we were the only two people alive.

Then headlights swept across the field.

Red and blue strobes splashed across the grass. Someone swore. Someone else tripped over a cooler. Sylvia yelled something unrepeatable and bolted for the trees before the siren even finished its first chirp.

Bobby was on his feet instantly, hauling me up with him, laughing like it was still a game.

It stopped being one when the flashlight found us.

The officer looked tired more than angry. "You kids think this is clever?"

Bobby tried to sound respectful and harmless at the same time. "Just hanging out, sir."

The officer's eyes dropped to Bobby's shirt. "You aware that's inside out?"

I laughed so hard I couldn't stop. Bobby turned crimson.

A minute later Sylvia came jogging back from the dark like nothing had happened, brushing grass off her jeans. "Did they leave yet?" she asked.

The officer just stared at her.

We got off with a warning. We always did.

Bobby kept his eyes on the road for a moment before he said, "Sylvia always ran faster than both of us."

Now, looking at the neat row of houses standing where that field used to breathe, I felt something close to grief.

"It feels smaller," I said.

"It was always small," Bobby replied. "We were just loud."

We turned onto his parents' street. The cul-de-sac felt both familiar and slightly diminished, the way childhood places do when you return as an adult. Pops' project cars still filled the driveway and side yard in various stages of repair. Hollyhocks still stood tall and stubborn in the sun. The spot beside the front door where Rowdy used to sleep in the evenings was empty, the concrete worn smooth there by years of the same warm weight, and I registered the absence the way you register an old ache, not newly painful, just present.

Bobby pulled in behind a newer Ford sedan parked near the garage. I noticed it immediately. Clean lines. Dark gray paint. No dents. No rattling hood. No duct tape holding the mirror in place.

He shut off the truck and stepped out, walking around to the sedan without a word. He opened the trunk and lifted out a worn leather briefcase and a slim black laptop bag. The way he handled them was practiced, careful. His shoulders squared slightly as he balanced the briefcase against his hip.

He'd built something while I was gone.

"Your car?" I asked.

"For work," he said, nodding toward the sedan. "Clients. Meetings. Turns out not everyone likes riding around in Blue."

There was humor in his voice, but something steadier beneath it.

Mama stepped onto the porch before we reached the steps. She crossed the yard and wrapped her arms around me without hesitation, pulling me tight against her chest. Her perfume, soft, powdery, entirely hers, rose around me and cracked something open.

For a moment I was five years old again.

First day at a new school. My mom had dropped me off with a cigarette in her hand and music blaring from the car. She kissed the top of my head without really looking at me and said, you'll figure it out. No one had told me how to get home.

At the end of the day the school emptied fast. Kids streamed toward buses and parents. I walked outside because everyone else did. Then I stopped. I didn't know which bus was mine. I didn't know the name of my street. I didn't know which direction to start walking. The parking lot emptied until it was just me standing there with my backpack digging into my shoulders, trying not to cry.

That's when I saw Sylvia.

She was halfway down the sidewalk arguing with a boy about something small and unimportant. Her hair was wild around her face. She walked like she knew exactly where she was going. I recognized her from class.

I didn't think. I just followed her.

She glanced back and caught me trailing behind. Instead of asking why, she slowed her pace. "Do you live this way?" she asked.

I nodded. It was a lie. I had no idea.

She kept walking. I kept following.

When we reached her house, she pushed open the door and called, "Mama, we've got one more."

Just like that.

Mama stepped into the hallway, took one look at me and opened her arms. No questions. Just room.

Now, standing in that same yard ten years later with her arms wrapped around me again, I realized something I hadn't understood then. Sylvia hadn't just let me follow her. She had chosen to slow down. And I had chosen to stay.

Mama pulled back and studied my face, her hands still resting on my shoulders. "You look tired," she said gently.

"I am," I admitted.

The house wrapped around me as we stepped inside. Coffee brewed in the kitchen; the faint trace of cigar smoke lingered in the walls. The height marks carved into the cabinet were still there: Bobby's, Sylvia's, and eventually mine.

Pops stood slowly from his chair and pulled me into a hug that felt steady and assessing all at once. His hand rested briefly at the back of my neck before he stepped away.

"'Bout time," he said.

"I know."

"You shouldn't have left."

I didn't argue. "Probably," I said.

At the table, Bobby set his briefcase beside his chair before sitting down. I noticed the small things. The way he checked his phone once, silenced a notification, then placed it face down on the table. The way one hand rested near the briefcase, like it mattered. Pops watched him with a quiet attention I recognized.

Mama set coffee in front of me. I wrapped my hands around the mug and let my eyes move around the kitchen. The same cabinets, same worn table, same patch of sunlight stretching across the floor.

Then I saw it.

One of my photographs hung on the far wall in a simple black frame. A rodeo shot: a rider just as the gate opened, dust lifting around the bull's hooves, the gloved hand locked in place as the world exploded beneath him. I remembered taking it in Cheyenne three summers ago.

Mama had framed it. Something tightened in my chest. Ten years gone, and my work still had a place on her wall.

"Have you been to Sylvia's yet?" Mama asked.

"Not yet," I said. "We came here first."

The truth pressed up before I could hold it back.

"She called me a few weeks ago," I said. "Said she found something strange at work. Said she needed help."

I stared into the coffee. The surface trembled slightly where my hands touched the mug.

"I told her I needed to finish a story."

No one spoke.

"I should have come anyway," I said. "Sylvia doesn't scare easily. If she said something felt wrong, I should've listened."

My grip tightened on the mug.

"She asked for me."

The words came out quieter than I intended.

Then, because the thought had been pressing at me for months, I added, "I was already thinking about coming back before she called. I've been living like a nomad for too long."

I looked down at my hands.

"I wish I'd done it sooner."

Pops shook his head before I could finish the rest. "I don't think it would've made a difference," he said. "We'll find her."

Mama's eyes flicked briefly toward the photograph on the wall before returning to my face.

Bobby reached across and took my hand. "Blame won't help us find her," he said.

I nodded, but the guilt didn't move.

Mama squeezed my arm once. "Come back tonight," she said. "I'll have dinner."

Pops looked at me steadily. "We're here, Shelly. We always have been."

Then he leaned back in his chair, and something in the room shifted.

"She didn't just stumble onto something strange," he said.

My head lifted. "What do you mean?"

"She called Bobby too," he said. "Not long after she talked to you. Said she thought something bigger was moving through the warehouse. Not just bad bookkeeping or late trucks."

A pause.

"She thought someone was watching her."

The kitchen fell silent.

Chapter Five
Breadcrumbs

We got back into Blue and pulled away from Pops' driveway, the door shutting harder than I meant it to. The sound echoed around the cab, then faded into the engine's steady rumble.

I pulled the seatbelt across my chest and clicked it into place. My hands were steady, but nothing else was. Sunlight poured through the windshield in harsh white bands, bleaching the dash and making everything feel too bright, too exposed. I fixed my eyes on the cracked vinyl until the tightness in my throat eased.

Bobby glanced at me once, then returned his attention to the road. "You want to talk about it or move through it?" he asked.

"Move through it," I said. "Let's go find Sylvia."

Blue rolled through the neighborhood and out toward the wider streets. The city gathered around us as we drove: traffic lights blinking through their cycles, delivery trucks double-parked near corner stores, lawn crews edging strips of grass that would grow back by next week. Kids rode bikes along the sidewalks, weaving between sprinklers and barking dogs.

When we turned into Sylvia's complex, Bobby eased off the gas and scanned the lot. He didn't need to say anything. The green Honda sat exactly where it should have been. My stomach tightened. Sylvia didn't leave without her car. She didn't take buses. She didn't hitch rides. Her car was freedom and fallback, the one thing she always kept close. Seeing it there without her felt wrong in a way that was almost physical.

"She keeps a lockbox," Bobby said, already pulling into a space two rows down. "And I doubt anyone's looked under the bumper."

The complex hummed with ordinary life. A sprinkler ticked across sunburned grass. A dog barked from behind a sliding glass door. Someone's radio drifted faintly from an upstairs window. It all felt obscenely normal.

Bobby crouched beside the Honda, retrieved the small magnetic box, and handed me the key without comment.

The moment I opened the driver's door, Sylvia's scent met me: faint perfume layered over stale coffee and the cinnamon air freshener she insisted made her car feel intentional. The interior was clean. She hadn't fled in chaos.

I checked the glove box out of reflex, then the center console, then the door pockets. I wasn't expecting anything obvious. Sylvia never used the obvious.

I stood there a moment, looking at the driver's seat. The realization didn't arrive dramatically; it settled the way habits do. Of course she would use the seatback.

I ran my fingers along the back seam of the driver's seat until I felt it — the subtle shift in tension where the thread had been opened and resealed. Carefully. Intentionally.

She wanted me to find it.

Bobby shifted beside me, leaning against the open car door. "Tell me that look means something," he said.

I didn't answer yet. My fingers were already working at the seam.

The thread slid free easier than it should have. Sylvia had never been careless with stitches. She had left this ready. For me.

I flipped the driver's seat forward and knelt, the pavement biting into my knee. My fingers slid along the underside of the seatback and found the loosened stitching immediately. It had been opened carefully and closed again, not ripped or rushed. Sylvia had always been precise. I reached inside and pulled out a small leather-bound journal — the kind she always carried. Tucked against it was an envelope made of thick purple paper, the kind you had to go out of your way to find. My name was written across the front in purple pen, neat and deliberate.

M&M.

My grip tightened around the envelope as I passed the journal to Bobby. This wasn't panic. This wasn't desperation. This was intentional.

"She knew you'd check there," he said.

"She knew I would."

As I stood, a cold awareness slid over me. The feeling was sudden and unmistakable — the quiet instinct that someone was watching.

"Bobby," I said, already moving away from the Honda, "we need to leave. Now."

He didn't question it. He shut the car door behind us as we moved quickly across the lot toward Blue. The air felt different suddenly — too still, too sharp.

We were halfway to the truck when the gunshot cracked across the complex. Glass exploded beside us and the side mirror on Blue shattered in a spray of shards. The sound echoed off the apartment buildings like a warning.

"Move," Bobby snapped.

We ran the last few steps. He yanked open the driver's door and slid inside while I moved into the passenger seat. The engine roared to life before my door was fully closed.

"Seatbelt."

I pulled the belt across and locked it in place as Bobby slammed the truck into reverse. Tires squealed as Blue lurched backward out of the space. Someone shouted across the lot. A woman ducked behind a parked car as Bobby spun the wheel and gunned the engine toward the exit.

I folded forward slightly in the seat, my ears still ringing from the shot, my hands moving to check the journal and envelope before my mind had caught up enough to tell them to. Both were still there. Both intact. I pressed my palm flat against my thigh, holding it there until the ringing faded and the world steadied around its edges.

We didn't slow until we were well clear of the complex. Bobby finally glanced over at me. "Seashell, you okay?"

"She left a breadcrumb," I said, holding up the journal slightly. "Her journal and a letter. We don't open it yet. Not here."

He nodded once and flipped down the visor, dialing Pops through the truck's Bluetooth. "We found Sylvia's journal and a letter in her car. Someone took a shot at us. We need to change cars."

Pops didn't argue. He told us to make sure we weren't followed and to meet him at Joe's.

Bobby drove for a while after that, looping through town and doubling back across side streets, checking mirrors and intersections the way someone does when they've learned not to trust easy exits. I stared at the purple envelope resting in my lap, holding it tighter than I needed to. The paper was thick. Deliberate. Sylvia had chosen it for a reason.

After a few minutes Bobby asked, "How did you know where to look?"

"Sylvia always hid things in the driver's seat," I said. "Not the glove box. Not under the mats. Too obvious. People check those first. Almost no one thinks about the seat unless they already know." I swallowed and looked back down at the envelope. "We built the system years ago. If something mattered, you left one breadcrumb somewhere personal but easy to overlook. Proof it wasn't random. Proof the other person was supposed to find it."

I paused, then added, "If you ever need to find me, look in the driver's seat of the RV."

He glanced at me quickly. "Really."

"Really."

Joe's garage sat back from the road behind a sagging stretch of chain-link fencing, three blocks off Central. The gate hung crooked on its hinges; the metal worn smooth where hands had pushed it open for decades. Two large dogs paced behind the inner fence, their movements slow and deliberate. They didn't bark when we pulled in. They simply watched, heads low, ears forward, deciding whether we belonged.

I'd been here before. The last time was the morning I left Albuquerque.

Joe had set me up with a small car, a full tank of gas, and enough cash to get out of the state without stopping. I doubted Bobby knew the details of that arrangement. Joe had never asked me why I needed to go, and I had never told him. He just handed me the keys, looked at me for a long moment, and said *you get one clean start.*

I had taken the highway north to Denver and disappeared.

Standing in the bay now, with a shot-out mirror on Bobby's truck and Sylvia's journal in my bag, I understood something I hadn't fully seen when I was nineteen. Joe hadn't just given me a car. He had kept the secret of it from everyone who would have tried to stop me.

That was its own kind of loyalty. The kind that didn't announce itself.

The metal bay door rattled upward as we approached. Inside, the air hung thick with burned oil, hot rubber, and that faint metallic tang that never left a shop where engines were opened and rebuilt every day. Joe stood near the far workbench beneath fluorescent lights that hummed overhead. He wiped his hands on a rag that had long ago surrendered to grease.

His eyes moved first to Blue's shattered side mirror, then to Bobby and finally to me. They stayed there a beat longer than necessary, long enough to say something he wasn't going to say out loud: some private accounting of the years between the morning he handed me a set of keys and this moment. Then he jerked his chin toward the back of the building.

"Inside," he said.

The small office behind the main bay hadn't changed in ten years. The linoleum curled at the corners. A metal desk sat against the wall, its surface scarred by decades of coffee cups and paperwork. The fluorescent light above it flickered intermittently. In the corner, an old soda machine hummed louder than necessary.

Pops was already there.

He stood near the desk with one hand resting on the back of a metal chair, his posture relaxed enough to look casual but tight enough that the tension showed if you knew how to read him. His coffee sat untouched on the desk, the steam long gone.

He looked first at Bobby. "You good?"

"We're fine," Bobby said. "Mirror's gone."

Pops' gaze shifted to me, scanning for injuries I didn't yet feel. "You hit?"

"No."

He held my gaze for another second, measuring whether I was lying. Only when he was satisfied did he nod once.

Joe leaned against the wall beside the door, folding his arms across his chest. The small room seemed to shrink with him inside it.

"Tell me, "he said.

I reached into my bag, setting the leather journal and the purple envelope on the desk. The paper looked almost defiant under the fluorescent light. Too bright and deliberate for a room like this, just like Sylvia.

"She hid it in the seatback," I said. "Exactly as we planned."

Joe's mouth tightened faintly. "Smart girl."

I opened the journal first. "She wrote the journal in code," I continued. "All of it. Her journals were always in code because she was afraid someone would read it." I glanced at Bobby. "No offense."

He raised one hand slightly. "I never read her journals. Not once."

"She didn't know that," I said.

I then opened the envelope and skimmed the note inside. "There is an address and what looks like a combination," I continued. "My guess is a mailbox place. Whatever she found, she stashed it there."

Pops picked up the envelope and unfolded the letter slowly. He didn't rush. He never rushed when something mattered. His eyes moved across the page once, then again, slower.

"They fired on you before you even opened it?" Joe asked.

"Yes."

Joe's jaw shifted.

"That means someone was watching the car," Pops said, not looking up from the paper. "Waiting to see who came for it."

The implication settled over the room. They hadn't known about the journal or the envelope. They had simply been patient, assuming that eventually someone who mattered to Sylvia would show up.

And when someone did, they acted.

Joe pushed off the wall and stepped closer to the desk. "Then we don't waste time," he said. "You follow her breadcrumb. Don't go back to that apartment. Don't talk in parking lots. Don't linger."

Pops set the letter down and met my eyes. Something in his expression had moved past concern into calculation.

"We move before they figure out you found something," he said. "Ready?"

The fear was still there, but it had shape now. Direction.

"Yes."

Joe reached for a set of keys hanging from a hook by the door and tossed them to Bobby. "You take the other car," he said. "Blue stays here a couple days. Let anyone watching think you're still on foot."

Pops gave a small nod of approval.

We weren't reacting anymore.

We were moving.

Somewhere ahead of us, in a mailbox behind a lock and a combination only Sylvia trusted me to decode, was whatever she had needed us to find.

Chapter Six
Following the Trail

Pops' car felt wrong the moment I slid into it. The banana-yellow Lincoln Town Car swallowed me instead of holding me; the leather seat giving beneath my weight with a slow cushioned sigh that felt too soft, too insulated from the world outside. It smelled permanently of cigars. Not fresh smoke but the ghost of it, sweet and stale, worked deep into the leather and seams, clinging to the headliner no matter how many times the windows had been cracked over the years. When the door shut, it closed with a thick, insulated thud that swallowed the outside noise completely. No engine rattle, no wind slipping through loose seals, no vibration under my feet. Just quiet, the kind that didn't calm anything, only made space for everything else to surface.

Bobby slid into the driver's seat and inhaled once before grimacing. "Damn it," he muttered. "I forgot how bad my dad's car smells."

I pulled the seatbelt across my chest and clicked it into place, the motion clean, practiced, something I didn't have to think about even as everything else pressed closer. Sylvia's journal rested against my thigh, the leather worn smooth from years of handling, the edges softened by time and use. The purple envelope lay on top of it, my palm pressed flat across both, holding them in place as if pressure alone could keep the moment from shifting into something I wasn't ready for yet.

Bobby rolled the windows down and eased the Lincoln into motion, his movements measured, deliberate, the kind that looked casual unless you paid attention to how little he had to correct once the car started moving.

The Lincoln floated instead of drove, gliding over the pavement in a way that made the world feel distant, as if we had stepped slightly outside of it rather than moving through it. Blue would have rattled and coughed, telling us exactly what the road was doing beneath us. This car erased all of that, smoothing everything into something almost unreal. With nothing external to anchor to, everything internal moved closer to the surface whether I wanted it to or not.

As we climbed out of the valley heading east, the city shifted around us in slow, visible layers. Cottonwoods thinned into wider streets and newer construction, stucco walls replacing chain-link fences, trimmed grass replacing hard-packed yards, irrigation ditches disappearing beneath concrete and landscaping designed to look intentional instead of inherited. The farther we drove, the more exposed it felt.

At a red light, my knee started to move before I caught it and stilled it, the motion cut off as cleanly as it had begun. Bobby's hand came down lightly against it, not pressing, not stopping, just there, a point of contact that grounded without asking anything in return. His eyes never left the road. The light changed and he eased forward with traffic, no rush, no hesitation, just movement.

The strip mall appeared, narrow and forgettable, squeezed between a dental office and a tax prep storefront that hadn't updated its signage in years. Beige stucco. Faded lettering. Windows coated with that faint film that never quite washes off no matter how often it's cleaned. The gym's sign buzzed faintly above the entrance, the sound nearly lost beneath the hum of traffic. There was one other car in the lot, and Bobby didn't pull in right away. He drove past once, slowly, his gaze moving across the windows, the roofline, the shadows that gathered along the edges of the building, then circled back and parked off to the side, angled toward the exit in a way that looked incidental unless you knew what you were looking for.

"You still good with this?" he asked, turning just enough to see me.

I unfolded the purple sheet again, checking the numbers, not because I doubted them but because confirming them narrowed everything down to something manageable.

"Yes," I said. "This is it."

He nodded once. "We go in, we don't linger. If anything feels off, we leave. No questions."

"Okay."

Inside, the gym smelled like rubber mats and disinfectant layered over sweat that had sunk too deep into the walls to ever fully leave. Fluorescent lights hummed overhead in a steady electrical tone that sharpened the quiet rather than filling it. One man worked out near the mirrored wall, headphones clamped tight, lifting in slow, controlled repetitions, his reflection doubling the motion across the glass with a slight delay that made it feel almost out of sync. Behind the counter, a woman scrolled on her phone, her eyes flicking up just long enough to register us before dropping again, the pause a fraction longer than casual. I mapped the room automatically, exit, secondary exit, mirrors, dead angles. Bobby shifted half a step to the side, placing himself where he could see both the entrance and the hallway without needing to turn his head.

"The numbers?" he asked quietly.

I looked down again. Locker numbers. My stomach tightened.

"It's in the women's locker room."

He nodded once. "Two minutes."

I held his eyes. "And if I'm not?"

His answer came without hesitation. "I'll come in after you."

The hallway stretched longer than it should have, the fluorescent lights overhead flickered once before settling into a steady hum. My footsteps echoed against the tile, each one landing exactly where I placed it, controlled, measured. The women's changing room was nearly empty, water running in the far shower, the steady rhythm of it filling the space just enough to blur smaller sounds. Rows of dented gray lockers lined the wall, the air cooler here, edged with stale perfume and damp fabric that never quite dried out. Locker 17. I crouched and turned the dial carefully, the metal cold beneath my fingers, each number catching with a small, precise click. When the lock released, the sound carried farther than it should have.

Inside sat another padded, purple envelope.

I didn't reach for it immediately. Sylvia hadn't rushed this. She hadn't panicked. She had built it, layer by layer, with the assumption that someone might be watching the first step and that I would still follow the second. She hadn't left fear behind. She had left directions.

I took the envelope, closed the locker, and stood.

When I stepped back into the main room, Bobby was leaning near the entrance, talking to the guy from the weight room, his posture easy but his attention anything but. He tracked me the second I came into view. I gave him the smallest nod. He let the conversation find its natural end and we walked out together, nothing abrupt, nothing that drew a second look.

Back in the Lincoln, the cigar smell closed in again as I opened the envelope. Inside was another sheet of purple paper, the same weight, the same deliberate choice. An address. A string of numbers. Recognition came immediately.

"The main library," I said. "Downtown. These are call numbers."

Bobby nodded and started the engine, pulling out of the lot after a quick check of the mirrors, then another, his movements consistent, controlled. He called Pops with one sentence, no details, just direction, then hung up.

"Makes sense," he said. "Nobody looks twice at a library."

"We used to talk about hiding things in library books," I said. "Books no one checks out. Travel writing. Regional history. Academic stuff that just sits."

He let out a short breath of a laugh. "You girls were nuts. What if someone checked it out?"

"We picked books nobody wanted," I said. "Obscure enough to be invisible."

Downtown pressed in as we drove, more movement, more noise, more people who had no reason to notice us and didn't. The parking garage echoed as we moved between concrete pillars, Bobby passing the first open space, then another, before backing into a spot with a clear line of sight to the exit. We crossed toward the library, a group at the bus stop laughing too loudly at something that didn't matter, someone lighting a cigarette, the city continuing without interruption.

Inside, the air was cooler, filtered, controlled. The hush settled automatically, voices dropping without instruction. Rows of books stretched in clean lines beneath soft lighting, the faint scent of paper and carpet cleaner holding the space together. I moved toward the travel section without hesitation, the call numbers guiding me exactly where they should.

An Iceland travel guide. Thick. Spine uncracked. The kind of book that had been sitting in the same place so long it had developed a relationship with the shelf.

I pulled it down and turned to page 47. Bobby stepped closer, his voice low. "Shell, you're not actually reading it."

"I might," I said.

The paper was exactly where it should have been, folded cleanly between pages 47 and 48.

Purple.

The key. Not something you could hold and turn, but something you could use. A reference point. A structure. The method Sylvia had left behind to make sure I could follow what came next. The system we had built on the hood of a red Tercel in the summer heat. *Library. Iceland. Page 47*, carried for ten years in a folded note in my jacket pocket, had just done exactly what Sylvia designed it to do.

Clarity settled in where pressure had been.

I folded the paper once and slipped it into my pocket. "Okay," I said. "I've got what I need. Let's go."

We didn't linger.

As we walked toward the exit, Bobby's hand closed around mine without comment, the kind of contact that didn't ask for anything but didn't leave room for doubt either.

Chapter Seven
Pressure Points

The drive back felt wrong from the beginning.

The code sheet rested in my hands, the purple ink already smudging faintly where my fingers had pressed too hard. I traced the symbols again and again, trying to wake up muscle memory that had once come as naturally as breathing. Sylvia and I used to build these systems on her bedroom floor with cheap notebooks and stolen highlighters, laughing at how dramatic we were being. We told ourselves we were preparing for spies or conspiracies, for secrets too big for ordinary hiding places. We never imagined we would be using them for something real. Now my hands shook badly enough that the paper rustled in small, controlled tremors. I pressed my thumbs flat against it, anchoring the paper to my knees. Bobby glanced over more than once, his jaw tight.

We pulled Pops' banana-yellow Lincoln into the driveway, and the sight waiting for us tightened something low in my gut. Joe's tow truck sat crooked near the curb, its winch cable coiled like a sleeping snake. Two Harleys leaned on their kickstands, their chrome flashing under the afternoon sun. Bobby's sedan, dark and clean and forgettable, sat off to the side like it didn't belong to any of this.

Bobby exhaled through his teeth. "We should've taken my car," he muttered as we climbed out. "We've been all over town in a baby-blue pickup and a yellow Lincoln. That thing disappears in traffic." He squeezed my hand once before opening the door.

The house felt crowded the moment we stepped inside. Cigar smoke hung in the air, thick and stale, settling into the curtains and clinging to the ceiling. The kitchen table had become a command post. Joe sat across from Pops, elbows on the scarred wood, two men flanking him who didn't pretend to be anything but what they were. One was young, barely twenty, wearing a biker jacket like armor he hadn't earned yet. The other was Hector.

He sat with his forearms on the table and his eyes already on me, the way they had always been. I hadn't seen him in ten years and he still looked at me like no time had passed and none of it had been good.

Mama moved through the space, setting down coffee cups no one really wanted. Ceramic touched wood with small, careful clinks. I didn't reach for mine.

Pops' gaze found me first. "Did you find everything you needed?"

"Yes, Pop."

Bobby filled in the details: how Sylvia had hidden the journal, how the envelope had sent us across town, how the library had held the cipher key. He even laughed once, trying to bleed some of the tension out of the room. "Crazy part is Shell knew exactly where to look. They planned this stuff years ago."

Hector made a sound. Not quite a laugh.

Joe leaned forward, the rag still in his hand though it wasn't wiping anything. "How long before you know what the book says?"

"I'm not sure," I answered. "I need quiet. I need my RV. The full key in front of me."

"Have you tried reading it with what you have?"

"A little. It's layered. It's going to take time."

Hector let out a slow breath through his nose and leaned back. "Jesus Christ," he said. "We're sitting here while she plays around with a goddamn notebook."

"It's not a notebook," I said. "It's the only thing Sylvia trusted enough to leave behind."

"Sylvia trusted you," he said. "Which tells me she was scared enough to reach across ten years and call the one person who bailed on everybody in this room."

"I came back."

"After she was already gone." His eyes moved over me, measuring. "You know what I think? I think you showing up here feels good. Like you're finally doing something right. But this isn't about you. Sylvia is missing. People are shooting at us. And you want quiet time."

"If we go kicking in doors at that warehouse before I know what she found," I said, voice level, "we could get her killed. She left this for me specifically. There's a reason for that."

"The reason," Hector said, leaning forward, voice tightening, "is that you two built a system when you were kids and she fell back on it because she didn't have anything else left. That doesn't make you special. That makes her desperate."

"Hector." Bobby's voice came out low and edged.

Hector didn't look at him. "You want to know what this is? You drove off in the middle of the night. Left a note under a coffee mug. I watched Bobby sit in that kitchen for two hours before he could stand up. This family carried you through the worst thing that ever happened to you and you walked away the minute you had a diploma in your hand." He paused. "Your mother was gone. Your father was gone. And you still left."

"That's not what happened," I said.

"It is." Something shifted in his face, something that had been waiting. "Your old man cried like the pussy he was. Right at the end. You were already gone by then, but we handled it anyway." He hesitated a beat. "Your mother was a two-bit whore who turned tricks for drug money and you've spent ten years pretending you came from somewhere better. You didn't. You came from the same gutter the rest of us did. The only difference is this family pulled you out of it and you forgot where you came from the second you hit the highway."

The room went completely still.

Bobby was on his feet.

"Sit down," Pops said. One word. Bobby didn't sit but he stopped moving.

I stood up slowly.

"Forget it," I said. "I'll find Sylvia on my own."

I reached for the journal and the envelope.

"Shell." Bobby started.

"No." I looked at him and then back at Hector. Something had cleared in my chest, cold and precise. "You were at the hospital," I said to Hector. "You went into that apartment with Bobby and packed my things. You know exactly what was in that room. You know what my father let happen to me in it." My voice stayed level. "And you just put my mother in your mouth to win an argument."

He said nothing.

"You want to come at me for leaving, come at me. You want to come at me for Bobby, come at me. But you used what you saw in that hospital room as a weapon. That's not family. That's just someone who's been keeping score for ten years and finally got a chance to collect."

"I said what needed saying."

"No," I said. "You said what you wanted to say. There's a difference." I looked at him steadily.

The sound Hector made wasn't anger. It was something quieter, more dangerous.

"Enough."

Pops' voice didn't rise. It didn't need to. It landed in the room like something dropped from a height, and everything stopped.

He didn't look at Hector. He didn't look at me. He looked at the table.

"We have one job," he said. "Find Sylvia. Everything else waits."

No one moved for a long moment. Hector's jaw was tight. Mine was tighter. Bobby stood between us like a man trying to hold two walls apart with his hands.

I sat back down, not because the fight was over. Because Sylvia didn't have time for it to continue.

The purple envelope lay in front of me, deliberate and bright. I pressed my fingertips against it and focused there, the texture, the slight give, the weight of what Sylvia had trusted me to carry. Hector's words hadn't changed what needed to happen. They had only made the ground underneath it sharper.

Pops refilled his coffee like the room had simply moved on. "Alright," he said. "Let's talk about what happens next."

Joe's eyes shifted to me. "What kind of RV?"

"Toyota Dolphin," I said. "Small. Old. But it's home."

"We can take it to the shop. Put it in a bay. Safer."

"No," Bobby said immediately. "She can't work there. Too many people coming and going. I'll move it behind my place."

Relief hit hard enough I had to steady my hand against the table.

Pops considered it, then nodded. "Hector and Jimmy go with you."

Bobby started to push back. I saw it. Then he stopped, recalculated, and nodded. "They stay in the bunkhouse."

"If there's trouble," Pops said, "I want you back in town."

Bobby nodded. "We're leaving. Shell needs to work."

Pops pointed at Jimmy. "You follow them. Call me if you see anything."

Bobby didn't wait for anything else. He took my hand and moved us out before the room could close in again.

The air outside felt cleaner, but my chest didn't loosen. We crossed the yard toward his sedan. He opened the door for me, waited until I was in, then circled to the driver's side and pulled away without looking back.

We had barely reached the end of the street when the Harleys came to life behind us, engines roaring one after the other before settling into a low, steady thunder that stayed with us as we turned onto the main road. I didn't need to look to know Hector was on the first one.

Bobby drove faster than he had before.

I curled into the passenger seat, knees pulled up, forehead resting against them. The tears came anyway, not clean grief, not clean fear, something sharper than either. I wiped my face before he could see how much.

His hand came off the wheel just long enough to rest against the back of my head. "Hang with me, Seashell." he said softly

"I'm just pissed," I said. "And scared."

"Yeah," he answered. "Me too."

I dragged my hands across my face, forcing everything back down where it could wait. Sylvia didn't have time for anything else.

"Hector's not all bad," Bobby said after a while. "We're going to need him."

"I know." I stared out at the passing traffic. "That doesn't make it easier."

A few minutes later he turned into the Smith's parking lot and parked far from the entrance, far from anyone else. The Harleys rolled in behind us, engines ticking as they cooled. Heat shimmered off the asphalt as we stepped out.

Bobby squared himself toward Hector. "We don't go in assuming it's quiet. If someone's already been there, this turns fast."

Hector lifted his jacket just enough to show the dull black grip of a .45. "I'm covered."

Jimmy tapped his thigh in confirmation. Bobby nodded. "Mine's in the glove box."

Hector's eyes shifted to me. "You?"

"I've got a .38 in the RV," I said. "I'll grab it when we stop."

"You know how to use it?"

"I wouldn't carry it if I didn't."

He held my gaze for a moment longer, something unreadable moving behind his eyes, then gave a small nod. No forgiveness. No apology. Just the acknowledgment that we were both still standing and there was work to do.

"Alright. What's the move?"

"We stop at the RV," Bobby said. "Shell grabs what she needs. Hector covers her. I grab gear. Dirt bikes out back." He looked at me. "Can you ride?"

"It's been a while," I said. "If we're not rushed."

"We'll be rushed." He didn't soften it. "You double with me or Hector."

"Whatever it takes," I said. "We have to find Sylvia."

Bobby nodded once, already moving. "Two minutes. In and out."

We drove the rest of the way without talking.

When Bobby pulled in behind the RV, his jaw tightened. "Shell. Something's off. Move fast."

I saw it the second I stepped out. The door hung wrong, the frame bent inward where something had forced it. Hector was already moving. "Stay back."

He went in first.

The seconds stretched.

Then he stepped aside and motioned me in.

I crossed the threshold and stopped.

My home had been taken apart.

The mattress lay split open, foam pulled out in rough chunks. The fabric I had stitched into the ceiling hung in torn strips, threads trailing where my hands had once pulled them tight and careful. One of my camera lenses lay cracked near the sink, the glass fractured into a spiderweb that caught the light in sharp angles. The air smelled like dust and insulation and something scorched from where they had forced the door. I stood there long enough to feel it, the violation of it, the deliberate dismantling of the one space I had built entirely for myself. Then I moved.

I went straight to the driver's seat and reached into the seam. My journal. The manila envelope. I put those into my bag with Sylvia's journal and the envelope. I strapped the holstered .38 to my ankle and added the box of ammunition to my bag.

"I've got what I need," I said.

The truck hit the street at speed before Hector could answer.

"Down!"

The first shots tore through the side of the RV, sharp cracks punching through the thin walls in a tight line. Glass shattered above me. I dropped flat, bag pulled tight against my chest, the floor shuddering with each impact.

Then the engine out back roared to life.

Jimmy's Harley shot past the property, chasing.

"Now." Hector hauled me up and pushed me forward.

We ran.

His bike waited just beyond the fence. I climbed on behind him, bag wedged between us, arms locked tight as he tore out across the dirt, the uneven ground bucking beneath us as we cut toward the ditch road. I held on, face pressed into his back, refusing to lose my grip.

We hit pavement fast. Turn. Another turn. Then the merge onto I-25 south.

Another engine came up beside us.

Jimmy.

His bike held steady but his left arm was dark with blood from the elbow down, the fabric soaked through, dripping at the edge of his sleeve.

Chapter Eight
Decoding

We rode to Socorro before anyone said much of anything. The highway stretched out in a long, sun-struck line, heat shimmering above the asphalt, the wind flattening my shirt against my back where I sat behind Hector and kept my grip locked hard enough that my fingers ached. Seventy-some miles of nothing but road and that particular kind of thinking that happens when you can't do anything else. By the time we pulled into a parking lot on the edge of town and cut the engines, the sudden silence felt unnatural. It took me a moment to adjust to standing still again. My legs were stiff when I climbed off the bike. Dust clung to my jeans. My jaw hurt from how hard I had been holding it shut.

Hector looked at Jimmy first. "You okay?"

"They winged me. I'm fine." Jimmy pushed up the torn sleeve of his T-shirt, revealing a long dried streak of blood running down his forearm. The shirt stuck to him in places, the fabric dark and stiff where it had dried. He tried to sound casual, but I could hear the strain underneath it.

"Let me see." I moved to him before he could argue. The bullet had only grazed him, a clean furrow through the skin above the elbow, ugly but shallow. Not deep enough to do real damage if we handled it right. I got a water bottle out of my bag and poured it slowly over the wound, washing the blood clear in thin pink streams that ran over his wrist and dripped onto the pavement. Jimmy hissed once through his teeth but didn't pull away. "It's not bad," I said. "We can clean it properly when we stop."

He nodded, then looked toward Hector. "Bobby went down the ditch bank. They didn't follow him. They came for you two." He paused, a grim kind of satisfaction touching his mouth. "I shot the driver. Did a better job on him than they did on me."

"Atta boy," Hector said, as if he was commenting on a well-executed pass.

Hector walked away and pulled out his phone. I could hear the low murmur of Spanish, his voice controlled and flat in the way it always went when he had already decided what mattered and what didn't. He came back a minute later with the same closed expression he carried when he didn't want anyone reading him too closely. "Pops wants us back in town," he said. Then he paused. "I told him no. Bobby's going to meet us. Joe's cousin is in Belen. He's sorting out a vehicle."

Jimmy and I both looked at him. Hector almost never went against Pops. That alone told me how serious he thought this had become. He didn't explain himself. He just dialed another number and walked away again, shoulders tight, boots scraping lightly against the pavement as he crossed toward the far end of the lot.

We moved to the McDonald's across from the gas station because it was open, anonymous, and full of the kind of people who minded their own business. Inside, the air-conditioning hit hard after the heat outside, carrying the smell of fryer grease, sugar, and old coffee. We found a table toward the back beneath a humming vent. The place was half full. A family with small children sat near the play area, one kid crying over spilled fries. Two men in work boots leaned over paper cups of soda near the windows. No one looked at us twice.

Hector went to order. Jimmy went to the restroom to clean up properly. I sat down and pulled Sylvia's journal, the cipher key, and a pen from my bag. The leather cover felt warm from being pressed against me all afternoon. I turned to the last entry. Whatever she had written most recently would hold the most immediate thing, the thing that had frightened her enough to leave a trail instead of a message. I flattened the page with one hand and started working through it, symbol by symbol, matching each one against the key and writing the letters carefully into the margins.

It was slow at first. Not because I didn't remember, but because remembering took a second to gather itself. Sylvia and I had built these systems in layers over the years, first as a game, then as a habit, then as something we trusted because adults made a mess of too many things and we liked having one world that belonged entirely to us. Once my mind found the rhythm again, the symbols began to resolve more quickly. Shapes turned into consonants. Repeated marks revealed patterns. Whole words began to emerge from what had looked like nonsense.

Hector set a tray down in front of us, burgers wrapped in paper, fries cooling in their cartons, empty cups stacked together. He looked at the journal, then at me.

"Iced tea," I said before he could ask.

He stood there for a moment with his back to me, one hand braced briefly against the edge of the table.

"I was out of line," he said. "Back at the house. Some of what I said."

I kept my eyes on the page for a second longer than necessary, finishing the letter I was writing before looking up. "You weren't wrong about most of it."

"Doesn't mean I had the right to say it the way I did."

His shoulders stayed closed. He didn't turn around. The apology existed in the space between us without requiring either of us to look at it directly. "We can talk about it later," I said. "After we find Sylvia."

He nodded once and went to get the drinks.

Jimmy came back with a clean arm and a fresh shirt, sat down, and ate two burgers in rapid succession while I worked. He didn't talk much. None of us did. The paper wrappers crackled. Ice shifted in plastic cups. The overhead menu boards glowed with pictures too bright to look at directly. After a while Jimmy reached across and stole three of my fries with the confidence of someone who had decided that being shot entitled him to certain liberties.

By the time I had decoded nearly a full page, the letters had begun to cluster into phrases that made enough sense to feel dangerous. Most of it confirmed what Bobby had already told me: the inventory discrepancies, the after-hours trucks, the sense of being watched. And then, near the bottom of the entry, something that made my hand stop moving.

I read it twice. Then I kept writing, because Sylvia hadn't stopped there either.

I heard Bobby's voice outside before I saw him, sharp and low, finishing an argument with Hector as they came through the door.

"...not the way we handle this. Pops isn't going to find Sylvia. All he'll do is get in the way."

"Boss is going to be pissed." Hector's voice carried the flatness of someone who understood the cost and was accepting it anyway.

"Yeah. Let him. He's not going to do anything to me, and you're with me. If we find Sylvia, everything else gets forgiven."

They reached the table. Bobby slid in beside me without asking and touched my face briefly. "How's it going?"

"Getting somewhere," I said.

He looked at the page, then at me.

"She mentions someone named Cap twice. Do you know who that is?" I asked.

Bobby read through what I had decoded, his eyes moving quickly over the lines. Something shifted in his expression, small but unmistakable. Recognition first. Then calculation.

"Yeah," he said. "I know Cap."

The room seemed to narrow around the name.

Bobby looked up. "We need to move. Jimmy, cops are looking for you. Someone saw you leaving and gave a description of the bike." He turned toward Hector without fully taking his eyes off me. "I've got a storage contact here in Socorro. We stash the Harleys and take the Jeep."

Hector didn't argue. "Fine."

"You're both coming," Bobby said. It wasn't framed like a question because it wasn't one.

"Obviously," Hector replied, already pushing his chair back.

I gathered the journal and the key and slid them carefully into my bag, making sure the pages stayed flat. We walked back out into the afternoon heat and I climbed into the passenger seat of the Jeep while Bobby gave Hector directions to the storage lot. The Harleys followed close behind us, their engines absorbed by the ordinary noise of the street.

At the storage unit, Bobby spoke briefly to a man who came out to meet us, a broad man in sunglasses who took one look at the bikes, then at Bobby, and asked no questions. Jimmy and Hector rolled both Harleys into an open bay. The metal door came down with a hard clatter and locked. Bobby got back behind the wheel.

"We're not going back to Albuquerque," he said, looking straight ahead. "Not yet. Whatever Sylvia found, Cap knows where it leads." Then he glanced at me. "You're with me?"

I thought about the RV. The split mattress. The torn fabric hanging from the ceiling. The cracked lens by the sink. Everything I had built and carried and trusted enough to call mine, ripped open and left exposed. I thought about Sylvia building trails through seats and lockers and library shelves because she knew someday someone might need to follow them.

"I've been with you since this morning," I said.

He put the Jeep in gear and we pulled out of the lot, leaving the bikes behind.

Chapter Nine
West

The storage yard sat at the edge of town where the highway bent toward the river, a chain-link fence wrapping around rows of metal units bleached pale by years of sun, heat shimmering above the gravel in slow transparent waves. Bobby punched in the gate code without slowing. The gate rattled open.

Jimmy and Hector rode straight to the back row, engines cutting out in quick succession, the sudden silence ringing in my ears after the steady thunder of the road. Bobby lifted the metal door of an empty unit and the Harleys rolled inside one after the other, chrome flashing once in the light before disappearing into shadow. The metal door slammed shut and the lock snapped through the latch.

Jimmy nodded toward the highway. "Cops can look all they want."

Hector didn't answer right away. He stepped away from the unit and scanned the road beyond the fence, his eyes moving slowly along the highway, across the empty shoulders, the distant shimmer of heat rising from asphalt. He stood there longer than necessary and when he finally turned back, his expression hadn't changed, but something in the set of his shoulders had tightened.

We climbed into the Jeep and rolled through the gate, leaving the bikes locked in the dark behind us.

Bobby turned west toward Magdalena and the mood inside the vehicle shifted almost immediately. Traffic thinned. Buildings disappeared. Radio stations faded into static. The mountains rose ahead like dark sentinels, their ridgelines blurring as the light began to fade. Bobby turned the dial twice before shutting the radio off entirely. The silence that followed didn't feel quiet. It felt like being cut loose.

I kept the journal open in my lap, but my attention kept drifting: to the road, to Bobby's hands locked on the wheel, to the mirror where Hector's eyes moved constantly, never settling in one place for long. He watched the road behind us, then the tree line, then the shoulder, then back again, the rhythm of it restless and precise. Bobby wasn't much different. His shoulders stayed tight beneath his jacket, his gaze fixed forward with the kind of focus that left no room for anything else.

We rolled through Magdalena without slowing. A diner with a flickering sign. A gas station with one lonely pickup out front. A scattering of buildings crouched low against the wind as if they had learned long ago not to expect much from anyone. Then the town fell away behind us and the forest closed in, ponderosa pines crowding the road, shadows stretching long between the trunks, the air colder and sharper, the kind of cold that seeps through glass even with the heater running low.

Hector broke the silence from the back seat. "So," he said, voice low, roughened by something that hadn't fully settled since the house. "I'm guessing we aren't going to the cabin."

Bobby didn't look back. "No. We're not." He paused just long enough to make the next part land. "I know where Sylvia is. I just need Shell to figure out how to contact him."

Hector leaned forward, forearms braced on his knees, the posture tight, contained. "Who?"

Bobby's hands shifted slightly on the wheel before settling again. "You remember that survivalist Joe used to deal with. The old gunrunner."

Hector let out a short, humorless breath. "That crazy bastard." His mouth pulled tight at one corner. "Never knew if he was going to shake your hand or put a round through you."

"That's the one," Bobby said. "He's out near Crownpoint."

Hector sat back slowly, the movement controlled but loaded. "And Sylvia?" he asked.

"With him."

For a second, no one spoke.

Hector shook his head once, slow and deliberate. "Then how's this gonna work?" he said. "If we roll up there, he won't wait to see who we are. He'll start shooting."

"Exactly," Bobby said. "So, we're not rolling up blind. We're going to Grants. Motel. Shell figures out how to contact him. No phones. No calls to Joe or Pops. This stays between us."

Hector held his gaze in the rearview mirror for a beat longer than comfortable, measuring it, then reached into his jacket and pulled out his phone. He handed it forward without a word. I added mine. Bobby dropped both into the center console, then reached for a third Jimmy passed up. The dull thud as they settled together felt heavier than the sound should carry.

I went back to the beginning of the journal, forcing myself to slow down and really see what Sylvia had done instead of trying to jump ahead to what I wanted it to say. The middle sections had been resisting me since Socorro. Page after page of lists. Cities. Numbers. Arrows. Too deliberate to be random, too fractured to be obvious. I could feel the structure beneath it, something layered and intentional, but it stayed just out of reach, like trying to remember a word that sat just beyond the edge of language.

Then I noticed it, a tiny number pressed into the crease of the page, almost invisible unless you knew where to look. Then another. Then another.

My pulse kicked up.

One digit per page. Hidden in the spine.

I flipped carefully through the journal, copying each number down in sequence, my pen moving faster as the pattern locked into place. When I finished, I looked up: "Area code, five-oh-five or five-seven-five?"

"Five-oh-five for most metro," Bobby said. "Five-seven-five for a lot of the rest."

"Five-seven-five," I said. "I think I've got a number for Cap."

Hector leaned forward, his eyes dropping to the notebook in my hands. "You're sure?" he asked, not doubting so much as testing.

"I'm sure enough to try it," I said.

Bobby nodded once. "We'll be in Grants in thirty minutes."

The code wasn't new. It was an evolution of what we had built as kids, something that only made sense if you already understood how Sylvia's brain worked: letters swapped for numbers, numbers tied to places, places tied to memory. A structure that looked like noise, until you knew what to ignore. As the Jeep climbed west I worked through the lists that had been resisting me, and the structure finally began to give. Every page started with a city — Albuquerque, Phoenix, El Paso, Denver — with columns of numbers and more cities beneath each one. Routes. Timing. Movement. The realization moved through me in pieces.

I pressed my fingertips flat against the page, grounding myself in the paper, the ink, the fact that this had been written down because someone had needed it to exist outside their own head.

Sylvia hadn't just found something wrong. She had understood it and then she stepped directly into it.

Bobby glanced over. "Anything yet?"

"Pieces," I said. "Enough to know she knew exactly what she was doing. Enough to know she planned for this."

Hector's voice came from the back, quieter now but tighter. "Planned to disappear?"

"Planned to be followed," I said. "Planned for me."

That shut the Jeep up again.

The Motel 6 sign buzzed unevenly, half its neon brighter than the rest. Bobby checked us in, his eyes moving constantly: lobby, hallway, parking lot through the glass, the reflection in the door. We drove around back where the lights were dimmer and the cameras barely reached. "Shared room," he said as we climbed out. "Short notice. Better we stick together."

Hector gave a small nod, but his eyes were already moving again, scanning the dark edges of the lot before following us inside.

The room smelled of industrial cleaner and stale carpet. Bobby locked the door, flipped the deadbolt, checked it once, then turned to me with his hand out. "Let me try that number."

I passed him my notebook and sat on the edge of the bed, my legs finally loosening as the adrenaline drained away.

Bobby dialed from the motel landline. The phone rang four times before someone picked up.

"Hey," Bobby said. "Cap? Bob Calderon."

He listened. His expression didn't change much, but something in his posture shifted — less guarded, more deliberate.

"Yeah," he said. "I'm in Grants. Hoping to talk business tomorrow."

He listened longer this time, his eyes flicking once toward Hector, then back down as he grabbed the pen and started writing. When he hung up, he slid the paper toward me.

Sylvia must have told him how to reach me if someone came looking.

The message was written in our old code. Letters only. No spacing.

Muscle memory took over.

My brain moved through the pattern without thinking, translating almost as quickly as I read.

Bobby didn't look at the page. He watched my face.

"She's with him," I said.

I read it again, slower this time, making sure I hadn't forced anything that wasn't there.

"And she's not alone."

My throat tightened before I could stop it.

"She took girls with her."

The room went still.

"It wasn't drugs," I said. "It was people. Girls. Young girls being moved from Mexico and further south." I swallowed once. "She figured it out and she stole the last shipment instead of letting them be sold."

Hector swore under his breath, low and sharp, the sound more reaction than language. He looked away immediately after, jaw tightening, one hand dragging briefly across the back of his neck before dropping again. He had spent his whole adult life in gray areas, had done things for Pops that weren't clean, had never lost sleep over the ambiguities of the world he moved through. But this was a different kind of wrong and the set of his shoulders told you he knew it without requiring him to say so.

Bobby stood without speaking, grabbed his jacket from the chair. "Let's eat," he said. "Cap'll be here in the morning."

Denny's was nearly empty, fluorescent lights buzzing overhead in that particular late-night hum that made every surface look slightly bleached. We slid into a booth near the back. The waitress poured coffee without really looking at us and drifted back toward the counter. Jimmy had the menu open before anyone else had sat down and was already pointing at the chicken fried steak with the focused attention of someone who had made this decision miles ago.

"What do you do now?" Hector asked after a moment, his tone neutral but his attention not.

"Photography mostly," I said. "Rodeo circuit. Ranch work sometimes. I follow the season." I turned the coffee mug slowly between my hands. "It was what I was finishing when Sylvia called."

Bobby studied me across the table. "That's what you've been doing all this time."

"Yeah." I paused. "I got my first real photograph the day I tried to call home. Almost a year after I left. No one picked up, so I left a message and went back to work. Caught a bull up close at the chute, full extension, dust everywhere. Sold it for enough to buy the RV."

I didn't say what I remembered about that day. The song playing over the arena speakers. The payphone outside the snack bar with a quarter in my hand and my throat closing. When the answering machine picked up I had left the message I'm okay, I miss you all and hung up before I could change my mind. I stood there for a second with my hand still on the receiver, the arena noise coming back in around me, and then I turned back to the bulls.

I picked up my fork and then stopped. Somewhere in the wreckage of the RV were my cameras. The laptop with the rancher interview. Six months of rodeo photographs I hadn't backed up. I had money saved. I could replace the equipment eventually.

Bobby watched my face. "You okay?"

"Yeah," I said. "Just thinking about what was left in the RV."

He nodded once, understanding what I meant and not pressing it further.

Hector didn't look at me, but I saw the slight shift in his posture, the way his shoulders tightened and then settled again, like he had noticed and decided not to say anything.

Across the table, Jimmy cut into his chicken fried steak with the satisfaction of someone whose priorities had been correctly ordered all along. He didn't say anything. He didn't need to.

We ate after that in silence.

Later, back at the motel, I lay fully clothed on the bed, listening to Bobby and Hector talk in low voices across the room. Planning around me, not over me. Their voices moved in a steady rhythm: strategy, routes, timing, the kind of conversation that built something forward out of whatever had just happened. I didn't follow the words. I followed the cadence of it, the way it held.

Sleep came in fragments. Thin, shallow pieces that never quite held.

Sylvia hadn't panicked. She had prepared. That was the difference between someone caught in a storm and someone who had studied the weather long enough to know when it would break. She hadn't just left us a trail. She had left us a way through.

Chapter Ten
Cap's Way

I woke out of a nightmare so fierce my whole body felt bruised from the inside.

The room was dark except for the dim yellow lamp by the table. Bobby was sprawled across the bed beside me, one arm thrown over the blanket like he had dropped mid-thought. Jimmy snored in the other bed, mouth open, boots kicked off but still on the floor like he didn't trust sleep to last.

Hector sat at the small table with a battered paperback in his hands, the lamp catching the edges of the pages. He looked carved out of shadow: still, upright, alert in a way that didn't match the hour.

I slid out of bed and padded toward the bathroom. Hector glanced up as I passed.

"Sounded like a rough one."

"Yeah," I said. "I don't ever sleep well." I nodded toward the book. "What are you reading?"

"Louis L'Amour." He held it up as if it might explain something about him. *The Shadow Riders.* "Probably read it ten times."

"Good book," I said. "I've read most of his. Wouldn't have guessed you read westerns."

He gave a short laugh. "You probably didn't think I could read at all. It surprises most people."

I grinned before I could stop myself and slipped into the bathroom.

Cold water. Motel toothpaste. When I stepped back out Bobby was awake, propped on one elbow, eyes gritty, hair wrecked.

"You should try to get a little more sleep," he murmured. "Tomorrow's gonna be rough."

"I will," I said. "Just needed to clear the dreams."

I curled back under the blanket and fell asleep hard. It wasn't rest, more like a blackout.

When I woke again it was to Bobby's ringtone, sharp and too cheerful for the room it was in. He paced near the window, talking low into the phone with his back half turned, the thin curtains glowing gray with early light. Hector sat at the small table in exactly the same chair, the paperback gone, his gun resting across his lap. The lamp threw a dull yellow circle across the table and one side of his face, leaving the rest in shadow. His posture hadn't shifted at all.

He had kept watch all night.

I didn't say anything. Neither did he. With men like Hector, you didn't thank them out loud. You just noticed and let the noticing stand.

I swung my legs off the bed and checked my bag. Journal on top, code pages folded tight, the purple paper tucked where I could reach it without looking, everything that mattered compressed into something I could run with if the room exploded.

Hector's eyes flicked down and back up, quick and controlled, followed by a quick nod.

Bobby ended his call and turned just as I pulled my jacket on. His eyes lingered on me a moment longer than necessary, something tight moving behind them before he looked away like he couldn't afford whatever that look wanted to become.

We filed out to the Jeep, boots crunching across gravel in the thin high-desert cold. Bobby slid behind the wheel and started the engine without a word. On the way to the freeway, he swung through McDonald's on instinct: coffee with cream and sugar, sausage McMuffins, hash browns. Jimmy's hand was already reaching before his bag was passed back. The smell of grease and hot bread filled the Jeep as I handed food and coffee back without turning around, then unwrapped a sandwich and held it out to Bobby. He took it one-handed, eating fast, as if the time between here and wherever we were going mattered more than the food.

Westbound I-40 opened in front of us, the sky widening into pale desert blue. The highway stretched straight toward the red-and-brown spine of the state, mesas rising in long, quiet layers along the horizon. Jimmy finished his coffee and crushed the cup against the floorboard. Hector said nothing, his eyes moving between mirrors and the road behind us, the rhythm steady, controlled, constant.

After his second sandwich, Bobby finally spoke.

"We're meeting Cap in Gallup."

His voice was steady, but his hands weren't. Death grip on the wheel. Knuckles pale. Tendons standing tight beneath the skin.

"I'm hoping Sylvia will be with him."

I turned toward him.

"Bobby."

"Yeah." He didn't look over.

"What's wrong?"

He exhaled through his nose as if the air scraped on the way out. "Nothing," he said. Then a long silence. The highway ran straight and unforgiving ahead of us and his hands stayed white on the wheel and he didn't speak again for a long time.

Then his hand came off the wheel and found mine where it rested on my knee, his thumb moving once in a slow, deliberate stroke. He held on for a moment. Then both hands went back to the wheel.

I looked back out at the highway and let the silence hold what neither of us was saying.

The restaurant parking lot was sun-bleached and half empty, wind pushing grit along the curb in thin scraping lines. Bobby killed the engine and turned toward the back seat.

"Stay sharp," he said. "I don't have a good feeling about this."

Hector checked his gun without drama, a quiet, practiced movement. Jimmy watched him and did the same, less smooth, more visible. Bobby took my hand as we walked in, his voice dropping close to my ear.

"Stay with me, Shell. If this goes south, I need you."

I nodded once. My stomach felt like it was trying to leave without me.

We rounded the corner and saw Cap.

He was already eating, like the world didn't get to interrupt him. A bowl of beans and green chile steamed in front of him. He tore pieces of tortilla and used them as a spoon, sopping up the juices, chewing slowly, eyes drifting across the room between bites.

Big man. Red hair. Beard like rusted wire. Camo that looked lived-in, not costume. A knife strapped to his thigh, like punctuation. Cap carried the kind of presence that didn't need to move fast to control a room. He didn't posture. He didn't rush. He didn't explain himself unless he chose to. That alone was its own kind of warning.

Hector and Jimmy stopped a step behind us, hands resting near their holsters. Hector's face was tight, controlled but strained, like he was holding something in place that didn't want to stay there. We slid into the booth across from Cap.

His eyes landed on Bobby first. Then Hector — something in them shifted there, not soft, but familiar, work done together that didn't need language. Then his gaze moved to me and paused.

Unknown.

Cap didn't like unknowns.

"What the hell is she doing here," he grumbled, voice rough as gravel. "We got enough damn females to deal with."

Hector's jaw tightened almost imperceptibly.

Bobby didn't flinch. "She's with me. You don't need to worry about her." He leaned forward just enough. "Where is my sister?"

Cap's mouth twitched like he might smile, but he didn't follow through. "I don't answer to you, kid. You aren't the boss."

Bobby held it. "You respect Pops."

Cap nodded once. "I respect Pops." His eyes moved back to Hector. "And I respect Sylvia." That landed differently. Hector's throat moved once, tight. Cap's gaze returned to me. "And I don't know you."

I held his eyes without blinking. Just steady, the way you look at something that might turn on you if you flinch.

"I'm here because Sylvia called me," I said. "She doesn't call unless it matters."

Cap leaned back slightly, studying me like he would turn a piece of metal in his hands, checking for flaws. "She did," he said. "And she doesn't do it for drama."

Bobby didn't move. "Where is she, Cap?"

Cap exhaled slowly. "You want to see Sylvia, you do it my way."

Nobody shifted.

Jimmy's foot tapped once under the table and stopped.

Cap took another bite, slower this time, deliberate. "Here's the situation. Whatever she found, whatever she interfered with, was bigger than a warehouse. Bigger than your father's reach. Bigger than Joe's garage games. People are looking. People are angry."

Bobby's eyes narrowed. "So she's alive."

Cap held his gaze. "She's alive because she's Sylvia. Because she's smart. Because she doesn't panic." He paused. "And because she planned for you."

He reached into his pocket and set something on the table.

A cheap purple hair tie, stretched thin.

"She left that on my counter," Cap said. "On purpose."

Bobby stared at it like it was something fragile. Hector didn't move, but something in his eyes shifted: sharp, protective, gone again just as fast.

"She wanted me to know she was still herself," Cap added.

Bobby swallowed. "What are the terms?"

Cap held up one finger. "First. You leave the Jeep in Gallup. Public lot. Somewhere boring."

Hector's shoulders tightened.

Cap didn't look away from him. "I know you don't like this, Hector."

Hector's jaw worked. He didn't answer.

A second finger. "Phones off. All of them. No calls to Pops. No calls to Joe." He let that sit. "Not because I don't respect Pops. Because I respect Sylvia's chances."

Bobby's voice sharpened. "You're saying Pops would make it worse."

"I'm saying Pops would bring a storm where you need fog."

A third finger. "You don't drive to my place. You ride with me."

"What are we riding in?" Bobby asked.

Cap nodded toward the window.

Outside sat a big Toyota Land Cruiser, dusty and scarred, reinforced bumper, heavy tires, the kind of vehicle that didn't ask permission from the road.

"If you want Sylvia," Cap said, "you do it my way. If you don't like my way, you walk out of this restaurant and go home."

Bobby didn't move. Neither did Hector.

Cap waited.

"Everyone goes," Bobby said. "I'm not leaving anyone behind."

Cap's brow lifted slightly.

He looked at Jimmy. "You'll do exactly what you're told."

Jimmy nodded. "Yes, sir."

Cap turned to Hector. "You're breaking your own rules."

"I don't break rules," Hector said, voice low.

Cap said nothing.

Hector's eyes flicked to the hair tie. "But I won't abandon her."

Cap held his gaze for a long moment. Then nodded once. "Good."

The waitress dropped the check without looking. Cap picked it up before anyone else moved, folded bills into it without counting, and stood.

Chairs scraped softly against the tile as we followed.

"Once we leave this parking lot," Cap said at the door, his eyes moving across each of us, "you follow my lead."

No one argued.

Outside, Bobby's hand found mine without thinking, fingers tightening once before letting go. Cap led us to the Land Cruiser.

"Phones off," he said again. "Weapons stay holstered. Nobody plays the hero."

Hector hesitated just long enough to make it visible. Then complied.

As I climbed in, I felt his attention flick to my ankle, quick and precise, a silent adjustment in where he placed himself.

Cap slid behind the wheel. Bobby took the passenger seat. I settled behind him, the leather hot from the sun. Hector and Jimmy climbed in beside me. The doors shut one after another, heavy and final.

Cap started the engine. The Land Cruiser rumbled low and deep, the kind of machine that sounded like it would keep moving no matter what tried to stop it.

We rolled out of Gallup and headed west.

Cap spoke without turning around.

"She didn't ask me to rescue her," he said. "She asked me to contain the damage."

Bobby's head snapped toward him. "Containment of what?"

"People who don't like losing inventory."

The word burned in the silence.

Cap's eyes lifted to the rearview mirror and landed on me. "She said something else," he added. "Said if you showed up loud, she'd know you weren't ready. Said if you showed up quiet," His gaze held mine. "She'd know Michelle was there."

My throat tightened, but I didn't look away.

Cap's mouth twitched. Recognition, nothing more.

"You've got about ninety minutes," he said, turning off the main road onto something narrower. "That's how long it takes for second thoughts to turn into bad decisions."

The landscape thinned almost immediately. Power lines faded. Pavement gave way to dirt. The sky widened until it felt like we were driving into something that didn't care if we made it through.

Inside the Land Cruiser no one spoke.

Hector sat rigid behind me, knuckles pale against his knees, breaking every rule he lived by and holding himself like it didn't show. Jimmy watched him and tried to match it, his knee bouncing once before he caught it.

Cap drove like he had done this his whole life.

Somewhere ahead, past Cap's control and ninety minutes of road that didn't allow for hesitation, Sylvia was waiting.

Chapter Eleven
Beneath the High Desert

The high desert opened in front of us, miles of scrub and stone stretched thin beneath a washed-out sky. The land was empty in the way only western New Mexico can be. Hungry empty, so that sound didn't travel right, distance felt unreliable, anything could disappear out here and leave nothing behind.

The Toyota Land Cruiser climbed steadily, the engine working low and constant under the hood. Tires ground over loose rock and washboard, vibrations running up through the frame and into the seats in short, controlled bursts. Cap kept one hand light on the wheel, making small corrections as the track shifted beneath us. He didn't hesitate at turns or slow to read the terrain. His eyes stayed forward, moving ahead of the vehicle, already choosing the next line before we reached it.

Behind me Hector sat rigid, shoulders squared, spine straight as if the movement of the vehicle didn't touch him. His eyes moved in slow, methodical sweeps between the rear glass and side windows, never lingering too long in one place. Jimmy watched him, tried to match the stillness, but tension leaked out anyway. His knee bounced once, twice, before he caught it and forced his foot flat against the floor, pressing down hard enough that his leg trembled.

Bobby hadn't spoken since we left Gallup. The quiet around him felt contained, like pressure building under something sealed. He stared through the windshield, jaw tight, the muscles in his temples jumping every few seconds. Once or twice he pulled in a breath like he meant to say something, then swallowed it back.

The road curved over a low ridge and Cap eased off the accelerator.

Two black SUVs sat ahead on the main track, angled toward each other, closing the space without fully blocking it. Anyone coming through would have to slow and pass between them. A man paced beside the closer vehicle with a phone pressed to his ear, moving in short lines, turning, pacing back. Every few seconds he lifted his head and scanned the horizon.

Cap slowed just enough to keep us moving, the engine dropping slightly in pitch. Then his hand disappeared beneath the seat.

The pistol came up smooth and practiced, his elbow braced against the wheel. The muzzle lined up through the windshield toward the man by the SUV. Cap's breathing didn't change. His shoulders stayed loose.

"I want to drop that fucker," he said. "But it would bring every level of hell down on me."

He held the aim a beat. Outside, the man turned, his gaze cutting across the ridge, not quite landing on us but close enough to register.

Cap lowered the gun slowly, deliberately, and slid it back beneath the seat without looking.

Then he cut the wheel hard left.

The Land Cruiser left the track and hit open desert; the tires striking uneven ground immediately, bouncing over rock and scrub as the road vanished behind us. Juniper branches scraped hard along the side panels, catching, dragging, then snapping free with sharp, hollow thuds. Dust surged up behind us in a thick rolling wall, swallowing the track within seconds, erasing the path we had just taken.

The terrain turned hostile fast. Deep ruts cut across at angles that shoved the vehicle sideways. Exposed stone forced the tires to climb and drop in uneven rhythms. Loose rock snapped under the weight and rang against the undercarriage in quick metallic strikes. There was no path here, no clear line. No signs. No fencing. Nothing that suggested this ground belonged to anyone.

Cap didn't slow. He worked the wheel in small, precise movements, letting the Land Cruiser move with the terrain instead of fighting it, choosing angles that kept momentum without losing control. The vehicle hit hard enough to drive my shoulders into the seat, the impact settling low in my spine.

My hands clenched in my lap, nails biting deep enough to dull the feeling in my fingers. For a second, the horizon shifted, the distance flattening in a way that made it hard to judge distance. I fixed my eyes on the line ahead and held them there until the ground resolved again into something I could read.

Cap never checked the mirror. He didn't need to. He read the ground ahead, guiding us deeper into the broken hills where the terrain itself would hide us.

No one spoke.

Then the wall appeared. At first, it didn't register. Just another rise of stone. Low and thick, built from rock pulled directly from the surrounding hills, fitted tight so the seams disappeared into the natural pattern. It didn't sit on the land so much as disappear into it.

A narrow gate cut through the center. A man stepped out beside it with a rifle slung across his chest. His stance was loose but balanced, ready without looking tense. His eyes moved over the vehicle, taking in details quickly. When they landed on Cap, something shifted. Recognition. The gate swung open.

Cap drove through without slowing.

Inside, the compound revealed itself in pieces. Outbuildings spaced wide so no one structure blocked another. Solar panels set low to avoid catching light. Dirt berms and stacked stone positioned to break wind and double as cover. Paths that curved and narrowed, forcing vehicles to slow and commit.

Nothing decorative. Everything had a function.

The Quonset hut at the center wore its age differently. Corrugated steel dulled by years of sun, seams reinforced and patched where time had tried to break it down. Cap drove straight toward it. The wide doors stood open.

The Land Cruiser rolled inside and the light dropped, desert glare giving way to a dim, cooler gray. Tires hummed across concrete before Cap shut the engine off.

Hot metal ticked beneath the hood, small sharp sounds echoing against the curved walls. Dust hung in the air, caught in narrow beams of light slipping through seams in the roof. The smell of oil, steel, and dry desert dust settled heavy in my lungs.

We climbed out and stood closer than we meant to.

Cap walked ahead and lifted a hand. "One at a time," he said. "Groups draw too much attention."

Bobby shook his head immediately. "No."

Hector stepped forward beside him. "That's not happening."

Cap didn't argue. He looked at me.

"You first."

Both men started at once. They were going to argue. I needed to stop them.

I turned to Hector.

"I'm going," I said.

It wasn't a question.

His jaw tightened, something shifting under the surface before he locked it back into place. His eyes searched my face, not for comfort, but for certainty.

After a moment, he gave a single nod.

I held his gaze, then nodded once in return.

Only then did I look at Bobby.

I didn't feel it until I saw it on him: the way his jaw set, the way he didn't move. That was what got through.

I stepped in close and squeezed his hand once, quick and firm.

Cap opened the door.

From the outside it looked like a workshop. Inside it opened into a compact kitchen that felt used, not staged. A heavy wooden table sat beneath a narrow window set high in the wall. Mismatched chairs sat around it. The counter along the far wall had been worn smooth at the edges by years of hands leaning there. Beneath the floor a generator hummed, steady and constant, its vibration faint but present through the soles of my boots.

"Sit," Cap said. "Don't move."

Then he left the room.

The silence tightened around me immediately. Each sound separated from the others. The scrape of the chair. The shift of fabric against my arms. The low vibration of the generator coming up through the floor. I placed my hands flat against the table and kept them there, watching the strip of sunlight on the floor inch forward.

The door opened. Jimmy stepped in, ushered quickly. His eyes moved — window, corners, doorframe — before landing on me. He crossed the room and dropped into the chair across from me, the legs scraping louder than they should have.

The door shut.

The generator hummed beneath us.

It opened again. Hector stepped through and stopped just inside, shoulders filling the doorway. His eyes moved immediately, checking everything. His hand hovered near his side.

Then he stepped in.

Bobby followed, and the air shifted with him, something protective and volatile settling into the space. Cap came in last and shut the door. The latch clicked, sharp and final.

Then he started talking.

"Sylvia called me out of the blue," he said. "Didn't explain much. Just said she was in trouble and couldn't wait." He leaned back against the counter. "I parked a horse trailer in the lot of that restaurant. She showed up in a van."

He paused.

"Fifteen girls."

I pictured the space without meaning to. Bodies pressed together. Air getting thin. I stopped it there before it could go further.

Bobby's shoulders tightened beside me. Hector didn't move.

"They were young," Cap said. "Some barely teenagers. Some younger. None of them spoke English. Spanish, a couple indigenous languages. Every one of them was scared enough they wouldn't lift their heads."

Jimmy shifted, then went still.

"They crowded into the front of the trailer. Wouldn't let go of each other. My men stacked hay behind them. Made it look right."

Silence held long enough for the image to settle.

"We didn't get lucky," Cap said. "Those SUVs didn't wander in. Somebody had a tracker on them."

Hector's jaw tightened.

"Once we got here everything changed," Cap continued. "Girls went underground. Clean clothes. Shoes. Blankets. Everything they came with burned."

My stomach tightened, not at the logic, but at what it erased.

"Not because it wasn't theirs," Cap said. "Because someone out there thinks it still is."

Bobby leaned forward. "And Sylvia?"

"You think she argued?" Cap shook his head slowly. "She burned her own things first. Phone included. Told the girls they were safe. That what they had now was theirs."

Bobby's hand curled into a fist.

"They're underground," Cap said. "Bunker. Old uranium-era construction. Reinforced concrete. Steel. Food, water, power, air filtration. I built it years ago." His gaze moved across each of us slowly. "I've been planning for the end of the world longer than most people have been pretending it won't come."

"This place doesn't advertise itself," he continued. "No heat signature worth tracking. No noise that carries. You could stand on top of the bunker and never know it's there."

"She's safe?" Bobby said.

"As safe as I can make her."

"She doesn't sleep much," Cap added. "Won't leave the girls. Counts them every hour."

I could see her moving through that space, touching shoulders, counting, making sure none of them disappeared.

"The SUVs showed up because someone knew their shipment vanished," Cap said. "They're looking." His eyes moved across us. "You don't get to be loud about this. You don't get to be brave in ways that make noise."

Bobby leaned forward. "You said we'd see her. That wasn't optional."

"I said she's here," Cap replied. "Seeing her comes later."

The room tightened again.

"She wouldn't have come to you unless she was out of options," I said.

Cap studied me.

"No," he said. "She wouldn't."

Silence settled, heavy and close.

"You're here because she trusted you," Cap said. "That buys you time. Not freedom. Rest while you can. Tomorrow you help me decide how this ends."

He stepped out. The lock slid into place with a heavy mechanical click.

For a long moment none of us moved.

Jimmy crossed to the counter, tore a tortilla, and dipped it into the beans. "If this is captivity," he muttered, "Well, I've had worse."

I stood and joined him. The food was plain, warm, grounding.

"They found them fast," Hector said. "Burning everything was the only move."

"That was Sylvia," I said. "She never half measures."

"And she never asks permission," Bobby said, voice rough.

He moved into the adjoining room. Four army cots in clean rows. A narrow aisle between them. A small bathroom tucked to one side.

He dropped onto one of the cots.

"She'd do that," Bobby said quietly. "Step into something like that and not look back."

He stared at the ceiling.

"You remember the river by the old bridge?"

"The one Pops swore would kill us."

"That one."

The memory came back sharp and sudden.

Late afternoon. Sky bruised from the storm. The river swollen, brown and fast, carrying branches and debris in a steady rush. Sylvia climbed over the guardrail first, boots slipping in the mud. Bobby shouted after her. She laughed and kept going.

I followed.

Hector came last. He hadn't hesitated, hadn't looked for the safest line in. He had looked at the current, looked at where Sylvia was already standing in it, and stepped in to put himself between her and whatever the river was going to do next.

The air smelled like rain and cottonwood. The ground slick under our feet.

"You're all going to die," Bobby said.

Sylvia waded in deeper.

The current hit her legs hard, pushing, testing, but she leaned into it and found her balance the way she always did. Not by fighting it.

"See?" she called. "Still here."

"And I followed you anyway," Bobby said.

The warmth of it settled into the room, filling the space between the cots, the low ceiling, the locked door, and for a moment, none of us spoke.

Chapter Twelve
What We Carry

Morning didn't so much arrive as force its way in.

Metal scraped against metal. A lock turned slowly, the sound thick and mechanical in the quiet, each tumbler engaging with a deliberate heaviness that suggested whoever held the key wanted us awake before the door opened. The hinges dragged with a long groan that sliced through the thin, shallow sleep we had managed to steal from the night, the sound filling the bunker and pressing against the low ceiling before fading into the corners.

Hector was already standing before the door had finished swinging inward. Bobby rolled upright beside me, his hand closing around my wrist without looking, fingers tightening just long enough to confirm I was there. Jimmy came off the cot in one smooth motion, shoulders squared, his gaze already sweeping the corners of the room before his feet were fully on the floor. There was dried blood on the cuff of his sleeve.

No one spoke.

Cap stepped in first carrying two heavy paper sacks, the kind that had already begun to bleed grease through the bottom folds. The smell of roasted chile, eggs, and dark coffee spilled into the bunker ahead of him, cutting through the stale recycled air and the particular sharpness that fear leaves in a closed space after a long night. He set the bags down on the scarred wooden table with a dull thump, casual in a way that felt considered, as if feeding us was just another part of the plan, one more variable he had accounted for before any of us arrived.

And behind him stood Sylvia.

I had prepared for broken. I had pictured Sylvia wrapped in a blanket somewhere in the dark, thin and trembling, eyes emptied out by too many hours of fear and isolation and the particular cruelty of not knowing whether anyone was coming.

Instead, she stood steady in the doorway.

Her hair was pulled back tight, a few curls escaping at her temples the way they always did when she had been moving too fast to care. Her face was thinner, sharpened by fatigue, shadows beneath her eyes deep enough to bruise. One sleeve carried a long streak of soot she had never thought to wipe away. But her eyes were fully alive in a way that had nothing to do with rest and everything to do with will. Her mouth was set in that stubborn line she had worn since childhood, the one that meant she had already made up her mind and was waiting for the world to catch up.

Her eyes found mine immediately, cutting across the room with the same directness she had always had, the kind that made you feel seen and measured and chosen all at once.

"M&M."

Just my name. The old one that she gave me when we were ten and I had dumped an entire family-size bag of M&Ms, skittering across the floor. The private one that belonged to bus rides and whispered plans and the long summers that once felt like they would never end. Ten years had passed between us. Not silence exactly, but distance. Phone calls that stayed careful, that skimmed along the surface of things because anything deeper risked opening doors neither of us had been ready to walk through. Updates arriving in short messages, clipped and safe, the way you write when you love someone but can't afford to say everything you mean.

For a moment neither of us moved. The bunker held the silence around us the way thick walls hold cold, absorbing it completely. Bobby stood beside me rigid and watchful; his hand still wrapped around my wrist. Hector had gone completely still near the wall, his gaze moving between Sylvia and Cap as if calculating every possible direction the next thirty seconds could take. Jimmy hovered near the table, unsure whether to move or stay invisible.

Sylvia broke first.

She crossed the room in three quick steps and pulled me into her arms so hard my breath left my lungs in a rush. I wrapped around her just as tightly, gripping the back of her shirt the way you grip something you were afraid you had lost, holding on past the point of comfort because letting go felt like a risk. She was warm. Solid. Real. Smoke clung to her clothes along with sweat and dust and the sharp acrid scent of the fire she must have stood beside while everything burned down to ash. Beneath it all was the smell I knew without thinking, the smell that had no name because it was simply Sylvia. Citrus shampoo and stubbornness and the faint permanent thread of green chile that seemed stitched into both of our lives whether we wanted it there or not.

For a moment neither of us spoke. We just held on.

"I thought I was too late," I finally said into her shoulder.

Her arms tightened immediately, fingers digging into the fabric of my jacket. "You weren't," she said, low and fierce against my ear. "You never are."

I pulled back just enough to see her face. Her eyes were rimmed red now, and there were lines there that hadn't existed when we were younger. She looked older than the girl I had left behind, sharper and more certain.

"I should've come sooner," I said. Not just now. Before. Back when leaving had turned into staying gone.

She didn't let the sentence finish. Sylvia shook her head once, firm and certain, and leaned forward until our foreheads touched. "We don't get to rewrite the last ten years right now," she said. "We get this."

Behind us Bobby had not moved. He stood a few steps away with his hands loose at his sides, but the tension in his shoulders betrayed everything his posture was trying to conceal. His body held itself like someone braced for impact.

Sylvia turned toward him.

For a moment neither of them spoke.

"I thought I was too late." Bobby's voice caught once before he steadied it. "I thought I was too late."

Sylvia crossed the small distance between them without hesitation and stepped into his arms. Bobby folded around her instinctively, one arm wrapping across her shoulders while the other hand came up to cradle the back of her head. His eyes closed.

"I didn't know where you were," he said. "I didn't know if you were hurt. Or if you were…"

"I know," Sylvia said softly.

"I didn't know you were in trouble."

"I didn't have time," she replied. "And I wasn't dragging you into it unless I had to."

His fingers tightened slightly. "You always say that," he said.

"And you always show up anyway."

He leaned back just far enough to look at her face, his thumb moving slowly across her temple. "Don't scare me like that again."

"I'll try, big brother."

For the briefest second her voice opened into something younger, softer, unguarded enough to hurt.

He pulled her into another hug, slower this time. Where the first had been panic breaking, this one held.

Hector stood a few feet away, motionless, his arms folded across his chest. He had not moved during the reunions, giving each one its space with the practiced restraint of a man who understood the difference between witnessing and intruding.

Now Sylvia turned and really looked at him.

Something passed between them before either one spoke. Hector's face stayed controlled, but his jaw tightened and his eyes softened just enough to betray what he would never say aloud.

"Hector," Sylvia said.

"Sylvia."

His voice came out rough, worn low. The space
between them changed, tightening around whatever had been
there long before any of us walked into this bunker.

Sylvia turned to Jimmy, who still hovered near the wall
beside the table. He had made himself smaller without
disappearing, a trick I suspected he had learned young. His
eyes stayed on her face, steady but alert, as if he understood
instinctively that this was not small talk and that whatever she
decided about him would matter.

"And you are?"

"Jimmy," he said. "I rode with them."

She studied him for a long second.

"Cops are probably looking for me," Jimmy added. His
voice was flat, but not empty. "Back in Albuquerque they shot
at Michelle's RV. I returned fire." His fingers flexed once at his
side. "Hit the driver."

"You kill him?" she asked.

Her tone didn't change.

"No." He looked at me then, only for a second, then
back at her. "But there were witnesses."

Sylvia nodded once, slow and thoughtful.

"You protected her."

"Yes."

"You stayed."

Jimmy held her gaze. "Yes."

"That's what matters."

Something eased in him at that. It was small but visible.
His shoulders dropped a fraction. He let out a breath through
his nose like he had been holding the weight of that moment
since the shots were fired and hadn't realized it until now.

Cap cleared his throat from the doorway.

"Eat."

We gathered around the table. The foil-wrapped
burritos were still warm enough to steam when we opened
them. Beans and eggs and green chile filled the small room
with a smell heavy and grounding, ordinary in a way that felt

almost impossible. The coffee was strong enough to burn all the way down and sat in the stomach like something solid. We ate standing. No one relaxed into a chair. No one turned their back fully to the room.

When the food was gone Sylvia set her cup down on the table and pressed both palms flat against the wood.

The room shifted with her.

The warmth of the reunion was still there around her eyes and mouth, but something harder had stepped forward and taken its place beside it. She straightened once, quiet and deliberate, and when she spoke her voice had changed. Not colder. Clearer.

"They're all from the same town," she said.

Cap's attention sharpened. It showed only a slight shift of weight, but I saw it.

"Small place just south of Tijuana," Sylvia continued. "Same church. Same school. Same market." Her jaw tightened as she laid it out, each detail placed carefully, like she had spent the night turning the pieces over until the pattern became impossible to ignore. "They didn't disappear all at once. One girl walking home from school, another helping her mother close the market, another waiting for a bus outside town. Weeks apart, different streets, different days."

She paused.

"But it's the same town."

The hum of the generator seemed to grow louder in the silence that followed.

"They were stolen," Sylvia said. "Right out of their lives."

No one interrupted.

"They don't know anyone here. Most don't speak English. A few speak Spanish well enough to understand me, but several speak Mixtec or Zapotec. They don't know where they are. They don't even understand what country they're in." Her voice softened, but only slightly. "All they know is they were taken from their homes and moved from place to place in the back of vehicles, treated like cargo because the people moving them had decided that was what they were."

Bobby's jaw clenched until the muscle along his temple jumped. Hector stared at the table, eyes fixed on the grain as if pinning the information there would keep it from escaping. Jimmy had gone very still. One hand rested against the edge of the table now, fingertips pressed white against the wood.

"They just want to go home." The words sat there. Simple. Final. Heavier than anything else she had said.

Sylvia lifted her chin.

"I'm taking them home," she said. "That has always been my plan. From the moment I understood what I was looking at, that was the only plan."

Cap gave one slow nod, the motion of a man who had heard the decision before she spoke it and had already begun building around it.

Bobby rubbed the back of his neck and paced two slow steps from the table before turning back.

"You're talking about getting fifteen girls home," he said. "Through territory you don't control."

"Yes."

He looked at her for a long moment. The worry was there but so was something else. The acceptance of a man who had spent his life watching someone he loved choose the hardest available road and had finally stopped being surprised.

"You always did pick the biggest fight in the room," he muttered.

Sylvia didn't apologize. She never had. She wasn't about to start.

Hector pushed off the wall and stepped closer to the table. "Then we move them," he said. "Staying here too long puts this place on the map."

Cap gave a small nod. "He's right."

Jimmy looked from Sylvia to Bobby to Hector, checking each face in turn.

"I didn't sign up for this," he said. His voice stayed flat, but his face had changed. Something in it had settled. "But I didn't sign up for leaving them here either."

He looked at Sylvia.

"You've got fifteen scared girls under this bunker who think you're the only person in the world who didn't lie to them." His throat worked once before he finished. "I'm in."

Bobby nodded once, reluctance and commitment locked together in the same movement.

"Alright," he said. "Then we do it right."

Cap studied the five of us in silence, his gaze moving across each face with the patience of a man who had learned to read people the same way he read terrain.

"Getting them here was the easy part," he said. "Getting them home will take planning, discipline, and every one of you doing exactly what you are told even when your instincts tell you to do something else."

Sylvia pushed away from the table. "Then we start planning."

Cap stepped forward and unfolded a large road map across the scarred wood, smoothing its creases flat with the broad palm of his hand. The bunker hummed steadily around us. Wind scraped faintly against the metal shell of the building above, thin and persistent.

"When you leave here," Cap said, his finger moving across the map, "you do it clean. No phones. No calls. No improvising because somebody feels brave and decides the plan can bend." He traced three separate lines with his fingertip. "You split into three vehicles. You stagger the departure by twenty minutes between each one. You take different routes for the first stretch — enough distance between you that you don't read as a group."

He pressed his finger to a point southeast of the compound. "First vehicle takes the county road south, then cuts west at the junction past Thoreau. The second vehicle goes north first, adds distance, then swings west on 40. The third vehicle takes the direct route but runs slow, well under speed, nothing that draws a second look." He looked up. "You are not in a hurry. People in a hurry get noticed."

His finger moved west across the map, tracing the long line of highway through mountains and high desert until it stopped at a small mark in the mountains southeast of Reserve.

"You regroup here. Morales' ranch. He's expecting you." Cap's eyes moved across each of us. "You have forty-five minutes from the time the first vehicle arrives. Forty-five minutes, and then you move regardless of who has not yet come in."

"We don't wait?" Bobby said.

"Waiting is how you turn one problem into three," Cap said. "Forty-five minutes. If someone hasn't arrived by then, the mission continues. The others will find their own way or they won't."

Bobby's jaw worked. He said nothing.

"At Morales' ranch you consolidate into one vehicle," Cap continued. "He has an old school bus he rebuilt himself. Ugly as hell. Loud. Looks like exactly what it is. Nobody looks twice at it on a rural highway."

Jimmy stared at him. "A school bus."

"Strength in numbers once you are past the first leg," Cap said. "The split is only long enough to break any pattern on the front end."

"And after Reserve?" Bobby asked.

"You go west," Cap said. "Through Arizona. Into San Diego." He looked up and met Bobby's eyes. "I have a contact there who has done this before. He will take the next step when you arrive."

Then he began assigning vehicles.

"Hector," he said. "You take the white Suburban. You drive Michelle and seven or eight of the older girls."

The assignment hit me before I could prepare, though some part of me had already known. The logic was there.

"Hector speaks better Spanish," Cap continued. "If you're stopped, he answers the questions. Michelle manages the back seat and keeps it calm."

He turned to Bobby.

"You take the green van. Sylvia rides with you. The youngest girls go in your vehicle."

Bobby's jaw flexed once. His eyes moved to Sylvia, then to me. I watched the calculation move across his face, not the tactical one, the other one. The one that had nothing to do with routes and everything to do with the fact that the plan was about to put distance between him and the people he most needed to keep in sight.

He turned to Cap. "You're splitting us wrong."

Cap looked at him without expression. "Explain."

Bobby's hand flattened against the map. "Three vehicles means three separate problems. No backup. No way to adjust if something shifts. If one vehicle gets stopped, the others don't even know it's happening."

"Three smaller targets," Cap said. "Not one large one."

"Or three isolated ones," Bobby said. "If something happens, we don't fix it. We just keep driving and hope." His voice flattened on the last word. "I don't accept that."

Cap studied him for a moment. "And Jimmy?" Bobby asked.

"He rides with me on the first leg," Cap said. "I split him south before Reserve and he comes in from a different direction."

The room held the silence.

I watched Bobby's hands on the map. Watched the way his eyes kept moving between the three route lines Cap had traced, trying to hold all of them at once, trying to build a position where he could see everything that mattered. I knew what he was actually calculating. It wasn't the routes.

I moved closer to him, close enough to keep my voice below the others.

"Trust the plan," I said quietly.

His gaze met mine.

"I know what you're doing," I said. "You're trying to figure out how to be in two places at once. You're thinking if something goes wrong with my vehicle you can't get to me." I held his eyes. "That's not a tactical problem. That's you trying to cover everyone and it's going to get somebody hurt."

His jaw tightened. He didn't argue.

"I don't want to be the reason you have to choose," I said. "Between me or Sylvia or those girls. I'm not doing this so you can spend the whole drive calculating how to save me if something goes wrong. I need you to focus on what's in your vehicle. That's the job."

He was quiet for a moment. The map lay between us, the three lines running west toward Reserve, each one carrying someone he couldn't afford to lose.

"I don't like it," he said.

"I know." I kept my voice level. "Trust Cap's plan. It got Sylvia this far."

Cap had been listening without appearing to. Now he looked at Bobby directly.

"I respect you," he said. "I respect what you did to get here. The instinct to act, to move, to put yourself between the people you love and whatever is coming. That has kept people alive before." He paused. "It will get people killed on this road." His voice carried no judgment. Only fact. "This mission does not need action. It needs discipline. It needs every person in every vehicle doing exactly what they are supposed to do and nothing else." He held Bobby's gaze. "Can you do that?"

The question sat in the room.

Bobby looked at the map for a long moment. At the three lines. At the point in the mountains where they converged again.

Then he looked at me. Something in him settled. Not gone, just placed somewhere he could manage it.

"Yes," he said.

Cap nodded once. "Good."

He folded the map carefully along its original creases, pressing each line flat with his palm.

"You have one hour," he said, his voice steady.

His eyes moved across each of us in turn, landing with the same unhurried weight on every face.

"After that, you don't belong to this place."

He let the silence sit before he finished.

"Once you leave here, you are ghosts."

Part III: Passage

"People live through such pain only once. Pain comes again — but it finds a tougher surface."
Willa Cather,
The Song of the Lark (1915)

Chapter One
Ghosts

Cap's hour did not feel like time. It felt like erosion.

The compound shifted almost immediately into motion, quiet and efficient as places built for survival always are, each person moving with the kind of purpose born from knowing exactly what happens when preparations fail. One of Cap's men hauled water containers from a storage shed and wedged them into the back of the green van, fitting them together with the practiced economy of someone who had loaded vehicles for long hauls through empty country many times before. Another stacked blankets and canvas supply packs along the tailgate of the Suburban, arranging them in careful rows, the packs ordinary and unimpressive looking, the kind of thing that would catch no one's eye at a checkpoint or a roadside stop.

The older girls came up from the bunker in pairs, blinking against the desert sun. Some clutched the small canvas bags Cap's people had given them. Others held nothing but each other, fingers wrapped around wrists, hands twisted into sleeves, the grip of people who had learned the cost of letting go. Their eyes tracked every adult movement with the quiet, exhausting focus of people who had survived by reading a room before a word was spoken.

One of them, taller than the rest with her hair braided close to her scalp and a stillness about her that looked older than her face, came up last. She counted heads the moment she cleared the door, a quick practiced scan, her dark eyes moving from face to face with the efficiency of someone who had been doing this long enough that it had become reflex. She did not stop until she had accounted for every girl in the group, and only then did she step fully into the light and let the door close behind her. I had heard Sylvia say her name that morning, moving among the girls as they came up from the bunker, her voice low and steady and careful. Marisol. Sixteen years old.

She had been the first one taken and the last one to stop watching the door.

The younger girls stayed close to Sylvia. They clustered around her like small children do around the one adult who's proven herself trustworthy in a space full of adults they can't read, hands twisted into the fabric of her shirt or gripping the belt loops of her jeans as if losing contact with her would undo some fragile agreement the world had made with them. One of them pressed her face against Sylvia's side and Sylvia bent immediately, murmuring something soft and deliberate in Spanish, her hand moving to the back of the girl's head in a gesture so automatic it had clearly been repeated many times through the long hours underground.

I stepped outside the Quonset hut for air.

The desert morning had sharpened while we were underground, the sun climbing high enough now to bleach color from the land and flatten sage and red dirt into a hard, dusty glare that made everything look both vivid and remote at the same time. The mesas in the distance rose jagged beneath a sky so wide and empty it seemed to operate at a different scale than the people moving across the ground beneath it, indifferent to all of it. Wind moved steadily across the open ground, carrying dust and the faint metallic scent of warmed machinery and the dry mineral smell that western New Mexico carries even on the calmest mornings. The compound wall cut low across the horizon ahead, and beyond it the land offered nothing. No trees thick enough to disappear in. No cluster of buildings to lose yourself among. No fold in the terrain that would swallow a vehicle or soften what happened when someone found you. If someone came through that gate, the desert would not help you and it would not hurry them.

Bobby followed a few seconds later. He didn't speak right away. He came to stand beside me, close enough that I could feel the warmth coming off him in the dry morning air. Behind us the compound continued its quiet, urgent preparation, engines testing and tires rolling slowly across gravel and voices low and purposeful. Neither of us turned. We stayed facing the desert as if the distance between the wall and the horizon could be studied and understood before we were asked to drive into it.

The silence between us lasted long enough that I knew he was building toward something.

"I don't like this," he said finally.

"I know."

"I don't mean the plan." He exhaled slowly through his nose, but the control was thin. "I mean all of it. The last two days. The last ten years." His jaw flexed once. "I mean standing here watching you get ready to drive away in a vehicle I can't follow and trying to convince myself that's okay."

I didn't answer. The wind moved across the open ground and lifted dust in thin pale sheets along the base of the compound wall, dissolving before they reached the height of the gate.

"You came back," he said, his voice lower now. "And I didn't know what to do with that. I still don't. You showed up at my gate and I just…" He stopped, his hand coming up to press flat against the back of his neck. "I had ten years of telling myself I understood why you left. Ten years of calling that peace. Then you got out of that RV and all of it fell apart in about thirty seconds."

"Bobby…"

"Let me finish." His voice wasn't sharp, but it wasn't steady either. "When they shot at the RV, I thought that was it. I thought I was going to watch you die before I got to say any of the things I couldn't say for ten years." He turned and looked at me, and there was nothing held back in it now. "And I still haven't said them."

Something tightened in my chest, fast and specific.

"You don't have to…"

"I know I don't have to." He looked back at the desert. "I just need there to be an after this. With you in it." His voice dropped. "I need to know you're not going to disappear on me again."

The words landed and stayed.

"I'm not," I said.

He searched my face for a long moment before he continued.

"If something goes wrong out there," he said, "and I'm not there…" He stopped himself. Tried again. "You handle things better than anyone I know. You always have. Ten years on your own, and you built something. You kept yourself together. You kept moving." His voice roughened. "That's not the point. The point is I don't want you to have to."

Something pushed back in my chest before I could stop it.

"I didn't want to," I said. It came out shakier than I had hoped.

He went still.

"I didn't want to handle it alone," I said, steadier now but carrying the edge. "I did it because there wasn't another option. Not because I was good at it."

The wind moved between us, lifting a thin line of dust across the ground and breaking it apart before it reached our feet.

"I know," he said quietly. And then, after a moment: "I'm sorry I wasn't there."

"You couldn't have been."

"No," he said. "But I'm sorry anyway."

Neither of us spoke for a moment. An engine turned over somewhere behind us and settled into a low idle, and then another one joined it.

Forty-five minutes at Morales, Cap had said. Regardless of who hadn't come in. The constraint sat in my chest, quiet and specific, the kind of deadline that doesn't negotiate.

"I'm staying," I said. "After this. I'm not leaving again."

He was quiet, the way he went quiet when something mattered enough that he didn't trust himself to respond too quickly.

"Okay," he said finally. Just that. But the word held everything he couldn't get the rest of the way to saying.

His hand found mine, his thumb moving once across my knuckles.

Then he stepped forward and pulled me into him, his arms wrapping around my back with more force than before, like he needed the contact to be certain. I leaned into him without thinking, my forehead pressing into his shoulder, my hand tightening against the back of his shirt. For a second everything else fell away.

Just this.

His chest rose and fell under my cheek, slower now.

"I need you alive," he said into my hair.

"You'll have me."

He pulled back just enough to meet my eyes.

He kissed me then, firm and deliberate, like he was putting something in place and trusting it to hold. When he pulled back, his forehead rested briefly against mine.

"If I don't make it there when I'm supposed to," he said, "you don't come looking for me. You stay with the plan."

"I stay with the plan."

He nodded once.

"Drive clean," he said.

"Keep her steady," I answered.

He nodded and stepped back, the control reassembling around him piece by piece. But his eyes stayed on me for one extra second before he turned.

I stayed outside.

Sylvia found me there.

She didn't say anything at first. She came to stand beside me and leaned back against the metal siding of the Quonset hut, arms crossed loosely over her chest, watching the loading with the quiet focus she brought to everything she needed to understand before she moved. The wind lifted a strand of her hair across her cheek and she brushed it away without looking.

For a moment she looked exactly like the girl I had grown up with. Not the woman who had pulled fifteen trafficked girls out of a supply chain. Just Sylvia, standing beside me in the wind the way she always had.

"You always pick complicated timing," she said.

"You always pick impossible missions."

That earned a faint smile, the real kind, quick and gone.

We stood shoulder to shoulder, the way we used to when we were younger, facing something uncertain and calling it a plan because calling it anything else made it harder to step into.

"You love him," she said.

It wasn't a question.

"Yes."

She watched Bobby across the yard for a long moment before she spoke again.

"You left him."

The words landed clean. No accusation in her tone, but no softness either.

My jaw tightened. "I left everything."

"That's not the same thing."

The wind shifted across the yard, carrying dust and the low hum of engines warming up.

"I didn't have a choice," I said.

Sylvia turned her head slightly, just enough to look at me directly. "You always had a choice. It just wasn't one you could live with."

That hit harder than I expected.

"I wasn't going to drag him into that," I said.

"You didn't give him the chance to decide that for himself."

Something flared up in my chest, sharp and immediate. "He would have followed me."

"Yes," she said simply.

"And he would have gotten hurt."

"Yes, but that would have been his choice."

The agreement took the ground out from under the argument.

I looked away, out toward the wall, toward the open land beyond it.

"I did what I had to do."

"I know you did," Sylvia said. "I'm not arguing the decision."

"Then what are you doing?"

She didn't answer right away. When she did, her voice was quieter, but it carried more weight.

"I'm asking you what you're doing now."

I turned back to her.

Her eyes were steady on mine.

"Because he's about to get in a vehicle and let you drive out of his sight again," she said. "And he's doing it because he thinks that's what you need."

The words pressed in.

"That's what the plan needs," I said.

"That's not what I asked."

Silence stretched between us.

"I told him I'm staying," I said.

Sylvia studied me for a long moment, reading not just the word but the shape of it, the weight behind it.

"Don't say that to make this easier," she said.

"I'm not."

"Don't say it because you feel like you owe him something."

"I don't."

Her gaze didn't shift.

"Then say it like you mean it."

I held her eyes.

"I'm staying."

The words settled differently this time, solidly.

Sylvia nodded once.

"Good," she said.

The tension eased just slightly, not gone, but contained.

"You and Bobby," she said after a moment, "that was never a complication for me."

"I know."

"I just need to know you aren't going to disappear on him again."

"I'm not."

This time it didn't feel like an answer. It felt like a decision.

She studied me one more second, then let it go, the way she had when we were kids deciding whether a situation could be trusted, weighing the thing behind the words against her knowledge of the person saying them. Then she nodded once, slow and complete.

"You're riding with Hector," she said.

"Yeah."

Her eyes tracked past me toward the Suburban, where Hector stood with the rear door open, checking the placement of the packs without looking like he was checking anything at all. There was something in the way she watched him that I recognized. I had known about it for years, longer than she probably knew I had. She probably didn't know I had been looking.

"He'll get you through," she said. The words carried more than the tactical fact. "He doesn't improvise under pressure. He executes."

I thought about the words he had said in that kitchen. The ones that had landed in the worst places. I thought about the way he had gone in first at the RV without hesitating. The way he had kept watch all night in that motel room with a paperback in his lap and his gun across his knees. The way his eyes had gone to that purple hair tie on the table and something in them had shifted before he locked it back down.

He had always been like that. Rough where he was rough. Steady where it mattered. I didn't have to like him to know that both things were true.

"Okay," I said.

Sylvia glanced at me sideways, catching something in my voice she hadn't expected. She didn't ask about it. She had always known when to leave a door closed.

A girl stumbled climbing into the back seat and caught herself on the doorframe. Hector's hand moved without hesitation, steadying her, then dropped away before it could become something anyone would notice.

"And you?" I asked.

Sylvia shifted her weight off the wall, her gaze moving once across the compound, counting without turning her head, taking in positions, distances, and timing.

"I improvise when I have to," she said.

That was the difference between them. Hector held a line. Sylvia stepped through it when it broke and built a new one on the other side.

She reached over and took my hand, her fingers closing around mine. Rougher than I remembered. There was dirt worked into the creases of her knuckles, a thin cut across one finger that had dried dark and been left alone.

"If something shifts," she said, "don't wait for it to settle. It won't."

I felt the pressure of her grip, the steadiness of it, the expectation built into it. Not reassurance. Instruction.

I nodded once.

Her thumb pressed against my knuckles, deliberate, like she was checking for something that couldn't be faked.

"And if I don't show," she said.

The words landed wrong. Not because they weren't true, but because she said them like they had already been decided.

Behind her, one of the younger girls said her name, soft and uncertain, then went quiet again when Sylvia didn't turn.

I kept my eyes on her. "I'll stay on it," I said.

Her eyes held mine a second longer, reading the shift, weighing whether it would hold.

"You don't come back for me," she said quietly.

Something in my chest tightened hard enough to make the next moment feel thin.

No. But yes. I didn't say it out loud.

My hand tightened in hers instead. That was the answer she got.

She watched me through it, and whatever she saw there settled something in her.

"Good."

The word carried weight. Final.

A truck door slammed somewhere behind us. The sound carried across the yard and flattened against the wall.

Sylvia released my hand.

"Don't let them see you hesitate," she said, quieter now. "They're watching everything."

I didn't answer that. I didn't need to.

She glanced past me, toward Bobby. He had stopped moving, just for a second, like something had caught and hadn't let go yet.

"Then don't make him watch it either," she said.

The wind picked up, pushing a sheet of dust across the open ground between us and the gate. It broke against the tires of the vehicles and curled upward before thinning out into nothing.

Sylvia stepped back.

"We don't get another pass at this," she said.

I nodded.

She held my gaze one last second, then turned, already moving, already shifting back into the role she had chosen, her shoulders straight, her attention snapping back to the girls as one of them hesitated near the van.

"Sylvia?" the girl said again.

"I'm right here," Sylvia answered immediately, her voice steady, already different, already for them.

She didn't look back.

I stood there a second longer, the place where her hand had been still warm, the sound of engines and low voices pressing back in around me.

Then I picked up my bag and walked toward the vehicle.

Near the Suburban, one of the girls sat on her canvas bag with her knees pulled tight to her chest, her arms wrapped around them, watching the compound wall with a stillness that had nothing to do with patience and everything to do with practice. She watched it the way you watch a door when you have learned what comes through doors.

She couldn't have been more than fourteen. Dark eyes set in a face still young in its shape but held in its expression, the way faces get held when they've been asked to carry too much for too long. She had made herself small in the way people do when they've learned that taking up space is a risk they cannot afford.

I knew that posture. I had worn it myself in rooms where the air felt wrong and the exits were not mine to use.

Her name was Nina. I had heard Marisol say it that morning, soft and precise, like she was placing it back into the girl's hands, reminding her it still belonged to her.

Nina didn't look at me. Her eyes stayed fixed on the wall, on the gate, on the space where something could come through and change everything without warning.

I adjusted the strap of my bag and kept moving. There wasn't anything I could give her right now that would hold.

I passed her without slowing.

The gravel shifted under my boots. I didn't look back.

Chapter Two
The Long Arc West

Cap's voice cut across the yard like a blade. "Load up."

The compound shifted into motion with the quiet efficiency of people who had learned long before any of us arrived that preparation was the only mercy the world ever offered. Wind moved steadily across the high desert, lifting dust along the perimeter fence and rattling loose tin against the side of the Quonset hut. The sky had hardened into that pale colorless blue that belongs only to desert mornings.

The older girls came up first. Seven of them. Eight. They gathered near the white Suburban in a tight cluster, shoulders angled inward toward each other, instinctively closing the space between their bodies. Their eyes moved constantly: adults, vehicles, open gates, back to the adults again. They were old enough to understand that movement meant risk. None of them cried. The silence in them worried me more than tears would have.

Hector opened the rear doors and checked the vehicle one last time, his movements slow and methodical. He looked under the seats, along the floorboards, into the rear hatch. He ran his hand along the seam of the rear panel as if reading the vehicle through his fingertips, then shut the hatch with a firm controlled click.

I stepped toward the girls, keeping my posture calm and my hands visible. "Mi nombre es Michelle," I said. "Vamos a manejar por unas horas. Todo estará bien." One of the girls, maybe twelve, watched me carefully. A faint bruise marked the edge of her jaw, half hidden beneath a strand of dark hair. Her gaze moved the way a grown person's gaze moves when they have already learned to take inventory of exits.

"¿A casa?" she asked. Not accusing. Just hopeful, as if hope were something fragile, she had learned to carry folded small inside her hands.

"A casa," I told her, letting certainty settle into the words even though my chest hurt with it. "Pero primero a un lugar seguro."

Hector stepped beside me and spoke to them in Spanish that flowed easier and smoother than mine. He explained the rules: they would ride without drawing attention, keep their heads down if told, and no one would open a door unless he said so. His voice wasn't harsh. It carried the kind of calm authority that implied control without needing to raise itself.

One by one they climbed in. Two in the back row. Three across the middle. Two more low against the seats with blankets folded across their laps. I passed out water bottles and small wrapped snacks Cap's men had packed. It wasn't much, but it gave their hands something to hold besides each other.

The youngest of the group hesitated at the door, her foot hovering over the step as if the space inside the vehicle might swallow her whole. I crouched so we were eye level, making myself smaller, less like another adult forcing a direction she didn't choose. "Escúchame," I said. "Yo no te voy a dejar." Her eyes flicked briefly to Hector then back to me, measuring the promise. After a moment she nodded once, so slight it barely moved her chin, and climbed in.

Hector closed the door. The sound echoed louder than it should have in the open air, metal sealing over breath, fear compressed into a vehicle that suddenly felt far too small.

Across the yard, Bobby and Sylvia were loading the green van.

The younger girls clung to Sylvia like she was the last solid thing left in the world. Small hands caught in the fabric of her shirt, fingers hooked through her belt loops, shoulders pressed against her legs as if proximity itself could keep the ground from disappearing again. Sylvia moved among them with calm authority, crouching to fasten a seatbelt, brushing a tangle of hair back from a small forehead, murmuring in Spanish that barely carried across the yard. Her voice had a rhythm to it, steady and patient, the kind of cadence that let frightened children borrow calm until they could find their own.

Bobby worked the rear cargo space with the same focused precision Hector had shown. Blankets were folded and wedged into corners. Water jugs were strapped down so they wouldn't roll if the road turned rough. He tested each strap twice, pulled at each latch with controlled force, the movements of a man trying to impose order on something that refused to be controlled.

Cap's Land Cruiser idled near the open gate, its engine rumbling low against the wind. Jimmy sat in the passenger seat with his back straight and his eyes fixed ahead, jaw tight enough to show through the line of his cheek. His hands rested on his knees, fingers still. The stillness wasn't calm. It was discipline.

Cap walked the perimeter of the yard one last time, boots crunching over gravel. He spoke briefly to the two armed men posted near the fence line. He didn't scan the horizon like a man hoping for quiet. He scanned it like a man expecting interruption. When he finished his circuit, he stopped in front of us.

"Morales knows you're coming," he said. "Pull in quiet. Don't linger by the ranch road. If there's anything off, you keep driving west."

Hector gave a single nod, small but absolute.

Cap's eyes moved to me. "You keep those girls calm."

"I will."

Then to Bobby. "Fifteen minutes after we clear the bend, you roll. Another fifteen before the Suburban moves." He paused just long enough to make sure the next part landed. "At Morales', don't wait longer than forty-five minutes. If someone isn't there, you move anyway."

The stagger mattered. Distance meant confusion. Confusion meant time. The weight of that settled across all of us.

Cap opened his door, slid behind the wheel, and pulled out without ceremony. The Land Cruiser rolled toward the gate, gravel crunching under thick tires as the engine settled into a steady growl. Jimmy sat rigid in the passenger seat, staring straight ahead. He didn't look back. The guards lifted a casual hand as the truck passed. The gate swung open, then closed behind them with a dull metallic thud that seemed louder once the Land Cruiser disappeared down the road.

For a moment the yard felt too large.

Wind moved steadily across the hard-packed dirt, lifting thin veils of dust that scraped along the fence line and curled around the parked vehicles. The compound settled back into stillness, the kind that carried tension, like the land itself was holding its breath.

Fifteen minutes feels different when you're waiting to disappear.

Bobby glanced at his watch once, his expression unreadable. Sylvia stood beside the van with one hand resting on the open door frame, the other threaded through the window to hold the smallest girl's fingers inside. She watched the horizon instead, her posture loose but alert.

When the time came Bobby didn't announce it. He simply moved, climbing into the driver's seat with the easy looseness falling out of his posture the moment his hands wrapped around the wheel. His shoulders set, spine straight, eyes forward. The transformation was quiet but complete.

Sylvia met my eyes across the yard. There was no speech, no reassurance we couldn't afford to offer. Just a small nod that carried more weight than words could.

See you there.

I nodded back, and the motion felt like sealing a promise neither of us had time to examine.

The van rolled forward, tires crunching over gravel. Dust rose behind it in a low cloud. As it approached the gate one of the guards lifted his hand in that same lazy gesture. Bobby returned it with the smallest lift of two fingers from the steering wheel, a movement so natural it would have looked careless to anyone watching. The gate opened. The van passed through. The gate closed again. Dust drifted back into the space the vehicle had occupied, the desert settling over the yard as if trying to erase the fact that anything had moved through it at all.

Another fifteen minutes.

Inside the Suburban, the girls sat too quietly. The older ones watched everything, their eyes moving toward every sound, the wind scraping along metal, the fading echo of Bobby's engine somewhere west of us, the low hum of machinery inside the compound. It wasn't calm. It was vigilance. I slid into the passenger seat, then pulled the door closed. Hector adjusted the rearview mirror slightly, angling it just enough to catch the back rows without making the movement obvious. His eyes flicked once to the center mirror, once to the side mirror, then out toward the road beyond the gate.

"You ready?" he asked.

"Yes," I said, and I meant it the only way it could be meant, ready because there was no alternative.

He gave a short nod and turned the key.

The Suburban rolled forward. The vehicle felt heavier than metal and passengers should allow, dense with breath and fear and the fragile weight of hope. As we passed the guards, I forced my shoulders to loosen and lifted a hand in a casual wave, my face carefully neutral. One of the men nodded back without much interest, chewing something slowly, his rifle hanging easy against his chest.

The gate opened for the third time.

And then the desert took us the way it takes everything, wide and indifferent, swallowing us into the open road.

For the first twenty minutes neither of us spoke. The road stretched narrow and sun-bleached ahead, a pale ribbon cutting through scrub and scattered juniper. The land lay open on all sides, low hills rising and falling like the slow breathing of something too large to notice us. Heat shimmered along the horizon. No other vehicles. No dust trails. No movement except wind pushing through brush and the occasional hawk gliding across the sky.

Hector kept the Suburban at a steady, forgettable speed. Not slow enough to look cautious. Not fast enough to look like we were in a hurry. His hands rested on the wheel but the stillness was deceptive. I could see the small adjustments, tiny corrections as the tires followed the ruts in the pavement, subtle pressure changes on the steering wheel, the quiet rhythm of someone driving with his whole body instead of just his hands. Every few seconds his eyes touched a mirror, then the road again. Center mirror. Side mirror. Horizon. He drove like he was trying to disappear.

In the back seat one of the girls shifted. The vinyl squeaked softly under her weight and the sound lifted three heads at once. Every movement carried weight now.

"¿Falta mucho?" she asked.

"Un poco," Hector answered without turning. "Unas horas."

The name drifted through my mind as we drove. Quemado. Burned. It fits the land out here. The hills looked stripped down to bone, sun-bleached rock and dry grass clinging to soil that never quite softened, the kind of country that made no promises and kept the ones it didn't make.

In the back seat the girls whispered to one another, the sound barely reaching the front. One of them had started a low repetition, the same phrases cycling back on themselves, small and rhythmic.

Casa. Familia. Pronto.

The words passed from one girl to the next, south of Tijuana, carried west through the high desert in a yellow school bus they hadn't yet boarded, toward a border they couldn't yet see. They had been stolen out of their lives and moved north across a country whose language they couldn't speak, every familiar thing stripped away. Now they sat in the back of a borrowed vehicle trying not to cry because crying felt like giving the world permission to notice them.

I kept my eyes forward, letting it steady me the way it was steadying them.

Quemado passed without incident. The town rose out of the open land almost without warning, a small scattering of buildings gathered close to the road as if they had learned long ago that nothing good came from standing too far out in the wind. A faded gas pump leaned beside a sagging awning. Sun-bleached signs clung to the sides of low storefronts. My pulse climbed when a pickup slowed at the intersection as we rolled through town, the driver's head turning slightly as he glanced toward the road. Hector didn't react, his hands loose on the wheel and the Suburban carried through the intersection at the same steady speed. After a moment, the pickup turned down a side street and disappeared.

The town slipped behind us as quietly as it had appeared.

The land began to change as we pushed closer to Reserve. The low desert gave way gradually to higher country where the hills rolled deeper and the ground became greener. Cottonwoods gathered in loose clusters along dry creek beds. Juniper thickened along the ridges. When Hector cracked his window the air that drifted inside carried a faint scent of pine and damp earth hidden beneath the sun-warmed dust.

I twisted slightly in my seat. "Dos horas y media," I said. "Encontramos a los otros. Después, juntos." One of the older girls nodded and repeated the words under her breath to the others, her voice carrying a little more confidence than it had before. The whisper moved through the back rows like a small current, fragile but steady.

Hector's gaze flicked briefly to the rearview mirror. "No vehicles behind us," he said. "But assume they'll adjust faster than we think."

He was right. The people who had taken these girls might not expect us to move west first. But men who lose something valuable rarely stop looking.

Reserve looked like a place the world had forgotten to update. A small cluster of low buildings sat along the highway, paint sun-faded and peeling, signage worn down to dull shapes and ghost lettering. Hector didn't turn toward the ranch on the first pass. He drove straight through town at the same steady speed, his eyes moving through the mirrors and the side streets. We crossed the far edge of town and followed a county road that curved behind a low ridge before looping back toward the highway.

When the ranch came into view it didn't look like safety. It looked like exposure. A stretch of fencing patched together with mismatched wire ran along the property line. A weathered house sat low against the wind. Several sheds and outbuildings stood farther back across the open ground. Hector slowed but didn't turn in. He drove past once, letting the Suburban roll by while his eyes scanned the property. Tire tracks near the drive. Shadows around the outbuildings. No extra vehicles. No strange tracks cutting across the dirt.

On the second pass he turned onto the gravel drive.

The tires crackled loudly over the rock. Hector eased the Suburban halfway up the drive and stopped short of the house. The engine idled, low and steady. No one moved.

The girls felt it immediately. Their breathing shifted behind me, quiet but uneven. One reached out without looking and found the hand of the girl beside her, their fingers locking together as if touch itself could keep them anchored.

The shed door opened slowly.

A tall man stepped into the light, his hat pulled low against the sun. His posture was relaxed but deliberate, the weight of his body settled comfortably over his boots. A rifle hung across his chest, not raised, not decorative. He watched us the way a man watches the sky when the weather starts to change, deciding whether what he sees is passing or moving directly toward him.

Hector cut the engine.

Wind moved through the cottonwoods near the creek bed. Somewhere metal creaked against metal. A dog barked once from somewhere behind the house and then fell quiet, as if even the dog understood that noise carried meaning out here.

Hector stepped out first. His hands stayed visible, his posture neutral as he closed the door and took two slow steps away from the vehicle. I followed and opened the side door for the girls.

"Stay close," I said in Spanish. "Cabeza baja."

They climbed out one at a time, moving carefully across the gravel, their shoulders angled inward toward each other as if the group itself was a kind of shelter.

We were first. Which meant we waited.

The rancher stepped forward from the shadow of the shed. He gave a single economical gesture toward the open doors. "Inside. Out of sight."

There was no urgency in his voice, but there didn't need to be. Hector nodded once and motioned the girls forward. We moved across the open ground and into the dim interior of the shed.

The air inside was cooler and thick with the smell of oil, dust, and old hay. The light filtered through gaps in the boards high along the walls, cutting narrow beams across concrete and packed dirt. And there, parked along the far wall beneath a thin film of dust and filtered light, sat a faded yellow school bus.

The paint had dulled into a tired matte from years of sun. Whatever school district once owned it had been scrubbed away, the lettering sanded down until only faint ghosts remained beneath the yellow. The license plates looked old on purpose, weathered just enough to seem ordinary. The windows had been darkened from the inside so that from a distance the vehicle would look abandoned, something left behind when a route ended and no one bothered to haul it away.

It wasn't abandoned. This was the next piece of Cap's logic made visible. Divide to escape the compound. Strength in numbers from here.

Hector moved to the edge of the shed opening, stopping just inside the line where shadow met sunlight. From that position, he had a clear view down the ranch road without exposing his silhouette. He simply stood there watching, the posture of someone who had spent years learning how to become part of a perimeter rather than stand inside one.

Jimmy wasn't here yet.

"Thirty-two minutes since Cap left," Hector said without turning. "Seventeen since Bobby."

Seventeen minutes was nothing on an open highway. It became an eternity when survival was measured in increments.

Behind me, the older girls had settled onto overturned crates and folded tarps stacked along the shed wall. They sat close together. The younger ones huddled closer still, their eyes moving between the adults and the dim interior of the shed as if they expected the next instruction to arrive without warning.

One of the smallest girls shivered, despite the warmth trapped inside the building. Her fingers twisted into the hem of her shirt so tightly the fabric stretched under her grip. I knelt in front of her and took her hands between mine. They were cold and trembling.

"Estamos juntas," I said. "No te vamos a dejar."

Her eyes searched my face with the raw seriousness only children carry when the world has stopped making sense.

"¿De verdad?" she whispered.

"Sí," I answered, slow and deliberate. "De verdad."

At twenty-three minutes, Hector stiffened.

A thin plume of dust had appeared along the far stretch of dirt track beyond the ridge. "Motorcycle," he said quietly.

Jimmy.

The bike crested the ridge fast, then slowed with deliberate control before the turnoff, the rider easing off the throttle so the dust trail thinned instead of rising. The motorcycle coasted the final stretch toward the ranch, engine cutting off before the sound could echo against the buildings. Jimmy swung off the bike in one smooth motion, helmet already coming free as his eyes moved across the property: tree line, fence posts, the road behind him. He didn't relax until he stepped inside the shed.

"Cap dropped me near the Arizona line," he said. "The bike was waiting. I doubled back twice. Took a dirt track south before cutting east. No tail."

"You sure?" Hector asked.

"Positive."

He rolled the motorcycle deeper into the shadows and covered it with a tarp; his movements tight and efficient. He understood better than any of us what it meant to be flagged somewhere north of here. If law enforcement stumbled onto this group before the story caught up, they would see only the simplest version of events.

At twelve minutes, my mind ran through the failures the road could produce. A routine traffic stop that stretched too long. A deputy following a van simply because the highway was empty. A blown tire on a curve where there was nowhere to pull off safely. Or someone farther up the chain widening the search beyond the normal corridors into the quiet stretches where people believed they were invisible.

At eight minutes, Hector checked his watch. The movement was small, almost careless, but it tightened the air inside the shed anyway. He said nothing. Jimmy said nothing. The girls watched us, their attention moving between our faces and the open doorway. Children learn quickly when adults are measuring something important, even if they don't know what it is.

At five minutes, my pulse had climbed high enough that I could feel it in my throat.

"If they're late," Jimmy said, "we stick to it."

"Yes," Hector replied.

Stick to it. Forty-five minutes, then move. No doubling back. No emotional decisions that could collapse the entire plan.

At three minutes, the wind shifted and carried dust over the ridge.

Hector stiffened slightly. I stepped beside him without thinking, my shoulder nearly touching his as we both looked toward the road. The plume was wider than the trail Jimmy's motorcycle had kicked up. It hung low against the horizon for a few seconds before the shape of a vehicle emerged beneath it. A van crested the rise, moving steadily, without rushing or hesitating. It turned onto the gravel drive.

Bobby.

The van rolled beneath the cottonwoods and slowed into the shade near the shed. The engine idled as the driver's door opened.

Bobby stepped out.

Alive.

Sylvia slid the side door open and began helping the youngest girls out of the van one at a time. They clung to her instinctively, their small hands gripping her sleeves as they stepped down. She crouched to their height before guiding them forward, speaking softly in Spanish and brushing their hair back from their faces. All the while she counted. Not aloud. Just a quick glance at each child before sending her forward.

The girls crossed the gravel and slipped into the shadows of the shed, where the others waited.

Forty-four minutes. One minute to spare.

Beside me, Hector released a slow breath through his nose. Not relief exactly, just the sound of tension settling back into control.

The rancher stepped forward, his eyes sweeping the tree line, then the narrow county road before he spoke. "You load now. You move as one."

The rancher handed Hector a folded county atlas, margins marked in pencil and grease. "Water, diesel, dry goods, trauma kits. All loaded. You stay small. Roads that don't show up in travel apps. More than two cars in ten miles, you adjust."

Hector unfolded the atlas on the nearest crate and ran his finger along a series of thin gray lines that curved west instead of cutting straight. "We keep moving through ranch land. No straight shots. No predictable arcs."

"Exactly," the rancher replied. "You don't look like you're fleeing. You look like you're just wandering."

Jimmy stood just outside the shed, binoculars raised, scanning ridge lines and fence breaks. "Clear," he said after a moment. "No movement on the north ridge. No dust trail behind."

"Good," the rancher answered. "Because once you're on that bus, you're committed to being visible."

Sylvia moved through the bus with quiet authority, guiding the younger girls toward the middle rows where they'd feel less exposed. She crouched to eye level with the smallest ones, pressing water bottles into small hands, speaking the kind of Spanish that didn't require fluency to understand because the tone carried everything. The older girls were more watchful. Marisol had counted them before boarding, the same practiced scan she had given the bunker door that morning, and the counting reassured the others the way it was meant to.

Bobby climbed the bus steps and checked the emergency exit, the latch on the back door, the spacing between seats. He didn't speak much. His silence carried its own weight.

Hector settled into the driver's seat and adjusted the mirrors wide, giving himself angles on the road behind and the approach from either side. He ran through the gauges with a mechanic's precision, glanced once at the atlas, folded it, and slid it beside him. "West," he said.

The rancher approached the bus door one last time and handed Sylvia a canvas bag. "Protein bars. Electrolytes. Sugar if the little ones crash." He looked at Hector. "You don't stop unless you have to. If you see the same vehicle twice in places it shouldn't be, you turn. Not fast. Not sudden. Just gone."

Hector nodded once.

"And if someone follows?" Sylvia asked, her voice calm but sharpened.

The rancher didn't hesitate. "You make them work for it. You don't show them fear."

Jimmy lowered the binoculars and rolled his shoulders once. "Cap dropped me clean. No tail from the line. If anyone's recalculating, they're behind."

Behind wasn't gone.

The bus door folded shut with a metallic hiss, sealing us into the smell of diesel and warmed vinyl. The engine's vibration traveled up through the floor and into my bones. It was louder than the van, harder to hide, but it held us all.

Hector eased the bus out of the shed and onto the gravel drive, tires crunching before catching packed dirt. The rancher stood back with his arms folded, watching until we cleared the tree line. He gave a single nod as we passed the gate.

We rolled west.

Not toward cities. Not toward interchanges. Toward open country that swallowed vehicles whole if you knew where to aim. The road narrowed to two lanes without markings, fenced pasture on one side, low brush and distant mesas on the other. The sky felt enormous above us, pale blue and indifferent. Heat shimmered across the asphalt ahead.

Inside the bus the girls leaned with the sway of the road. Nina sat pressed against the window with her knees drawn up, her fingers laced through the hand of the girl beside her, her eyes tracking the open country as it moved past the glass, watching the desert the way you watch something that has held you and has not yet decided to let go. The older ones whispered to the younger ones, translating fear into smaller pieces. Sylvia moved down the aisle, counting without counting. Bobby remained near the rear, one hand braced against a seatback, scanning through tinted glass. Jimmy sat forward enough to watch the mirrors from Hector's blind angle, binoculars resting against his thigh, ready.

Hector drove with steady restraint, never pushing the engine harder than necessary. He let faster vehicles pass when they appeared, which was rare. He didn't accelerate into open stretches. He didn't brake hard when curves tightened.

Blend. Not flee.

We had slipped free of Cap's land. Now we were committed to the long arc west, toward a border city where an associate waited, toward a crossing that would not be obvious, toward families who didn't know yet that their daughters were alive and moving closer with every mile the bus swallowed beneath its worn yellow frame.

Chapter Three
Across the Line of Heat

The state line came and went without ceremony. Arizona opened flat and wide around us, scrub stretching in brittle waves beneath a sky that felt too large to belong to anyone. The bus rattled in a low, steady rhythm, diesel humming through the floorboards, seeping into our bones. Consistent, if nothing else, and consistency was its own kind of camouflage.

Hector drove first. He handled the bus the way he handled everything else, no wasted motion, no unnecessary acceleration, no dramatic corrections. His hands rested lightly on the wheel, but nothing about him was relaxed. He checked mirrors without appearing to check them, measured distance between vehicles, allowed faster traffic to pass without contest. The bus looked exactly like what it was meant to look like: sun-bleached, dull, forgettable.

Bobby moved through the aisle slowly; one hand braced against a seatback as the road dipped and climbed. He checked on the girls, adjusting a blanket, tightening a seatbelt, handing out water, and moving on. He never drifted far from the center of them. There was tension in the way he moved, not obvious on its own but carried through every motion, contained because it had nowhere to go.

Sylvia sat near the youngest, her voice low and steady in Spanish, translating the sway of the bus into something harmless. Every bump became normal. Every shift in engine tone became nothing to fear.

Jimmy rode further back, binoculars resting against his thigh, his eyes cutting between horizon and mirrors. He was quieter than usual. The jaw said the rest.

By late afternoon the heat had thickened, pressing against the windows in waves. The interior carried the smell of warmed vinyl and dust, cut occasionally by the citrus wipes Sylvia kept passing back to sticky hands. The older girls whispered softly in Spanish, the rhythm of it steadying. The youngest leaned into shoulders and laps, exhaustion finally outweighing adrenaline.

I took the front seat on the door side, close enough to watch the mirrors and the road without crowding Hector at the wheel.

"You good?" I asked quietly.

"Define good," he replied without looking at me.

"No consistent vehicles?"

"Nothing that repeats. Two trucks passed twice. Different plates. Different drivers." He adjusted the rearview mirror slightly. "We are not interesting."

"That's the goal."

"Yes," he said softly.

I leaned back and let my eyes rest briefly, not to sleep, just to steady the constant hum of vigilance. When I opened them again Sylvia had slipped into the seat beside me.

"You figured out what you needed," she said quietly.

"I had to."

She let that sit.

"And now?"

That was the part that mattered.

I looked past her toward the aisle, toward where Bobby had paused a few rows back, one hand braced against a seat as the bus shifted.

"Now I know I can stand on my own," I said. "So, if I stand next to him, it's because I choose to."

Sylvia watched me carefully, not the words but the way they landed.

"He's still going to try standing in front of you."

"I know."

"And?"

The answer sat there for a second before I let it settle into something I could actually stand behind.

"I'm not disappearing again to stop him from doing it."

Sylvia's gaze held mine a second longer, measuring.

"Good," she said.

Bobby didn't move, but I felt the shift in him anyway.

"I can hear you," he said quietly.

Neither of us apologized.

We rotated drivers east of Kingman. The stop was brief and unremarkable, fuel and restrooms, the bus sitting at the far edge of the lot away from the pumps while Hector paid inside without lingering. To anyone glancing over, we were nothing worth remembering. When we pulled back onto the highway Bobby took the wheel. Hector moved into the seat directly behind him. I stayed in the front seat on the door side, and the three of us settled into the quiet arrangement of people who understood what the front of the bus was for.

Bobby drove differently. Not recklessly, but instinctively. He read the road in a way that didn't rely entirely on what he could see, adjusting speed when something felt off before it had time to show itself. His hands held the wheel a little tighter than Hector's had. Not enough to draw attention. Enough that I noticed.

For several miles no one spoke.

"I didn't leave because of you," I said.

The words came out steady, but they didn't feel that way.

His shoulders shifted, just slightly.

"I know," he said.

Too fast. Like he needed to get there before I did.

I watched the back of his neck, the tension sitting there with nowhere to go.

"I left because I was afraid of what staying might do," I said.

The engine hummed under us. The road stretched out, flat and exposed.

"I was afraid of him," I said. "Of what he might do if I stayed close to anything that mattered to me."

My throat tightened. I kept going.

"And afraid of me."

He went very still.

"I didn't know where he ended and I started anymore," I said. "Not by the end."

The words hung there longer than I wanted them to.

"I was angry all the time," I said. "Not just at him. At everything. At things that didn't deserve it." My jaw tightened. "At you."

I forced myself not to look away.

"If I had stayed," I said, "I would have put that on you. I would have made you carry it." My voice dropped. "And you would have let me."

That landed.

"I was afraid I'd pull you under with me," I said. "Or that I'd disappear anyway, just slower, and you'd have to watch it happen. I didn't know which version of myself would show up when things got hard. I couldn't let you be the one who found out."

That was as close as I had ever come to saying it out loud.

"I didn't leave to get away from you," I said. "I left so you wouldn't get pulled into it with me."

Silence settled in, thick and uneven.

"I thought you didn't trust me," he said.

There was no control left in that. Just something that had been sitting there too long.

"I didn't trust what I was living in," I said. "And I didn't trust what it was turning me into."

His hands tightened on the wheel. This time he didn't hide it.

"I would have followed you," he said.

"I know."

"And I would have gotten caught in it anyway."

"Yes."

His jaw flexed, harder now.

"I would have taken it from you," he said.

My chest pulled tight. "I know you would have."

"And I wouldn't have let it go."

"I know."

The words came out quieter. Heavier.

His breath shifted, just slightly. Not enough for anyone else. Enough for me.

Hector's hand came forward and rested once on Bobby's shoulder. Not a grip. Just contact. Then it was gone, and Hector was looking out the window like nothing had happened.

Bobby's hands loosened on the wheel. Not completely. Enough.

"You both would have survived," Hector said evenly.

"You don't know that," Bobby said.

His voice wasn't steady now.

"Yes," Hector replied. "I do."

There was no argument in it.

Bobby gave a small nod, but he didn't answer.

Sylvia had moved forward by then, settling into the passenger seat.

"You didn't have to come," she said quietly.

"Yes, I did."

"For Cap?"

"No."

"For me?"

He didn't answer right away. His eyes stayed on the road ahead, the desert running flat and open on either side, the kind of country that made you choose your words carefully because there was nothing else to fill the space if you got it wrong.

"For the girls," he said first.

Then, after a beat, quieter, "And because I don't leave you in something like this."

That one stayed. She let it.

"You're breaking rules," she said.

"Yes."

"Bobby." Her voice was quiet but direct. "For what?"

He didn't hesitate.

"For what matters."

The bus rattled over a rough stretch of pavement, the sound carrying through the frame and into the silence that followed.

Jimmy shifted from somewhere further back. "You all do this every road trip?" he muttered under his breath.

"Better now than at the border," Sylvia replied.

He didn't argue with that.

As we crossed into California the light changed first. The sky deepened into amber, mountains cutting sharp silhouettes against the horizon. Traffic thickened gradually, more vehicles, more unpredictability. The anonymity of open desert gave way to layered movement and the particular tension of being visible in a way the highway hadn't required.

Hector leaned forward slightly. "They're moving," he said quietly. "Act like it."

"They'll watch their corridors," Bobby replied.

"Yes. But desperation narrows thinking."

Jimmy's voice came from further back. "Still nothing."

"Good," Hector said. "It stays that way."

The girls had grown quieter. Some slept. Some watched the lights multiply in the distance, unfamiliar and overwhelming. Sylvia moved down the aisle, counting without counting, her hand resting briefly on each shoulder as she passed. The gesture was so practiced by now that it had become automatic, the way a person checks a lock they've already checked, not from doubt but from the need to confirm that the thing they're protecting is still there.

The lights of San Diego spread wide against the darkening sky as we came down out of the mountains. I stood midway down the aisle, bracing one hand against a seatback and watched them multiply. Somewhere ahead a contact waited. A quiet exchange. A crossing that wouldn't show up on paperwork. Behind us the people who had lost these girls were still recalculating.

Bobby glanced back at me through the mirror.

I nodded once.

The tension didn't ease as the lights grew closer.

It sharpened.

Chapter Four
Tidal Lines

San Diego did not feel like safety. It felt like exposure layered over noise.

The air shifted first: salt, diesel, seaweed rotting in the pilings, metal and machinery that never shut down. Traffic thickened as we pushed south, brake lights stacking into red rivers that pulsed, stalled, and surged again without warning. The bus felt too large now, too noticeable, too full of everything we could not afford to lose.

No one spoke for the last mile.

Bobby drove. Hector stood braced near the front, one hand gripping the metal pole behind the driver's seat, watching mirrors instead of the skyline. Jimmy sat just behind them, posture loose but eyes alert, scanning for the one vehicle that didn't belong. Sylvia and I moved through the aisle, checking faces without counting out loud.

Fifteen. Still fifteen.

The dock Cap had arranged sat south of the main commercial piers, tucked into a working stretch of waterfront that survived on routine. Forklifts beeped. Gulls screamed. Men in reflective vests smoked near loading ramps and didn't look twice at passing vehicles. Ordinary was camouflage.

Bobby didn't pull in immediately. He passed once, then circled a neighboring block lined with low warehouses and faded signage. Hector never stopped scanning. Jimmy watched cross streets like he expected headlights to hesitate and turn. Nothing lingered. On the second approach Bobby eased the bus into the lot.

The dockhand stood near a stack of shipping containers, collar up against the wind, hands in his pockets. Late fifties, maybe early sixties. Sun-creased skin. Thick forearms. The posture of a man who had spent decades lifting things heavier than conversation. His eyes tracked the bus before his head moved. He didn't wave. He waited.

Bobby cut the engine.

The girls shifted in their seats, sensing change before understanding it. One of the older ones reached for the hand beside her and held on tight. Hector stepped off first, movements controlled and unhurried. Jimmy followed, glancing once toward the street before turning his attention to the dockhand. Bobby came down last, closing the bus door softly behind him. Sylvia and I remained inside long enough to steady the girls.

"Otro vehículo," Sylvia said quietly, moving through the aisle. "El mismo de antes. Tranquilas."

I crouched near the youngest. "Juntas," I said. "Nadie habla. Seguimos juntas."

They didn't answer. They didn't need to. Their hands found each other in the dark.

Outside, the dockhand approached. "You can't take that bus across," he said evenly.

"We didn't plan to," Bobby replied.

The man nodded once, as if that confirmed something already decided. "Two vans. Landscaping company. Real plates. Real work orders. They cross twice a week. Nobody thinks twice about men who look like they're headed to sweat."

"How many?" Hector asked.

"Seven and eight," the dockhand answered. "Tools in the back. Tarps. You tuck the girls low. Keep it boring."

We stepped aside to confer without making it look like a conference.

Hector spoke first. "I'll drive one."

"I'll drive the other," Bobby said immediately.

Jimmy shrugged lightly. "I ride with whoever wants the extra pair of eyes."

"With me," Hector replied.

The dockhand gestured toward the vans parked along the fence. White. Dust-streaked. Logos for a real landscaping company stenciled on the sides. Racks on top. Tools visible through rear windows.

"We ride in back," Sylvia said. It wasn't dramatic. It was practical.

"With the girls," I added. "Both vans."

Bobby's jaw tightened slightly. "You don't need to be under tarp."

"Yes," Sylvia said quietly. "We do."

Hector watched the exchange. "If they open the rear doors," he said evenly, "they see women first. Not men."

"And we're going south," Jimmy said.

"Exactly," the dockhand confirmed. "Nobody cares what you're taking into Mexico."

We split the girls carefully. Eight in Hector's van. Seven in Bobby's. The older girls went with Hector, old enough to follow whispered instructions instantly. Marisol climbed in last and positioned herself at the interior end of the row, her back against the panel, where she could see all of them. She didn't need to be told. The youngest rode in Bobby's van, where Sylvia's voice could anchor them if fear spiked. Jimmy climbed into the passenger seat of Hector's van.

The dockhand opened the rear doors of Hector's van first. The smell of cut grass and gasoline wafted out from the tools stacked along the side panels. Tarps were folded neatly along the floor. Coolers wedged into corners. We loaded in layers. Water bottles first. Then blankets. Then girls, two at a time. They climbed in without being told twice, tucking themselves low along the interior wall. Sylvia moved among them in Bobby's van, adjusting positions, making sure no small foot stuck out past a tarp edge. I did the same in Hector's van.

"Stay close," I whispered. "Heads down if someone knocks."

One of the older girls looked up at me. "¿Y si nos separan?"

"No," I said firmly. "We are not separating."

When all fifteen were settled, eight under the tarp in Hector's van with me crouched near the door, seven in Bobby's van with Sylvia seated among them, the dockhand handed paperwork to both drivers.

"Regroup at the last light before the contractor lane," he said quietly. "Four minutes apart. You roll in together. Look annoyed. Look tired. Don't overperform."

"What if they flag one?" Jimmy asked.

"Then the other keeps moving," the dockhand said. "Because hesitation draws attention."

Bobby didn't like that. I saw it in the way his shoulders tightened before he slid into the driver's seat. But he didn't argue. He trusted the plan, or at least he trusted that arguing now would cost more than it gained.

Hector closed his door and started the engine. I pulled the tarp higher, settling into the narrow space between two girls. The van interior was warm and smelled faintly of fertilizer and rubber matting. I could hear Jimmy adjusting his seatbelt in front, and I could feel Hector's steady rhythm through the steering column.

Across the lot, Sylvia did the same in Bobby's van, her back against the interior panel, one arm wrapped loosely around the smallest girl. She met my eyes through the open rear doors for one second before Bobby shut them.

The dockhand stepped back and folded his arms. "Four minutes."

Hector's van rolled first. The gate opened. We pulled into San Diego traffic like we belonged there.

I felt the shift immediately, the way urban flow replaced open roads. Engines idling. Motorcycles slipping between lanes. Sirens far enough away to be unrelated but close enough to spike adrenaline. In front, Jimmy's voice drifted back low and controlled. "The left lanes clean. No follow yet."

Hector didn't answer. He didn't need to.

Under the tarp, one of the girls' hands found mine in the dark. I squeezed back once.

Four minutes behind us, Bobby's van would be moving. Ahead, the border lights glowed artificial and unforgiving against the darkening sky. We would regroup before the contractor gate. Then we would cross.

Together.

Chapter Five
The Line

The border did not announce itself so much as gather. Traffic thickened by degrees, lanes tightening into concrete channels, brake lights bleeding into one another beneath the glare of floodlights humming awake against the darkening sky. Steel barriers waited in silent readiness. Cameras perched overhead. Nothing about it felt chaotic. It felt measured. Controlled. Designed to compress movement into scrutiny.

Hector kept the van in the contractor lane, hands loose on the wheel, posture relaxed in a way that was entirely deliberate. Jimmy leaned back in the passenger seat, elbow resting near the open window, paperwork visible on the dash as though this were just another end-of-day return from a job site. Every movement in the cab was calibrated to look ordinary.

Under the tarp, the air felt thinner.

The girls were silent, not because they weren't afraid, but because fear had compacted into something disciplined. Their shoulders pressed together in the dark, breaths shallow and synchronized. I could feel the tremor running through them the way you feel vibration through metal before you hear the sound.

"Respiren despacio," I whispered. "Slow breathing. Lento. Como antes."

I shifted slightly, bracing myself against the interior panel as the van crept forward another few feet.

Ahead of us a white pickup was redirected to secondary inspection. Cones slid into place behind it with mechanical precision. A dog circled the truck slowly while its handler watched without expression. Hector did not look at it. He let the van idle.

Four minutes behind us, Bobby's van would be in the same funnel of light. The thought settled under my ribs like a second pulse.

The booth came into sharper focus. A uniformed officer stepped forward, scanning windshield, plates, driver, passenger in one fluid sweep. Another officer stood several yards back, arms crossed, gaze drifting lazily across the line as though boredom were its own tactic.

Hector rolled down the window before being asked. "Evening," the officer said.

"Evening," Hector replied easily, his tone steady and familiar. "Landscape contract. Rancho del Sol." He handed over the paperwork without hesitation. The officer glanced at it, then at Jimmy.

"Tools in the back?"

"Yes, sir," Jimmy answered. "Mulch and edging tomorrow. Early start."

The officer's eyes lingered a half-second too long on Jimmy's forearm, where the scar from earlier in the week had not entirely faded. My pulse kicked once, hard. Under the tarp, one of the girls' fingers dug into my sleeve.

"Anyone else in the vehicle?" the officer asked.

"Just us," Hector replied.

The officer stepped back and tapped the rear panel twice with his knuckles. The sound echoed through the metal like a gunshot.

Inside the dark, everything froze. The tarp did not move. No one inhaled.

Bootsteps circled toward the back of the van. I could hear them clearly, the slow scuff of rubber soles on asphalt. The officer tried the handle once.

Jimmy shifted slightly in his seat, enough to look unconcerned. "You want us to open it?" he asked, casual, almost bored.

The question hung between them.

Hector didn't speak. He waited.

The officer studied the company logo again. The dust along the lower panels. The ladder rack. The clipboard wedged between the seat and console.

He stepped back from the rear doors. "No," he said finally. "Keep moving."

Hector did not accelerate abruptly. He let the van roll forward at the same steady pace it had maintained in line. No surge. No visible relief. We passed the final barrier. The last camera. The floodlights. The pavement dipped slightly and the signage shifted from English to Spanish.

México.

Not safety. Not yet. But movement.

"Estamos cruzando," I whispered. We are crossing.

The girls' fingers tightened around one another.

Ahead, the road widened into the layered noise of Tijuana traffic, vendors weaving between lanes, music drifting from open windows, headlights cutting sharp angles through dusk. Hector drove two more blocks before turning onto a dim side street as arranged.

We waited. Then the second white van rounded the corner.

Bobby.

He did not honk. Did not wave. He pulled in behind us and cut the engine. Neither vehicle moved. Then Hector stepped out. Bobby did the same. They met between the vans, close enough to confirm what mattered without dramatics.

Jimmy scanned the street again. No one lingered. No one slowed.

Sylvia opened the rear of Bobby's van first. The youngest girls blinked against the change in air but stayed close together. They did not scatter. I pushed the tarp aside in our van and helped the older girls sit up one at a time. Marisol was the last one up. She looked at me for a long moment before she nodded once, the same nod she had given the bunker door that first morning.

"Ya está," I told them softly. It's done.

Bobby climbed briefly into our van, eyes scanning faces. "Everyone okay?" he asked.

"We're good," I answered.

He nodded once, jaw tight. Hector closed the rear doors again. "We don't stop long."

"No," Sylvia agreed.

We had crossed. Now we had to disappear.

The vans rolled again, deeper into Tijuana, into streets that swallowed unfamiliar plates and foreign faces without comment.

Somewhere north of the line, someone would realize their shipment had not shifted. It had vanished.

And ahead of us, fifteen families were one long drive closer to being whole.

Chapter Six
The Road Back

The parking lot just south of the border smelled like asphalt, diesel, and frying oil. The vans idled beneath a sagging awning while traffic moved around us in uneven waves. Horns, music, voices layered over each other until they blurred into something constant and pressing. After the stillness of the desert, it felt like stepping into a current that didn't slow down long enough to catch your breath.

No one had followed us across. That didn't mean no one would.

Hector stood between the vehicles, reading traffic without fixing on anything long enough to draw notice. Bobby leaned against the driver's door, watching the world through reflections. Jimmy made a slow pass along the edge of the lot and came back clean.

"No tail from inspection," he said quietly.

"Or they weren't there yet," Sylvia replied.

Neither of those options settled anything.

We folded back into a single van, and the shift was immediate. The tight, compressed silence from before didn't return. The girls sat up now, no longer tucked into themselves, their attention moving outward instead of inward. Voices surfaced in low, overlapping Spanish, tentative at first and then easier, names of streets and places slipping back into their mouths like something remembered rather than relearned.

I sat with Sylvia in the middle row, close enough to feel the change move through them in small, quiet ways: the way one girl leaned just a little closer to the window, the way another turned instinctively toward Marisol's voice. She translated where she needed to, steady and unhurried, keeping them oriented. She didn't have to hold them together the way she had before, but she was still watching.

I recognized that instinct. I didn't think it went away.

The van pulled forward, easing into traffic.

Tijuana pressed close at first: bright storefronts, unfinished walls, painted murals broken by concrete and dust, wires sagging overhead. But it didn't stay that way. Gradually the buildings dropped lower, the noise spread out instead of stacking, and the road opened into something that felt less compressed, even if it wasn't empty.

"They'll look north first," Jimmy said from the back, his voice low.

"They always do," Hector answered.

"And when that stops making sense," Sylvia said, her gaze still on the passing streets, "they'll start asking better questions."

The words settled into the space between us and stayed there.

The girls began pointing things out as we moved deeper into the city, small things, but theirs. A church with a red roof rising above the houses. A market near a water tower painted in peeling blue. A mural stretched across a long concrete wall, the colors faded but still recognizable. Their voices lifted with each one, not loud, not careless, just lighter, as if something inside them was remembering how to move again.

"They'll be safer here," I said, more to myself than anyone else.

Sylvia glanced at me briefly, then back at the road. "They won't be invisible."

No. Not after this.

Bobby adjusted slightly in his seat, not looking at any of us. "We don't all go to every house."

"We split them," Hector said. "Different streets. Engine running."

"I stay with the van," Jimmy added.

It settled into place without discussion, the same way everything else had.

The town came into view gradually, the road narrowing as the houses closed in: faded blues and greens, laundry strung between rooftops, a dog barking somewhere just out of sight. Kids paused mid-game as we passed, their attention following us in a way that felt curious, not suspicious.

We stopped a few blocks short of the first house.

"We walk from here," Sylvia said.

Marisol leaned forward, giving directions in quick, quiet Spanish, her hand lifting once to indicate a turn before dropping again.

The first two girls stepped out and paused on the curb, not moving right away, just taking in the street, the doorway, the distance between where they were and where they needed to go.

I stepped out with them.

A woman stood in front of a small house, sweeping dust into the street. The motion stopped when she looked up. The broom slipped from her hands and hit the ground, and then she was moving, fast and uncontained, the sound she made carrying farther than it should have.

The girls broke toward her at the same time.

They met in the middle of the yard, arms wrapping tight, voices overlapping, names repeated again and again as if saying them made everything real. People came out of nearby houses, from the street, from behind gates, drawn in without being called. The space filled quickly, bodies closing in around them, not crowding, just holding.

I stayed at the edge of it.

Sylvia stepped forward just long enough to speak low and firm. "Protégelas. No las dejen solas."

The woman nodded fiercely, gripping her hands.

We didn't linger.

Back in the van, the air felt different, heavier in a way that wasn't fear and wasn't relief either.

By the second stop, people were already waiting.

A man stood from a chair outside his gate before we fully stopped, removing his hat as his granddaughter reached him and pressing it against his chest while he held her. His eyes lifted once, meeting Bobby's through the windshield, steady and direct.

Acknowledgment.

With each stop, the town changed.

Men appeared at corners. Arms folded. Eyes on the road.

Not watching us. Watching for anything that might follow.

Nina's street was narrow, the houses close together, a low blue gate set slightly back beneath a fig tree. She stepped out slowly and paused, her gaze moving over the gate the same way it had moved over the compound wall, measuring it, deciding.

Then a girl came around the side of the house. Same age. Same hesitation. They stopped a few feet apart, both of them still.

The other girl said something I couldn't hear, and Nina's face shifted in a way that was small but unmistakable. She moved through the gate.

I felt that in my chest before I could stop it. I had stood like that once, at the edge of something that might be safe, not knowing if I was allowed to trust it, not knowing how to step forward without bracing for it to give way.

The gate closed behind her.

We moved on.

Jimmy shifted in the back, subtle but deliberate.

"There's a pickup," he said. "Dark. Slowing."

I didn't turn.

"Local?" Hector asked.

"Maybe," Jimmy said. "Could be nothing."

The truck rolled past us slower than it needed to, the driver's eyes lingering a second too long before moving on.

Jimmy watched it until it disappeared.

"Gone," he said.

No one answered.

Marisol's street came next.

She went still as soon as we turned onto it, but not in the way she had before. This wasn't control. This was recognition so immediate it caught her breath.

A woman stood at the far end of the block, wiping her hands on a towel. She froze when she saw us. Marisol was out of the van before we fully stopped. She didn't run, but she moved straight toward her.

The woman dropped the towel and came down the steps, and they met in the middle of the street, holding on in a way that made everything else fall away.

I didn't look away.

She had held everyone together when there was nothing to hold onto. She had kept them moving when stopping would have meant breaking. This was hers.

By the time we reached the final stop, the light had dropped low, turning everything gold at the edges. The church stood at the center of town, doors open, bells ringing.

The youngest girl hesitated before stepping out, her fingers tightening around the strap of her bag.

"¿Se van?" she asked.

Sylvia crouched slightly, meeting her at eye level. "Sí. Pero ya no estás sola."

The girl nodded, then stepped out into the movement gathering at the church doors.

People spilled out and stopped as they saw what was happening, the realization moving through them quickly, hands lifting, voices breaking, names spoken aloud. The priest stepped forward, listening as Sylvia spoke, then nodded once and turned to the crowd.

"Se organizan." And they would.

As the last girl disappeared into her mother's arms, something in my chest loosened, not gone, not finished, but no longer held as tight.

We climbed back into the van. It felt too large without them.

Bobby pulled us out of town without a word.

In the rearview mirror, people were already gathering in the church courtyard, men standing close together, phones out, voices low and urgent, patterns being remembered.

"They won't be easy prey now," Jimmy said.

"No," Hector answered.

Sylvia watched the town until it disappeared behind us. "They'll try something," she said quietly. "Maybe not here."

Bobby didn't look away from the road. "They'll notice."

Chapter Seven
Paper Trails

We took one room.

The motel sat three blocks off a main drag in Tijuana, close enough to noise to disappear into it and far enough from the tourist corridor that no one asked questions they didn't already know the answer to. The paint on the walls had gone flat with time, a tired cream that held every scuff and corner mark, and the air carried the layered smell of bleach and old air-conditioning that never quite cleared, no matter how long the unit ran. A single window faced the street, the curtains thin enough that passing headlights moved through the room in slow, uneven bands, light and shadow sliding across the floor and up the walls without ever settling.

We locked the door, then checked it again, not because we thought it would fail, but because the act of checking gave us something to do with the awareness that we were no longer moving. The girls were home now, folded back into houses that had held their absence like something unfinished. The quiet that followed didn't land as relief. It settled wrong. Too still. Too open. Without motion, there was nothing between us and whatever came looking.

Stillness lets things find you.

Sylvia sat cross-legged on one of the beds, her notebook open in her lap, the purple cover worn soft at the corners from being handled too often in too little time. She had built it carefully, piece by piece: names, routes, fragments of plates, times that only aligned if you knew how to read them, patterns that didn't look like patterns until you stepped far enough back. It wasn't just notes anymore. It had shape now. It held.

Bobby stood near the window, pulling the curtain aside just enough to see the parking lot without being seen, his body angled so anyone looking in would only catch a shadow if they looked too long. Hector sat in the chair with his boots planted wide, forearms resting on his thighs, still in a way that read as relaxed until you noticed how deliberate it was. Jimmy held the edge of the other bed, quiet, watching without pretending he wasn't taking in everything: the way Bobby kept his sightline narrow, the way Hector listened without moving, the way Sylvia kept her hand on the notebook even when she wasn't writing.

No one settled into the room. No one let themselves.

"They're going to know it was me," Sylvia said.

She didn't sound uncertain. She sounded like she was placing something where it belonged.

Hector didn't hesitate. "They won't know how," he said. "But they'll know where to start."

"They'll retrace the warehouse," Bobby added without turning. "Inventory logs. Staff rotations. Who asked questions. Who stopped showing up when the shipments did."

Sylvia nodded once. "I didn't leave quietly."

"They'll connect the girls," she continued. "Same town. Same church. Same route. It narrows fast once they look at it the right way."

"And whoever was running that segment," Hector said, "is already feeling it."

"Feeling it turns into pressure," Bobby said.

Hector's voice lowered slightly. "Pressure turns into mistakes."

That sat in the room for a moment, not a pause, just something that settled and stayed.

I leaned forward, resting my forearms on my knees. "If they're going to trace it back, then we decide what they find when they get there."

Hector's gaze shifted to me, steady and assessing.

"Right now, they can call it whatever they want," I said. "Internal theft. Interference. Something they can contain. But if this gets out, if there's a record that doesn't disappear, then it stops being something they handle quietly. It becomes something they can't control."

Bobby let the curtain fall and turned toward me. "You want it public."

"Yes."

Jimmy shifted slightly. "That makes everything louder."

"It makes it harder to bury," I said.

"It also makes people move faster," Hector said.

"They're already moving," Sylvia replied. "We're just deciding if we stay ahead of it."

I met her eyes. "I have someone."

That pulled all of them to me.

"A journalist," I said. "Independent. Long-form investigations — cross-border labor, trafficking routes, dock work. She verifies before she publishes."

"Do you trust her?" Bobby asked.

"Yes."

Hector leaned forward slightly. "Then we control how she gets it."

"We don't send anything from here," I said. "We don't call from here. We move first."

"Back across," Bobby said.

I nodded. "San Diego. Clean entry. Clean devices. If it breaks from the U.S. side, it forces attention."

Hector exhaled once. "Attention cuts both ways."

"It always does," I said.

Sylvia closed the notebook halfway, her hand still resting on it. "Then we make sure it says what it needs to say."

No one argued with that.

"So how do we move?" Jimmy asked.

"Not together," Bobby said. "No group. No pattern."

"Small," I added. "Separate enough to disappear."

Jimmy nodded, then looked at Hector. "If something shifts?"

"You cut loose," Bobby said. "No hesitation."

That sat in the room for a second.

Jimmy's jaw tightened once, something settling into place behind it. "I'm not going anywhere," he said.

Hector didn't respond right away. He didn't look at Jimmy. He didn't need to.

Then, quiet enough it almost didn't carry, "Neither am I."

Sylvia looked at him.

Something in the room shifted, something older than this.

"You remember Fenton," she said.

Hector's mouth moved, almost a smile. "You didn't think."

"I didn't hesitate."

"You didn't check the current."

"I knew where I was."

"You thought you did."

The exchange sat between them, and I could see it as they spoke. The river moving faster than it looked from the bank, Sylvia already in the water before anyone else had decided what was happening, Bobby going in after her without stopping, and Hector still on the edge, not frozen, watching the current, where it pulled, where it let go.

"You told me not to fight it," Sylvia said. "If it pulled me under."

Hector didn't answer.

"You said let it take me until it slowed."

Bobby looked up at that, something sharp in his expression. "I wasn't going to let her go under."

Hector's eyes stayed on Sylvia. "You wouldn't have had a choice if she had."

The room didn't tighten so much as deepen.

Sylvia held his gaze for a second longer than she needed, then looked down at the notebook, her hand flattening against the page as if to steady herself.

Hector leaned back again.

No one tried to resolve it.

Bobby exhaled slowly. "Once we're across, we find a vehicle. Something neutral. No names."

"I'll handle it," Hector said.

"Then we call Pops," Sylvia added.

Bobby glanced at her. "You want him in this?"

"Yes."

Hector nodded once. "He should hear it from us."

"And he needs to know what this actually is," Sylvia said. "Not what someone else turns it into."

I looked down at the notebook. "If we give this to my contact, she's going to pull on everything."

"We don't bring the girls back into it," Sylvia said immediately.

"No," I agreed. "We give her enough to follow without putting them back in it."

Jimmy leaned forward slightly. "Once she starts pulling threads, people notice."

"They're already noticing," Hector said.

Sylvia flipped to the middle of the notebook, tracing a line with her finger. "These routes intersect near the docks. Not just one."

"Of course they do," Bobby said.

I met his eyes. "Which is why this doesn't stay small."

Outside, something cracked sharp against the pavement.

All three men went still, not reacting. Listening.

Footsteps moved along the walkway outside, slower than they needed to be, then stopped just past the door. The shadow at the bottom of the frame shifted, held, and then moved on.

Jimmy let out a quiet breath. Bobby's hand rested briefly against the curtain before dropping.

Sylvia closed the notebook. "We need to make sure it says what it needs to say," she said again.

Hector nodded once. "We control what we can."

"And we move before we have to react," Bobby added.

I reached for Sylvia's hand and squeezed it once. "Then we do this right."

Later, after Hector and Jimmy stepped outside to check the perimeter and Sylvia fell asleep sitting up with the notebook still open in her lap, Bobby crossed the room and sat beside me.

He didn't speak right away. He leaned forward, elbows on his knees, his hands hanging loose between them, turning one over and then the other like he was trying to work through something heavy that had been sitting there. It wasn't nervous, not hesitation exactly. It was the kind of stillness that comes when you know the next thing you say is going to change the shape of something, even if you don't know how much.

"I need to say something," he said.

"Okay."

He nodded once, but didn't go on. The silence stretched, as he tried to decide where to start, or maybe how much of it he was willing to let out.

"I heard you," he said finally. "On the bus."

Something in me tightened before I could stop it, not enough to show, not enough to move, just a shift under the surface, the kind that starts in your chest and settles lower, where it stays.

"You and Sylvia," he added. "I wasn't trying to. There wasn't anywhere else to be."

I didn't answer. There wasn't anything to say that didn't turn it into something smaller than it was.

He let that sit, like he knew it mattered, then drew in a breath and let it out slowly.

"I was angry when you left," he said. "Not at you. Not exactly."

A small pause.

"I told myself that," he corrected. "That it wasn't about you."

His thumb pressed once into the side of his hand.

"It was."

He didn't look at me yet.

"I was angry because I was sure," he said. "Not hoping. Not wanting it to work. Sure." His head tipped slightly, a small, almost frustrated movement. "That you'd stay."

His voice dropped, quieter now.

"That I was enough."

The words didn't land cleanly. They settled, heavier than that, pulling something with them.

"I thought that meant I understood you," he went on. "That I knew you well enough to know what you would do." A breath. "It didn't."

He shook his head once.

"It meant I was only seeing what I needed to see."

I stayed still, but something in my chest had already shifted, tightened in a way that felt too familiar, like stepping into a room where you already know how the air is going to feel before you breathe it in.

"I told myself I respected your leaving," he said. "That I understood."

He looked at me then.

"I didn't."

He didn't try to explain it past that. Didn't soften it. Just left it there.

"I thought if I stayed steady enough, you wouldn't need to go," he said. "That if I didn't push, didn't ask, didn't make it harder, you'd stay anyway."

Something in me reacted before I could catch it, small and automatic. My shoulders tightened just slightly, the old instinct to go still, to take up less space, to wait for whatever came next instead of moving first.

He saw it. Not the reason. Not the shape of it. But enough.

"That sounds like respect," he said quietly. "It isn't."

He didn't look away.

"It's still control."

The word hit harder than anything else he'd said, not loud, not sharp, just precise, landing exactly where it wasn't supposed to.

My hand tightened against my leg without meaning to, fingers pressing in once before I forced them still again, but it was already there, the echo of something older, the kind of quiet that wasn't safe, the kind that watched you back.

He noticed that too.

"I didn't see it then," he said. "Or maybe I didn't want to."

That felt closer to the truth than anything else.

"I'm sorry," he added, quieter now. "Not just that you left. That I didn't see what you were leaving."

That caught somewhere deeper than I expected, not clean, not immediate, but real enough that I felt it settle.

He wasn't asking. He wasn't trying to name it. He was leaving space for it.

"You didn't make me leave," I said.

"No," he said. "But I didn't give you a reason to stay that didn't cost you something."

That sat between us, and I didn't push back against it, didn't try to reshape it into something easier.

He reached for my hand then, slower this time, like he was giving me time to pull away if I needed to. When I didn't, his fingers settled around mine, not tight, not claiming, just there, his thumb moving once across my knuckles like he needed the contact to steady what he was saying.

"I love you," he said. No buildup. No softening. Just the words themselves.

"I always have."

He held my gaze, and there was something different in it now, not certainty, not expectation, not the kind of belief that assumes an outcome.

"Not the way I did before. Then, I thought it meant holding on."

A small shift of his hand.

"It doesn't."

He let that sit, and didn't try to fill it.

"I know who you are," he said. "And I'm still here."

That was it.

No promise. No ask.

Just that.

Something in my chest eased, not all at once, not clean, but enough that I felt the difference in the space it left behind.

"I know," I said.

A small breath of something like a laugh left him. "You always say that."

"Because it keeps being true."

He leaned forward then and rested his forehead briefly against my temple, not tentative, not asking, just there long enough for it to register before he pulled back, the contact quiet and deliberate in a way that didn't need to be anything more than what it was. Not a kiss. Not a question. Something steadier than both, something that didn't ask for an answer or try to define itself before it had the chance to settle.

Chapter Eight
North of the Line

We didn't cross together. That was the first rule.

Sylvia and I folded ourselves into the pedestrian current moving north, our shoulders angled forward like everyone else's, our pace unremarkable. The fencing rose high and layered on both sides, steel, concrete. Cameras angled downward like they had already seen every version of fear and boredom a human could produce. The air smelled like exhaust and hot metal. I kept my breathing even. Nothing rushed. Nothing hesitant. Just two women walking back into the United States on an ordinary afternoon.

Bobby and Jimmy crossed ten minutes later. Hector came last, separate from all of us, unhurried and clean, carrying nothing that tied him to the rest of the group if someone decided to start pulling threads.

We regrouped three blocks north in a narrow park wedged between a convenience store and a bus stop. The grass was burned flat from heat. The picnic tables were dented and carved with old initials. A palm tree leaned toward the street like it had grown tired of pretending to offer shade. It was unremarkable. That was the point.

Hector was already there when Sylvia and I arrived. He stood near the sidewalk with his posture loose but alert, his eyes cutting across faces and traffic patterns without lingering long enough to invite attention. When Bobby and Jimmy joined us, Hector handed Bobby a cheap burner phone. "Cash," he said quietly. "No cameras inside."

Bobby nodded once and stepped away before dialing. I watched his shoulders as the line rang.

"Pops."

A pause long enough that I could feel the weight of it from where I stood.

"It's me," he continued. "No, sir. You didn't."

His jaw tightened slightly as he listened. "We're in San Diego." Another pause. "No. We handled it."

"We need to move north. Phoenix."

He turned slightly while he waited, scanning the park, watching the sidewalk traffic like he could physically intercept anything that came too close.

"No," he said after a moment. "Cap didn't tell you?"

Something shifted in his posture at that, less tension, more calculation. "Yeah," he said quietly. "That's what I figured."

He listened another beat, nodded once even though Pops couldn't see him, and said, "We'll be there tonight."

He ended the call without ceremony, crushed the SIM card beneath his heel, and slipped the useless shell of the phone into his pocket.

When he walked back toward us, I met him halfway.

"He didn't know," Bobby said before I could ask.

"About Cap?"

"About any of it." He exhaled once, slow and controlled. "He's not thrilled."

"He'll get over it."

"Maybe." The corner of his mouth moved slightly. "He'll make arrangements in Phoenix. Safe place. No questions on a line."

He looked at me then, not the way he had been looking at everything else for the last two days, calculating exits and angles and threat levels, but actually at me. Like he was checking that I was still the same person who had climbed into that Suburban at Cap's compound.

"You holding, Seashell?" he asked quietly.

"For now."

He nodded, accepting that as the honest answer it was. "The journalist," he said after a moment. "You still want to move on that."

It wasn't a question, but I answered it anyway. "Yes."

Sylvia's notebook was still in my bag. Names. Routes. Dates. Patterns. Not guesses. Records. The kind of thing that didn't stay buried once someone who knew what they were looking at got their hands on it.

"We don't bury this," I said. "We drag it into daylight."

Bobby studied me carefully, the way he always did when he was weighing something he already knew the answer to. "You trust her?" he asked.

"She doesn't print what she can't verify. She protects her sources. She doesn't get bought." I held his gaze. "Yes."

"Then we do it smart," he said. "Through Pops first. We don't go public without protection in place."

"Agreed."

He was quiet for a second, looking at the street rather than me, the way he did when something wanted to come out and he was deciding whether to let it. "I can handle whatever comes," he said finally. "Heat. Confrontation. Whatever they throw. I just can't handle you being in it alone."

"Then don't let me be alone," I said.

He stepped in close and kissed me, firm and deliberate, the kind of kiss that wasn't asking anything, just confirming something that had already been decided. When he pulled back his forehead hovered near mine for a fraction of a second.

"Phoenix," he said softly.

"Phoenix," I agreed.

We rejoined the others.

Sylvia stood a few feet from Hector; arms folded loosely across her chest. She held herself together the way she always did, discipline before feeling, but the edges were thinner than she would admit. The last several days had cost her something she hadn't finished counting yet.

Hector didn't crowd her. He angled slightly in her direction the way he always positioned himself near something he was keeping watch over, present without pressing, close enough to matter.

"You burn the phone?" she asked Bobby when he rejoined us.

"Yeah."

"Was he surprised?"

"Completely."

Something moved across her face, relief and something harder beneath it, the particular exhaustion of someone who has been right about a dangerous thing and finds no satisfaction in it.

Hector saw it. He always saw it.

"You good?" he asked quietly.

"Define good," she said.

His mouth tightened slightly. "Sylvia."

"I'm fine, Hector." The word came out with just enough friction to signal she wasn't entirely. "I'm here. I'm thinking. That's enough for right now."

He looked at her for a long moment, reading what she wasn't saying. She turned and met his eyes. "I'll be better when we're moving again."

He reached out and adjusted the strap of her bag where it had twisted on her shoulder, the gesture automatic, practical, the kind of thing you do for someone without thinking because you've been paying attention to them for years.

"You're not carrying this alone anymore," he said.

Sylvia held his gaze for a moment. Then she nodded once, small and certain, and let that be enough.

Jimmy pushed off the tree and stepped closer, hands in his pockets. "So, Phoenix," he said. "And then what?"

"Then we regroup," Bobby answered. "Lay low. Figure out next steps."

"And we call the journalist," Sylvia added, glancing at me. "Once we're stable."

"After Pops sets the perimeter," Bobby clarified.

Jimmy nodded slowly. "You really think exposure helps?"

"It shifts the field," I said.

Hector's jaw tightened slightly. "Exposure cuts both ways."

"I know."

Bobby looked at Jimmy. "You've got an out in Phoenix."

Jimmy shook his head once. "I'm in."

"You don't have to prove anything," Hector said evenly.

"I'm not," Jimmy replied. "I just don't quit midstream."

Hector held his gaze a moment longer, then nodded. Approval earned.

We left the park separately and converged two blocks later on a side street where the foot traffic was thin enough to talk without being heard. The afternoon sun had flattened the sky into a harsh California blue. It felt too open out here, too much light, not enough cover.

Hector stopped at the corner and scanned the intersection once before turning back. "We move," he said. "Same way we came in. Nothing that reads as a group."

Bobby nodded. "Car rental's three blocks. We don't arrive together."

We split without discussion, the way we had learned to do everything else over the last several days. Sylvia and I took the near side of the street. Bobby and Jimmy crossed and walked the other. Hector went ahead, already half a block up, already invisible in the ordinary movement of the afternoon.

As I walked, I felt it again — that low persistent awareness that someone somewhere might already be recalculating. Phoenix wasn't an ending. It was a staging ground. And when we called the journalist, when those names in Sylvia's notebook began surfacing in print, the traffickers would stop treating this like a missing shipment.

They would treat it like betrayal.

Chapter Nine
The Long Road to Phoenix

The rental office Pops arranged sat two blocks from the park, tucked between a laundromat and a payday loan storefront. The place smelled like old carpet and overworked air conditioning. It wasn't the kind of place that invited questions, which was exactly the point.

Bobby handled the paperwork. The rest of us spread out without discussing it. Hector near the door, Jimmy watching reflections in the window glass, Sylvia beside me against the far wall close enough that our shoulders touched. The clerk had an address in Phoenix and a confirmation number. That was it. No questions. No curiosity.

I couldn't tell if that restraint came from trust or from a calculation I wasn't seeing yet. I let it sit.

All I knew was that we were heading east.

The SUV they handed Bobby was dark gray and completely unremarkable, the kind of vehicle designed to dissolve into traffic and leave nothing behind but distance. Hector walked it once, slow and methodical, checking seams, running his hand beneath the rear bumper, pressing against the spare tire mount. He crouched near the rear wheel well and stayed there a second longer than the rest, like he was listening as much as looking.

"Nothing obvious," he said when he stood.

That didn't mean safe. It meant not careless. There was a difference, and all of us felt it without saying it.

We loaded in with silent coordination. Bobby took the wheel first. Hector settled into the passenger seat. Sylvia and I slid into the middle row. Jimmy folded into the third, his body already angled so he could watch the rear glass without making it obvious. The doors shut one at a time, the sound heavier than

it should have been, each one closing with the sense of
something sealed rather than secured.

We didn't speak until we were merging onto the
freeway.

San Diego flattened behind us in layers giving way to
dry brush and rising hills as the air shifted from salt and diesel
to heat and dust and something metallic from the engine
pushing harder under the climb. I kept watching the side
mirror, tracking the rhythm of traffic as cars accelerated and
fell back, telling myself it was ordinary, that the patterns were
what they always were. Every few minutes something in my
chest disagreed, quiet but persistent.

"Pops didn't know," Bobby said finally, his eyes fixed
on the road ahead.

I watched the landscape widen through the window and
let the words sit without answering. I didn't know what Pops
knew. I didn't know whether Cap had kept him outside it or
whether this was something else entirely, another layer we
hadn't uncovered yet. The uncertainty didn't press. It just stayed
there, waiting.

"He sounded surprised," Bobby went on. "Not angry.
Just… surprised."

"That won't last," Hector said, not looking at him.

Traffic thinned as we climbed out of the coastal basin,
the highway opening into long, exposed lanes beneath a sky
that offered nothing to hide under. Out here there was no noise
to dissolve into, no turn that made you anonymous again. We
were just a gray SUV moving east, and anyone who knew
where to look wouldn't need much more than that.

A silver sedan held three cars back longer than chance
explained. I tracked it for two miles before it peeled off onto an
exit. My shoulders dropped a fraction without my permission.
Beside me, Sylvia's hand was pressed flat against her thigh,
fingers splayed slightly, and I knew she had been watching it
too.

"They'll retrace it," Hector said after a while, voice even. "Loss, routes, manifests."

Sylvia didn't hesitate. "Yes."

"They start inward," Bobby added. "Then widen."

Sylvia leaned her head back against the seat and closed her eyes, not resting, just holding still long enough to think without interruption. "They'll assume it was deliberate."

"It was," I said.

The desert outside stretched wider as we moved, emptier in a way that made everything feel more visible rather than less.

"We follow the money," I said after a stretch of silence.

Bobby shifted slightly in his seat. "Walk me through it."

"Not the girls," I said. "Not first. We don't lead with that." I watched the horizon, the heat rising from the road in wavering lines. "We lead with structure. Shell companies. Contracts. Leases. Freight that doesn't match what's documented. You expose the money and suddenly it's not a missing shipment. It's something bigger. Something people have to respond to."

Hector nodded once. "Federal."

"Yes. You freeze assets. You trigger audits. Banks start asking questions. When banks ask questions, people start making mistakes."

Jimmy shifted in the back seat; eyes still fixed on the road behind us. "People mess up when they're rushed," he said. "We just… pay attention."

I nodded, keeping my eyes on the road ahead.

"We give her the framework first," I said. "Dates. Addresses. Names tied to transfers. Once that holds, she builds out from there."

"And your names stay out of it," Bobby said immediately.

"Yes."

The SUV hummed beneath us, steady and unremarkable, the road stretching forward in long, heat-bent lines. I checked the mirror again. A black pickup had held the same distance for several miles now: not gaining, not falling back, just there, steady in a way that felt like patience.

I didn't say anything yet.

We crossed into Arizona without much to mark it: a sign, a subtle shift in pavement, the air turning sharper, drier, the light hardening as the sun dropped lower. The pickup was still there when I glanced again.

"Hector," I said quietly.

"I see it."

Jimmy adjusted slightly, not turning fully, just enough to keep the truck in view without making it obvious.

Bobby's hands settled more firmly on the wheel. He didn't speed up. Didn't change lanes. Just stayed where we were, letting whatever it was either reveal itself or disappear.

After another mile the pickup moved into the passing lane. It came up alongside us slowly — too slowly — the window dark enough that I couldn't see inside. My pulse climbed.

It held there longer than it needed. Then it accelerated. It moved ahead, shrinking in the windshield before disappearing around a bend in the road.

No one said anything at first.

Jimmy shifted again in the back. "It's all going to feel like that, isn't it?" he said. "Like something's off even when it isn't."

"Everything could be," Hector replied.

The highway stretched on, empty and unyielding.

An hour later Bobby pulled into a rest area carved out of rock and scrub, nearly empty except for a semi idling at the far end, its engine a low constant vibration that carried through the pavement. Wind dragged grit across concrete. A man sat alone at a picnic table eating from a paper bag, not looking at us.

We switched drivers without a word. Bobby stepped out first, scanning the lot in a slow arc before circling the SUV again. Hector moved into the driver's seat. Jimmy exited last and walked a loose perimeter, checking under the vehicle, checking the wheel wells, repeating everything Hector had done earlier.

Sylvia and I stayed inside.

"You're holding a lot," she said quietly.

"So are you."

She didn't argue.

The wind rocked the vehicle once, then eased. She watched the horizon, and I followed her gaze. The man at the table finished eating, folded his bag carefully, then stood and walked to a sedan a few spaces down. When he drove away, the lot felt emptier, not safer.

"I missed you," she said.

"I know. I missed you too."

She was quiet for a moment. "I thought about you every time I used the system. Every time I hid something, every time I wrote something down." A small shift at the corner of her mouth. "I kept thinking you'd find it. You'd know where to look."

"I almost didn't come," I said.

"I know." She glanced at me. "But you did."

The wind shifted again, then settled.

"The seat worked," I said quietly.

"The seat always worked." A beat. "We were very strange children."

"We were very smart children."

She laughed then, quietly.

"I don't regret it," she said when the quiet came back.

"I know."

Hector slid into the driver's seat. Bobby took the passenger side. Jimmy climbed back in. Doors shut. The engine turned over. We pulled back onto the road.

Dusk crept in slowly, turning the sky violet and then charcoal, headlights cutting narrow tunnels through the dark. The desert felt different at night, not emptier, but more aware, the kind of dark that didn't give anything back once it took it in.

Sylvia shifted closer, her voice low. "When we get to Phoenix, you call her."

"Yes."

"You don't soften anything."

"I won't."

She studied my face. "You understand this escalates."

"Yes."

"They'll adjust," she said. "Not right away. But they will."

"Then we stay ahead of it," Bobby said from the front seat.

The lights of Phoenix appeared as a faint glow against the horizon, growing as we descended, the desert giving way to structure again: gas stations, overpasses, traffic thickening around us in slow layers. The anonymity of open land shifted into the different anonymity of a city at night, and I wasn't sure which one offered less cover.

Chapter Ten
When the Storm Breaks

The rental unit in Phoenix didn't feel like refuge; it felt like something temporary lodged against the ribs. The walls were beige and unmarked, the carpet vacuum-lined but already worn thin along the high-traffic paths. The air smelled faintly of industrial cleaner and something stale beneath it, like too many short-term stays stacked on top of each other. Nothing here belonged to us. Nothing held memory.

Which meant everything that happened inside it would.

We were still standing in that unfamiliar living room when the knock came. Not tentative. Not polite. Solid. Controlled.

Pops.

Bobby's shoulders tightened before he moved. Hector's gaze went to the door frame, then to the window, instinctively mapping exits even here. Jimmy shifted his weight. Sylvia stood very still beside me, hands loose at her sides, chin slightly lifted.

Bobby opened the door.

Pops stepped in first, filling the frame. He looked older than he had even a week ago, eyes darker, jaw set hard enough to crack bone. Mama came in right behind him, one hand pressed to her mouth, the other reaching instinctively toward Sylvia before she'd even taken in the rest of the room. Joe followed last, quiet, scanning all of us before closing the door firmly behind him.

For a long second nobody spoke.

Pops' eyes went straight to Sylvia. "What the hell did you do?"

The question wasn't shouted. Worse. It was low and furious, coiled with something deeper than anger, fear building without answers for days.

Mama didn't wait. She crossed the space and pulled Sylvia into her arms. Not a sob at first, just air leaving her lungs all at once. She cupped Sylvia's face, kissed her cheeks, her forehead, her hair, then pulled Bobby in too, then me, her arms trying to gather all of us at once as if we were still small enough to fit.

"You are home," she whispered, even though we weren't. "You are home."

Hector stepped back half a pace without meaning to. Mama saw it. She reached for him too. "Come here," she said, voice thick.

He hesitated, just a flicker, but then let her pull him into the edge of the embrace. Jimmy stood awkwardly to the side until Joe clapped a hand on his shoulder and guided him forward. Mama cried over all of us. Not delicately. Not quietly. She cried like women do when the worst thing they imagined doesn't come true.

Pops didn't move.

"Cap wouldn't answer," he said finally, eyes never leaving Sylvia. "I called him twice. Then he went dark." His jaw flexed. "You want to tell me why?"

Sylvia pulled back from Mama's arms but kept one hand wrapped in hers. "I intercepted a shipment," she said evenly.

The room shifted.

Pops blinked once. "A shipment of what?"

"Girls," she said, quietly.

The word landed heavy and final.

She didn't rush the story. She didn't dramatize it. She told it straight. How she traced the movement pattern. How the same town kept appearing in manifests that didn't list names, just numbers. How she followed it alone. How she found the van. How she saw them, fifteen girls from the same small town south of Tijuana, taken in pieces over weeks. Same church. Same market. Same school.

"I couldn't let them move north," she said quietly. "Not again."

Pops' anger didn't disappear. It shifted shape. "You went alone?"

"Yes."

"You didn't call me."

"No."

"You didn't call Bobby."

"No."

His voice sharpened. "You didn't call anyone."

"I didn't have time," she said. "And I wasn't dragging you into it unless I had to."

"You don't get to decide that," Pops said. This time the anger broke through fully. "You don't get to decide what risk I take for my own family."

"It wasn't about you," Sylvia shot back, fire flickering now. "It was about them."

"Don't you dare," he snapped. "Don't you dare make this about mercy like that erases the fact that you put yourself in the middle of something bigger than this family."

He turned on Bobby. "And you. You went without telling me."

Bobby didn't flinch. "She was already at Cap's."

"So, you followed."

"Yes."

"And you," Pops said, eyes landing on Hector. "You went with them."

Hector met his gaze evenly. "Yes."

"You're supposed to be the one with sense."

"I was," Hector replied quietly. "Once I knew."

Pops' eyes shifted to Jimmy. "And you. You put yourself in the middle of it and fired a weapon in Albuquerque."

Jimmy straightened but didn't look away. "They shot first."

"That doesn't matter to a prosecutor."

Silence pressed in.

Joe stepped forward slightly, voice measured. "Let them finish."

Pops exhaled hard through his nose but didn't interrupt again.

Sylvia told him about Cap. About burning everything. About the bunker. About splitting vehicles. About the bus. About crossing west. About walking those fifteen girls back into the same dusty plaza they'd been taken from. Mama listened with her hand over her heart.

"They ran to their mothers," I said softly when Sylvia's voice caught for the first time. "All of them. Same town. Same street corners. They didn't even wait for us to leave before they were pulling doors open."

Mama's breath hitched.

"They're safer now," I continued. "Because they're together. Because family will close ranks. Because whoever took them won't expect them to be returned."

Joe nodded slowly. "Not expect mercy," he murmured.

Pops stared at the floor for a long moment. Then he looked up. "You just burned someone's money," he said quietly.

"Yes," Sylvia answered.

"And you didn't just burn inventory," he continued. "You burned a supply chain."

Joe's eyes sharpened. "Follow the money."

I stepped in then. "It wasn't random," I said. "The ledger she built shows a pattern. Small towns. Repeated pulls. Same transport corridor. Same holding sites. It's layered — shell companies, trucking routes, small cash infusions that look like agriculture payments. They're laundering through produce contracts and independent haulers."

Joe's attention locked onto me. "Do you have proof?"

"Enough to map," I said. "Not enough to indict yet. But enough to follow."

Pops' anger came back fast. "You stole fifteen girls from a pipeline that runs on profit," he said. "Do you have any idea how many people that touches?"

"Yes," Sylvia said quietly. "I do."

"You didn't just poke a warehouse," Pops continued. "You embarrassed someone upstream." The room went still. "And they will know it was you."

Sylvia didn't look away. "Yes."

The truth of that hung between us.

Mama's hand tightened around Sylvia's.

"They will come," Pops said. Not a threat. A fact.

"Maybe," Hector replied calmly. "But they'll have to work."

Pops' eyes flicked to him. "You broke formation."

"Yes."

"And you," he added, looking at Bobby. "You shut me out."

Bobby held his gaze. "Yes."

"Why."

"Because you would have tried to run it," Bobby said. "And it wasn't yours to run."

The silence that followed was a different kind than what had come before. Pops' jaw tightened but he didn't argue. Because Bobby wasn't wrong and both of them knew it.

Pops' eyes shifted to Jimmy. "You are a liability," he said bluntly.

"I know," Jimmy replied.

"And you stayed anyway."

"Yes."

A beat. "Then you stay under my roof until we decide what to do about it."

Jimmy swallowed once. "Yes, sir."

Joe stepped in fully. "They brought them home," he said quietly.

That landed.

Mama moved then, wiping her face, stepping back just enough to see all of us at once. Her eyes lingered on Bobby and me, just a fraction longer than necessary: on the way my hand had found his without either of us noticing, on how his body angled subtly toward mine even in confrontation. Then her gaze shifted to Sylvia and Hector. Hector wasn't touching her. He never would in front of Pops. But his attention was anchored there in a way that had weight. Protective. Not possessive. Present. Mama saw it. She had always seen the things that mattered before anyone else named them. She said nothing.

The confrontation didn't end so much as exhaust itself, the anger burning down to something harder and more permanent. Pops looked at Sylvia one last time.

"You don't move like that without telling me," he said quietly. "Not again."

Sylvia met his gaze. "No."

It wasn't surrender. It was acknowledgment. And in the silence that followed, something in the room recalibrated without ceremony.

Pops turned and walked toward the kitchen with Joe. Bobby and Sylvia drifted after them. Mama took Jimmy by the arm and guided him toward the small table near the window, already asking about food in the way she asked about everything that mattered.

The room emptied by degrees until only Hector and I remained near the far wall.

"I owe you something," he said finally.

"Not just for the kitchen," he said. "I already said what needed to be said about that." His jaw worked once. "For longer than that."

I didn't help him. He hadn't made it easy for me for years. I wasn't going to make it easy for him now.

"I was there," he said. "At the hospital." He looked at the wall rather than me, which was the most honest thing I had ever seen him do. "I stood in that hallway for three hours. Bobby couldn't sit down. Couldn't stop moving."

The kitchen sounds drifted through, Mama's voice low and steady, the scrape of a chair, Sylvia's brief tired laugh at something Pops said.

"I went with Bobby to the apartment to pack your things," he continued. "I carried boxes. I peeled those photographs off your mirror one at a time and put them in a bag because Bobby couldn't do it without losing it completely." His voice stayed level but something beneath it had weight. "I folded your mother's sweater."

"After you left," he said, "I spent about six months making sure Bobby didn't do something stupid. Just kept him moving. Making sure he ate. Making sure he showed up to class. Making sure he didn't drive out to wherever he thought you might have gone." He paused.

"I knew about the drinking," he said. "Both of them. I knew what that house was long before any of it came to a head. I'd known for years." He paused. "I watched you come to Pops' house when you were a kid. Watched you sit at that table and eat like you hadn't eaten all day. Watched Mama put food in front of you and not say a word about it because saying something would have made you feel ashamed." His jaw tightened. "I knew all of it."

"Then why?" I asked. He looked at me then.

He was quiet for a moment, and I could see him choosing whether to answer honestly or deflect. Hector had spent his whole life choosing deflection. This time he didn't.

"My father killed my mother when I was six," he said. "Then he killed himself. I was in kindergarten. Joe came and got me. That was it." He said it the way you say something you have repeated to yourself so many times it has stopped feeling like a story and started feeling like weather. Just a fact of the atmosphere you grew up inside. "Joe gave me a roof and work. He wasn't cruel." He paused. "But he wasn't family."

The kitchen sounds continued. Bobby's voice now, low and even, answering something Pops said.

"I watched the Calderons for years," he said. "The way Mama called everyone mija. The way Pops made room at that table without making anything of it. The way Bobby and Sylvia just accepted people without discussion or conditions." Something tightened around his eyes. "It looked easy for them. Natural."

"And then you showed up," he said. "A kid from a bad house with a worse father. And within a week you had a chair at that table. Within a month Mama was braiding your hair." He stopped. "Within a year you were more theirs than I had ever managed to be in all the time I'd known them."

"I was there first," he said quietly. "And it never looked like that for me."

The words landed in the space between us and stayed.

"So, I made it your fault," he said. "I told myself you were soft. That you were a liability. That Bobby was making a mistake." His jaw worked. "I told myself you didn't deserve what they were giving you because it was easier than admitting I wanted it and didn't know how to ask for it." He paused. "I'd never known how to ask for it."

"I knew what you came from," he said. "I knew exactly what that house was. And I still stood in the hallway that day when you were fourteen and told you it wasn't a shelter. Like you were a problem instead of a kid." He stopped. "That wasn't tactics. That wasn't protecting Bobby. That was me being cruel to someone who hadn't done anything except need a place to land." His voice stayed flat but something beneath it had gone tight. "And I knew it when I said it."

I didn't speak. He wasn't finished.

"After the hospital," he said, "I told myself I had done enough. That folding your things and keeping Bobby steady squared the account." The corner of his mouth moved, not quite a smile, not quite anything. "It didn't."

"I told myself it was because you were a liability," he continued. "Too visible. Too emotional." He paused. "That was easier than admitting I didn't know what to do with someone who had been through what you'd been through and still came out the way you did."

I held his gaze. "And now?"

"Now I've watched you cross a border under a tarp with eight terrified girls in the dark," he said. "I've watched you hold them steady when your own hands were shaking. I've watched you come back to people you left behind and not ask them to make it easy for you." Something shifted in his expression, not softness exactly, but the absence of the guard he usually kept in place. "I was wrong about you."

"You weren't entirely wrong," I said. "I was a liability sometimes."

"Maybe," he said. "But that wasn't why."

We stood in the quiet for a moment.

"What I did after you left," he said carefully. "I don't want your thanks. That's not why I'm saying it. But I need you to know it wasn't just duty. They all needed to pay for what they did to you." He paused then, looking directly at me. "And to our family."

I understood what he meant without him having to finish it. He had decided I belonged to the family long before I came back to claim it. He had stood in that hallway for three hours. He had folded my mother's sweater and put it in a bag so Bobby wouldn't have to. He had spent six months keeping Bobby moving so he didn't drive into the dark looking for someone who wasn't coming back. None of that had been duty.

It had been the only way he knew how to be family.

"I know," I said quietly.

He nodded once.

Not closure. Not absolution. Just two people who had spent years circling the same damage from opposite directions, finally standing still long enough to acknowledge it.

Then he turned and walked toward the kitchen, and I stood there alone for a moment in the quiet of the emptied room before I followed.

Chapter Eleven
The Countermove

Nobody slept much.

By morning, the rental unit had settled into the stillness of a place where people had been awake for too long in too small a space. Coffee cups lined the counter. The blinds were still closed. The air conditioner rattled every time it kicked on, as if resenting the demand.

Pops had been up before anyone else. He stood near the kitchen counter when I came out of the small back room, shoulders squared, jaw set, but the volcanic fury of the night before had burned down into something colder and more deliberate. Joe sat at the dining table with a legal pad in front of him, pen in hand, already working. Mama had made eggs that nobody had finished eating.

"Sit down," Pops said when he saw me. Not unkind. Just done with waiting.

The others filtered in over the next few minutes. Bobby came in from the back room with his hair still damp, running on whatever sleep he'd managed. Sylvia came last, moving carefully, the way you move when your body is exhausted but your mind won't stop. Hector was already at the far wall. Jimmy sat at the table across from Joe.

Pops looked at Sylvia. "Walk me through it," he said. "All of it. From the beginning."

"I didn't stumble onto it," she said. "I followed a pattern."

Joe shifted slightly. "What pattern?"

"Duplicate freight manifests," she replied. "Agricultural shipments, produce, livestock feed, machinery parts. Same carrier numbers. Same weight class. Same route identifiers. But the invoices were processed twice."

"Mistake?" Jimmy asked.

Sylvia shook her head. "Not at that scale."

She leaned forward, forearms on her knees, her voice steady in a way that made my chest tighten. "It was always clean numbers. Three hundred thousand. Four hundred thousand. No odd cents. No variation. Always routed through holding accounts in Arizona first, then consolidated into accounts in Nevada and Texas. Shell LLCs registered under different names but tied to the same filing agent."

Joe's expression shifted in recognition. "How much?" he asked.

"Three point eight million in six months."

Pops' hands tightened on the counter.

"Not street money," Joe muttered. "Not drug money."

"No," she said. "Structured. Predictable. Routed like legitimate commerce."

Pops' hands tightened further. "And you decided to follow it."

"Yes."

"How."

She didn't hesitate. "I tracked the carrier switch outside Gallup. The driver thought he was meeting a secondary freight transfer. Instead, he met me."

Joe's head snapped up slightly. "You were armed?"

"Yes."

"Backup?"

"No."

Hector's jaw moved, but he didn't interrupt.

"I redirected the truck," Sylvia continued. "Cap had a horse trailer staged. We moved the girls before the next scheduled checkpoint."

Joe leaned forward. "They will recalculate," he said quietly. "Because three point eight million in predictable revenue doesn't vanish. It flags. It triggers review. Someone upstream is already asking where the loss is."

"They'll assume misallocation first," he said. "Internal theft. Logistics error. Corrupt handler."

"And when they rule that out?" Jimmy asked quietly.

"They escalate," Joe replied.

Hector finally spoke. "They already have," he said. "They were at the compound before we got there."

Pops turned sharply. "They were at Cap's?"

"Black SUVs," Hector confirmed. "Positioned. Not parked."

Pops looked at Bobby. "And you still moved west without telling me."

"There wasn't time," Bobby said. "Movement keeps people alive."

Pops' eyes settled on Jimmy. "You're already flagged. You discharged a weapon in Albuquerque. You made yourself visible."

"Yes, sir."

Hector's voice cut in, low and controlled. "He held position under fire," he said. "He didn't fold."

Pops turned back to the room.

"So, we don't wait," I said flatly.

They all looked at me.

"We don't sit here and let them recalculate in the dark," I said. "We take it public."

Pops' eyes narrowed. "Excuse me."

"A journalist," I said. "Someone who follows money. We give her the ledger, the routes, the shell companies. We expose the financial architecture before they can bury it."

"You want to go to the press," Pops said flatly.

"Yes."

"With information that ties back to this family."

"With information that ties back to a trafficking network," I said. "The family connection disappears into the background once the scale of it becomes visible."

"It doesn't disappear," Pops said. "It will get examined."

"Everything gets examined," I said. "The question is whether we control when and how."

Joe held up a hand before Pops could respond. "Walk me through the logic," he said. His voice was measured, neither approving nor dismissing. He wanted to hear it out.

"Right now, they're looking for a single point of failure," I said. "One person. One disruption. They find Sylvia, they find us, and it ends quietly. No one outside this room ever knows what happened to those girls or where the money was going." I looked at Pops. "But if this becomes public, if the financial structure is exposed, it stops being a private dispute and becomes a liability they can't manage. Federal attention. Asset freezes. Audits. Journalists pulling threads they can't unravel."

Joe's eyes moved to Pops.

Pops was quiet for a long moment. "You paint a target on Sylvia," he said.

"Sylvia is already a target," I replied. "This changes what kind."

"How," Pops demanded.

"Right now, she's a loose end," I said. "Someone they want to silence. If this goes public, she becomes a source. A whistleblower. Silencing her after the story runs makes them look guilty of everything the story alleges."

Joe leaned back slowly. "She becomes expensive to touch," he said.

"Yes."

"And if they move before the story runs?" Bobby asked.

"Then they confirm everything," I said.

Pops stared at the floor. The air conditioner rattled once and settled.

"Who?" he asked finally.

"A journalist named Lena Torres," I said. "Investigative desk, national syndicate. She follows money trails, offshore holdings, and laundering fronts. She built her reputation on cases like this."

"You trust her," Pops said. Not a question.

"Yes."

"Why."

"Because she's careful," I said. "She doesn't print what she can't verify. She protects her sources. She doesn't get bought and she doesn't get scared." I paused. "We met three years ago at a rodeo in Wyoming. She was chasing a story about cattle subsidies masking land acquisitions. I gave her photographs that confirmed a paper trail she'd been building for months. She could have burned me to get ahead. She didn't."

Joe and Pops exchanged a look that lasted less than a second but carried a full conversation inside it.

Pops studied me carefully. "You've changed," he said.

"Yes."

"You're not asking for permission."

"No."

Something passed between us then, not forgiveness or approval, but recognition. He held my gaze a moment longer, then nodded once. "Fine," he said. "We move to the next step."

"And that is?" Jimmy asked.

Joe answered. "We follow the money." He looked at me. "Make your call."

I stepped toward the sliding glass door, angling my body slightly away from the room, and pulled out my phone. I scrolled through my contacts and dialed.

She answered on the third ring. "If this is about another bull rider breaking his collarbone, I'm busy," she said.

"It's not," I replied.

A pause. Not long. Just enough. "Michelle?"

"Yes."

"You don't call unless it's something."

"It is."

"I need secure," I said.

"You always need secure," she replied dryly. Then her tone shifted. "How bad?"

"Multi-state. Structured transfers. Shells. Likely international."

Another pause. "Human?" she asked.

"Yes."

She didn't react emotionally. That was why she was good.

"Talk to me."

"Not over open lines," I said. "I can give you this: freight carriers routing through Arizona. Consolidation accounts in Nevada and Texas. Clean numbers. Predictable schedule. One loss event."

"Loss event?"

"Shipment diverted."

She inhaled slowly. "Diverted by who."

"Doesn't matter," I said. "What matters is they're missing revenue. That means they're looking."

"And you're connected."

"Yes."

"How deep are you in it?"

I didn't answer that directly. "I have the ledger," I said. "Full notebook. Codes broken. Dates, carriers, account references."

Now she was silent for real. "Send nothing electronically," she said finally. "Not yet."

"I won't."

"Where are you?"

"Phoenix."

"You stay put. I need to confirm something before I move."

"What."

"If this is what I think it is, you didn't just trip over a trafficking ring," she said. "You stepped on an operation, not a ring. An operation."

I glanced back into the room. Pops watched me. Joe listened without appearing to. Hector had not shifted. Sylvia sat forward, hands clasped, eyes sharp.

"That's what I'm afraid of," I said.

"Michelle," Lena continued, her voice lower now, more focused, "once I start pulling on this thread, they'll know someone is looking."

"They already know someone is looking."

"Not at the federal level," she replied.

There it was. The threshold.

"You send me a summary," she said. "Handwritten. Photograph of the page. No files. No attachments. I'll cross-reference corporate filings quietly first. If this is what it smells like, I will escalate."

"And if it's bigger?" I asked.

"It's always bigger," she said. "The question is whether you want it bigger now or later."

"I want it now," I said.

"Then don't disappear," she replied. "And don't get dead before I call you back."

She hung up.

When I turned back to the room, Pops was watching me.

"She's in," I said.

Joe nodded once. "She'll trace the shell structures first," I continued. "Quietly. Corporate registries. Filing agents. Bank consolidations. If she finds overlap, she escalates to federal."

"And once federal's in?" Jimmy asked.

"They don't protect us," Joe said before I could answer. "They protect jurisdiction."

Sylvia looked at me. "She won't sensationalize it."

"No."

Hector shifted his weight for the first time in several minutes. "And when the story runs," he said quietly, "they will know who cost them money."

"They already know that," Sylvia replied. The words didn't carry heat, just fact.

Mama stood, crossing the room slowly. She stopped in front of Sylvia first, cupped her face in both hands, and pulled her close. The hug was not soft. It was desperate. Protective.

She cried openly, over Sylvia, over Bobby, over Hector, over Jimmy, over me. Over the fact that they had crossed lines that could not be uncrossed. When she stepped back, her eyes moved between us.

"I see things," she said quietly.

No one asked what she meant. But I felt it anyway.

Bobby's hand found the small of my back, not claiming, not possessive, anchoring. He didn't look at me when he did it. He didn't need to. Across the room, Hector stood near Sylvia but not touching her. His body angled slightly toward her without his permission. When she shifted in her seat, he adjusted his stance without looking like he was doing it.

Mama saw that, too. She said nothing.

Sylvia drifted to where I was standing, close enough that our arms touched. She wasn't looking at me. She was watching Hector across the room, the way she watched him when she thought no one was paying attention. Steady, certain, the kind of looking that had been going on for so long it had become part of how she moved through a room.

"You know why the cat is his," she said.

It wasn't a question.

"I know he found it," I said. "I never knew the rest."

She was quiet for a moment. Outside the air conditioner rattled once and went still.

"It was raining," she said. "One of those heavy spring rains. The acequia was running fast and the shed at Grandma's was flooding." Her voice stayed level, the way it did when something mattered. "I heard something from the doorway. I looked in and Hector was on his knees in the water."

She paused.

"He had a kitten tucked inside his jacket. Just his hand curved around it, keeping it against his chest. His face." She stopped. "He didn't know I was there. He looked…" She stopped again, searching for the word but not quite finding one that fit. "Like himself," she said finally. "The version of himself he never lets anyone see."

The sounds from the kitchen drifted through. Bobby's voice. Joe's low response. The scrape of a chair.

"He carried it inside and put it by Grandma's stove and never said a word about it," Sylvia continued. "Never told anyone. Never made anything of it." The corner of her mouth moved slightly. "Grandma fed it for twelve years."

I didn't speak.

"That was the day," she said.

She didn't say which day. She didn't need to. I had known for years — in the way she tracked him across rooms, in how her attention shifted when his name came up, in the careful distance she kept, as if closeness was the thing she was most afraid of wanting.

Now she had said it out loud.

Hector looked up from across the room then, just briefly, the way people do when they feel the weight of attention. His eyes found Sylvia's for one second before moving away. She didn't look away first.

"Okay," I said.

She nodded once. That was enough.

Joe turned to Sylvia. "Walk me through the ledger," he said. "Every pattern. Every account. Every carrier."

Sylvia nodded and moved toward the table. Hector stepped closer without being asked, close enough that his shoulder almost brushed hers. She did not move away. Bobby remained at my side.

For the first time since Phoenix, we were not reacting. We were building something.

Chapter Twelve
The Work

Lena's instructions were simple. Handwritten summary. Photograph of each page. No files. No attachments. She would call back when she had confirmed what she needed to confirm from her end.

She did not say how long that would take.

Joe heard the instructions when I relayed them and nodded once like they were the only sensible approach. He was already pulling the legal pad toward him. "Sylvia," he said. "Sit down."

Sylvia sat. Jimmy pulled his chair around to the other side of the table without being asked, already reaching for a pen. Joe glanced at him once, then handed him a second legal pad without comment. Jimmy uncapped the pen and waited.

That was enough. Joe nodded and turned back to Sylvia. "Start from the beginning," he said. "Every number. Every name. Every carrier."

Mama put coffee in front of both of them without being asked and then returned to the kitchen, where she began doing what she always did when the world was threatening to come apart. She cooked. Within twenty minutes, the rental smelled like green chile and eggs and something sweet on the back burner that nobody had asked for but everyone would eat. The smell of it moved through the beige rooms, reminding us of home.

Pops stood near the window with his coffee. He had positioned himself there after the briefing and he hadn't moved much since. With one hand on the curtain edge, his eyes tracking the parking lot and the street beyond it in slow methodical sweeps. The anger from the night before hadn't gone anywhere. It had just stopped having anywhere useful to direct itself. He watched the street the way a man watches a horizon where weather is building: not panicking, not relaxing, just keeping eyes on what he couldn't control and waiting for it to show him what it intended.

Bobby came in from the back room with his boots already on. Hector was behind him, jacket in hand.

"Grocery run," Bobby said.

Mama turned immediately. "Tortillas," she said. "The thick ones. And cilantro. And…" She was already moving toward her purse.

"I've got it," Bobby said, interrupting her before she got there.

"You don't know what to buy."

"Then write it down."

She wrote it down on the back of an envelope. Bobby folded it without reading it, slipping it into his shirt pocket. Hector was already at the door. Bobby looked at me before he went. Not asking anything, just checking.

"Go," I said.

He nodded once and they left.

The room settled into a different rhythm without them. Quieter and more concentrated.

Sylvia opened her notebook to the first coded page and set it in front of Joe. She didn't explain the system from the top. She had already walked him through the structure in the morning briefing. Instead, she picked up exactly where that conversation had left off, pointing to a column of symbols in the left margin.

"These are carrier identifiers," she said. "Three digits, then a letter. The letter corresponds to a route segment, not a company name. Each segment has a fixed transit window; I mapped those against the invoice processing dates." She turned the page slightly so Joe could see the full column. "When the invoice processes outside the transit window, that's a flag. When it processes outside the window and the declared weight doesn't match the carrier class, that's a pattern."

Joe studied both columns carefully. "You built this from the invoice logs alone?"

"Invoice logs, carrier manifests, and the accounts payable ledger," Sylvia said. "I had legitimate access to all three. Nobody thought to restrict them because nobody thought an accountant would know what to do with the freight data."

"But you did."

"Freight billing runs through accounts payable," she said simply. "You can't do the job without understanding what you're paying for."

Joe's expression shifted with the attention of someone recalibrating what they're working with. He looked at the page again with different eyes.

"Walk me through the account structure," he said.

Sylvia turned to a later section of the notebook. "Three tiers," she said. "The first tier is the operating accounts, legitimate freight revenue, genuine clients, and real cargo. That operation is actually profitable. It gave them infrastructure and cover." She moved her finger to the next set of entries. "The second tier is the holding accounts. Arizona registered, all of them. Ninety-day lifespan on average before dissolution and re-establishment under an adjacent LLC with a different name but the same filing agent and the same registered address." She looked up at Joe. "That's the first place most people would stop. The churn looks like a tax strategy."

"But you didn't stop," Joe said.

"Because the transfer timing was wrong," Sylvia said. "Legitimate tax-motivated account cycling follows a calendar pattern. End of quarter. End of year. These transfers were irregular. They clustered around specific dates that didn't correspond to any financial calendar I recognized." She paused. "Until I mapped them against the missing persons reports."

The room went quiet.

Jimmy's pen had stilled without him realizing it.

"The transfer spikes preceded the reports by seventy-two to ninety-six hours," Sylvia said. Her voice stayed steady. Professional. The voice of someone who had already spent weeks living inside the horror of what she'd found and had learned to hold it at the distance required to keep working. "Pre-payment. The money moved before the transport. Which means the accounts weren't processing proceeds. They were processing orders."

Joe sat back slowly.

"Third tier," Sylvia continued, "is where it consolidates. Nevada and Texas. These accounts have longer lifespans, eighteen months to two years. They're blended with legitimate agricultural disbursements, commodity payments, and produce contracts. The amounts are large enough to absorb the trafficking revenue without flagging standard monitoring thresholds." She closed the notebook carefully. "That's the architecture."

Joe was quiet for a moment. "You built all of this by yourself."

"I'm an accountant," Sylvia said, quietly. "This is what I do."

It wasn't pride in her voice. It was the particular gravity of someone who understood that her professional training had led her somewhere it never prepared her to go.

Joe looked at Jimmy. "You follow all of that?"

"Most of it," Jimmy said honestly.

"Then start with the carrier identifiers and the transit window discrepancies," Joe said. "One line per flag. Date, carrier code, declared weight, actual weight class, invoice processing date, transit window variance. Leave a column for the account reference."

Jimmy picked up his pen and began.

It was careful, quiet work. Sylvia moved Joe through the notation system section by section, answering his questions with the precision of someone who had built the system to be auditable, not just legible, but defensible. Joe asked questions the way he did everything, direct and specific, never the same question twice. Jimmy wrote steadily, his handwriting neater than I expected, the kind of neatness that comes from someone who learned early that sloppiness has consequences.

I sat across from them with my phone ready and photographed each completed section as Joe finished reviewing it. Sylvia checked each image before I moved to the next, her eyes as precise on the photographs as they had been on the original pages. We developed a rhythm without discussing it. Sylvia translated, Joe verified, Jimmy transcribed, I photographed.

Pops watched from the window.

At some point Mama set a plate of eggs and tortillas at the edge of the table without interrupting the work. Jimmy ate while he wrote. Joe picked up a tortilla and continued talking to Sylvia without acknowledging the food at all, which was the highest compliment he could have paid it.

An hour passed, then another.

The ledger had more layers than the first read had suggested. What had looked like a disciplined double-billing scheme opened into something more architecturally sophisticated the further Joe followed it. The account cycling wasn't random; it followed a rotation pattern designed to stay below automatic monitoring thresholds at each individual institution while moving significant cumulative volume across the network. The agricultural disbursement blending wasn't crude, it was calibrated, the trafficking revenue absorbed into commodity payment streams at ratios that would look unremarkable to a standard audit.

"Whoever designed this understood banking compliance," Joe said at one point, sitting back.

"Yes," Sylvia said.

"Not street level."

"No," she said. "This was built by someone who understood how compliance monitoring works and designed around it deliberately. The ninety-day account cycling, the threshold calibration, the agricultural blending, those aren't improvisations. That's a system." She paused. "Which means somewhere above the freight operation, there's a financial architect."

Joe tapped the page. "Someone with institutional knowledge."

"Or someone who bought it," Sylvia said.

Joe was quiet for a moment. Then: "The SAR that was filed and never acted on."

"Yes," Sylvia said. "That bothered me too."

Jimmy looked up briefly. "Did someone bury it?"

"Or someone with access to the reporting system flagged it as low priority before it could escalate," Sylvia said. "I can't prove that from the ledger. But the timing is wrong for it to have been missed accidentally."

The room held that.

Pops turned from the window at that. He looked at his daughter for a long moment. Her controlled posture, the pen moving over the page, the particular expression she wore when she was doing something she had decided was worth doing regardless of cost. Something moved in his face that wasn't anger and wasn't pride exactly but existed somewhere in the territory between them.

He crossed to the table and pulled out a chair.

He didn't sit at the working end. He sat at the corner, adjacent but not in the middle of it, close enough to follow but not inserting himself. Joe glanced at him, then back at the page without comment. Sylvia looked up once, registered his presence, and returned to the notebook.

Pops sat there quietly for a long time.

Bobby and Hector came back around noon. The grocery bags made it onto the counter and Mama was already sorting through them before the door had finished closing. Bobby scanned the room when he came in and understood without asking. He got himself coffee and leaned against the counter near the window. Hector set two bags down and then moved to the far wall and resumed the position he had held all morning as if he had never left it. His eyes made a circuit of the room and settled.

The work continued.

By early afternoon Joe had three legal pad pages of clean, organized documentation. Carrier identifiers mapped to routes. Account numbers with corresponding dates and transfer amounts. The transit window discrepancies laid out in a column that made the pattern undeniable. The account cycling rotation charted against the monitoring thresholds it was designed to avoid. Sylvia's notation system decoded line by line, the shorthand rendered into plain language that a financial investigator, or a federal prosecutor, could follow without needing to understand how a twenty-eight-year-old accountant had taught herself to read a criminal operation from the inside.

Jimmy flexed his writing hand once and picked his pen back up.

"Last section," Sylvia said.

I photographed each of the three legal pad pages twice, from two angles, making sure every number was legible. Sylvia checked each image with the same precision she had applied all day. Joe reviewed the final page one more time, running his finger down the columns, then set his pen down.

"That's enough to follow," he said.

Not enough to convict. Enough to follow. Lena had said the same thing.

I put together the message to Lena. No text. Just images, one after another, the legal pad pages in sequence. I sent them through the secure channel she had specified and then set the phone face up on the table.

We waited.

Mama put lunch on the table. Real food, the kind that required plates and forks and sitting down: rice and beans and the green chile she had been tending all morning, warm tortillas in a cloth-lined bowl. Nobody said anything ceremonial about it. We just sat down and ate, all of us around the table, the legal pad pages stacked neatly to one side, the phone face up beside them.

Jimmy had three helpings.

Pops ate in silence but he ate, which was its own signal. When he finished, he set his fork down and looked at Sylvia across the table. She met his eyes.

"You should have called me," he said.

"I know," she said.

"Before it got that far."

"I know, Pop."

He was quiet for a moment. "I would have helped you."

Sylvia's jaw tightened slightly. "I know that too."

The admission cost him something and she knew it and they both let it settle without making more of it than it was.

Bobby reached under the table and found my hand without looking.

My phone lit up at 2:47 in the afternoon.

Lena.

I picked up before the second ring. "Tell me."

"I've got three of the LLCs confirmed," she said. She was moving fast; her voice carried the focus of someone who had been working without stopping. "Same filing agent. Different registered agents, but the formation dates cluster within a six-week window two years ago." A brief pause. "The freight broker at the center of your carrier map has a civil judgment in Arizona from four years ago. Cargo fraud. Small case, settled quietly." Another pause. "He's also listed as a silent partner in two of the agricultural disbursement accounts. Which means he's not a contractor. He's a participant."

"So, the money trail holds," I said.

"The money trail goes further than I expected," she said, and something in her voice became tighter, more focused. "I cross-referenced the Nevada consolidation accounts against public political contribution records." A pause. "Three of them show up as pass-through sources for PAC contributions to a sitting state senator in Arizona. The contributions themselves are legal since the amounts are below reporting thresholds. But the routing is the same pattern your accountant documented. Clean numbers. Irregular timing. Agricultural cover."

The room was very quiet.

"Someone in elected office is connected to this," I said.

"I can't say that yet," Lena said. "What I can say is that money from accounts connected to this network has flowed into political infrastructure. Whether that's knowing participation or whether someone's PAC was used as a laundry point without their knowledge. That takes more reporting to establish." A beat. "But it explains the SAR."

"The one that was filed and never acted on," I said.

"Filed six months ago by a compliance officer at a regional bank in Tucson," Lena said. "The officer was transferred to a different branch three weeks later. The report sat in a queue without escalation." Her voice was level. "That's not a bureaucratic delay. That's management."

I looked at Pops across the table. He was watching me with the expression he reserved for decisions that couldn't be taken back.

"How high does it go?" I asked.

"I don't know yet," Lena said. "High enough that someone felt comfortable burying a federal compliance report. High enough that the financial architecture was designed by someone who understood institutional monitoring from the inside." A pause. "Michelle, I need you to understand what this means. When I publish, I'm not just exposing a trafficking network. I'm putting documented evidence of political money connections into the public record. That changes the nature of what comes back at the people connected to this."

"I understand," I said.

"Your source," Lena said. "The accountant. She built this from inside a legitimate operation, using access she was authorized to have, documenting what she found through her own professional analysis. That's a whistleblower by any legal definition." A pause. "I'm going to need her to be characterized that way in the piece. It protects her and it protects the story."

I looked at Sylvia. She was watching me. She already knew.

"She'll agree to that," I said.

"Then I need forty-eight hours to finish building the structure," Lena said. "I won't publish without giving you a window to get clear."

"How will I know when?"

"I'll send you two words," she said. "Just two. You'll know what they mean."

"What are they?"

She told me.

I closed my eyes for a second.

They were the two words Sylvia had put at the top of the first page of her notebook, the day she started keeping it. The two words she had written before she understood exactly what she was looking at, when she still thought it might be a clerical error worth reporting.

Tell someone.

"She sent me a photograph of that page," Lena said. "Separately from the others." A pause. "She wanted me to understand why it started."

I looked at Sylvia across the table. She looked back at me, clear eyed.

"Forty-eight hours," I said.

"Forty-eight hours," Lena confirmed. "Be careful."

She hung up.

I set the phone down on the table and looked at the room.

"She's building," I said. "Forty-eight hours." I looked at Sylvia. "She's going to characterize you as a whistleblower. Formally. In the piece."

Sylvia held my gaze for a moment. Then she nodded once.

"The money connects to political contributions," I continued. "PAC routing. A state senator in Arizona." I looked at Pops. "And the SAR was buried. Someone with access to the compliance system managed the escalation."

Joe set his legal pad down carefully. "That's not a regional operation," he said.

"No," I said. "It's not."

Pops exhaled slowly. Bobby's hand tightened around mine and then released.

"Then we wait," Hector said.

Mama stood and began clearing plates. The ordinary motion of it filled the silence: the scrape of ceramic, the soft sound of water in the sink, the rhythm of someone who has spent a lifetime keeping a household steady while difficult things happened inside it.

Jimmy stacked the legal pad pages carefully and handed them to Joe.

Outside, Phoenix continued in the afternoon heat, indifferent and bright.

Somewhere in the next forty-eight hours a story would move from Lena's desk into the world, and nothing after that would be exactly the same as what had come before.

We didn't talk about that. We just let Mama feed us, stayed where we were, waited for the two words that would tell us it was time.

Chapter Thirteen
When the Story Breaks

The article goes live at 6:12 a.m.

I know the exact minute because I'm already awake, sitting at the small kitchen table in the Phoenix rental with the laptop open and the blinds cracked just enough to let in the flat gray-blue wash of desert morning. The air conditioner hums unevenly in the wall. Every sound feels sharper than it should. The coffee in front of me has gone cold. I haven't taken a sip.

Pops stands at the sink with his back to me, his coffee untouched beside him. I don't know if he slept at all. He hasn't spoken since I sat down. Neither have I. The kitchen holds us both in the particular silence of people who are waiting for the same thing without saying so.

When Lena's email comes through my pulse hits once, hard.

Subject: Tell Someone.

No commentary. No reassurance.

I open it.

The headline is restrained, deliberately so. No dramatic language. No accusations that could be challenged. Just structure laid bare in clean, documented lines. Shell companies threaded through Arizona and California. Freight brokers whose routes don't match declared cargo. Account transfers that spike in the days before clusters of missing-persons reports. A pattern of inventory moving north in increments too small to draw attention until someone overlays the money.

At the center of it all, referenced carefully but unmistakably, is a shipment that vanished.

Not stolen. Not seized. Vanished.

I don't call out right away. I read the first two sections twice, feeling how the story tightens around the numbers rather than the narrative. Lena didn't speculate. She traced. She followed wire transfers through holding accounts, layered through construction firms and agricultural suppliers that never filed the right tax forms. She quoted a former customs analyst about cargo masking and staggered transport. She cited federal review of financial irregularities within private logistics networks.

Months of quiet investigation, exposed all at once.

Pops turns from the sink. He has been watching me in the window's reflection.

"It's up," I say.

He crosses to the table and looks at the screen. He doesn't read the article like the others will. He scans it like he reads everything that matters, looking for the shape of the damage before the details.

"Wake them," he says.

I push back from the table. "Bobby," I call toward the back rooms.

He appears in the hallway doorway within seconds, already dressed, like he has been lying on top of the covers rather than under them. Hector comes right behind him, moving with the quiet economy of someone who was already awake and waiting for a reason to step forward. Joe emerges from the small side room with his legal pad already in hand, reading glasses pushed up on his forehead. Jimmy comes slower, blinking, but the moment he sees our faces, whatever sleep he managed drains out of him. Sylvia steps in last. She doesn't ask what happened. She just looks at me, and I turn the laptop so they can see.

Mama comes from the bedroom doorway, her robe pulled tight, her eyes going immediately to Sylvia's face before settling on the screen.

We gather around the table, shoulders almost touching. The rental feels smaller with all of us leaning in over the same screen.

Sylvia reads in silence, her eyes moving steadily down the page. Bobby's jaw tightens the further he goes. Hector doesn't shift at all, but I see the slight narrowing of his eyes when the article reaches the section on layered banking transfers and third-tier accounts. Joe reads faster than anyone else in the room, his finger moving along the text, not pointing but tracking, the habit of a man who has spent years following numbers through systems designed to obscure them. He reaches the bottom before the rest of us and straightens slowly.

Pops doesn't read it. He watches our faces instead, taking his information from our reactions like he always has.

"That's going to hurt," Sylvia says quietly.

"Yes," Bobby answers, just as quietly. "It will."

I scroll further, and at the bottom of the article, a single line tightens something deep in my chest.

Federal authorities confirm that a multi-agency task force has been reviewing related financial activity for months.

Months.

"They were already building a case," Jimmy says.

"Yes," I reply. "We just forced it into daylight."

Joe sets his legal pad on the table. "They'll move on the Arizona accounts first," he says. "Those were the thinnest structures. Easiest to freeze without a full evidentiary package."

Pops' eyes cut to him. "How long before they work up the chain?"

"Days," Joe says. "Maybe less if the Treasury is already coordinating."

The phone in my hand vibrates.

Unknown number.

The room goes silent instantly. No one tells me to answer. No one tells me not to.

I step away from the table before I pick up. "Yeah."

Lena's voice is tighter than it was two days ago, moving faster now that the dam has broken. "It's moving."

"How?"

"Yuma. Mesa. One warehouse outside Tucson. They hit them before seven. Treasury froze three accounts before the story even finished syndicating."

Behind me I hear Bobby exhale slowly.

"That's not reaction," Lena continues. "That's coordination. They were waiting for something to trigger public justification."

I look at the screen again, at the clean lines of numbers that now feel less abstract and more explosive. "How high does it go?" I ask.

"Not high enough yet," she says. "But someone upstream is scrambling. We're seeing wire reversals and emergency withdrawals. They're trying to pull liquidity out before it locks."

Money. Always the money.

"Michelle," she says more quietly, "if your source was right, they're cornered."

"I know."

"You safe?"

"For now."

I end the call and turn back to the table. "They've hit three sites already," I say.

Joe nods once, unsurprised. "Pre-positioned," he says.

Pops' jaw tightens. "Which means federal wasn't just waiting for justification," he says. "They were waiting for cover."

Bobby's phone buzzes against the counter.

Cap.

Bobby answers and moves toward the sliding glass door. This time he opens it.

"The vehicles pulled off my fence line about twenty minutes after the story syndicated," Cap says. Not relief in his voice. Assessment. "They didn't leave because they gave up. They left because the story made them visible."

"They'll regroup," Bobby says.

"Yes. But not here. Not today." A pause. "You stirred something bigger than a warehouse, son. Federal presence changes the calculation. They'll consolidate before they move."

"And you?"

"I'm fine. I'm always fine." The faint suggestion of something dry in his voice. "You just make sure yours are."

He ends the call.

Bobby closes the sliding door. "Cap's clear for now," he says. "Vehicles pulled back after the story broke."

Joe nods once. "They didn't want to be photographed near a federal story."

"No," Bobby agrees.

Joe's phone buzzes on the table.

He picks it up without excusing himself, reads the screen once, and steps away from the table to answer. His voice stays low. "Yes." A pause. "How many?" Another pause, longer. "Understood."

He ends the call and stands for a moment with his back to the room before turning.

"Three more facilities cleared overnight," he says. "Not raided. Emptied. Personnel pulled. Records burned. Someone high up moved before sunrise."

Jimmy swallows. "They're cleaning house."

"They're cleaning liabilities," Joe replies.

The air in the rental shifts. Not panic. Pressure. A sense of something large recalibrating out of sight.

Sylvia folds her arms tightly across her chest. "They'll assume internal betrayal first."

"Yes."

"Or Cap."

"Yes."

"Or Pops," she adds quietly.

Mama's head lifts sharply at that. Pops doesn't turn from the window. His silence is its own answer.

Joe speaks carefully. "If they trace it to the family, it comes through Sylvia first. Which means Sylvia needs to be positioned as a whistleblower before they can frame her as a conspirator."

"The article does that," I say.

"The article suggests it," Joe replies. "Federal corroboration makes it fact."

Pops turns from the window then. His eyes move across the room, settling briefly on each of us. When they reach Mama he holds her gaze for a moment, something passing between them that belongs only to people who have been through decades of difficult things together.

"We don't move yet," he says. "We let it run."

The article is already being picked up by national outlets. Financial blogs map the money trail in red threads across the Southwest. A congressional aide has posted a vague statement about disturbing logistics patterns. Exposure spreads faster than we expect.

Mama crosses the room quietly and fills the coffee mugs without asking. She sets one in front of Pops when he returns to the table, another in front of Joe, one more in front of Sylvia. The gesture is so ordinary it aches. She is doing what she always does when the world is dangerous. She is making sure the people she loves have something warm in their hands.

"They won't come loud," I say, finally.

"No," Joe agrees. "They'll test."

"How?" Jimmy asks.

Sylvia answers before anyone else can. "Pressure. Traffic stops. Quiet audits. People asking the wrong questions in the right offices."

"They'll see who flinches," Bobby adds.

Outside, Phoenix continues as if nothing has shifted. A neighbor's door slams. A car alarm chirps once and goes silent. A garbage truck grinds its way down the street and disappears. Ordinary sounds layered over something that was anything but.

My phone lights up again with a new notification. The article has moved to the front page of a national outlet. The money theory is trending.

Somewhere in a building with tinted windows and locked floors, someone is reviewing internal access logs and shipment deviations. Someone is asking who knew enough to move product and who had the nerve to disrupt flow. Someone is deciding whether this is a leak or a threat.

Bobby looks at me. "Second wave?" he asks quietly.

"Yes," I answer.

Arrests. Or retaliation. Or both.

Pops sets his coffee mug down with a quiet, deliberate click. "Then we prepare," he says. Not to anyone in particular. To the room.

Joe picks up his legal pad. Sylvia reaches for the notebook. Hector straightens from the wall.

The rental feels thinner now, as if the walls are no longer insulation but suggestion. We are still safe. No one has knocked. No one has followed. Cap is intact. The girls are home.

But the story has broken.

We don't hear thunder yet. But the air tastes metallic. And this time when the storm moves it won't come as noise.

It will come as strategy.

Part VI: Home

"Now I understood that the same road was to bring us together again. Whatever we had missed, we possessed together the precious, the incommunicable past."
Willa Cather, *My Ántonia* (1918)

Chapter One
The Road Home

Pops' Escalade sat alone in the parking lot, broad, dark, and dusty from the drive down, a vehicle that belonged to a man who had learned long ago that reliability mattered more than appearance. Hector had returned the rental an hour earlier without ceremony, sliding the keys across the counter and walking out without looking back. Now we stood in the flat Phoenix morning loading whatever we had carried into the back while the air conditioner ran and Mama arranged the cooler she had packed that morning from what remained of the Phoenix kitchen, as if the act of feeding people on the road home was simply the next logical step in a week that had required her to be useful in every way she knew how.

"There's green chile stew in the thermos," she said to no one in particular, tucking it between the cooler and a folded blanket. "And tortillas, wrapped in foil. Don't let them get cold."

Nobody argued with Mama about food. Not even Pops.

Pops took the wheel. Joe settled into the passenger seat, his legal pad already open, reading glasses pushed up on his forehead. Mama slid into the middle row first, taking the window seat behind Pops. Bobby climbed in beside her. I took the seat on the other side, the three of us filling the middle row with our shoulders almost touching. Sylvia, Hector, and Jimmy took the back row.

The doors closed one at a time.

Pops pulled out of the lot without a word and pointed the Escalade north toward the interstate.

Phoenix dissolved behind us in layers: strip malls, car dealerships, the vast geometry of suburbs that had no memory of desert before they arrived. The sky was already hard and bright, the kind of morning light that didn't soften anything. I watched the city thin through the window and felt something in my chest begin to loosen that had been coiled tight since the moment I pulled into Bobby's driveway in what felt like a lifetime ago.

Joe's phone buzzed once. He glanced at the screen, read something, and set it face down on his legal pad. "Treasury confirmed three additional asset freezes this morning," he said quietly. "Domestic accounts tied to the Nevada structures. They're moving up the chain."

Pops' eyes flicked briefly to the road ahead. "Sylvia?"

"Federal corroboration came through this morning," Joe replied. "Two congressional offices have requested the financial documentation. Her name is on record as the source." He paused. "She's a witness now. Not a suspect."

The distinction settled through the Escalade without anyone marking it dramatically. It was the thing they had been working toward since the motel room in Tijuana. Hearing it said plainly on a highway in Arizona felt smaller than it should have, which was how important things usually arrived.

"Jimmy," Pops said from the front, his voice steady.

"Sir."

"The situation in Albuquerque. The weapon discharge." He didn't look back. "Joe has a name. You'll meet with him when we get home."

"Yes, sir."

"You do exactly what he says."

"Yes, sir."

Pops said nothing more about it. That was how he handled things that were already decided.

The interstate opened in front of us and the desert took over, the land flattening and widening into the particular emptiness of the Arizona stretch before New Mexico began. Saguaro gave way to scrub. The sky doubled in size. I watched the distance and thought about nothing specific, which was the first time in days my mind had been willing to do that.

Mama passed the thermos of green chile stew backward over her shoulder and Bobby unscrewed the lid without being asked. The smell filled the Escalade immediately, warm and sharp and completely at odds with the highway and the dry air outside. Something about it cracked the silence in a way that nothing else could have. Jimmy accepted a cup without comment. Joe set his legal pad aside. Even Hector leaned forward slightly from the back row.

Jimmy held the cup in both hands and stared at the steam for a moment. "The shell company structure," he said, not to anyone in particular. "The way the accounts were layered. I kept thinking about it while I was transcribing the ledger." He paused. "How do you learn to read something like that? The way you did."

Joe glanced back at him over the seat. "You study," he said simply.

"Where?"

Joe was quiet for a moment, the legal pad open in his lap. "Law school, if you want the legitimate version. Financial crimes unit, if you want the practical one." He looked at Jimmy steadily. "You have the right kind of mind. I noticed it when you were working through those columns."

Jimmy absorbed that without responding immediately. He took a slow drink of the stew. "I don't have a record," he said carefully. "Not formally."

"Then you have options," Joe replied.

Pops said nothing from the driver's seat. But his eyes moved briefly to the rearview mirror and back to the road, which was its own kind of answer.

"Mama," Sylvia said, tearing off a piece of tortilla, "you are the only person in the world who packs a full meal for a rescue operation."

"I packed it for the drive home," Mama said placidly. "I knew you'd all be hungry."

Bobby caught my eye and the corner of his mouth lifted. I looked away before it became something larger than the moment deserved.

We crossed into New Mexico without announcement, the state line marked by a sign that seemed too small for what it meant. The landscape shifted almost immediately, redder, older, the mesas rising in long slow layers along the horizon. I had driven this stretch of highway more times than I could count over the last ten years, always moving through, always pointed somewhere else. Now I watched it the way you watch something you are finally willing to let belong to you.

I had turned slightly to say something to Bobby when I saw it in the back row: Hector's hand resting on the seat between him and Sylvia, close enough that the distance between them was a decision. Then Sylvia, without looking at him, moved her hand and covered his. It was small. Deliberate.

I turned back to the window and said nothing. Jimmy was still looking out at the desert. Pops and Joe were talking quietly in the front. Bobby hadn't seen it.

For once, it belonged only to them. And to me, who knew enough to keep it.

The miles accumulated quietly. Joe worked. Jimmy watched the desert go by, the exhaustion of the last week finally giving way to something quieter in his expression, like a man beginning to understand what he wanted to do with what he had just been through. Bobby and I sat close enough that our knees touched when the road curved, and neither of us moved to change that.

Somewhere past Gallup, Bobby said quietly, "You going to stay?"

He wasn't looking at me when he asked. His eyes were on the passing mesa country, the same landscape we had driven through on the way out under completely different circumstances.

"Yes," I said.

He nodded once, like he had expected the answer but needed to hear it anyway.

"I was thinking about it before any of this happened," I said. The words came out easier than I expected, like they had been waiting for the right road and the right speed to say themselves. "I've been living on the road for a long time. It suited me for years. I needed it. But somewhere along the way I started feeling the absence of something."

Bobby turned his head slightly toward me.

"Roots," I said. "A place that knew me back." I looked out at the Sandias rising on the horizon, still distant but already familiar, the shape I had carried in my memory for ten years without admitting why. "I can still travel. I'll have to, for work. But it would be good to have somewhere to come home to."

Bobby was quiet for a moment. Then he said, simply, "Yeah. It would."

From the back row, Sylvia said nothing. But I felt her attention shift toward me and hold there for a moment before returning to the window.

Pops said nothing from the front seat. But something in his shoulders eased slightly, almost imperceptibly, and Joe glanced at him once before returning to his legal pad.

The Sandias grew larger as we descended toward the valley, their ridgeline sharpening against the afternoon sky. Albuquerque spread below us in its familiar grid of streets and cottonwoods and low adobe buildings that never quite decided whether they belonged to the desert or the city. The Rio Grande caught the light somewhere to the west. The smell of roasting chile drifted through the vents even before we reached the valley floor, as if the city was announcing itself.

Pops took the exit toward the North Valley without being asked. He eased the Escalade through familiar streets, past the corner store, past the church, past the cracked stretch of sidewalk near the old vacant lot that had never been fixed in all the years any of us could remember. The neighborhoods sat low and quiet in the afternoon light, unhurried and unchanged, as if nothing extraordinary had touched the word beyond their edges.

He turned onto their street and pulled into the driveway and shut off the engine.

For a moment nobody moved.

Then doors opened one at a time and people climbed out into the warm North Valley air that smelled of dust and someone's dinner already on the stove somewhere down the block. Mama went straight to the trunk to retrieve her cooler. Joe stretched and rolled his shoulders. Jimmy stepped out slowly, taking in the street and the house and the porch with its wind chimes moving faintly in the breeze. He had been inside that house once before, in the worst hours of the week, and standing in the driveway in ordinary afternoon light it looked different. Smaller. More like what it actually was, a home rather than a command post.

Bobby came around the front of the Escalade and stopped beside me.

I looked at the house. The porch light was on even though it was still afternoon. It was always on.

I was reaching into the back for my bag when I saw Hector lift Sylvia's bag out ahead of her and hold it out. She took it, and when she did, their hands stayed connected a moment longer than the exchange required: not dramatic, not hidden, just there in the open afternoon light of the driveway.

I straightened slowly.

Pops had come around the back of the vehicle to help Mama with the cooler. He straightened and turned and saw it.

Not a glimpse. Not a suspicion. The full thing, in afternoon light, plain as the driveway beneath his feet.

He went very still.

Sylvia met his gaze without flinching. She didn't explain herself or look away. She simply stood there in the driveway of the house she had grown up in and let him see exactly what he was looking at.

Hector held Pops' gaze steadily. He didn't step back. He didn't look apologetic. He looked like a man who had already made his decision and was prepared to stand in it.

The moment stretched.

Mama appeared at Pops' elbow with the cooler handle in her hand. She looked at Sylvia and Hector. Then she looked at Pops.

"Come inside," she said quietly. "Dinner needs finishing."

She walked toward the house without waiting for anyone.

Pops watched her go. Then he looked at Sylvia once more, something working behind his eyes that hadn't reached his mouth yet. He picked up the cooler, turned, and followed Mama up the porch steps without speaking.

The screen door opened and closed behind them.

Sylvia exhaled slowly.

Bobby looked at her. "You okay?"

"Yes," she said.

She wasn't entirely. But she would be.

I had spent ten years moving through places that didn't know my name. Places that were beautiful and temporary and sufficient in the way that things are sufficient when you have decided not to want more.

Albuquerque knew my name.

I picked up my bag and walked toward the porch.

Nobody needed to say where we were going. We were going home.

Chapter Two
Settling

The room that had always been mine at Mama and Pops' house felt smaller than I remembered, the way rooms shrink when you come back to them as an adult and realize your childhood made everything larger than it was. But the window faced east and caught the morning light in a way that suited me, and Mama had put fresh flowers on the dresser without saying anything about it, which was how she communicated most things that mattered.

I had been there three weeks.

My cameras lined the shelf above the bed the way they had lined the shelf in the RV, the only constant in the inventory of my life. Everything else was borrowed or replaced or slowly being rebuilt from scratch. The RV was gone, totaled in the shooting at the trailer park, the insurance claim still crawling its way through a process that moved slower than anything else in my life. I had Bobby's old hoodie in the closet and three pairs of jeans and enough camera equipment to work, which meant I had enough.

I had started shooting the neighborhood the first week. Not for any assignment. Just to get my eye back. The North Valley in the early morning, when the light came low and sideways across the irrigation ditches and the cottonwoods threw long shadows across dirt roads that hadn't changed in forty years. Old men drinking coffee on porches. Kids cutting through the vacant lot on their bikes. The particular way this part of Albuquerque existed slightly outside the city's self-image, unhurried and unimpressed and entirely itself.

The investigative work with Lena was developing alongside it, slower and more deliberate. She called every few days with updates, another corporate filing confirmed, another account traced to a known shell structure, the federal case building layer by layer toward something that would hold in court. I sent her photographs when she needed them. Documentation. Evidence that didn't require words.

Bobby stopped by most evenings. Not always for long. Sometimes just long enough to sit at the kitchen table while I edited photos and drink coffee and talk about nothing consequential. Sometimes we drove out toward the river where the cottonwoods were beginning to turn at the edges, the first suggestion of fall coming into the valley. He didn't push for anything. He was patient in the way he had always been.

One Tuesday afternoon I came back from shooting the old elementary school, the cracked basketball court, the chain-link fence leaning inward, the hoop that still sagged from years of kids hanging on it, and noticed Hector's truck parked in front of the house. Not unusual on its own. Hector came and went from Pops' house the way he always had, part of the operation's rhythm rather than any social arrangement. But it was two in the afternoon on a weekday and Pops' car was the only other vehicle in the driveway, which meant Mama wasn't home, which meant whatever was happening inside wasn't happening around the softening influence of food and conversation.

I stayed in Bobby's truck for a few minutes before going inside.

When I did, the house was quiet in a way that meant people were talking somewhere rather than the quiet of an empty house. The garage door was cracked at the bottom, a thin line of light visible from the hallway. I didn't go closer. I set my camera bag on the table and made coffee and waited.

Hector left twenty minutes later. He came through the kitchen without looking surprised to see me, gave a single nod, and walked out the front door. His face was controlled like always, but something in his posture had the set of a man who has said something difficult and is carrying the having-said-it rather than the unsaid weight of before.

Pops came in from the garage a few minutes after that. He washed his hands at the sink with the slow, deliberate movements he used when he was thinking. He didn't look at me directly. He poured himself a coffee and stood at the counter and looked out the window at the back yard where the hollyhocks were still blooming against the fence.

"You need anything?" he asked finally.

"No," I said.

He nodded once and took his coffee down the hall.

I sat at the table, looked at my own hands and understood that whatever had happened in that garage, Hector had walked toward it rather than waiting for it to find him. And that Pops, who had built his entire life around the principle that men were defined by what they were willing to stand in, had recognized that. It wasn't acceptance. Not yet. But it was the beginning of something that could become it.

The call from Lena came on a Thursday morning while I was shooting along the river. I had been there since early, working the light on the water and the cottonwoods and a great blue heron that had been standing in the shallows for twenty minutes. My phone was in my jacket pocket on silent. When I felt it vibrate, I almost didn't answer. Then I saw her name.

"It's done," she said the moment I picked up.

I lowered the camera slowly.

"Federal indictments came down this morning," she continued, her voice carrying the controlled energy of someone delivering news they have been building toward for months. "Seventeen counts. Trafficking, money laundering, conspiracy. Three principal figures arrested before six a.m. Assets frozen across four states."

Without warning, the heron lifted from the water and crossed the river with slow, heavy wingbeats before disappearing into the cottonwoods on the far bank.

"Sylvia?" I asked.

"Formally designated a protected federal witness," Lena said. "Her testimony was central. It's in the record." A pause. "She's on the right side of this, Michelle. Publicly and permanently."

I stood at the river's edge and let that settle.

I had left this city in the middle of the night because staying felt like drowning. I had built a life from motion and distance. From the discipline of never needing anything I could carry. And somewhere in the years between then and now, my best friend had looked at a set of numbers that didn't reconcile and followed them into something enormous and dangerous because she couldn't look away from what they meant.

"The story's being picked up everywhere," Lena continued. "National syndication. Two major outlets running follow-up investigations. Congressional inquiry announced this morning." A pause, and then her voice shifted, quieter and more deliberate. "This is the story I came into this work to find," she said. "I want you to know that."

"The photographs you sent," she added. "The documentation. I want to credit you."

"Credit Sylvia," I said. "She built the map. I just helped read it."

I understood what she meant. Not the indictments or the syndication or the congressional inquiry. The fifteen girls from the same town south of Tijuana. The accountant who had read the numbers and couldn't look away. The notebook that had started with two words written before anyone understood what they were looking at.

After I hung up, I stood at the river for a long time without taking any photographs. Cottonwoods moved in the breeze. Water ran brown and steady over the stones the way it always had. Somewhere behind me, the city carried on its ordinary business, completely unaware that something large had just finished. I thought about fifteen girls in a bunker beneath the high desert, counting each other in the dark. I thought about Sylvia burning her phone. I thought about Hector's hand on the wheel of a faded yellow school bus, driving west through country that swallowed everything. Then I raised my camera and photographed the river and the light and the empty space where the heron had been.

Sunday dinner at the Calderon house had always been its own institution, governed by rhythms so steady they no longer required words. Mama started cooking by noon. Pops appeared at the head of the table at six regardless of what else was happening in the world. The food was abundant in the way that said feeding people wasn't hospitality but love spoken in the only language that didn't ask for vulnerability.

This Sunday the table was full. Bobby beside me. Sylvia across from us, sharper and steadier than she had been even a month ago. Testifying publicly had cost her something and returned something in equal measure, the way difficult things do when you walk through them rather than around them. Joe at the corner, already talking to Pops about something logistical. Jimmy at the far end, less careful than he had been in Phoenix, beginning to understand that a place at this table meant something that didn't have to be earned repeatedly.

Hector arrived at six fifteen.

He came through the door the way he always came through doors, scanning the room once before stepping fully inside, his presence filling the space without announcing itself. He set a six-pack on the counter. Mama handed him a plate without being asked. He sat beside Sylvia instead of the edge of the room.

Pops watched from the head of the table.

He didn't speak. Didn't nod. He picked up his fork and continued eating, and in the silence that followed I understood that this was how Pops accepted things he couldn't change, things he didn't entirely disapprove of. Not with words, not with gestures, but with the simple act of continuing. Of not stopping. Of letting the meal go on.

Mama refilled his glass without comment.

Somewhere between the main course and dessert, Jimmy set down his fork and looked at the table rather than any one person and said, "I'm going to apply to UNM. Pre-law."

Pops looked at him from the head of the table.

"Joe thinks I have a shot," Jimmy added.

"Joe's right," Pops said, then went back to his plate. That was all. But at a table like this, that was everything.

The conversation picked up again around the table, overlapping voices, Sylvia's laugh at something Bobby said, Jimmy asking Joe a question about something I didn't catch, the ordinary noise of people who had been through something together. I reached for my camera on the empty chair beside me. Nobody noticed.

I photographed Mama's hands passing the bread. Bobby's profile in the kitchen light. Sylvia's smile, unguarded for once, directed at something Hector said quietly beside her. Pops at the head of the table, serious and present and entirely himself, the man who had bent down to my eye level when I was a terrified child and told me I was safe here and meant every word of it. I photographed Jimmy watching the family around him with the careful attention of someone learning a language they have wanted to speak for a long time. I photographed the window behind Pops' chair, the evening light coming through it in the particular way North Valley light arrived at that hour, warm and slightly golden and entirely unrepeatable.

These were the photographs I had always wanted to take. Not the eight seconds before something tried to throw you. The ordinary. The people in it. The light on their faces when they didn't know anyone was watching.

Mama found her moment after dessert, when Pops had moved to the living room with Joe and Bobby and the younger voices had drifted toward the back of the house. She touched Sylvia's elbow at the sink where they were washing up together, a small and deliberate gesture, and Sylvia turned. I sat at the table with my coffee and my camera, close enough to hear.

"Your father went to the garage," Mama said quietly.

Sylvia dried her hands on the dish towel. "I know."

"Hector came to him," Mama continued. "He didn't wait. He came." She let that land for a moment. "You understand what that means to a man like your father."

Sylvia was quiet.

"He won't say it," Mama said. "You know him. He won't find the words for a long time, maybe never. But he's not fighting it." She looked at her daughter carefully. "That's not nothing."

Sylvia's jaw worked once. "He doesn't approve."

"No," Mama agreed. "Not yet." She folded the dish towel with the slow precision she brought to everything that required her hands. "But he's adjusting. And with your father, adjusting always comes before accepting, even if no one ever sees the moment it changes."

Sylvia looked out the window above the sink at the back yard where the hollyhocks leaned against the fence in the evening air.

"I'm glad you chose someone who stayed," Mama said softly. "Whatever else he is. Whatever your father thinks about the rest of it." She touched Sylvia's face once, brief and certain. "He stayed."

Sylvia pressed her lips together briefly, then she nodded. Mama kissed her cheek and went to find Pops. I sat at the table with my coffee going cold and my camera in my hands and didn't pretend I hadn't heard.

Bobby found me on the front porch after everyone had gone. The night had cooled and the wind chimes were moving softly in the breeze that came down off the mountains after dark. The street was quiet. A dog barked somewhere down the block and stopped. The ordinary sounds of a neighborhood that had held its own rhythms for decades regardless of what moved through it.

He sat beside me on the porch steps without being asked. For a while neither of us spoke.

"Lena called this morning," I said finally.

"I know," he said. "Sylvia told me."

"It's done."

"Yes."

The word settled between us simply.

"She's protected," I said. "Publicly. It's in the record."

Bobby looked out at the street. "Good," he said. Just that. The word carried everything it needed to carry without asking for more space than that.

We sat together in the dark for a while longer, our shoulders touching, the wind chimes doing what they always did, the mountains somewhere behind the city holding their particular shape against the sky.

"I was thinking," Bobby said after a while, his voice quiet and careful in the way it got when something mattered, "about the spare room."

I looked at him.

"At my place," he said. "I cleared some stuff out. If you want, when you're ready, there's space."

He wasn't asking me to decide anything tonight. He was simply letting me know the door was open and he had already made room for me behind it.

I looked out at the street where we had grown up, at the porch light casting its soft circle across the driveway, at the city spread out around us familiar and imperfect and entirely ours.

"Not yet," I said. "But yes."

He nodded once, the way he nodded when something had been settled without requiring ceremony. "Okay," he said.

And we sat there together on the porch steps of the house that had first shown me what safe felt like, while the wind chimes moved and the night held everything steady, and for the first time in ten years I was not passing through.

I was here.

And here was enough.

Epilogue
Late Summer

The river was lower than it had been in spring, the water running clear over stones that had been hidden under the runoff months earlier. The cottonwoods stood full and heavy along the bank, their leaves catching late morning light in shifting patterns that moved with every breath of wind off the mountains. I had been there since seven, working the light as it shifted, the camera finding things I hadn't known I was looking for until the shutter closed around them.

This was the work now.

Not the rodeo circuit, not the next county fairground, not the narrow shelf of cameras in a vehicle pointed somewhere else. The investigative work with Lena was ongoing. She called twice a week, the trafficking story continuing to unspool through federal proceedings that would take years to fully resolve.

The photographs I took in the mornings were mine. The North Valley. The river. The city as it actually was, unhurried and imperfect and entirely itself. I had started a project documenting the neighborhood, the families who had been here for generations, the irrigation ditches and the cottonwood corridors and the particular quality of late summer light on adobe walls that existed nowhere else in the world quite like this.

Bobby's house had a darkroom now. He had converted the old shed out back, the one that smelled of pine and old wood and decades of accumulated use, into something precise and deliberate. The shelves he had built himself, dimensions wrong on the first attempt and corrected without complaint. The smell of fixer and developer permanently settled into the walls now alongside everything else the shed had ever held. My prints hung drying on the line he had strung across the back wall, and the sight of them there, my work in his space, still surprised me sometimes when I walked in.

I had been surprised by a lot of things lately.

By how easily I slept in a room that didn't move. By how quickly the neighborhood had come back to me, the corner store and the church and the cracked sidewalk near the old vacant lot were as familiar as my own hands. By the way, Bobby moved into a shared life without making it feel like territory, leaving room for me.

By how much I had missed this river.

I was crouched at the water's edge photographing the way the current moved around a cluster of stones when I heard footsteps on the path behind me. I didn't look up. The light was doing something particular to the water and I wasn't ready to lose it.

"You've been here since before breakfast," Sylvia said.

"The light doesn't negotiate," I replied.

She dropped down onto the bank beside me, pulling her knees up, her arms wrapped loosely around them. She looked different than she had a year ago, not older exactly, but more settled inside herself. The federal proceedings had been hard. Testifying publicly had been harder. But she had done it with her chin up and her eyes clear. She had come out the other side with her name on the right side of the record, that knowledge sitting visibly in her posture.

"Hector's parking," she said.

I lowered the camera. "You brought Hector to the river."

"He brought himself," she said. "I just told him where I was going."

The distinction was very Sylvia.

I heard another set of footsteps on the path and then Bobby appeared through the cottonwoods, two coffees in his hands, his boots already dusty from the walk down from the road. Cisco ranged ahead of him, nose down on the path, checking everything. He reached me first, pressed his nose briefly against my shoulder in greeting, and then moved to the water's edge to conduct his own assessment of the river.

Bobby handed me a coffee without ceremony and sat on the bank on my other side, close enough that our shoulders touched.

"You could have told me you were leaving before sunrise," he said.

"I left a note."

"The note said, "gone to the river." That's not information. That's a location."

"Same thing."

He shook his head, but he was almost smiling.

Hector came through the trees a minute later, moving with the quiet economy that never changed regardless of circumstances. He scanned the bank automatically before his posture settled. Some habits never switch off. He found a spot on the bank a few feet from Sylvia and sat, forearms resting on his knees, eyes on the water.

Cisco finished his assessment of the river and settled beside Bobby with his chin on his paws, watching the current.

The river moved past us steadily.

For a while, nobody said anything. The cottonwoods shifted above us in the warm breeze and the light moved across the water in the way it does late in summer when the angle has begun its slow change toward fall without having arrived there yet. A hawk circled somewhere high above the valley. The city existed beyond the tree line, ordinary and continuous, going about its business the way cities do.

"Lena called yesterday," I said after a while.

"The Pulitzer," Sylvia said.

"She won."

Sylvia was quiet for a moment. "Good," she said.

Bobby's hand found mine on the bank between us.

I turned toward him slightly, not enough to interrupt the moment but enough. "I love you," I said quietly. It wasn't the answer to anything he had asked or a response to anything in the air. Just the thing that had been true for a long time, finally said in the right place at the right time, with the river in front of us and nothing left to be afraid of.

He didn't say anything. He squeezed my hand once and looked back at the water. That was enough. That was exactly enough.

Hector picked up a flat stone and turned it over in his fingers without throwing it. After a moment he set the stone down again.

"Cap called this morning," he said.

We all looked at him.

"He's coming through Albuquerque next month," he said. "Wants to see how things settled."

Sylvia's mouth curved slightly. "Tell him Mama will feed him."

"Already did," Hector said.

Bobby laughed, fully and without restraint, the sound carrying across the water and into the cottonwoods. Something in the ease of it, in the way it belonged to the morning and the river and the four of us sitting on this bank together, tightened something in my chest in the best possible way.

I raised the camera.

I photographed Bobby's laugh and Sylvia watching him with the fond exasperation of a lifetime of being his sister. I photographed Hector almost smiling, the expression arriving and departing so quickly that if I hadn't been watching through the lens I would have missed it. I photographed Cisco at the water's edge, his pale eyes on the current. I photographed the river and the cottonwoods and the light doing what it does in late summer in the Rio Grande valley, something that doesn't translate into words but translates perfectly into silver and shadow on photographic paper.

Then I put the camera down.

We sat there for another hour, the four of us. Sylvia's new position at a firm that didn't require her to look at freight manifests. Bobby's latest construction contract, a school building in the North Valley that Pops had wanted for years and finally secured. Hector said almost nothing, as usual.

When we finally walked back up the path toward the road, Bobby's hand was in mine and Sylvia was ahead of us already talking about where to get breakfast and whether Frontier was worth the wait on a Saturday and Hector was half a step behind her. Cisco moved between all of us on the path, ranging ahead and doubling back, making sure the group stayed intact.

Pops' Escalade was parked at the road's edge when we came through the trees.

He was leaning against the hood with his arms folded, hat low against the morning sun. Mama stood beside him with a paper bag that smelled unmistakably of green chile and eggs.

"Figured you'd all be hungry," Mama said.

Sylvia stopped when she saw them. Something moved across her face, brief and unguarded, before she recovered it.

Pops pushed off the hood and straightened. His eyes moved across the group, settling briefly on each of us. When they reached Hector they stayed there for a moment, the way they always did now, measuring, assessing, the calculation behind them still visible even if its conclusion had shifted.

Then Pops reached into the Escalade, produced a cold bottle of water and held it out.

Not to Bobby. Not to Sylvia. Not to me.

To Hector.

Hector took it without hesitation. He unscrewed the cap and took a long drink and nodded once in the way he nodded when something had been received and understood.

Pops turned and opened the tailgate and began passing out the breakfast Mama had brought, the ordinary work of feeding people he loved, and nobody said anything about what had just happened because nothing needed to be said.

I raised my camera one more time.

The shutter closed.

The river moved behind us, steady and indifferent and entirely beautiful, the way it had always moved through this valley, through all the years and all the leaving and all the coming back, holding nothing against anyone, just running clear over the stones toward whatever came next.